NECESSARY DECEPTIONS: THE WOMEN OF WYATT EARP

NECESSARY DECEPTIONS: THE WOMEN OF WYATT EARP

PAMELA NOWAK

FIVE STAR
A part of Gale, a Cengage Company

LIBRARY OF CONGRESS CATALOGING-IN-PUBLICATION DATA

Names: Nowak, Pamela, author.
Title: Necessary deceptions : the women of Wyatt Earp / Pamela Nowak.
Description: First edition. | Waterville : Five Star, 2022.
Identifiers: LCCN 2021035969 | ISBN 9781432888015 (hardcover)
Subjects: LCSH: Blaylock, Mattie, 1850-1888—Fiction. | Earp, Josephine Sarah Marcus—Fiction. | Earp, Wyatt, 1848-1929—Marriage—Fiction. | LCGFT: Western fiction. | Biographical fiction.
Classification: LCC PS3614.O964 N43 2022 | DDC 813/.6—dc23
LC record available at https://lccn.loc.gov/2021035969

First Edition. First Printing: February 2022
Find us on Facebook—https://www.facebook.com/FiveStarCengage
Visit our website—http://www.gale.cengage.com/fivestar
Contact Five Star Publishing at FiveStar@cengage.com

Printed in Mexico
Print Number: 01 Print Year: 2022

For Ilka and Danika . . .
Daughters of my heart and treasured friends

ACKNOWLEDGMENTS

I could not have completed the complicated research in this book without the help of so many people. I relied on much of the research done by other historians, searching through the discrepancies for common ground. I am especially indebted to Sherry Monahan and E.C. (Ted) Meyers for igniting my interest in Josie and Mattie and for being willing to correspond with me about their research. Their heavily documented work saved me innumerable hours. Karma Heim Lanning and Shirley Vinsand (descendants of Mattie's sister, Tony May) generously shared the few family recollections they had and provided clarity and ideas. Linda Aylward, Special Collections Assistant at the Bradley University Library in Peoria, Illinois, assisted me with copies of records from police magistrate docket books, and Peoria Historical Society member Kaleb Nieman spent hours of volunteer time going through documents searching for mention of Celia/Mattie that might have been missed.

My in-person critique group (Alice, Brenda, Carla, Cate, Denee, Janet, Kay, Peggy, Robin, Steven, and Thea) stayed with me chapter by chapter and helped me make these women sympathetic despite their very real issues. Email critique partners Debby and Karen offered guidance from the Women's Fiction perspective. Janet, Karen, and Liz served as beta readers for the entire manuscript and their suggestions for improvement made this a far better story. Deni, my developmental editor with Five Star, put in hours to trim my words and fix Mattie's voice. I hope you all know how much I appreciate you.

And Ken . . . I could not have found a more patient and supportive partner in life.

Allie

The world likes to think it knows all about Wyatt Earp and everybody around him but it don't. There ain't a soul alive who knows the truth about my brother-in-law. The legend pure gobbled up the truth.

Oh, the family knew but we all kept our mouths shut.

The lies started with his last wife, Josie. She never did want folks to see the truth about the early days, as if she could change where she came from and the things she done. And then there was Mattie, lying to herself about things so she could live with it all. Once Wyatt shoved Mattie aside, it was like Josie was trying to change the past completely, like she could make Mattie disappear if nobody said her name no more.

It was all ever about deceiving folks, protecting Wyatt, making sure the world didn't know about all the trouble he got into. It was never about the family. It was about Wyatt and her making him into something he wasn't. But I garbled up what I told anyway, just like she knew I would, until nobody knew the whole story.

There was so much that got left unsaid, about Wyatt, sure, but mostly about the Earp women and what Wyatt cost them. Tombstone changed us all, leaving some of us to rebuild what got shattered and others to grab what wasn't theirs. In the end, deception seemed necessary to most of us.

It shames me I done it. The stories ought to have been told. Now, all that's left is lies and a whole lot of supposing.

Prologue

Mid-1930s
Allie Earp's house

"What did you tell that man?"

Allie stared at her sister-in-law, the words rankling her. There was no cause for Josie to be getting all uppity. That snooty tone was all Josie, same as it had been all these years, but the hostile glare in her eyes got Allie's dander more than anything.

Allie grabbed the papers off the kitchen table. Knowing Josie, she might take 'em and all Allie's hours of talking would be gone. That writer fella shoulda taken the notes with him.

"What d'ya mean?" Allie snapped. "I told Frank Waters my story, same as Wyatt and you told that man who interviewed you." She reckoned Virgil Earp could have his biography done same as Wyatt had, him being in Tombstone, too.

Josie stalked behind Allie, crowding her.

"Yes, but what did you tell him? He asked you about Wyatt, I know he did."

Allie shoved the papers into the cupboard and slammed it shut before she turned. "You ain't got no call to be poking into what I said. Waters is writing about me and Virgil."

"Which means he's writing about Wyatt."

Oh, lord, the woman never quit harping on Wyatt Earp. Nobody had even cared about what happened in Tombstone until all them books came out. And Josie'd controlled what the biographers learned about Wyatt—and her and Mattie—so that they left out all the bad stuff and told all lies that made Wyatt into a saint. What with Wyatt dying and Josie suing folks right and left every time they said something she didn't like, the truth got pure changed up.

"The whole world don't spin around Wyatt Earp," Allie said. Except now there were movies and the rest of the Earp brothers, her Virge along with 'em, were shunted off into obscurity.

Josie wrinkled up her nose and rolled her eyes just like she'd done for years. "Oh, posh. He wouldn't even care about you and Virge if it weren't for Wyatt. Did you tell him about Missouri? About Kansas?" Josie paused. "About Mattie and me?"

"I answered his questions, sure enough." In truth, he hadn't asked too much about any of it, though she suspected he'd turn more to Wyatt before all was said and done. There *was* some talk about Mattie. That was when Allie had teared up.

"So you did tell him?" Josie pressed.

Allie hedged her way around Wyatt's widow. There was no need for her to answer that direct. So what if she talked about Mattie? "He ain't writing about Wyatt and you and Mattie."

"Allie?" Josie all but screamed.

"Don't you go using that tone with me, *Sadie.*" *There, let her chew on that for a while.*

"Don't call me that!"

Yep, that stopped her alright. "It's your name, sure as snow is white. It's your name same as Josephine is. 'Til you showed up on Wyatt's arm, Sadie's all anybody ever called you."

Josie's jaw clenched. "I left that name behind a long time ago, and everything that went with it."

Used to be, everybody knew all about Sadie Marcus. Now, she'd invented a whole new story. It would serve her right if Waters wrote it down in his book.

Josie just pretended none of that life ever happened. Rewriting history was what Josie was doing. It wasn't right.

"You tell everyone you came from class but it ain't so. Your pa wasn't a merchant and you weren't a society girl who got stranded by a dance troupe like you tell everyone. And not saying anything about Mattie don't erase her from Wyatt's life. You ain't got one thing up on her and what you done to her won't go away on account of you pretending she didn't exist. And nothing you make up is gonna make Wyatt any purer than you."

Josie caught Allie's arm and spun her around.

"If you tell the truth about any of it, the family will be hurt. Don't you see that? The world wants heroes and I made Wyatt one. You take that away, and there's nothing left."

She sighed and blew the anger out like Allie'd seen her do before.

"You tell that man about our pasts and you'll ruin *all* our lives," Josie continued. "We'll all suffer for it. Not only me, but the reputations of all the Earp women. They'll make whores of us and criminals of our husbands. Is that what you want, Allie?"

Allie shrugged. Was that the truth of it? She sure didn't want to besmirch Louisa and Bessie. They'd done nothing but marry Morgan and James Earp, same as she'd married Virgil. Maybe it *would* be better not to dredge up those early days, even if the women were both long gone. Lou and Bessie came from hard lives, had done things that weren't respectable. Even if the Earp family was full of scoundrels, she didn't need to dig up any of the details—not when they'd put them in the past.

"Please, Allie, I don't care what you tell him about yourself, about you and Virge, but don't you say anything about what happened to Wyatt before Tombstone. There's nothing about those beginnings anyone needs to know."

Allie nodded, feeling cornered but agreeing all the same.

★ ★ ★ ★ ★

Part One: Early Days Dismissed

★ ★ ★ ★ ★

ALLIE

Beginnings make us what we are.

When Wyatt and Josie first started telling about their lives, Josie had lots of stories about her beginnings. She mixed up the details, depending on who she told, but the gist of what she made up was the same: naïve and bored with life as a daughter of a wealthy German merchant, she ran away with a dance troupe and got herself abandoned in Arizona. Being a dutiful girl, she went back home but then she got lured back by a diamond ring and promises of marriage and met Wyatt the very day she got to Tombstone.

Like most things Josie said, the truth was plumb manipulated into something it wasn't.

Chapter One: Josephine/Sadie

Appearances are everything, or so Mama always said. And sometimes, it's necessary to tell a few small lies to maintain them.

1871

San Francisco

There wasn't much to recommend about San Francisco's eighth ward. It was bad enough Papa had broken his promises yet again, but moving us to *this* squalid neighborhood was about the worst thing he could have done. How on earth was I going to land a husband of any means living here?

Sure, I was only eleven. But Mama had started in on the topic of husbands the minute my bosom budded and she hadn't eased up one bit given how fast I was growing out. No matter her fussing, though, the eighth ward held none of the prospects she said were important in a fiancé.

In one fell swoop, I'd lost any hope for a decent future along with my house, my playmates, and interesting surroundings. I was none too pleased about any of it.

"You'd best quit your pouting and get on to school," Mama advised from across the room, the pile of laundry in her arms hiding her face. It didn't matter much. I knew there were lines etched in it—lines of worry and fatigue and crossness. Thanks to Papa, Mama's life hadn't turned into much and now mine wouldn't either.

"I ain't never going to school again." I couldn't see much point in it.

"*Ach,* stop it, now, Sadie. You will go to school and make something of yourself." She dropped the laundry and it billowed about her like a pile from the ragman's cart. "You and I, we dream of such castles in the clouds for you, but you want it all the easy way. *Mein Gott,* go to school."

I smothered a giggle at how her words didn't match the cloud-of-rags picture in front of me. It wasn't funny anyway, not when I thought about it.

"My life is ruined. I'll never meet a boy from a decent family here."

"Josephine Sadie Marcuse! If you don't go to school, you'll be so ignorant that even the boys from lesser families won't look at you. Education, culture, those are the things you need."

"It ain't gonna matter none." Not when we said *Marcuse* instead of *Marcus.* Even if I could convince them to abandon the Jewish name, Mama and Papa still carried accents that betrayed our Polish heritage. Speaking German mattered little—the real Germans saw through it. It reminded folks we were nothing but lower-class.

"And there you go. Listen to yourself. *Ain't.* Everyone will know you're baseborn."

She was right. I *was* baseborn but I didn't have to sound so common. My accent was American and there was no need for me to speak as though I was ill-educated. Words made a difference. I might not like school but I was smart and I'd best learn to speak like the lady I wanted to be. "I wish we'd never come here. I wish we'd stayed in New York."

"*Ach,* there was nothing for us there. In San Francisco, there are prospects. It's not your papa's fault this time. If Dobrzensky had known how to run a business, your father would still have a job and we'd still be living on Powell Street." She stepped out of the laundry pile and pulled me into a hug. "He'll find something soon, Sadie. Then we'll move out of this neighborhood, back to somewhere finer. In the meantime, you'll go to school and learn to be a lady."

"All right, I'm going."

I shrugged out of her arms and grabbed my schoolbooks. It wasn't education I needed, just the semblance of one. All a person had to do was convince others they were educated, cultured. That was what was important.

Once outside, I slammed the door shut behind me and headed down the block, kicking at a rock with each step. Dirt swirled into the air.

Dusty, dirty, grimy neighborhood.

Powell Street had been a fine place to live. Well, not exactly rich-fine. It had been adequate. Perfectly sufficient, with bright row houses, each with a single family, most in decent repair. Mama called it a place of opportunity and it was colorful and full of life, devoid of drudgery. Everywhere, there was something to see, a bustling neighborhood where everyone appeared to be doing well. But here, people were sour, toiling the entire day. There was nothing but shabby tenements, leaning one against the other, as if bracing themselves so they wouldn't tumble down the hill into San Francisco Bay.

I turned the corner on to lower Fourth Street and stared at the primary school across the way. Its unadorned weathered brown brick wasn't much to look at either.

Papa had said life in California would be better than New York, that he'd have his own bakery. We were supposed to live in a grand house, painted up real pretty. Mama was promised servants to help her with the chores. Instead, Papa had lost his job yet again and there was no grand house anywhere in the future. And worse, San Francisco was a place where such things mattered far more than they had in New York, where everyone a person knew was poor and no one even thought about rising above their station.

Here, the wealthy were close enough to spit at, except they were all busy spitting on us.

I sent the rock flying down the hill. If there was any luck in the world, it would hit some toff in the head. Once it rolled out of the neighborhood.

"You kick that rock any harder, it's gonna break somebody's window."

I started and whipped around to face a girl about my age, her heart-shaped face framed by blond braids. She was staring at my ringlets, still flying about me in a sable whirl. "So what?"

"You gonna pay for it if it does? I'll bet your papa don't have a dime to his name."

She had no call lecturing me, standing there in a patched dress that was at least an inch too short for her. "And yours does?" I wrinkled my nose and stood a bit straighter so she could see my dress was more fashionable.

"Ain't got no pa so I guess that's for sure."

Well, that spoke volumes, I guessed. But I still didn't like it that she'd placed me in the same barrel. "I bet your ma doesn't have a dime, either." *There, that would put her in her place.*

"Ain't got no ma neither."

That took the wind out of me. No father *and* no mother? My gaze swept over her. "You're an orphan? I never met an orphan."

"Don't stare so hard. Your eyes are liable to get stuck that way and you'll go around forever with your eyeballs bulging out."

It sounded so much like something Mama would say that I couldn't hold back my laughter. It rose up out of me like a burp, an embarrassing guffaw that made my cheeks heat up.

The girl grinned at me. "You live around here?"

"On Clara Street. We just moved in."

"I live over a few blocks, on First Street. I'm Ella Howard."

"Josephine Marcus." I offered the Americanized version of my Jewish last name. Only the lower classes retained their Old World names. "But everyone calls me Sadie."

"Sadie? That's a long ways from Josephine."

"My middle name's Sarah. Germans place a great store on middle names." She didn't need to know I was Polish. Germans were higher class, after all.

Ella nodded, asking nothing further. She didn't need to—everybody knew Sadie was a nickname for Sarah. "You headed for the school?"

"Supposed to be. I don't much care whether I go or not."

Ella shrugged her shoulders. "Me neither. How about we just not go?"

It struck me as a fine idea. At Powell Street Primary, I'd skipped school so often that the principal had taken to bringing me in to slap my palms with a ruler. It hadn't made much difference. There'd been far more interesting things to see outside of school and I learned more, too.

"Where are we headed, Ella Howard?"

"We can go over to Rincon Hill, where all the rich folks used to live. They ain't there no more. They all moved to the new part of town, but all their fancy houses are still there. They are nothing but boardinghouses now, smack full of poor folks like me and my sister."

We skirted through alleys, working our way between brick and wooden tenements. Above, wet shabby clothes hung on lines strung from one window to another. Echoes of bustle and business filled the cramped corridors, draymen selling wares, people rushing to and fro. It was like a section of New York got plunked down on the other side of the country.

We climbed, emerging atop a hill, panting. Ella pointed to a large house, faded bric-a-brac decorating its front. "That's

Rincon House. Used to be some well-to-do family lived there. The widow Holt rents it from them, and we rent a room from her."

"You and your sister?" I liked Ella, her blunt way of speaking and her spunk.

"And her husband. She's fresh married but saddled with me 'til I can fend for myself."

"You're sharing a room with newlyweds? That must be something." I knew all about newlyweds, my own sister being one. All they did was hold hands and gaze into each other's eyes. "Ew."

"Sometimes at night, I stick my fingers in my ears."

I knew about the other stuff, too, the stuff that happened in the dark. Not firsthand, of course, but I had an idea. You don't live too long on Powell Street without learning about that. Still, I wasn't sure on the details involved or exactly what Ella meant. But I nodded like I knew.

"They root around like animals."

I tipped my head sagely at that, too, even though it made little sense. I knew men and women paired up, did things with each other, but had no firsthand clue how it bared any resemblance to cats mating in the alleyways.

We explored the once-fancy neighborhood for a while, sharing bits about ourselves, until the morning was gone and we'd covered most all there was to do. "Let's go up Powell Street," I suggested. I knew there was a lot to see there. Plus, it would impress Ella, show her how worldly I was. Impressions were important after all. "I'll show you where I used to live."

We tackled the hills, headed northwest before angling north up Battery Street. Some twenty minutes later, I turned left on Clay and meandered through the area folks called Chinatown. Brilliant red and blue and gold fabrics drew our attention, Chinese kimonos and brocaded slippers and long dark ponytails.

I reminded myself to tell Ella this was the Oriental area—that sounded fancier than "Chinatown."

Ella's eyes widened. "You lived here?"

"Well, a few blocks over. But I thought you'd like to see this."

We passed a crowded shop and the scent of incense drifted out from the doorway, mingling with the noodles and fish being cooked in an apartment above. Against one building, a man lounged with an ivory pipe in his hand, his eyes glazed. I hurried Ella past the opium den and stopped in front of an older woman a few doors down.

"Ming?"

She looked up. "Miss Sadie Jo." Ming bowed, then straightened, at least as much as she could. "Oh so good to see you."

I bowed back as my mouth stretched into a wide smile. I didn't correct her on my name—she'd always mangled it up and it didn't really matter. "I've missed you." My eyes stung. I hadn't realized how much I'd yearned to see her.

"You come to visit? Have some lunch?" She rushed to usher us in the door and I introduced Ella.

"Sit, sit," Ming insisted. She spun around the tiny room, then shoved bowls of rice into our hands. "Eat."

I took the chopsticks she offered and demonstrated to Ella how to hold them. She messed up the first few efforts but finally managed to grasp them correctly. Picking up the rice was an entirely different matter and Ming finally sighed and handed her a porcelain spoon. Lord, how I loved eating Ming's rice. I didn't know what it was she cooked it in but I was glad we'd ended up passing her place at lunchtime. She chattered on, telling me about her neighbors, and I nodded as if I knew every single one of them. It was always better to appear wise than stupid. Then, we carried our bowls to the rough wooden counter.

"I'm sorry, Ming, but we have to go. Thank you for the rice." We'd need to be back home by the time school let out and we still had things to see and a good half-hour walk back.

"You come back. Visit me again," Ming chimed.

I hugged her, then bowed before we stepped back into the sunlight. I took Ella's hand and led her down the block, winding through the busy community. We emerged a few blocks later, now on Jackson Street. Ahead lay Powell.

At the corner, I pointed right. "We lived there, in the middle of the block."

"Ain't we going by?"

"Nah, that block is dull. This way is more exciting." We turned back south, toward Washington, and I knew the moment Ella saw because her mouth dropped open.

I was glad we'd delayed until early afternoon. Mornings on Powell Street were empty of activity. But in the afternoon, things came alive.

Women in richly crafted taffeta strolled the block, their fine silk parasols protecting their faces from the sun. Velvet hats with bright feathers and ribbons perched on their heads. Paisley shawls draped from their shoulders.

"Oh, my!" Ella said.

"If you're quiet, and listen real hard, you can hear the rustle of their skirts."

We stood, watching the women glide down the sidewalks, chatting among themselves.

"Who are they?" Ella whispered.

"Mama calls them painted ladies."

"Fallen women?"

"Mama told me to walk around this block but I never did."

"These are brothels?"

"Fancy ones, nearly every house on the block. In the afternoons, the women all come out and parade around like ladies in the rich neighborhoods, except right here on Powell

Street. I wasn't going to walk around the block and miss all this."

"They don't look like fallen women, not like the ones I've seen before."

"Come on." I strode off, leaving Ella to catch up with me. Along the way, the ladies smiled at us, offering pleasantries. Piano music drifted out from open windows, and from a few of the houses, soft melodies floated out on soprano voices. "Oh, how I wish I could sing like that."

"Why don't you take voice lessons?" Ella asked.

Hah! Papa couldn't even afford to keep us housed in a decent neighborhood. There was no way he'd be able to pay for a luxury like that. "I wish I could."

I winced at the wistful tone in my voice. Thank goodness Ella didn't ask me about it. It was bad enough to be poor without having to admit it to anyone.

"I could ask James if he'd teach you," she said.

"Who?"

"My brother-in-law."

I fought to keep my excitement in check. "Your brother-in-law teaches music?"

"Well, he works as a draftsman but he wants to get a job in a music store. He plays piano around town, at special events, and gives a few lessons. I bet he'd teach you."

"I don't think my folks can afford for me to take music lessons." There, I'd said it.

"He wouldn't charge much, not since we're best friends and all."

Her words warmed me. I hadn't had a best friend since we left New York. "Is that what we are? Best friends?"

"Seems like it to me."

We strolled the street, me thinking how much more cultured I would be if I could sing like the songbirds inside the windows.

"You know any of these women? Like you do Ming?"

How I wished! Maybe if I did, some of their fineness would rub off on me. "There's a few I know by name but mostly just nodding acquaintances." I made light of any implied shortcomings for not having met them. In truth, they'd never much paid attention to kids like me. "They move in and out a lot."

"Look at that!" Ella pointed to a third story window, where a woman perched in a silk wrapper that drooped off her bare shoulder. "I swear she don't have a stich on under that thing."

The woman looked down, her eyes smoky with kohl, her lips red and plump, even from a distance. She caught our gazes and blew a kiss.

"Oh, lordy! That one's fallen for sure," Ella said.

She looked pretty secure up there on the window ledge so I wasn't quite sure what Ella meant—not entirely—but something told me I shouldn't ask. I didn't want to look dumb, after all, not in front of my new best friend.

We cleared the block, a few of the ladies even smiling at us. Maybe I was growing up and not such a kid anymore. We nodded back and headed home to the eighth ward.

But I couldn't get the image of the woman in the window out of my mind. Even dressed as she was, she'd been stunning. I imagined meeting her on the street, attired in her finest, and couldn't picture her being any more beautiful than she'd been in her silk wrapper.

What a life those women had, milling the streets just to show off their fancy clothes and lounging at the window in their underthings without a care in the world.

Maybe I shouldn't worry so much about attracting the right husband. None of those women had one and their lives seemed just fine to me.

★ ★ ★ ★ ★

1873 (two years later)

Over the next two years, Ella's landlady relocated twice, Ella and her sister moving with her. My family had moved once. By the time it was all over, we lived just a block apart and were thick as fleas. I'd managed to convince Mama into letting me take voice lessons from Ella's brother-in-law and adored the attention James paid me while I was there. If there were more men like him around, the neighborhood wouldn't be so glum.

The eighth ward was still one of the dirtiest, poorest parts of town but I'd given up expecting Papa to move us out of there. He'd worked mostly as a peddler with a few scattered bakery jobs and I lost hope that he'd ever become anything more.

I was thirteen, after all, and saw things more clearly. I'd been right all along. It wasn't so much what you were but what people *thought* you were. And Mama worked real hard at convincing folks who didn't know us that we were better than we were. When life dealt a bad hand, you did what you could to bluff your way past it.

"I want you to practice the aria this next week. With a tad more dedication than you and Ella give your schoolwork."

Next to me, Ella giggled at her brother-in-law's remark and I threw her a look. Just because it was true didn't mean we had to acknowledge it. Especially to James.

"Yes, Mr. Rhind," I promised. Lord but that man was dreamy. I'd never met anyone quite like him and I guessed Ella hadn't either. He had an easy way about him, relaxed with females rather than all fussy and worried like the boys at school.

"You still taking those dance lessons?" James asked.

"Both Hennie and I." When the McCarthy sisters opened a dance academy, I'd pressed at Mama so hard she'd finally given in, using her egg money to pay for occasional lessons for me and my younger sister. So we could learn to dance properly, like the ladies we weren't—one more way to pull the wool over society's eyes. We didn't tell Mama about how we were learning the Highland Fling and the Sailor's Hornpipe—just about the ballroom dances.

James handed me the sheet music, his glance lingering on me. "That's good. A lady needs to know how to sing and dance."

Exactly what I'd told Mama.

"Like they do at the fancy houses?" Ella prompted.

I glanced at her and saw how she smirked, holding back her laughter.

"Don't make fun, Ella." James frowned at her and I wished she hadn't distracted him. "Many of those women are more cultured than the wealthy women who condemn them."

James had a sort of allegiance to brothels now that he was a "professor of music" in them. Once Ella and I started chatting with the ladies on Powell Street, we learned about how touring musicians provided entertainment in the evenings. Ella had tipped off James and he'd secured employment, moving from one brothel to the next. The ladies called him "professor."

We had called him that once, to his face, but he hadn't been too pleased. He had a day job at a musical instrument store now and said he wanted to keep his other job quiet, like he was ashamed of it.

"You keep your distance from those places," James advised. "Never mind how refined the ladies are, you girls still have no business interacting with them."

It was an odd thing to say, after his comment about how cultured they were. To me, they put society ladies to shame. They were all that rich women were without the snooty overtones.

"They got a better life than most around here do," Ella said.

"The ones you've seen do and some of them are the finest

women around, but not all of them." James's brow knit. "There are others that don't have such an easy time. Despite the finery and what you see as easy lifestyle in those parlor houses, it isn't something you girls need to focus on."

I rolled my eyes at Ella.

"We gotta go, James." If there was one thing Ella was good at, it was deflecting conversation. "Are you done with Sadie?"

"Practice!"

"I will," I promised, then followed Ella out the door and sat on the stoop with her. "When did he get to be such a wet hen?"

"About the time I started sprouting titties."

I snorted. That was when the boys at school had started acting different, too. And when we started our monthlies, Mama and Ella's sister Mae had gotten all particular about our behavior. Now, we had to focus on fooling them, too.

"Mae told him to stop talking about his 'employers' because it wasn't a fitting topic to discuss with young ladies. I don't think he ever told her we're the ones who got him the job."

"You ever catch him looking at yours?" I asked her.

"My titties?"

"Yeah."

"Lord above, Sadie. He's married to my sister."

"Being married doesn't stop men from looking."

Ella shrugged. "No, I guess it don't. But I ain't got that much to look at. Not like you."

I puffed out my chest. Mama said I'd "bloomed early" and most times, boys stared at my bosom like it was something to be afraid of.

"Does he look at yours?" Ella asked.

"Sometimes."

Except he didn't look afraid, like the boys did. Men looked at them different. Like they wanted to touch them, or nibble on them. I'd seen my brother-in-law do that to Rebecca once and she'd gasped out loud as her head fell back and her eyes got all glassy. Maybe I'd have let James do that to me if he wasn't married to Ella's sister.

Ella looked around, then bent her head close. "Joe looks at mine sometimes. He asked me if he could touch them."

"He didn't!"

"He did."

I tried to imagine having a boy ask that. But, then, Joe wasn't a boy—he was nineteen and Ella's steady beau. "Did you let him?"

Ella closed her eyes, a soft smile forming. "Oh, Sadie, it felt so good."

"Ella Howard!"

"Well, it did." She peered at me from beneath her fluttering lashes. "I knew it would. I share a room with James and Mae for Pete's sake."

She'd told me more about James and Mae, what they did at night. I tried to imagine my folks doing that, or even my sister, but couldn't quite make a picture of it with my relatives. But James . . . I could see him touching a body, imagine him caressing mine. Ella said Mae made sounds, like she liked it. Goose bumps rose on my arms and I shivered.

"You all right?"

"Yeah," I said. "Just thinking about it is all." I knew I wasn't supposed to have such thoughts. Mama said good girls didn't dwell on such things.

We sat, quiet, until Ella spoke. "You never did anything yet?"

"Nope. The boys around here don't tempt me one bit." They were childish, still teasing and pulling hair. I wanted a grown man, like James, somebody who would treat me like a woman instead of a girl. Someone who knew breasts were designed for more than pinches and stares.

"You need somebody like Joe. He knows lots more than the

boys our age."

I sat up straight. "Lots more?"

"I might have let him do a few more things than just touch my titties," she whispered.

"Like what? Ella Howard, you tell me this minute."

"I might have let him touch me other places."

Warmth flooded me and I quivered. "Like James touches Mae?"

"And other things."

I thought about what she might mean and finally decided it was better to know straight up. "Did you fornicate with him?"

"Not yet . . . but I might." She sighed. "It ain't like I gotta save myself for some high-class fellow. I'm dirt poor and I'm not gonna marry anybody who expects anything. There's no such thing as 'soiled goods' around here."

"You sure about that? Mama takes great stock in telling me I need to stay pure." She harped on it every time I looked sideways at a boy, or one looked at me. Still, I wasn't convinced it was so wrong, not when it made me tingle so much when I thought on it.

"Not in my circles. Maybe you got a chance. You might meet somebody and get out of here. But I'm not going anywhere and we both know it."

Was she right? Were girls from the eighth ward fated to lives of poverty? "It doesn't seem like you're setting your sights very high."

"Why pretend? I like Joe, he likes me. Maybe I'll end up marrying him. If not, at least I'll go into marriage knowing what to expect and how to enjoy it."

We sat there in the growing dusk, not saying much while my mind wandered, wondering if I had a chance for a decent life or if I, too, would end up trapped.

I wanted more than that, much more, and I'd be damned if

I'd sit back and be a victim. Ella had the right view on things, making her own choices rather than letting life decide for her.

I just needed to figure out what it was I wanted and I could do the same.

Spring 1874 (six months later)

My ears hurt.

Mama had warned me but I hadn't paid much attention. She'd forbidden me to have them pierced but my thoughts had mostly focused on how I wasn't about to let her deny me. I'd gone ahead and done it anyway, nearly a month ago. But ever since yesterday, when they started swelling, I'd been worried.

Ella and I had had it done on Powell Street where a dark-skinned Chilean prostitute named Maria had iced our earlobes and stuck a needle through them. I hadn't cried a bit, even though it had stung like the dickens.

Ella said it stung less than when Joe took her maidenhead. Then she'd bounced away with pearl ear fobs dangling on either side of her face.

Maria had laughed at her and plunged the needle through my lobe. When it was done, she'd inserted the fine jade drops I'd picked up in Chinatown.

Neither Ella nor I had been able to afford the jewelry ourselves. Joe had bought hers the night she'd given herself to him. Mine had been paid for by a friend of Joe's who'd been happy to part with the money in exchange for time with my bosom in the alley behind Ming's place. Both Ella and I had been pleased with the bargains.

"It's sore, little one, but not an infection." Hattie Wells, the madam of the house, patted my hand. "Don't tug so much on the earrings. You are tempted too much by the shiny things."

In the side chair, Maria giggled.

We'd worked up the courage to ask Maria to pierce our ears, after we'd been unable to resist prying about her earrings. She'd told us one of her customers had offered the gorgeous silver fobs. That's when Ella had the idea to ask Joe. I figured letting his friend touch me a little wouldn't hurt.

Now, I just wished my ears pained a little less.

Mama had been mad as a hornet.

"Josephine Sarah Marcuse, what have you done?"

"My friend's *abuela* did it. The girl from the dance academy." It was a lie, but one Mama would swallow. I'd become pretty skilled at convincing her as easily as I did the endless parade of boys my sister marched me in front of on the nights she took me to the theatre. They all knew we were only there because her husband's employer had a box but they had no idea I was a poor Polish girl.

"After I forbade it."

"But all the girls are doing it. All the upper-class girls, anyway. I wanted to fit in, so the boys would think me one of them. She even gave me the earrings."

Mama had mellowed and fingered the jade drops and the fine gold filigree. "She gave you those?"

"She said she wanted me to have them. She might even invite me to one of her parties. Can you imagine that, Mama? Me, going to a fancy party where I can meet the right boys?" That would quiet her protest, for sure.

"*Ach,* that would be something. You are fourteen and it is time we start matching you with someone. What that would be, to have a good German boy notice you. We could avoid the matchmaker then."

Good lord! "The matchmaker? Oh, Mama, no."

"You don't want a good match? You want some dirt-poor boy to take you home to his Mama? *Nein,* I think it better we scrape together the money and find a Yiddish matchmaker to at least give you a chance."

I'd rolled my eyes. "We don't even go to synagogue, Mama. What would a good Jewish boy want with me?"

"Just because we work the Sabbath to make ends meet doesn't mean we need to deny tradition. We will find you a tailor, established in his trade. Someone older, perhaps a widower, who does not care so much your family is not wealthy. With such a bosom, you will be sure to catch a man's attention. It will not be easy and it will cost us money we do not have, but it will be better you have a match than marry a tinker off the street or some Gentile without a dime."

And wouldn't such a good Jewish businessman be pleased to know I had my ears pierced in a brothel after letting a dirty Gentile boy touch my breasts in exchange for jade earrings?

Maria's madam, Hattie Wells, cleared her throat, drawing me back to the present. "It's getting late, girls. Maria needs to get ready for the evening and you both need to head out of the neighborhood."

Hattie did that regularly, shooed us away once the afternoon began to wear away. We knew better than to argue with her. We were fortunate she tolerated us hanging around. I grabbed my schoolbooks while Ella got our shawls and we headed back to our own neighborhood.

Ella said little, a marked difference from her usual chattering.

"Something wrong?" I asked.

"Nah."

"Is, too. You've barely said a word in the last four blocks."

"Just thinking is all."

"About what?"

She stopped and caught my gaze. "James and Mae want to get their own place, start a family. They told me last night that it was time I found a job and went out on my own."

My heart sank for her. "Oh, Ella! You're not even fifteen!"

"Mae said she was on her own at my age and she found a way."

"What's she expect you to do?"

"That's up to me. My birthday's at the end of the year. By then, I need to have a job and find a place of my own."

She took off down the block, me chasing after her.

"That isn't right," I choked out when I caught up. "Mae found a husband."

"That wasn't until later, after Ma died and she got saddled with me. Besides, she didn't marry James for that. They love each other."

I struggled for alternatives. "What about Joe? Has he talked about marriage?"

"Joe hasn't spoken to me for three weeks."

"What?" Ella hadn't said a word.

"He said he isn't interested in a girl who would offer herself for a pair of earrings."

Hot anger boiled up inside me. "He was sure interested enough to give them to you."

"I shouldn't have asked him, shouldn't have done any of it. He was like a fish on the line as long as there was bait. Once he got the worm, he hasn't been interested in the hook."

I didn't know what to say. I had no experience with this. "There are plenty of other fish out there," I finally offered. It sounded weak.

"And I'm spoiled goods. Mae told me this would happen if I let Joe have his way. I thought it wouldn't matter but it does." She marched away again, muttering. "She warned me."

I strode along, grasping for another bit of wisdom. "Do you see Hattie and Maria suffering? They have all kinds of men fawning over them. You need to find some other beau."

"Sadie, don't you see? Joe's told everybody he knows. I've had five of his friends offer to buy me trinkets in exchange for a poke. There isn't a male in the entire eighth ward who hasn't heard by now." Her face reddened.

"You think your chastity matters that much?"

"What matters is that I *sold* it."

Deep down, I knew she was right and that we both should have listened to our elders' wisdom.

Two boys had stopped me on the street last week, promising me charms and ornaments of my own but it hadn't grown into a problem. I'd laughed at them, told them the rumor was ridiculous. Everybody knew I'd received my earrings from a wealthy girlfriend—Mama had announced to the world that I had such a friend from a good family. I'd told them I'd never let a boy from this part of town touch me. No one had to know what had really happened.

"So what are you going to do?" I asked her.

"I'll get a job in a shop or something. Maybe as a laundress or a seamstress if I have to. Then I'll move to another ward, where nobody knows me. I can't stay here. I've seen it happen to other girls. The boys will just keep coming round, asking me until I do it again."

"It's six months until you have to move out. Things can change a lot in six months."

"Or get a lot worse. All I know is that I don't want to end up turning johns in back alleys or some dark little crib somewhere. I want more from life, don't you?"

I nodded, wondering what would have happened if Mama and I hadn't crafted a good reputation that could stave off any negative rumors. No, I wouldn't have any problems, not like what Ella was having.

After all, I'd not given up my virtue and no one in the eighth ward knew any of the men the matchmaker would find for me.

God willing.

Chapter Two: Josephine/Sadie

Respectability was hard to come by, back then.

Fall 1874 (six months later)
San Francisco

By the time school was back underway, Ella and I had formed a plan to solve her situation. Now, we just needed to find the courage to set it in motion.

Despite our delusions to the contrary, Joe had continued to run his mouth and his pals had kept up the pressure to bed us. For me, it wasn't so bad. I continued to feign arrogant innocence, told them I didn't know what they were talking about, that someone must have made up the whole tale. In time, they stopped bothering me and no one was the wiser.

A good lie went a long way and I learned a valuable lesson in creating a false truth in advance of trouble.

But for Ella, it was different. Lies were of no benefit to her. She hadn't had a ready story and no one would have believed her anyway. There was little she could deny. She and Joe had been an item and folks had seen how they acted together. There wasn't a soul out there who believed she wasn't easy; everyone knew she didn't have money of her own for pearl earrings, and she'd already bragged they were real.

The gossip spread. Boys and men came to Ella's boarding-house, stopped her on the street when she was looking for a job. Potential employers turned her away, not wanting to risk her turning tricks from her place of work. She couldn't move to another ward until she earned enough money for a place to live and she couldn't get an honest job until she moved to another ward. Without honest work, there was but one other way to earn the money.

My heart wept for her and I recognized the stab of guilt that prickled when I thought about it too much. I'd grown up learning to craft my versions of the truth in advance, and I wished I'd thought of doing so for Ella. But I hadn't and now it was too late.

The way we looked at it, she had two choices. She could either live her life as a victim of that soiled reputation or she could take charge of it and create her own path. She'd chosen the second option. We headed up Powell Street the same day she decided. Mostly because she was determined to prevent herself from backing out. I went as moral support.

We rang the bell of Hattie Wells's fine carved oak door and waited to be admitted.

Hattie answered herself, wrapped up in a comfortable Chinese silk robe no doubt from the shops near Ming's place—the robe a vivid blue that complemented Hattie's azure eyes. "Well, look who's here! We haven't seen you two in a month of Sundays. You lost?"

Ella exhaled a heavy breath. "No, we have something we want to talk about."

"My, that seems ominous." Hattie waved us into the house and led the way into a well-appointed parlor, the peacock robe sweeping the floor in a wide tail. She sank onto a brocaded chair in a single fluid movement. Even in a wrapper, she was elegant with sophistication I craved.

Ella and I perched on a red velvet settee like two plain little wrens.

"You're here earlier than you normally are and you look

pretty serious. I suggest you spit it out. One of you in trouble?"

I glanced at Ella, unsure what Hattie meant.

Ella blushed and shook her head. "No, ma'am, not in the way you mean."

"But there *is* trouble?"

"You remember when Maria pierced our ears?" Ella clasped her hands together, as if she was forcing herself not to touch her earrings. She trembled and the pearl fobs tapped her face.

Oh, Ella.

Hattie crossed her arms. "You didn't tell your parents where you had it done, did you?"

"No, ma'am," I said. Did she really think we were that dumb?

"Then?"

"We couldn't afford the earrings," I explained.

"And?" Hattie drew out the word.

"Sadie let a boy feel her up. I let one have me."

"But you're not pregnant?"

"No. But I might just as well be."

Hattie relaxed her arms and her lips turned up in sympathy. "The bastards told everyone who would listen, didn't they?"

"It's not so bad for me," I said. "Hardly anyone that matters believes it."

"And for you?" Hattie turned a soft gaze on Ella.

"It's taken over my life." Her eyes glinted. "My reputation wasn't good in the first place. I don't much have one at all now. No one will hire me and I'm not likely to land a husband. In three months, my sister is sending me out on my own and I refuse to become a streetwalker."

Hattie leaned forward, grasping Ella's hand. "And so you're here?"

"If the only course open to me is prostitution, then I want to work out of a parlor house."

"That makes sense."

I was glad she hadn't made Ella beg. It was bad enough she'd had to make such a choice. Hattie was more than just an elegant woman; she was compassionate. She'd treat Ella right. Coming here had been a good decision.

"Tell me about yourself . . . your education, skills?"

"My skills?" Ella blushed again.

Hattie laughed and patted Ella's hand. "We'll teach you those, darling." She pulled away and waved her hands in a wide gesture. "Singing, dancing, musicianship, foreign languages? Entertaining in a parlor house is much more than lying on your back."

"I've had some voice lessons and I can play a little piano. My brother-in-law taught me." Ella paused. "James Rhind."

Hattie smiled. "Ah, yes, James. He's played here on occasion. I didn't realize you were related. I haven't seen him in a while."

"He got a new job, selling musical instruments, and gives lessons at the store. Says he needs to stay respectable if he's to keep those customers."

"That's true, I'm sure. Let's see what he's taught you. Piano's in the music room." Hattie pointed to a side room.

I squeezed Ella's hand and held my breath as she rose and seated herself on the piano stool. She wasn't much of a pianist, barely adequate. Her voice was a shade better. I'd shown her a few dance steps but not enough to qualify her as a dancer. A good fit of nerves and she'd be done for.

She plunked out a couple tunes, making a few errors.

My own pulse skittered and I could only imagine what Ella's heart was doing.

I jumped from the settee and joined her. The way she was shaking, she couldn't possibly play. "Here, let me do this. You sing." I launched into a popular song James had taught us.

Beside me, Ella steadied, her voice solid and confident.

Once through the tune, I shifted to an aria.

Ella kept up with that, too, doing far better than she had with the piano playing.

I snuck a glance at Hattie. She wasn't frowning.

"Can you two sing a duet?" she asked. "I'd like to see how your voice blends with others."

I chose another song, taking alto to Ella's soprano.

"Hmmm." Hattie joined us in the music room. Behind us, she waited for us to turn.

I held my breath. *Please, please, please don't make her beg.*

"You've potential, Ella. You're a bit limited but we could mold you. I don't believe you're ready to fit in here in San Francisco, but I do have a connection in Prescott, Arizona. I'd apprentice you there, then bring you back once you've honed your skills. All of them."

This time, Ella's face didn't redden. "You would?"

"I'm taking a group of girls there in October. I see no reason not to include you." She caught my gaze. "Either of you."

My heart nearly stopped at Hattie's words. I spent the rest of the meeting in a stupor and trudged back to our own neighborhood barely listening to Ella. I tried to imagine what such a life would be like. I'd spent years of my life walking through that two-block stretch of parlor houses envying those who lived there, thinking about how much better their lives were than mine.

But joining them had never crossed my mind.

Until now.

"You're not listening," Ella said.

"I'm thinking."

"You're considering it? Sadie, you're a good girl. Why would you even think about it?"

"Because those women are elegant and cultured and have exciting lives. They control their own destinies. They aren't shackled to husbands who promise them heaven, then renege. They don't live in squalor."

"But you'll marry and move out of the eighth ward."

"The current plan is to hire a matchmaker and wed me to a middle-aged man with a trade. I'll never become wealthy. Worse, I could end up with someone like Papa—a man with a trade but no ambition to pursue it."

"They'll find you a young man, someone with prospects."

"The young men with prospects don't need matchmakers. They are surrounded by girls of their own class. Educated, cultured girls from proper German families—girls whose parents have the right accents. Girls with pert noses." I stared cross-eyed at my nose. Papa had called it bulbous and said I'd never get a match. "It's only the ones that have something wrong with them that need matchmaking. It's only the desperate ones that would settle for a poor Polish girl."

"What if you're wrong? What if you get one with all the wealth and social status you've ever dreamed of? You'd go to the opera and the theatre and have new dresses all the time. And servants to keep your big fancy house."

"That's not the kind of man who needs to use a matchmaker. Don't you see? It'll be a widower of modest means with a litter of kids who needs someone to raise them while he works. Or maybe some mama's boy who's never married, maybe even one who prefers men but who needs a wife to bow to his mother's control and take care of her when she's bedridden. Maybe he'll beat me because I won't kowtow to his control."

"Sadie—"

"I cringe every time Mama says 'matchmaker' and no boy in the neighborhood catches my eye."

"And you think life in Hattie's parlor house is the answer?"

"I think a life of independence and wealth is worth consideration. Tailored clothes, lives of leisure, music and culture."

"And what about the men?"

"What about them? You think it would be much different having some old man I can't stand forcing himself on me every night? Someone I'm chained to for life? The girls at Hattie's don't stay forever. Why not live well and be able to move on after a few years?"

"And do what? They're fallen women, soiled doves."

"Only if they're bad liars. Lie well and one can change the truth."

I left the house in my plaid dress, schoolbooks in hand. My heart pounded. I glanced back, waved to Mama, and choked back my tears. Would she ever speak to me again? In time, she'd forgive me. I had to hold on to that. I patted my smart Dutch braids, tied up with a ribbon that matched my dress. I looked good, too good for the hang-jowled butcher who'd come calling last night. I told myself if that was the best the matchmaker could do, I was making the right choice.

By the time I walked the short distance to Ella's place, I'd churned up a healthy dose of resentment. For the life of me, I couldn't imagine how Mama thought it would be a good thing to tie me to a man like that. He was so fat he didn't fit on the chair and when he'd kissed my hand, I'd noticed bits of meat trapped under his fingernails. I had to wash three times to get rid of the reek that lingered from his touch.

I shuddered. It gave new meaning to meaty paws.

Ella sat on her stoop, waiting. "Ready?"

"Ready."

We took off up Fourth Street, passing the school and leaving it behind us. We were both quieter than usual but our steps were determined. We were masters of our destinies and there was a life of adventure in front of us, we were sure.

At Hattie's we were ushered into the parlor, where a gaggle

of girls near our own age was already gathered. Seamstresses were at the ready with measuring tapes, a pile of dresses heaped over the settee.

"Let's get those dresses off, girls."

I glanced around as we stripped our frocks, shedding school dresses and girlish petticoats to the floor. Naked, we eyed one another—our curves and lack thereof—and I fought to keep from covering myself. I wouldn't, couldn't, be the first to do so. I looked down, then raised my eyes and stared boldly at the other girls. One by one, we were called behind a screen.

"Sadie, you're next."

I walked toward the corner, my underthings in hand, fighting my fear.

Ella nodded at me and mouthed reassurance. "A doctor," I think she said.

Beyond the screen, a man sat me on a wooden stool, checked my hair, pronounced me lice-free, and asked about my monthlies. My face heated at his other questions. Bare in front of him, I trembled but held steady. Then he told me to lean back, opened my legs, and looked *there*.

Oh, dear lord.

I fought to keep still, to behave like Hattie would expect. I'd chosen this.

"That's all," he said. "Head to the seamstress."

I let out the breath I didn't know I'd been holding, stood, and put on my shift. When I went around the screen, I was a bit more confident. I'd survived this man seeing my body. I'd survive the rest of it.

Hattie motioned me over and one of the seamstresses set to work, taking my measurements and making notes on a scrap of paper. Whisk, whisk, then she was done and sending me to the milliner in the corner who perched first one, then another hat upon my head. She *tsked* at my braids and waved me on.

I glanced at Ella, still being measured, then at the pile of dresses.

Those are for us?

The array of silks and satins drew me. A woman with a dark complexion sorted through them, eyeing the notes from the seamstress. She glanced at me and picked up a ruby gown.

"This here color will be fine with that sable hair." She handed it to a younger woman, along with the paper. "Let out the bodice some." Then she turned to me. "You come with Aunt Julia now. We gotta do something with that hair. Hair like that don't belong in braids."

She sat me in a chair and pulled the ribbon from my head, dropping it on the floor. Around the room, other girls were having their hair styled into elaborate coiffures while seamstresses altered dresses. When the gowns were ready, we were assisted into them. One by one, we ceased being girls, most of us too overwhelmed to say much.

I turned to a mirror and staggered at the image. The transformation was stunning. I was no longer Sadie Marcus. I looked just like the women who'd awed me for so many years.

"You girls look absolutely breathtaking." Hattie stood in the parlor arch, drawing our attention. "I've advanced five gowns for each of you, along with undergarments, robes, and shoes. Aunt Julia will see everything is packed into trunks, then join us at the wharf." She glanced around the room, smiling at each of us in turn. There were nine of us. "You can get acquainted in the hacks and on the steamer. We've not much time, girls. Come along."

She led us from the house to the street. We paired up, chattering. I caught up to Ella.

"My goodness!" I said.

"She doesn't waste any time, does she?"

"What do you mean?" I asked.

"The rush of it."

"We're running late. We have a steamer to catch."

Ella sighed. "Inside of two hours, we all owe her for more clothing than I've ever owned in my life."

"She's generous, wanting us to have the best."

"There's nothing generous about this, Sadie. She didn't give it to us, she *advanced* it. We owe her now. There's no going back. That's why we're scurrying to the steamer, before we change our minds."

"That's awfully harsh."

"Maria warned me we'd be in her debt. I just didn't think it would be this hurried."

"Look at us. Stylish, sophisticated. People are noticing us, envying us. We are wealthy, cultured, independent women. Just like we wanted."

"I have a hunch we're none of those things."

"You're thinking too much. Just enjoy." I fingered the fine fabric of my dress and couldn't fathom why she was doubting this. We'd finally have the lives we'd envied for so long.

We boarded the hacks, Ella wrapped up in her private thoughts. The horses clomped down the hill to the wharf. I expected we'd take the steamer across the bay, then board a train for the trip south and west. Around me, other girls chatted, none of them showing any of the doubt Ella was exhibiting.

"I'm Alice Johnson," the girl next to me announced.

She was petite, with hair so blond it was near-white piled atop her head. Someone had powdered and rouged her face. At first glance, she appeared to be about eighteen or so. Then I looked closer and realized she was younger than I was.

"Who're you?" she asked.

"Josephine Marcus—Sadie."

"Those your real names?" someone asked.

I looked up into the eyes of a woman I recognized from

Hattie's. A chaperone? I choked back a giggle.

"Of course," I said.

"Change it."

"Why would I want to do a thing like that?" I'd worked hard to cultivate Marcus as my name.

"Change part of it or the whole thing, but change it. If you ever decide to leave the business, you'll be thankful of it."

It made sense, seeding a story, crafting a lie, just in case—advice well worth heeding.

Besides, she was right. I wasn't Josephine Sarah Marcuse anymore, that was for sure. I just wasn't sure who I'd become.

Chapter Three: Josephine/Sadie

Sometimes, no matter how many lies you tell, it doesn't change things.

October 1874 (a few weeks later)
Wickenburg, Arizona

We girls were old friends and already tired of one another by the time we reached Arizona. We'd crossed into the territory some hundred miles west, ferried across the Colorado River at Ehrenberg, a brush and adobe town deemed a city by Arizona standards. But calling it a city didn't make it one, and Wickenburg had little more to recommend. We pulled up to Grant's Stage Station in a cloud of dust.

There were five of us remaining: Hattie, "Aunt Julia" Burton, the newly named Minnie Alice, Ella (who had retained her own name), and me. The others had veered off to another of Hattie's branch houses. Hattie and Aunt Julia would settle us girls in Prescott, then return to San Francisco.

Along the way, I'd become Sadie Mansfield. I'd conscripted the last name from two broad-shouldered brothers who loaded our trunks onto the steamer in San Francisco, simply because it sounded elegant.

We alit the stage, our stylish gowns now travel-worn and stained with perspiration. Sand swirled in the dry desert air.

Ella snorted.

"What?" I snapped. I'd be glad when we arrived and out of

the confined travel space. I stretched and watched the dust settle. Oh, to breathe clean air again—air that wasn't stagnant and full of body odor. Stagecoach was a horrendous method of travel. Every muscle ached and I'd lost count of the bruises raised by the constant bumping against my seatmates.

"We could have stayed in our own dresses and we'd still be the most sophisticated women in town." Ella nodded toward the plainly dressed women near the station.

"It's just a stopover. Prescott will be refined, you'll see."

"Prescott won't be nothing more than the last three towns. Hot, dusty, and forlorn."

With each mile, Ella had grown more derisive. I knew she was second-thinking her decision but I resented her contempt. This was our way out of a life of drudgery and poverty and it would serve us well to retain our optimism, despite the harsh environment. Her constant barbs were making me doubt myself and I didn't want to—couldn't—do so.

If I did, I'd break into tears.

"Stop it," I hissed. "When did you get to be such a wet hen?"

"About the time I started adding up the cost of the clothes and the trip and the meals and comparing it to the desolation and utter lack of wealthy men. Every mile we travel into Arizona, I'm more and more afraid we'll never earn-out the debt."

I pasted a bright smile on my face and told myself she didn't know what she was talking about. "Prescott will be different. It has mining wealth and it was the territorial capital."

"Yeah, it *was* . . . until they moved it to Tucson. And every town we've passed through has been a mining town. Have you *seen* those miners?"

"Prescott is different. Hattie said—"

"Hattie says a lot of things. Don't be so naïve."

"Don't be so cynical."

"Girls . . . bickering doesn't become you." Hattie stood in

front of the stage station, some twenty feet away. "Smooth out your dresses, stand straight, and gather your things. We'll spend a few days here so I can review operations at my Vulture City enterprise."

"Vulture City?" Ella curled her lips. "That must be a wonderful place to live."

"It's another mining town," I told her, "named for the mine." At least that's what Aunt Julia had told me and I had no reason not to believe her.

We grabbed our satchels and followed Hattie, who'd disappeared down the dusty road into town with Julia and Minnie.

"How many places does Hattie own anyway?" I asked Ella.

"I don't know. A few, I guess. Most of them in the middle of nowhere, it seems."

I heard the sarcasm in Ella's voice and held back my own comments. Deep down, I knew we'd both believed Hattie's other brothels would resemble the one on Powell Street, but saying it out loud would only amplify that we'd been misled.

I pasted a smile on my face and focused on staying positive. "Mining towns are full of men. They don't look too fancy but where the mining is good, they have money. Don't brush that aside just because they're covered with dirt. I'd guess her places do well."

"Hattie likely turns a good profit. But I don't think we will, Sadie." She sighed.

We wouldn't, not if we became sour gloomy souls determined life was against us. What had happened to Ella on this trip?

I left her standing there and hiked into town after the others. Ella could come or not, but I wouldn't spend another minute trying to coax her into optimism.

Ahead, the hotel beckoned. It wasn't one of the sumptuous brick hostels of San Francisco, but it was in good repair and the best the town had to offer. I told myself we'd be comfortable enough. Prescott wasn't far beyond. Things would be better there.

Ahead, a darkly handsome man held the front door. Now that was a pleasing sight. His brocade vest marked him as a gentleman of some wealth. A very charming gentleman.

I entered the foyer, flashing him a smile.

"Ma'am," he said.

"Miss," I corrected. I fished for a demure expression, fitting for a lady. After all, he had no idea I'd be entering the trade soon. And if he *was* rich, maybe I wouldn't need to.

"I stand corrected," he said, "as well as pleased. I'd not wanted to hope. John Harris Behan, at your service." He stepped inside and took my hand, kissing it. His lips tickled the back of it ever so slightly, and I shivered.

Life would be something with a man like that. Lord, he must be thirsting for a decent woman. I could be that woman. As long as I acted fast.

"Miss Sadie Mansfield," I told him. The new name rolled off my tongue as if it had been mine for a lifetime. I lowered my eyelashes and hoped Ella was still shuffling along on the road somewhere. I didn't need her storming in and interrupting things.

"I am most enchanted," Behan said. He held my hand a moment longer than was proper and my breath hitched.

Instead of reaching for the handle of the second door, I remained in the foyer and drew on every flirtatious tip Hattie had relayed to us during the trip. "As am I."

He drew closer. "Are you traveling alone, Miss Mansfield?"

"I'm with Miss Wells's party."

"Ah, the lovely Miss Wells. Then I am indeed glad I've met your acquaintance. Are you engaged for dinner?"

Well, crap and hellfire. If he knew Hattie, then he knew all of it. Damnation. Still, he'd be a fine man to take as my first.

"I would love to dine with you, Mr. Behan, but my schedule is not my own. You would need to speak to Miss Wells." There, I'd said it. Now all he had to do was pay her and the night would be his.

Instead, his face fell.

"I was afraid you'd say that. Miss Wells and I are not on good terms. Might you be able to get away later? Perhaps for an evening stroll? I could meet you at the livery."

My heart pounded. "I should like that, Mr. Behan. Shall we say eight o'clock?"

"I shall be waiting."

I gave him a small smile, one that promised more, and moved past him, catching up with Hattie and the others at the reception desk. Moments later Ella strode in, brushing her hair from her brow. She hadn't even noticed Behan, I didn't think.

Hattie distributed keys, *tsked* at Ella for her late arrival, and sent us to dress for dinner. I chose my gown carefully, trembling at the thought of the handsome, cultured, and very well-dressed Johnny Behan. A man of wealth and refinement . . . out here in the middle of nowhere.

Ella might have her head too buried to notice him and the opportunity he presented, but I certainly didn't.

Dinner was agonizing in its delay, despite the skill of the cook. I excused myself, feigning a headache, as soon as I could get away. Slipping into the hallway next to the stairs, I made my way to the back door and exited into the pleasant October evening. Despite all we'd heard of the blazing heat in Arizona, the weather was a delight.

Behan lounged against the side of the building, a cigarette in hand, thin wisps of smoke curling about him. A slow smile stretched his lips as I neared. He dropped the cigarette and ground it with his boot, his gaze never leaving mine.

He had the merriest twinkle in his eyes.

Delicious tingles crawled up my spine. Would I be able to convince him I wasn't yet in the trade, that I was still available?

"I didn't know if you'd come," he said.

I laughed, a light tinkling, just as Hattie had taught us during the trip. "Not come? I wouldn't have missed it for the world."

"It wasn't you I was doubting." He glanced toward the hotel.

"Hattie?"

He nodded. "As I said, Miss Wells doesn't care for me."

I took his arm, determined to make light of things. There was no need for him to get all serious. "I can't imagine why not."

"A past business dispute—minor—but she does guard her girls from me."

"But I'm not one of her girls, not yet." I let the comment lie for a moment, so he could think about it, then swayed my hips and squeezed his arm just so. "You could steal me away."

He said nothing for a moment, just gazed at me, his dark eyes growing ever blacker.

I'd been too bold, shocked him. Now, he'd laugh, call me a silly girl, I knew it.

But he stopped and spun to face me. "I might, dear Sadie, I just might. I'm taken with you. My heart is pounding." He grasped my hand and laid it on his chest. Under my palm, his heartbeat throbbed.

Stunned, I dropped my head against him. Oh, lord, had the hint really taken root?

"You're truly not yet a fallen woman, then? I could really take you away from that life?"

I lifted my face. "Pure as the driven snow, Mr. Behan."

"Oh, hell. Johnny, please." He drew back. "You are a jewel to behold."

I let my eyes drift closed, the way I'd seen some of Hattie's girls do, so that my eyelashes just graced my cheeks. Then I peered back at him for a moment before I glanced down as if embarrassed.

He groaned and pulled me close.

"Fate has brought you to me, Sadie. Let me take you away, court you properly."

My heart pounded. Could it really be this easy?

"You don't even know me."

"There are times when one just knows, don't you think?"

"And you believe this is one of those times?"

"If you'll let me, I'll spend the rest of my life with you." His arms surrounded me, one arm at my waist, the other sliding behind me until his hand cupped the bustle of my dress. Without the crinoline still packed in my trunk, I was flush against him. I felt him shift, adjust to my shorter height. He pushed the bustle out of the way, molding his hand to my body, and pulled me against his hardness.

I gasped.

His mouth crushed mine, hungry, greedy, and I mewed into his mouth.

Oh, lord, this was what Ella meant when she said her sister made noises!

Johnny turned us so I was against the wall of the hotel. He moved his hips and my knees buckled.

"Let me take you away from what Hattie has in mind for you, Sadie. Let me make you mine forever."

I couldn't get my breath.

"Please, Sadie. I'll give you so much."

He leaned in, kissed me again, ground against me. I sagged in his arms, surrendering, unable to believe I'd found my dream this easily . . . a wealthy husband all the way out here in Arizona.

"John Behan, you let that girl go. Don't you think I don't know what you're about." Hattie's voice broke through the haze in my senses as Johnny pulled away from me.

"Damn," he said.

Hattie stalked toward us, a scowl on her face. "Inside," she ordered me.

"But—"

"Go, now. If he offered marriage, you'd best open your eyes. He's already got a wife and the only thing he has in mind is getting a free first poke at a new girl."

I stared at her, not wanting to believe her words. I stared at Johnny, saw the reality in his hangdog expression.

I drew a breath and straightened my clothing. "No worries, Hattie. I was playing with him. Giving him something to think about. Maybe he'll pay extra for me." I threw a smirk at Johnny and sauntered back to the hotel, swinging my derriere just enough to make both of them think it was true.

But my eyes stung and I damned myself for my naïvety. There was no room for such innocence in the life ahead of me.

We pulled into Prescott the last week of October and arrived at Jennie Roland's house late in the morning. Jennie, a slender redhead, ushered us into the back door and directed Minnie, Ella, and me upstairs.

"Pick any of the rooms with open doors," she told us.

We clambered up the narrow staircase, still stiff from the bumpy ride. Minnie chattered, happy as a lark. Ella brooded. I was pensive.

Fool that I was, I'd almost given Johnny the best asset I had, all because I fell victim to impossible dreams, dumb enough to fall for a line. Marriage indeed. I'd since learned Johnny had both a wife and two children here in Prescott. He was running for sheriff, and was well known throughout Yavapai County for both his ambition and his fondness for young women. Hattie had guarded both Minnie and me more carefully during the remainder of our stay in Wickenburg.

I followed Ella down the hall and turned into the middle doorway. The room was small but papered with a floral design. The iron bedstead needed a new coat of white paint. A commode sat in one corner, a battered chifforobe in another. Atop the wooden commode was a chipped metal pitcher and basin set. Jennie's hired man brought in my trunk and set it on the floor next to the bed. A worn blue quilt covered the lumpy-looking mattress.

Home sweet home.

I choked back disappointment. I'd wanted the place to be grander, like Hattie's brothel on Powell Street. The house was plain by any standards and the bedroom even more so. But, then, there wasn't much reason for the bedrooms to be fancy. Once upstairs, the men were hardly focused on the trappings of the house. It was clear this was no parlor house; it was a run-of-the-mill brothel. But this was Arizona, not San Francisco. I didn't plan to be here long.

I peered into the scratched mirror over the commode and re-pinned my hair. Lord, with the fancy upsweep, I looked nothing like the schoolgirl who'd left the house just weeks ago. I'd learn quick, prove myself, and be back at Hattie's grand house in no time.

"Girls?" Jennie called. "Come on down to the kitchen."

We emerged from doorways, each of us feigning self-assurance, none of us sure what would happen next.

Once we were seated around the kitchen table, Jennie stood in front of us. Hattie and Julia were already on their way back to San Francisco. "Welcome to Prescott, ladies. We have only a few hours before business starts flooding in. Tonight will be busy. I doubt there's a man in town who hasn't heard about your arrival. They'll be here vying for you before you know it."

Ella swallowed. Minnie looked excited. I tried to look confident. Truth was I felt like Ella looked. And poor Minnie, she didn't have a clue, I don't think.

"While you're in my house, you'll take music and dance lessons, learn to speak a little French, and how to conduct yourselves as proper ladies, practice dinner etiquette. Your lessons will be billed to your accounts as have been your travel, gowns, and accessories. Room and board will be added as those costs accrue. If you have need for additional items, you can purchase them as needed from local merchants and bill them to my account. For the time being, your earnings will be credited toward your debts. Once the debt is paid, you will begin to accrue your earnings, paying for room and board and any items purchased, of course. The faster you learn, the sooner you can stop paying for lessons and the closer you'll be to returning to San Francisco."

"How much do we get paid, ma'am?" Minnie asked.

Jennie's mouth stretched wide. "That, my dear Minnie, depends on you. Exact amounts hinge on what customers ask for. The girls will go over all that with you in a little while. These first weeks, I expect you'll make a tidy amount. You're young, fresh. Once you're broken in, things will slow down and won't pick up until you hone your skills." She eyed each of us in turn.

Ella nodded, sober. I did the same, knowing what she meant but wondering how in the world I was expected to learn. Minnie still had no clue.

Jennie looked at Ella. "Hattie said you've had a man?"

"Once."

"Well, we can fake that. You'll go with Pearl. She'll explain how and some of the technicalities you'll need to know."

A woman we hadn't noticed stepped forward and motioned for Ella to follow her upstairs. Then Jennie glanced at Minnie. "How old are you, girl?"

"Twelve," Minnie said.

"Oh, dear lord," Jennie whispered, "what a find! You go on with Polly. She'll tell you what to do. For tonight, we'll keep your training minimal. Given your age, the men will like it better that way, anyhow."

Minnie stood and skipped away with another woman.

I glanced at Jennie and she smiled at me. "You're a virgin?"

I nodded.

"The men won't believe it, not with that set of tits! You know what will happen or are you as innocent as that little girl I just sent upstairs?"

"I know what goes where."

"You know how to make a man feel good? How to touch him, get him ready? What to do with your mouth?"

"Of course," I lied.

"Yeah, sure you do."

"I know how to flirt. Hattie taught us during the trip."

"There's a lot more you'll need to know. Minnie will do fine as a shocked virgin. You . . . with the way you're built, they'll expect you to know all about being a temptress but to offer the surprise of a girl unused. There's things about men Hattie couldn't teach in a stagecoach. You come on up to my room and I'll show you what that involves."

I gawked at her.

"Come on, honey. The john's waiting on us."

That night, I waited in the parlor with the other girls, still trying to wrap my mind around everything I'd witnessed in the past few hours. Though I'd not yet had a man, I was no longer innocent, that was for sure. I'd sat in a chair, watching Jennie and her good-natured partner demonstrate what I would need to know.

I'd had no idea.

Ella flitted through the room, every ounce of movement

calculated seduction. I knew she didn't like doing it, but she was good at it. What she lacked in musical skill and culture, she more than compensated for in raw sexuality. Everything about her promised a good time.

Jennie had prepared me for the same but cautioned me to walk a thin line between sensual and innocent. It wouldn't be as hard as she might think. Dressed as I was, with my breasts hefted high by my corset, my appearance was all she'd encouraged. My face was painted, my hair slightly tumbledown. All I had to do was sway my hips a little and keep up the flirtatious behavior Hattie had taught. My nervousness, though not obvious, was still apparent. Jennie said it would lure the men in and assure I brought a good price tonight.

They'd dressed Minnie in a silk gown that hugged her not-yet-mature body. Her near-white hair was pulled back from her face by a bow, flowing down her back. She looked like a girl playing dress-up. Exactly what she was. I hoped they'd told her enough about what was coming that she wouldn't be taken by surprise.

"It's time." Jennie smiled at the three of us, then unlocked the front door, greeting several gentlemen who were already on the stoop. Through the next hour, we flitted among the gathering crowd of men—the first of the bunch had been well-heeled and smelled of bay rum. But as the hour advanced, the men grew shabby and reeked of sweat. Jennie had determined we would make them all wait. Despite the hopes of those who came early, arrival time would not play a part in determining who would take us upstairs.

"Gentlemen, your attention please."

The men turned to Jennie.

"By now, you've all met Ella, Sadie, and Minnie." She lifted her glass high, saluting us. The men followed suit, a few toasting us while some let loose catcalls.

My cheeks burned.

"It's not every day such lovely girls make their way to Prescott. I'm offering each of them for the entire evening, should any of you desire that option. If not, they will be on the regular menu. However, due to their innocence, I have chosen a bidding system to determine each's first guest rather than my usual 'as available' practice. You'll find three jars on the bar. If you wish to bid on Ella, place your name and bid in the jar with the blue ribbon. For Sadie, the red ribbon. Pink for Minnie. If you don't know which is which, the ribbons match their dresses. I'll check the jars in thirty minutes."

Ella rolled her eyes as the men made a mad scramble to the bar. Minnie's eyes widened.

"Quite a show, huh?" Ella whispered.

"Jennie warned me it would be."

"Are you ready for this? Sure about it?"

"It's a little late, now. I just hope whoever gets me isn't rough."

"Me, too."

"I feel sorry for Minnie. I don't think they told her much," I said.

"*You* know, right?"

"Yeah. There was a moment earlier, when I wanted to run, but Jennie said to let my mind go, not take any of it personally."

"A means to an end. If we do it well, we get the life we want. If we don't, we won't make it as parlor house girls. I don't aim to live on the street, Sadie, or even in a brothel like this. I want the good life."

"Me, too."

"Then, cheers to us." She turned and grabbed two flutes of champagne from a tray. Clinking hers against mine, she downed the contents in a gulp.

I sipped, the bubbles tickling my nose before they danced

down my throat. Across the room, Jennie nodded. She'd advised a drink or two to loosen our inhibitions.

We milled among the men, sipping drinks and flirting—each of us in our own way—until Jennie slipped behind the bar and removed the jars.

The champagne in my stomach began to churn in frantic bubbles.

A few short minutes later, Ella glided across the room on the arm of a paunchy mustached man I'd heard was a banker. She faltered once, on the stairs, but regained her step amid a tinkle of laughter. The banker never suspected a thing.

Minnie beamed as her gentleman ushered her forward. He was less well-dressed but had the air of someone who was used to being in charge. She chattered like a child all the way up the stairs.

Then, Jennie signaled to the man who'd bid highest for my initiation. He strode forward as if he enjoyed power. Like the others, he was on the higher end of the financial ladder. We'd expected as much, what with soldiers, cowboys, and miners being outbid by businessmen, politicians, and gamblers. I suspected he was one of the latter—too much of a dandy to be either of the other two.

"You know my name," I purred. "May I ask yours?"

"Just call me Ed. We won't be doing much talking." We gained the second floor and he stopped. "Which one, doll?"

I pointed to my open door and he pushed me in, locked it behind him.

I flinched at the sharp click.

"You know what you're about here or you want me to just take you?"

"I know enough and imagine you'll teach me the rest." I stepped forward, touched his chest. "Let's start with you telling me if I'm yours for the night or if we're doing something from the menu." I referred to the menu of the house, which listed various individual acts.

"I paid for whatever I want, however long I want to take with it."

"Then how about we get comfortable while you decide what you want to start with? Or maybe you want me to start?"

I removed his jacket, folding it carefully and laying it across a chair I hadn't seen earlier. The room had been subtly decorated since I'd left it. The chair, scattered silk scarves, dimmed lamps. I bent over the chair, my rear in his direction and bent one leg like Jennie had shown me so my derriere bumped out more.

Ed groaned and stepped behind me, cupping me with his hands.

I swiveled my hips against his palms.

"You sure you're a virgin?"

"Am I doing it wrong?" I let doubt play in my voice. "Jennie said to do this, to make you hungry. Didn't I do it right?"

"Girl, any more right and I'd be spilling my load on the floor." He shrugged out of his clothes, done with me helping him.

I watched, letting my eyes widen as each layer came off. When he dropped his drawers, I let my mouth fall open and I swallowed.

"She tell you about this? About what I'm going to do with this?"

He grabbed himself and stroked. I swallowed again, all acting gone. He was going to put that oversized thing inside me?

He was bigger than the john I'd watched with Jennie. His pecker stood straight out, like it was pointing the way. Jennie had warned me they'd all look different but my mind hadn't pictured what she meant.

"Get over here. On your knees."

I did as he ordered. It was my job, the first step in gaining the life I wanted. But when he stuck it in my mouth and shoved my head forward, I gagged and tried to push away.

"Do it," he growled.

I relaxed my muscles, moving on him, letting my lips and tongue do the work so he'd ease up on pushing my head so much. He tasted of soap and salt and I told myself I was lucky I'd landed a clean man. Thinking of what might have been, I lost concentration, choked, drew back.

Relax and remember the more you work at pleasuring him, the less likely he is to control you.

I hated this already, hated the decision I'd made and hated the lifetime ahead of me. In that moment, I knew that no matter how hard I worked at this, I'd never be in control again.

I sucked at him, dreading he might come in my mouth, that I'd be forced to swallow. He pumped, panting and grunting as his pace quickened. Then, he stalled and thrust me away. I landed on the floor on my butt.

"On the bed."

I rose and started to unfasten my gown but he tossed me on the mattress and shoved the dress over my head. He jerked my hips to the edge of the bed and slammed into me. Pain ratcheted through me and I bit back a scream. He pumped, hard and fast. On the bed, under my upended skirt, tears streamed from my eyes as he growled his release. It didn't take long.

"Good God, you were a virgin after all. What d'ya know!"

He pulled out and I heard him donning his clothes, then the jingle of coins hitting the table next to the bed.

"Thanks, whore," he said, just before he closed the door.

Chapter Four: Josephine/Sadie

The biggest lies are the ones we tell ourselves.

1874 (a few weeks after Sadie's first night)
Prescott, Arizona
Those first weeks in Prescott were rough. Though the town had only a few hundred residents, Jennie did a brisk business. Until Jennie had opened her brothel, most of the trade operated out of rooms above the saloons. Her nondescript wooden house was the best Prescott offered and the lure of three young girls brought men in every night.

Most customers wanted to be with us.

It was a rocky start, the older girls losing business to the newcomers and jealous because of it. We were sore and dead tired. Already, I'd become mechanical, flirting without any real sentiment and simply doing what they demanded. Once I'd been deflowered, my price had dropped and my clientele became more ordinary. Miners were the bread and butter of the trade, as Ella had predicted. I learned to put up with their unwashed bodies and ignore the lice.

Whiskey helped. Barely.

Ella had been right about a lot of things. It wasn't the life I'd imagined and regret tasted bitter. At this rate, I despaired of ever being able to pay off my debt. It didn't take long for me to learn I'd best start perfecting what I offered or I'd be in Prescott forever.

Three weeks after our debut, Minnie got beat up bad. They took her off the line so she could recover. That next night, I paced the parlor, dreading who might slip in the front door.

"Well, if it isn't the flirtatious Miss Sadie." A silky voice cut through my worry—one I knew. My pulse picked up.

"Well, if it isn't the equally flirtatious Johnny Behan." Married he might be, but he was also a member of the territorial legislature, owner of a home on Capitol Hill, and held business interests in several local saloons—the sort of man that might benefit a girl. More, he excited me. Few of my customers held my appeal. It would be a welcome change to bed a man who did.

And Johnny Behan definitely caught my interest.

A shiver formed at the base of my spine. "Have you come to finally get your taste?"

"I'd have preferred my taste back in Wickenburg, before everyone else got a sample."

I was glad he hadn't taken my innocence. I wouldn't have known how to enjoy him. *Not like now.*

"You'd have been disappointed, Johnny. I've seasoned just enough to satisfy you." I neared him and cupped his groin, brazen and not a bit ashamed of it. My heart pounded. "Come on upstairs and I'll show what I've learned."

Johnny laughed, rich and hearty. "You're sassy. I like that." He searched the room, caught Jennie's gaze, and nodded to her.

Moments later, she was next to us. "Sorry about the election, Johnny."

"Me, too. I was looking forward to being sheriff. Still, it will give me more time for other pursuits. Like visiting Sadie. Met her on her way here but Hattie wouldn't let me steal her away."

"You would have, too, stolen her right out from under us, if I know you." She turned to me. "Why don't you head upstairs while Johnny and I settle on a price?"

"See ya soon." I winked and sauntered away. I could feel his eyes on me even as I took the stairs. For the first time since arriving in Prescott, my body tingled and all dread was gone.

If I played this well, Johnny would be back and he'd be back often.

February 1875 (a few week after Johnny's first visit)

"I envy you," Ella said as I primped before the cracked mirror a few weeks later. "You're going to make good money."

"What's more, I get to go out!" I'd fairly danced with anticipation since Johnny'd made the arrangements. Dinner and a variety show was the best Prescott had to offer and it wasn't often a john took a girl out of the house for a night. Tonight, I would enjoy myself, maybe explore the possibility of an exclusive arrangement.

I smoothed my blue satin dress, the most modest of my gowns, and prayed it would be suitable. The whole town knew who I was so I wasn't sure why it mattered so much.

I told myself I shouldn't crave their approval. A lie, but one I forced myself to believe.

"Does he still treat you good?" Ella asked.

"As long as I don't let him drink too much. That and listen to him complain about his wife." Johnny made me pant with desire but his time did come with costs.

Hell, everything came with costs.

"Word is his wife isn't too happy about all the time he spends here."

Ella was right about that. "I don't think Victoria Behan is happy about much of anything. Johnny's a womanizer. It's just that his attention is focused on only one woman for a change."

"You don't think there will be trouble, do you?"

"Tonight? She's out of town." I shrugged, feigning a lack of concern. A tinge of regret drifted through me at the loss of the friendship Ella and I had shared for so long. In brothels, one didn't have friends. It was too much of a risk, too easy to get hurt. Better to shutter oneself off.

I blinked against threatening tears.

Don't dwell on it. Be tough.

"She's not going to like it, when word gets around that Johnny took you out in public."

I found the edge again and seized on it. "She doesn't like it when he doesn't."

"How much do you think he's paying Jennie?"

"I don't know. It's not about the money." Sure, the money mattered but I adored Johnny. He was attentive, focused, and a damn good lover. And . . . if things went well, I might coax him into paying off my debt and setting me up as his mistress. But I wasn't about to tell Ella *that.*

I couldn't. Not anymore.

"How can it not be about the money?" she said, her voice taking on that brittle tone I'd grown to hate. I knew it was her own way of guarding herself but it grated on me nonetheless. "At this rate, we'll never make it back to San Francisco. My earnings don't even meet my expenses, let alone the debt from Hattie setting us up."

"We've only been here a couple months. Pretty soon, we'll turn a corner." I offered an encouraging smile despite the pitiful truth of it. Thank God I wasn't taking dance or voice lessons to add to what I owed. Johnny always left me extra but I figured it was best not to mention it, even if it was Ella. If word got out that I had cash, one of the girls would toss my room for sure.

"Well, on that note, I'd best head downstairs." Ella swept from the room, a much harder girl than she'd been when we were friends.

We both were.

The life we had was not the one we'd expected. Aside from the gowns Hattie had purchased, there was no fancy clothing. Dresses and undergarments had become tattered and mended. This was not the lifestyle we'd envisioned. We didn't spend our days in cultured ease. Bruised and worn thin, we never fully recovered from the nights spent under one man after another. My body ached and my soul had long since quit looking forward to the next day.

But, a half hour later, none of it mattered.

I was on Johnny's arm and we were pushing our way into Prescott's fanciest restaurant. A few women raised their eyebrows. I nodded at each of them and squeezed Johnny's arm tighter, gaining pleasure as their faces reddened. We took our place at a secluded table and ignored them.

Halfway through dinner, a man approached, doffing his hat. "How do, Miss Sadie?"

I shivered and pasted a smile on my face. Charles Goodman was a frequent customer at Jennie's place, a man I couldn't abide. Devious, with beady eyes and furtive movements, he never failed to raise a chill up my spine. Still, I couldn't afford to antagonize him.

"Fine, Mr. Goodman. And you?"

"Just fine. Must be something to have a night out, huh?"

"I am enjoying myself immensely. Everyone deserves a night on the town now and again." What in the world was he playing at?

"Didn't think we'd see any of you out and about, though."

"Jennie is quite accommodating, for a price," Johnny interrupted. "It was good to speak to you but if you don't mind, let's let Miss Mansfield return to her dinner before it cools."

"Oh, yep, sure thing." Goodman hustled away, muttering to himself.

"I dislike that man," I told Johnny. "Never can figure out

what he's thinking." More than likely, he'd be telling Mrs. Behan all about us the moment she returned to town. But I wasn't about to ruin the evening by bringing *that* up.

"Everyone in the room is curious," Johnny said. "They're all looking at you."

I felt it, hated it. But I wasn't about to let anyone see how I felt. "Like they've never seen a woman before."

"Not one like you."

I leveled my gaze. "Don't be insulting, Johnny."

"You're gorgeous. How could they not have their eyes glued on you?"

Ah, Johnny, clever as always. "That's a very smooth escape." By now, I recognized his smooth words for what they were. I was no longer the innocent I'd been.

"It's true." He grinned, that infectious smile making him look like a mischievous youth instead of a seasoned man of thirty, and I shivered. I always forgot he was twice my age.

I pushed my roast beef away, done with the cold remains. Moments later, we were out in the crisp winter air, strolling up Granite Street. I figured Johnny was full, satisfied and loosened by two glasses of wine—feeling good but not yet drunk. An agreeable mood.

"Are you saying you'd take me out again, if you had the chance?" I asked, edging a slight purr into my voice. "That you don't mind having a girl like me on your arm?"

"It delights me to have you with me."

I squeezed closer. "You know . . . there are some men who keep their favorites privately . . . without the stigma of a house."

"Mistresses, you mean?"

"Mistresses, courtesans, whatever label you choose."

Johnny paused. "And?"

His voice held annoyance at the too obvious manipulation. *Hellfire.* I caught his gaze and went for the straight-up approach.

"I've heard such women spend more time in public than do those in brothels. Somehow, the exclusive nature of the arrangement is more acceptable to society."

"Is that what you want, Sadic? To be my courtesan?"

"You saw how they looked at me." Too late, I heard the weakness, hated it, hated the flush that crept up my neck. Hated that I'd lost control by being so direct.

I took his arm again and started us walking. "I would love to devote myself to you, without the mess of having to bed other men." That would have to do.

"And you'd expect me to provide a place for you? Support you?" He sighed.

And I bristled. "That is generally the arrangement, is it not?"

"Hell, Victoria is mad enough as it is. There's been no end of fighting about my 'catting around.' She'd have my hide for sure if I took a mistress."

"Given how much you likely dole out to Jennie every time you come to see me, it'd likely save you money."

"It's not the money, Sadie. I've got the money to do whatever I want. I was county recorder for three years, managing tax records—you think I didn't squirrel some of that away for myself? I've got money enough for whatever vices I choose to pursue, whores included."

I flinched.

Whore.

Except for the looks from the women in the restaurant, I'd never felt like a whore with Johnny. Not until then.

We walked the last block to the music hall in silence. Once there, Johnny ushered me in. We were ahead of curtain time, with time to purchase a couple of tickets for the Grand New Year's Gift Enterprise drawing. I laughed as Johnny made a show of buying the raffle tickets for me.

But the evening was spoiled. Completely and thoroughly spoiled.

Spring 1875 (a few weeks later)

I settled for what I could get. I didn't have much choice. But I made damn sure I got as much as I could—hating how callous I'd become, knowing survival demanded it.

It was no easy feat.

Victoria had returned home only to encounter rampant gossip—fueled by Goodman, of course—about Johnny's night on the town with his pet prostitute. She'd been mad as hell, threatening Johnny with divorce, vowing to destroy him politically and financially.

He'd stayed away for a while, but he always came back. I was a habit he couldn't break and I fed his addiction the only way possible. Each time he strayed, I consulted Jennie to learn new skills d'amour.

I also fed his animosity with his wife. What I'd learned today should have Johnny eating out of my hand out of sheer gratitude alone.

"Did you like that, lover?" I asked.

"Now what do you think?"

I laughed, feeding his ego. "I think if you'd come any harder you'd have blown your brains out your cock."

"You have a way with words, Sadie, but oh, what you do with your body."

"Is Victoria back?" I knew the answer but I wanted to rile him. It was shameful and self-defeating, the way I enjoyed playing with him, but the heady surge of power took over my common sense. I felt it deep inside, a twitch as strong as desire itself and it grew in orgasmic waves.

"Goddamn bitch. She wants the house and the mines. She's

got Goodman signed up to testify I'm unfaithful and now she claims I abuse her."

"It's no secret you cheat and no one's going to believe you hit her. She'd have bruises."

"She said she'll tell the judge I yell at her, threaten her."

"You *are* an angry drunk, dear."

"I don't need to take shit like this from you. There are plenty of other whores I can visit."

My eyes stung. It was time to pull things back, settle his anger.

"Oh, but there aren't many that take you where I do." I ran my fingernail across his buttocks, teasing.

A slow grin stretched across his mouth. "You are a vixen, you know that?"

"And you love every minute of it." I let my voice shift back to the purr he loved.

But his gaze was firm. "Did you mention Victoria just to get my back up?"

"A little." He was getting to know me too well. "You can spank me for it if you want."

"She'll bring you into it, too, you know."

I blew out a breath. "Hell, Johnny, the whole town knows where you spend your time." She would do what she wanted and nothing I could do would make any difference.

"She just makes me so mad, carrying on like it's a surprise to her that I like women. She knew that when I married her. She ought to be glad I did. I could just have easily told her I didn't care about the kid."

My mind seized on a bit of gossip, a chance to control things once and for all, and I sat up. "Maybe you should have."

"Not taken responsibility for Henrietta?" His eyes shuttered.

"Exactly."

"I don't shy from my duty."

I pressed on, following the temptation. "And if the duty wasn't yours?"

"What do you mean?"

"Oh, just a little rumor I happened to hear."

"What? For God's sake, Sadie, get to the point!"

I quivered, the rush flooding me. "She can't ask you for child support for Henrietta if you're not Henrietta's father."

"Not . . . ?" He dropped the question, incredulous.

Power swarmed me and I leveled my gaze. "Word among those who know Victoria has it that she wasn't faithful during your courtship."

Johnny shook his head. "She was just seventeen when we were married."

"Seventeen and pregnant. If I have my information right, you were pretty busy at the time?"

He paused, thinking. "I was."

"And being 'just seventeen' really means very little. After all, it'll take two more years before I reach that mark."

"Who'd you hear it was?" An edge of anger crept into his tone.

"No names dropped, just lots of innuendos about Victoria's lack of virtue."

"Good lord, she trapped me!"

"If that girl isn't yours, Johnny, you shouldn't have to pay support for her. Victoria can grouse as much as she wants about your infidelities and all it does is make her more sympathetic. Maybe it's time you raise a bit of a stink about hers."

"You little witch! Maybe I will make you my mistress after all."

I settled into his arms, basking in the moment, secure for the first time in months.

Maybe he'd make me his wife . . . after all, in a few months, he'd be a free man.

February 1876 (a year later)

I clutched my shawl tighter and half ran down the block to the mercantile. Who'd have thought Arizona could get so cold? My throat ached with a persistent scratch, likely from breathing in the constant chill. January and February were bitter, as frigid as things were between me and Johnny. As raw as my life had become.

Damn John Behan. I'd been a fool, played my hand too soon, and I was paying for it.

As soon as his divorce had become final, Johnny had turned his full focus to political ambitions and left me out in the cold. He no longer wanted anything to do with me.

Having his name connected to mine wasn't "productive."

I hated him, hated him with a passion I hadn't known I possessed.

Aside from emptiness, it was the only thing I felt these days.

In months, my income had dropped off quicker than I'd imagined possible. One of the girls—I never discovered which and I prayed it hadn't been Ella—had found my stash of money, leaving me completely dependent on Jennie. Last week, I'd had to purchase new stockings on her account, a john having ripped my last good pair. All in all, I was still looking at months of work before my debt to her would clear.

This morning, when the sore throat hit, the hopelessness of my situation hit me full force.

Minnie had committed suicide, Ella had been transferred to Vulture City. I was completely and totally alone and no longer anyone's favorite. I wasn't spending nights out, wasn't being loved as a woman should be, and saw no hope for a return of that status.

When my throat started swelling up, it dawned on me that no one would come offering hot tea or compresses to ease the pain. No one even knew my name. Even if they looked for me, my family would find no trace. I'd referred to myself as Mansfield since I left San Francisco nearly eighteen months ago. No one knew Sadie Marcus. All I could do was continue to bed men I hated and hope to finally pay off my debt.

Worse, parlor house life no longer held any appeal. Johnny had dropped me on my ass and I could no longer maintain the lie I'd been telling myself. I'd lost all control over my life.

All I wanted was to go home.

I wanted it so bad I could taste it.

I opened the door to H. Asher and Company's fine establishment, shivering as I made my way into the warm interior. At the counter, Mrs. Asher raised her eyebrows and sighed. She didn't much like us girls in her store but she wasn't about to turn away the money. Especially since she marked on extra for the bother of dealing with us.

The only other customer stood at the counter, whistling "Darling Nellie Gray." He was Al Sieber, an army scout from Fort Whipple, well known around town. But as far as I knew, he'd never visited the house and was unlikely to know me. I ignored him and wandered toward the back of the store, where I'd seen the silver spoons last time I was in.

There they were, a full set of solid silver German tablespoons. The label in front of them demanded 162 dollars. Silver that pure could buy me a ticket home.

I passed the spoons and fingered a comb and brush set with ivory handles. Up front, Mrs. Asher was factoring Sieber's bill. I swallowed and returned to the spoons, careful to keep my footfalls quiet. I reached for the spoons, my heart thundering in my ears.

In a flash, I had the box under my shawl and strode toward the door.

I was halfway out when Mrs. Asher grabbed me.

It was all over quicker than a whore's poke.

Mrs. Asher screamed for the sheriff and he hauled me off to the jail, Sieber trailing us.

I eyed the empty cell, tears stinging. Why hadn't I thought out my actions more?

"You're not really going to put her in there, are you?" Sieber asked.

"That's generally where we put lawbreakers." The sheriff grinned. I knew him well enough from his monthly visits to Jennie to collect the fees for our business licenses. He'd defeated Johnny for the office in November and Johnny had complained about him plenty.

"You put one of Jennie's girls inside, you know Jennie'll make trouble."

I stared at the scout and a wave of small desperate hope began to build.

"Aw hell, Sieber," said the sheriff.

"Let her go. What good will it do to lock her up? Just take her before the judge and be done with it. No sense keeping her in the jailhouse. Unless you're trying to prove a point you don't need to make."

The sheriff sighed and glanced at me.

I let the pent-up tears roll. Might as well do what I could.

"Oh, hell," the sheriff muttered—just as I'd intended.

Seiber's expression was soft. "I'll take her up to Jennie's. You can let her know the trial date once it's set."

"Go on, then, get her out of here before I change my mind."

"Come on, Sadie. You heard the man."

I sniffled and followed Sieber to the door. Hell, I'd follow him anywhere. Once outside, he took my arm and guided me up the street.

"That was a damn fool thing to do, girl," he lectured.

"So was coming here in the first place." I muttered the words, then wanted to grab them back. A stranger didn't need to know things like that.

But he didn't latch on to the vulnerable revelation the way I thought. He just slowed and settled his jacket over my shoulders. "Where you from, kid?"

Tears welled in my eyes. "San Francisco."

"Your folks know you're here?"

I shook my head.

"Sadie Mansfield your real name?"

"What do you think?" The hard tone crept back into my voice, a habit.

Seiber sighed. "I'm about the only one on your side. How about you try being civil?"

He was right. But it'd been longer than I could remember since someone had offered me something without demanding a price. "I'm sorry, Mr. Sieber. Thank you for your help."

"Does the judge frequent Jennie's place?" he asked.

"Every now and again." My throat burned.

"Then I would expect you won't have any problems. Plead not guilty. If it even goes to the point of him asking you what happened, tell him you expected Mrs. Asher to put the spoons on Jennie's account. I doubt it'll even get that far, though."

I stared at him. "Why are you doing this for me?"

"Because you seem like a decent kid caught up in something she didn't see coming. If you were my sister, I'd want someone to step in."

He continued on and I hurried to keep up with him.

"Thank you," I murmured.

"You do know there's a telegraph over at the fort, right?"

"A telegraph?" I touched my swollen throat and felt the sting of the tears in my eyes. Lord, how I yearned for Mama right now.

"What's your name, Sadie?"

"Josephine Sarah Marcus," I told him in a rush. "But it doesn't matter. My mother will never retrieve me, not after this. I've prostituted myself for well over a year and the reputation she's created for our family won't withstand my return. There's no sense even trying."

Chapter Five: Josephine/Sadie

The problem with lies is that one often necessitates another and, over time, it becomes more and more difficult to keep track of them all.

March 1876 (a month later)
San Francisco

"Are you going to putter around all evening?" Rebecca chastised. My older sister's dominion had become routine.

"I'm well aware of the time." I slammed the drawer of the dressing table shut with a bang and spun away from the mirror. "I'm not a child anymore."

"Then don't act like one." She glanced at the drawer and shook her head.

I fought humiliation. I wouldn't act that way if she didn't constantly pick at me.

"Do you have to constantly order me around?" I asked. "I'm sixteen, old enough to have lived on my own for the past year and a half."

Rebecca pursed her lips for a moment. "On your own? You didn't run your own life, Sadie. That woman who 'employed' you did. You couldn't even maintain your health. Mama swears you had scarlet fever when we found you. You'd probably be dead if we hadn't."

She turned away and I fought sticking out my tongue like the child she said I was.

Acting like one wasn't getting me anywhere and it was time I realized it. If I didn't behave like an adult, I'd never be treated like one. I'd be under her thumb forever.

Rebecca and Aaron had made arrangements for my return the same day they got Sieber's telegram, paying for my stage and rail tickets from their own pockets. She lauded her generosity over me at every turn and controlled my every movement. She'd bought and paid for me just like any of the johns who'd had me in Arizona. I was in debt to her as much as I had been to the madams. I didn't know whether Aaron had paid what I owed to them in addition to my way home. Maybe I was still somehow liable and Hattie would send her "man" to pick me up on the street.

I shivered and turned back to the mirror. Either way, I needed to quit acting like a kid. Rebecca needed stroking as much as those johns had. Much as I hated to admit it, she was right. It was time I acted my age. I needed to focus on finding a way to control my own life again.

Rebecca and Aaron were taking me to the opening of Lucky Baldwin's theatre. Baldwin was one of the richest men in town and the newspapers were full of gossip about his grand new establishment. Outings like this might be my only chance to meet eligible men.

A couple more pins and my hair felt secure. I looked prim, not at all like I'd looked a few weeks ago. My dress was demure and Rebecca had styled my hair in a formal style. It reeked of lack of adventure but at least it would get me out of the house.

I finished primping and less than an hour later, we stood in Baldwin's grand lobby.

I had to admit I appreciated Aaron's employer providing him with theatre tickets. Especially tonight. The new venue was elegant, brocade upholstery and gold pillars, imported carpets, crystal-enhanced gaslights, and prominent people everywhere a person looked.

"Aaron, Rebecca! How wonderful to see you here."

I spun and recognized Lucky Baldwin. He looked just like the pictures that flooded the newspapers, distinguished, mustached, albeit older than I'd imagined. Still, he had to be a youthful man—he'd married his third wife a few months ago and she was the same age I was.

"Congratulations, Lucky. Such a wonderful building." The words dripped from Rebecca's mouth as if she'd been born to status. Apparently, we had more in common than I'd thought. Mama's influence, I was sure.

"And this must be your sister." Lucky smiled at me, interest in his eyes. "She's lovely. Where have you been hiding her?"

"Josephine has been with our aunt, in New York. We're so pleased to have her back with us." The lie dripped from her lips, clearly prepared for just such questioning.

"Ah, New York!" He grasped my hands, kissing each one with elegant flare. "At least you were somewhere with culture. Were you able to take in the theatre?"

Somewhere with culture, my ass! But Lucky's attention drew me in and my pulse danced. Lord how I'd missed men.

"Oh, I saw a lot of acting. None of it first-rate. I'm afraid opportunity was more limited than I would have preferred. My aunt is not well connected."

Next to Lucky, Rebecca beamed, pleased I'd followed her lead with the story she'd invented. A brief smirk crossed Aaron's mouth as he digested the double meaning of my words.

"Will you join me in my box for the first act?" Lucky directed the question to Aaron, who nodded. The honor was unmistakable, the boost in social prestige significant. It might be enough to gain several invitations to call for Rebecca.

We retired to Lucky's private box. I focused on charming him, fielding questions about New York, drawing on memories and filling in fabrications as needed. The man was a delight and I warmed to his attention. Had I known Rebecca ran in such social circles, I might have never run off.

Except I knew she didn't really run in such circles.

Still, I'd caught Lucky's eye—I knew I had.

He could introduce me to a lot of people . . . men who were cut far above those the matchmaker might offer. That would be next on Rebecca's list, I suspected. If I played my cards right, I might be able to focus her attention on the theatre crowd instead.

Lucky was twice divorced and who knew how long he'd stay with the current wife? I should keep my options open. He'd be a catch beyond my farthest imagination and wouldn't care a hoot that I wasn't pure. I shifted closer and allowed him to place his hand on mine. I turned, so my palm was up and stroking the underside of his. It wasn't much and I knew Rebecca wouldn't notice but it was enough. Lucky's eyes widened, recognizing the invitation.

At intermission, Lucky left us, caught up in conversation with others. But his gaze had tracked me all the way down the elegant foyer.

Once we retired to our own seats, Rebecca beamed at me. "You did very well, Sadie."

"I'm not a dolt. I know how to conduct myself and I most certainly know how to lie." I wondered, for a moment, if she meant something more, if she'd noticed Lucky's interest.

"Thank God for that. Mama never told anyone you ran away. She spread the New York story from the time you left. You know how people are. They'll be looking to trip you up, discover the slightest gossip. It helps that you've returned with such a measure of culture."

"And why wouldn't I?" The words had more of a bite than I'd intended and I softened them with a smile.

Rebecca eyed me, then went on. "To be truthful, I had no idea how you'd come back, what condition you might be in."

My smile slipped at her tone. "My condition is fine. I really am not a little girl anymore, Rebecca. I have a great deal of experience in a great many things and I will not be pushed around."

I stared at her, damning my lack of control.

Comprehension crossed her face and her lips settled into a hard line.

Hellfire. Now I'd done it.

My retort nearly cost me my freedom altogether and I rued my inability to control my tongue.

Rebecca was determined I wouldn't leave the house again until I learned my place. She was smart enough to read between the lines and was afraid I'd embarrass her. But Mama's idea of giving me a bit of freedom by sending me back to school wasn't what I had in mind.

"I don't see the point in it," I told her.

Mama waved her hand, chasing the comment away like a bothersome fly. "Going back to school would do you good, let you leave the house like you've been begging."

That wasn't what I'd meant and we both knew it. "There isn't a thing I'd get out of school."

"But you need to finish! You didn't graduate, even."

Oh, I'd graduated all right. Poor Mama hadn't any idea the education I'd received. "Close enough, Mama," I told her. No sense adding fuel to the fire. "So I didn't finish eighth grade."

I couldn't fathom if this had been Mama's idea or Rebecca's but it didn't matter much. My answer would be the same either way.

"And what about Normal School? I always wanted you to go on with your education."

Me, learning Latin and Greek? Parsing out nouns and verbs. No, I was by far better suited to the interesting French phrases and seductive movements I'd already learned. I shook my head. Life had hardened me and I couldn't bring back the carefree girl I'd been or the innocence she'd once known.

A whisper of grief stung my eyes and I choked it back. Those days were in the past.

I forced regret into my voice and focused on where I was now. "We can't afford that."

"I was saving for it. It doesn't cost so much now. The state, it gives money to the schools so they don't have to charge so much."

"Mama . . ." I paused. My tone was too argumentative. I needed to reason with her, not start a fight.

"You'll at least finish with the eighth grade. I insist. You will start again in the fall and you will finish it this time."

"I'm two years older than the other girls. Do you know how much that will embarrass me? They'll all be gossiping about me . . . have you got a story for that? A reason for me not finishing in New York when I 'visited my aunt'?" The words spilled out, despite my intent to hold myself in check.

"Everyone knows your aunt was not well, how you gave up your school to nurse her. *Ach,* there will be praise for how you set aside your last year for your family."

"I don't want to."

"I don't care. I have decided."

I glared at her, rational persuasion now well beyond my reach. "I will not go back to school and you can't force me."

Shock crossed her face. I'd never opposed her, not openly. "I am the mother. You will do as you are told."

"I will not."

"Josephine Sadie Marcuse, you will." Stubborn resistance set her jaw.

Oh, hellfire. This was getting me nowhere.

I drew a breath and let it flow back out. You didn't argue with Mama. I *knew* that. I clamped my mouth shut, anger pulsing. I was *not* going back to school. I wasn't.

Then it dawned on me. All I had to do was give a little. I'd go to her damn school but I'd get what I wanted in the bargain.

"I'm sorry, Mama. I should not have argued with you." I let my lips tremble. "It's just . . . there won't be anyone my age. How am I going to find a husband this way?"

Mama's expression softened and she pulled me into her arms. "*Ach, liebling,* it will be all right. We will find you a match."

"I saw so many fine men when Rebecca and Aaron took me to the theatre. At school, there will be only boys." I choked back what passed as a sniffle.

"*Ach,* I will ask her to take you again. There must be young men with prospects there. Cultured men."

"I guess I wouldn't mind going to school so much, not if I found a beau at the theatre."

"It is settled then. You will go to school like a good girl and they will take you with them to the theatre whenever they go."

"Then I'll finish eighth grade, Mama. As long as I get to go to the theatre, I'll be happy."

I'd graduate, as promised, but that didn't mean I planned to attend.

Two weeks later

The old neighborhood hadn't much changed. It was still a ramshackle collection of rental houses and tenement buildings. The Fourth Street Primary School had remained the same, too. In fact, the entire eighth ward was as dirty and grimy as it had been the day I'd left with Ella for what we thought was a grand life at Hattie Wells's parlor house.

Oh, what I'd give to have those days back . . .

I sulked, staring out the window into my memories until we were excused for the day. I grabbed my books and stormed out the door. I'd attend often enough to avoid problems at home but no more. Tomorrow, I planned on spending the day at Lucky Baldwin's theatre, backstage with the stagehands. Maybe even the rest of today.

"Sadie Marcus! Wait up."

I quickened my pace. The last thing I wanted to do was socialize with my classmates.

"Sadie!"

This time, there was a pull on the sleeve of my plain calico dress, one of many Mama had insisted upon. I looked like a fool. "What?" I demanded.

The petite girl with her hand on my arm winced at my tone and withdrew her grasp. She was shorter than I was, barely five feet tall, and younger. Everybody in the school was younger.

The disappointment on her face shamed me.

"I'm sorry," I said. "I'm in a bit of a hurry."

"I'm Dora Hirsch. You probably don't remember me but I always thought you were so sophisticated. Your father used to deliver for my father's bakery, over on Third Street."

Hirsch. I vaguely remembered the name. He'd died a few years back and Papa had lost his job. Dora had been a couple years behind me in school. Not anymore.

"Yes, I remember."

At my words, her eyes brightened. "I was surprised to see you back."

I grew wary, unsure of what she wanted. To be friends or was she seeking gossip fodder? I hadn't had a friend since Ella and I sure didn't need to feed rumors. I strove for a neutral answer. "After I came back from taking care of my aunt, Mama insisted I finish up."

"Didn't you used to take dance lessons? And sing?"

I shifted my posture. "Dora, I really do have to go."

Her enthusiasm faltered. "Oh. All right. But I noticed you were all alone most of the day and I thought we might become friends."

Oh, hell. I didn't need friends. They were complicated, especially if they were ones who'd expect me to be at school every day. Next thing, they'd be at my house asking Mama where I was. "I like being alone," I told her.

"You do?" Her eyes widened.

"I was alone a lot when I was with my aunt. I got used to it."

"That doesn't sound like much fun."

Sorrow pinched. Little of it had been fun, except for the times I'd been in Johnny's good graces. That, I missed. "I didn't have time for fun."

"How awful. I relish having fun. And I thought we'd have so much in common. I saw you at Lucky Baldwin's theatre on opening night so I know we both like plays. And dancing. And music, too. My mother teaches voice and piano."

"Well, I'm not taking lessons anymore if you're trying to gain her another student."

"Oh, you're funny. Do you want to come with me to the theatre on Saturday? Mother said I could invite a friend."

I swallowed. No one had invited me to join them for anything since the days Ella and I had roamed the neighborhood. "And you're inviting me?" A sting welled in my eyes.

"I thought you'd enjoy it. I'd love to hear all about New York. I want to become an actress and it would be divine to learn what it's like there. So I know before I go there."

Dora had passion, more than I'd encountered for a long time. It was difficult to resist her. And she was right, we did have interests in common.

I shifted, looking at her more closely. "You plan to go to New

York and become an actress?"

"I do." She was pert enough to do it, that was for sure. Confident, too. She reminded me a bit of Ella on that day we first met.

My resistance slipped. "You want to come along, over to Baldwin's theatre? I was going to see if they needed any help backstage."

"At Baldwin's?" She cocked one eyebrow.

"Lucky is a friend of my brother-in-law." It was a fib, but given Lucky's interest in me, I figured I could get away with it. "He lets me spend time there."

Dora bit her lip. "I guess I could come, but I should tell my mother."

A good girl, then? Obedient and rule abiding didn't exactly fit my bill. "You coming or not?"

She nodded. "I'll come. Mother will understand."

We headed north, up and down the hills of the eighth ward, chatting about dance and theatre. Dora was determined to make her life in the theatre, and most of her former friends had dropped away, unwilling, or forbidden, to damage their reputations. Actresses were just a step above prostitutes, after all.

By the time we had walked to Baldwin's theatre, I suspected we'd be fast friends.

A few months later

"Ah, there are two of my favorite young ladies!"

Dora and I turned at the sound of Lucky's voice. His words were cordial but his eyes held smoldering interest. Dora was convinced his frequent attention was related to her acting potential but I knew otherwise. Lucky was interested in far more than onstage talent.

It was an interest I'd cultivated.

Over the past few months, Dora and I had attended the theatre more and more often, chaperoned by either Rebecca or Mrs. Hirsch. Tonight, we'd convinced each mother we were attending with the other party. We'd met at the theatre, free of chaperones. Dora wanted to make connections for a future career; I hoped to advance things with Lucky.

I flashed him a seductive smile and shuttered my eyes just enough.

His breath hitched a bit more than usual.

Maybe he's tiring of that young wife of his.

"Lucky! How wonderful to see you. I didn't know you'd be here tonight," I said for the benefit of those around us. "You remember Dora Hirsch?"

"I do indeed. I'm hoping to see her audition. I'm hearing great things about her talent."

Dora beamed but was uncharacteristically silent.

Good heavens! There were times it was painfully evident she was only fourteen. If she wasn't going to pursue the opening, I supposed I'd need to do it for her. Who knew when we'd have another opportunity. "Is there a show she'd be good for?"

"There are several roles for juvenile actresses this season."

I nudged Dora in the ribs.

"Really?" she finally asked. "I'd love to hear more."

"Why don't the two of you join me in my box? I'll introduce you to the directors."

Dora's eyes widened. "How wonderful. Of course we'll join you." As always, once she jumped past her initial fears, her pertness propelled her. Once Dora was engaged with the directors, I'd have Lucky all to myself, an opportunity to explore what I'd seen in his eyes.

"Do I need to ask your mother?"

"We've been allowed to attend on our own tonight," I said.

"As regular as we've been attending, Mrs. Hirsch trusts all will be well."

I took Lucky's proffered arm, smiling as Dora took the other, and he escorted us to his box.

"I've a few other guests tonight," he told us. "Three directors and an out-of-state investor and his son. I'm sure you'll find him them all delightful, as they will you." Lucky's upper arm brushed my breast and I tightened my fingers where I held his forearm.

"Indeed," I purred.

We entered the elegant box, moving past the gold brocade curtain to the plush velvet seats. Lucky had installed several double seats and I hoped he'd be sharing his with me.

Introductions were made and Dora settled into the front row, happily chatting with several directors and one wife. Within seconds, they were already discussing upcoming roles. Lucky then steered me to the back row.

"I'll put you in the care of my guest while I finish up with obligations. We still have a good deal of time before the show starts and I'm needed downstairs until then. You'll be all right, by yourself?"

"Of course, Lucky. I'm not a child." I let the back of my hand brush against his thigh as I moved past him toward the seat.

"No, indeed you are not." He guided me into the row, close behind. "Allow me to introduce you to one of my newest business partners, Mr. John Behan, and his son, Albert. John, I present Miss Josephine Marcus."

My legs weakened as Lucky's words registered and I fought to stay steady as I raised my eyes to meet Johnny's. Lord, he had to see my heart beating under my low-cut bodice . . . the lowest I'd been able to talk Mama into, anyway. It thundered like a racehorse.

"Miss Marcus, I'm delighted." He took my hand, lifted it to his lips as he'd done back in Wickenburg not quite two years before. His mustache tickled, as it had then, but his tongue slipped out, circling briefly in the dim light before he pulled his lips away and lowered my hand. "Say hello, Albert."

Albert stared at me. He wasn't yet five, I didn't think, so I doubted he would remember seeing me in Prescott. At least, I hoped not.

Behind me, Lucky patted my shoulder and drifted away.

I nodded to Albert. "Master Behan."

"Good evening, Miss," he said, well trained. He bowed slightly, no recognition in his eyes. Relief flooded me.

"Go ahead and sit, son," Johnny said. "Miss Marcus, do you need to visit the ladies' retiring room before the show begins? I'd be willing to escort you there. Albert, will you be all right here?"

At the boy's nod, I swallowed.

"Oh, well, that might be wise." I stumbled with the words and limply allowed Johnny to escort me from the box, back toward the hallway.

He paused in the shadows of the entry to the box, closed the curtain behind us, and drew me into his arms. His mouth was hot on mine, hungry but quick to pull away.

"Good God, Sadie," he whispered, "you're the last person I expected to see Baldwin come in with. I had no idea where you'd gone. I searched all over for you."

"You wanted nothing to do with me, last I noticed." I hissed the words at him and strode away, marching down the hall.

Johnny followed, tucking my arm around his and stopping me in my tracks. "I couldn't. Not if I wanted to gain office. You understood that."

"Are you back with Victoria? Or do you have some other trollop on the hook?"

"Stop it, Sadie. You never owned me."

"But you pretty much owned me."

"The hell I did. You were in it for what you could get."

"We had a good thing, for both of us. You tired of me and used the campaign as an excuse."

"I didn't tire of you. You simply weren't patient enough to wait things out."

"You didn't answer my question, Johnny."

"I'm a man, honey. Of course there have been others. But there's no one regular, not like you. As to Victoria, the shrew remarried as soon as she'd milked me for what she could." He stared at me, intent, his breath audible. "God, I've missed you."

With no further words, he ushered me down the carpeted hall, polite, distant, yet urgently moving me. We passed the ladies' retiring room as his pace increased.

"Johnny, that was—"

"Hell, Sadie, that was an excuse and we both know it." He moved to the end of the hallway, glanced around the now empty expanse, and opened a door to a dark stairwell. "Good thing Lucky gave me the grand tour earlier." Before the door slammed shut, he had pulled me into his arms and edged me into the corner of the landing. Then his lips met mine.

Hungry, demanding, probing, and all Johnny. All residual thoughts of Lucky flew from my mind as familiar lust heated my body. God, how I'd missed this man.

His fingers brushed my nipples and they grew hard. He worked my breasts out of the top of the bodice and suckled me, that glorious tongue of his flicking my nipples until they ached.

I reached for his trouser fly. He was erect, ready, and I popped the buttons open to let him spring free. He filled my hand and I stroked him, touching the familiar rigid velvet length, his soft head. I gasped.

In an instant, he was pulling up my dress and his fingers were inside me. I spasmed as an orgasm hit, then another.

I realized nothing more until he entered me, pumping fast and deep. I rode him, my legs around his waist, my back against the wall, and everything else disappeared.

Late summer 1876
San Francisco

"Sadie, are you all right?"

I met Dora's gaze, saw concern etched in her eyes. "I'm fine."

"That isn't fine." She glanced at my hand. "You're doing it again."

Hellfire. My fingers were twitching for the third time that day, like I was milking an invisible cow. I had no idea what was going on and it scared me. "Nervous twitch," I said.

"Nervous about what?"

My tongue darted between my lips with a life of its own and I turned my head so Dora wouldn't see it. *That* had started today. I couldn't form words around my thoughts and the damn twitches made me look like a bumbling idiot. A ball of dread tightened in my gut.

"Don't know."

"Sadie?"

"I miss Johnny." I blurted the words without intending them. That was another issue, words just spilling out.

"Mr. Behan? The man at the theatre last month?"

"Yesssssss." I nodded and the movement took on a life of its own, a ragged staccato. I gulped air and the head bobbing ceased as suddenly as it had begun.

"You don't shake with a palsy when you miss someone and you know it. Besides, you never said a word about the man before now."

I didn't want to think about the palsy and the blurting and

the shaking so I focused on Johnny. I'd been in misery after seeing him. We'd snuck away three times that night on one pretext or another and I'd relived each coupling again and again. My nerve endings were on fire and my stomach rolled. His touch lingered on my breasts and I'd tossed and turned with erotic dreams ever since he'd left. Half the time, my legs were so weak I could hardly walk.

Damn, why in the world had I said anything? Now that I'd mentioned him, Dora would probe until she got more. "I didn't know if I should say anything. We talked a lot. I liked him."

She clapped her hands and leaned forward. "That's wonderful. He was charming and he's a businessman. In some little town in Arizona Territory but in business nonetheless. And he must be doing well, to invest with Lucky Baldwin. Or was it Lucky investing in Behan? I don't recall. Is he interested in you as well? Oh, this is perfect!"

Her reaction astounded me, though I guess it shouldn't have. This was Dora, after all. If there was any hint of a fairy tale, she usually found it.

"Mama wouldn't like it," I said.

She *tsked.* "How would she even know?"

Well, tarnation. Now I'd gotten her started. I fished for a story that would placate her; I couldn't tell her the truth. "He asked me to correspond with him but I don't dare. I've been on pins and needles over it. But if I write him and he writes back, Mama will confiscate the letter."

That much *was* true, anyway. There was no way Mama would allow me to reignite my "other life." If Johnny and I had only had more time, we might have explored my return to Prescott, this time on different terms.

But we hadn't. We'd had three magnificent pokes and then he was gone.

"So have him send the letters to my address. Mother won't

mind. She adores you and hasn't a kind word at all about how your parents shelter you. They should be encouraging the interest of such a fine man instead of you fretting and throwing away the chance to snag him."

"Dora, that's perfect!" I jumped up to offer her a hug only to have my knees buckle from under me. The last thing I remembered was the shock on Dora's face as I foundered to the floor.

"Saint Vitus's Dance."

Confused, I stared at the doctor. "Saint what?"

"Saint Vitus's Dance, a disorder of the nerves. The medical term is chorea. We see it from time to time among those who have had acute childhood infections, rheumatic fever, things of that sort. In adult women, it sometimes happens in pregnancy but, of course, that wouldn't be the case here." He turned to Mama. "You said she might have had scarlet fever awhile back so that might be the root of it."

"*Ach,* is there a cure?"

There damn well better be one. I couldn't even walk without looking like a puppet on a string. I had no control over any of my limbs anymore. As for being pregnant, I doubted that was the case—it was only three pokes and I'd had no signs. Besides, if it were, it could be treated—I'd learned how to do that a long time ago.

The doctor packed up his bag. "It seems to last a few months, up to two years in rare cases, and should disappear as fast as it appeared. Keep her quiet as much as possible. If she goes out, she should have someone with her, in case she stumbles."

Go out? Like this? That thought was almost as bad as having to stay at home for months. Almost, but not quite.

"*Ja,* we'll keep her at home. Quiet."

"Can I . . . I . . . I . . . I . . ." *Hellfire.* I let the stutter pass, then tried again. "Vis . . . vis . . . visi . . . tors?"

"Highly encouraged! She's not contagious and it will help her pass the time."

Thank heavens. This was going to be bad enough but I'd kill myself before I'd become an isolated prisoner in this house. I needed to write Johnny and I needed to do it now. He'd come to me, I knew he would.

July 1877 (the following summer)

"There's a letter!"

Dora stood in the doorway of the bedroom I shared with my younger sister, eager curiosity in her eyes.

Thank God for Dora. She'd been a beacon through months of oppression. Johnny hadn't come—not with raising Albert on his own and getting the business on its feet. He wrote monthly and never failed to brighten my day. I dutifully shared them with Dora—since they were mailed to her house, after all—omitting racy sections and references to my time in Arizona.

"From Johnny?" I asked, though I knew the answer.

"Who else would it be from? You didn't traipse out and meet someone else behind my back, did you?"

"Hah!" I made light of her comment but it riled me that I was unable to traipse anywhere. I needed to recover my strength. Johnny and I had plans.

Dora entered and closed the door, then sat on the bed next to me. "Rough day?"

"My legs haven't worked well all week. But the hand tremors are better and at least I can talk without babbling." Most of the symptoms had faded by now but even after a year, my legs continued to buckle without warning and Mama didn't trust me beyond the house without a cane. This morning, I'd given up after falling twice and gone back to bed.

"Mama finally agreed I don't have to go back to school. I'm

free as a bird." I flapped my arms dramatically.

Dora patted my legs. "Yeah, I see that."

I laughed, then stretched at my hand for the letter. "Are you going to give it to me or not?"

"In a minute." She smirked at me. "I have news before you get all mushy over Mr. Behan's missive."

I rolled my eyes at her. "Hurry it up, then."

"I got in!" She jumped in excitement, shaking the mattress under us.

"You did? Oh, Dora! I'd jump up and dance if I could. With Lucky's company?"

She beamed and my heart swelled for her. She'd wanted this so much!

"I'll be a stock actress for the fall season, taking on roles in several of the plays. You just need to hurry and get over this so you can come see me."

"You'll be rehearsing all summer?"

"Most of it."

That meant she wouldn't be visiting as much. Another reason to regain my strength. I offered her a smile, though, biting back a nip of envy. "I'm happy for you."

"Now, are you ready? Ta-da." She presented the envelope to me with great flare, laying it on my lap as though it was a treasured gift. Which it was.

She watched with anticipation as I slipped open the folded papers beneath the seal. As was usual, I skimmed the lines before I shared anything out loud.

The lines I read crushed my heart. His ex-wife's daughter had died.

"What?" Dora prompted.

"His daughter died. There was an outbreak of scarlet fever. She and Albert both caught it and it turned into meningitis, whatever that is."

"Scarlet fever . . . isn't that what you had last year?"

Oh, Johnny, I wish I'd been there. I nodded and read deeper into the letter.

"He says it's been running rampant there. Albert's settled in his ears. He went deaf. Henrietta passed away earlier this month."

"That's awful. He must be devastated."

The tone of his letter was *full* of sorrow, such a contrast to his usual suggestive comments and increasing hints of marriage. This one spoke only of the children and how difficult the last weeks had been. I read none of it aloud.

I had to find a way to him. He needed me. How in the world was he going to deal with parenting a child who'd lost his hearing? Would Victoria attempt to take Albert away, now that she'd lost her daughter? Damnation . . . her daughter, not Johnny's daughter. Still, until the divorce, Johnny had thought himself her father. He'd still mourn for her, I knew.

"I need to get to Arizona."

"Arizona? You can't even get out your front door."

"As soon as I'm strong enough, I need to go." And nothing would stop me.

March 1879

But, of course, I didn't go. The effects of the Saint Vitus's Dance lingered and it was another year before I recovered enough strength to leave the house for any length of time. By then, Papa had lost yet another job and we'd been forced to move in with Rebecca and Aaron. Then, I had two eagles watching over me.

At least Dora had helped persuade Mama that dance lessons would help me regain my leg strength. Dancing the hornpipe helped. It was all the rage, with the *H.M.S. Pinafore* craze across the country. Dora talked of joining a traveling troupe and leaving San Francisco after her current season at Lucky's. I envied her.

"Sadie, you have a caller. A gentleman." Rebecca stood in the doorway, concern evident in her voice. "He says you've been corresponding."

Johnny! He'd come. He'd finally come. I leapt from the window seat and grabbed for hairpins. At the mirror, I tidied my hair and evaluated my dress."

"Who is he, Sadie?" Rebecca demanded.

"John Behan."

"And you've been exchanging letters without Mama's knowledge? Without Papa's consent?"

"He's a businessman with experience in politics. Lucky introduced us—they've partnered in a few ventures."

"But you didn't think to have him scrutinized by your family?" Her implication was clear.

"He's a gentleman, Rebecca. Exactly the type of man Mama has been trying to match me with. I'd think you'd be pleased rather than finding fault with me."

"Did you know he was coming to call?"

"What do you think? I look dowdy as a pumpkin." I glanced at the faded ginger dress and scowled. There was no time to change. I couldn't risk leaving Johnny all alone with Mama and Rebecca.

I strode past her. She tagged behind me, firing questions the whole way. I ignored her and stopped at the parlor door, tingles flooding me as I saw Johnny on Rebecca's worn settee.

He stood. "Josephine."

"Hello, John." I stifled a giggle at our formal exchange. "I didn't expect you."

"I wanted to surprise you. I hope this isn't an inconvenience."

I eyed Mama, perched in a chair. There was no evidence of

disapproval in her expression though she was clearly puzzled by the turn of events.

John caught the action. "You didn't tell me your mother was so charming."

Mama blushed and waved her hand.

Rebecca marched forward to stand toe-to-toe with him. "Sadie says you met at Baldwin's theatre. We had no idea you'd been corresponding so you will have to forgive our shock."

I was mortified. "Rebecca!"

Johnny drew back, flashed that smile I fell in love with, and poured on the charm. "Mrs. Marcus, Mrs. Weiner, I do hope you'll allow me to finish the call, despite the sudden revelation of our correspondence."

"Obviously a covert one," Rebecca muttered under her breath.

"Ja," Mama said, hooked like I'd been. "Let's sit and give Mr. Behan a chance. It's not so often we have such a gentleman in our house."

Rebecca snorted but settled into a side chair. I sat next to Johnny. It was all I could do to keep my hands in my own lap.

Johnny cleared his throat. "Forgive me for appearing so suddenly. My trip was unplanned and the opportunity presented itself."

"What brought you here?" Mama asked.

And why oh why did you wait so long?

"My son is deaf. I brought him to see a specialist."

"Your son? You are a widower, then?" Mama's mouth dipped in sympathy.

Silence stretched and I knew Johnny was evaluating how best to respond.

Finally, he leveled a gaze and Mama and told her, "My wife was unfaithful. I divorced her."

Rebecca drew in a long hissing breath. "Divorce?"

My heart stuttered and I prayed she wouldn't make a huge to-do.

"It's not a route I would have chosen, Mrs. Weiner. But it was a necessary one. Marriage demands loyalty."

I fought back a laugh at Johnny espousing loyalty in marriage. But it seemed to pacify Rebecca. She sat back in the chair, her stiff posture softening.

"How long have you known my daughter?" Mama asked.

Johnny slid me a glance. "We met a few years ago, before Josephine's illness. I'd intended to visit long ago but with her delicate condition and my son's illness, I thought it best to delay. Besides, it gave us a chance to get to know one another better through our letters."

They chatted, then Rebecca leaned forward. "It doesn't speak well of the situation that you've been circumspect in communicating instead of forthright."

"I gave him Dora's address, knowing you'd react just this way. Johnny didn't realize it wasn't our address until recently."

"It's not an auspicious—"

"Rebecca, may I see you in the hallway?"

"We can talk later, Sadie. It wouldn't be polite for us to—"

"Now, Rebecca." I rose and strode out of the room.

She followed, her step echoing mine.

"What are you doing?" I demanded. "John Behan is a fine catch and you are ruining my chances with him."

"I'm not as naïve as Mama is. She might not notice the way you two look at one another but I see every nuance. You did *not* simply meet at the theatre."

I blanched. "We might have met more than once."

She sighed and marched down the hall, muttering again.

I returned to the parlor and found Mama and Johnny deep in conversation. I sat, listening as Johnny drew her in, told her about his business interests, his connections with men of influence. When they finally paused, Mama turned to me.

"*Ach, liebling,* your Mr. Behan is charming. While you and Rebecca were out, he declared his intentions. I am giving him leave to talk to your papa this evening."

"Like hell," Rebecca announced from the hallway. In her hand, she held the packet of Johnny's letters, my neat pink ribbon untied. "Sadie had these in her dresser drawer. She's not going anywhere with him. Behan's nothing but a scoundrel she picked up in Arizona."

Chapter Six: Josephine/Sadie

There are lies to impress and mislead the world, lies to achieve, and lies borne of desperation.
Some are more difficult than others but in the end, all are necessary.

September 1879 (six months later)
San Francisco

My family sent Johnny packing.

I seethed at Rebecca. Without her interference, I was convinced Johnny would have had no problem swaying my parents to consent to marriage. Had she no idea what a catch Johnny was? She'd simply seized on the probability that I'd met him "in the trade" and plowed ahead under that assumption.

Never mind that she was correct.

How I met Johnny was not important in the least. It was the security he'd offer me as a businessman and successful politician. Not to mention the electric physical passion we shared. Damn Rebecca to hell and back.

The summer had been miserable, with Mama convinced I needed a chaperone again. I chafed under the hawkish watch. Worse, Mrs. Hirsch had been alerted to report any letters received. I craved his correspondence and ached for his touch, becoming more determined each day to make a life with him.

One way or another, I'd find my way to Arizona and our future together.

Thank God they still let Dora visit. She lay on my bed, staring at the ceiling while I lounged in the chair by the window.

"She simply *has* to let you come to *Pinafore*! You can't miss the event of the season."

Doubt smothered me and I blew out a heavy breath. "Fat chance of that."

She sat and glanced my direction. "Surely they'll let you come if Mother is there."

"They've all but banned me from the theatre."

"But it's *Pinafore*!"

I slumped further into the chair. "Have your mother ask, then. But I suspect she'll have to include Rebecca in the invitation."

Dora tucked her legs to the side and arranged her new grown-up skirt around her. "I still can't believe what happened. What got into them, turning away such an eligible businessman?"

Over the months since Rebecca had sent Johnny packing, Dora had probed, seeking more details. She knew there was more to the story but I couldn't reveal anything else, no matter how our friendship had deepened. I straightened and framed the response I always offered.

"Rebecca heard rumors about him. She suspects he's not what he claims to be."

"Whatever did she hear?"

I rose with a whoosh. "Stop, Dora. I don't want to talk about it."

"You're a wet dishrag sometimes."

Guilt pinched at me and I fiddled at my dresser. I knew Dora meant well, that she was only trying to be supportive, but I couldn't afford to trust her. Trust backfired on a person—I'd learned that a long time ago. I waved a hand, brushing the topic away. "It just churns up bad thoughts. I need distractions."

"Then we must get you to the *Adelphi* for the show," she chimed, ever full of enthusiasm.

I'd never met a more optimistic person than Dora and I loved that about her.

Driven, she plunged on. "They'll only be playing for a few more weeks. Agnes Sterns told me that Pauline Markham and her husband have bought out the English Opera Company and they're taking the show on the road. 'Pinafore on Wheels' they're calling it. Agnes is auditioning." She paused. "I think I might, too."

Shocked, I whipped to face her. "You'd leave San Francisco?"

"That was always my plan. It could be the chance I've been waiting for."

"Markham is headed for New York?" I envied Dora the chance to seize her dream.

"Well, no. But it's a traveling troupe. And it's the *Pinafore.* I think the plan is to do shows in Arizona, then on to Colorado. If I can reach Denver, it would be a step closer. From there, maybe I can join a different troupe, head east to Chicago and New York."

My heart skipped a beat, my mind frozen on the first few sentences she'd uttered. *I think the plan is to do shows in Arizona.*

I swallowed and crossed the room to sit next to her. "Denver might be just the place to catch attention. It's big enough that the theatre is catching on, small enough that you'd get noticed. I think you should do it. I'll come along to auditions, for moral support."

My heart thundered. My entire future hinged on the next few hours.

After four weeks of honing my hornpipe steps under the guise of helping Dora with hers, I sat with her in a crowded auditorium while handfuls of eager girls were called to the stage to display their dancing skills for Mrs. Markham. Beside me, Dora was biting her nails.

Her worry was making mine all the worse. I pulled at her arm. "Stop."

She exhaled a heavy breath and stuck her hand below her thigh. "They're so good."

I stared at the dancers with a critical eye. "They're inexperienced. They can do the dance but they can't follow the choreography instructions beyond it. Dance lessons but no stage experience."

Dora sat up straighter. "I didn't notice."

Nerves, I supposed. If anything, the same issue would be my downfall. Still, I told myself I'd sat in enough rehearsals at Lucky's—before Mama had put the kibosh on such trips—to recognize how to follow instructions that varied the usual movements of the dance. I hoped I'd learned enough. This was my way out as well as Dora's and I *had* to land a role.

"That's us!" Dora piped. She grasped my hand and pulled me to my feet.

We trod up the stairs and onto the stage, formed a line with the other girls, and readied ourselves. In the dark theatre, Mrs. Markham gave instructions. Like the other sets, we'd start with the basic hornpipe steps. In seconds, the pianist started and we were off.

I told myself to relax, to let my feet follow the music, not to think about the movements.

Minutes later, the music stopped and we stilled. From the auditorium, Pauline Markham thinned the numbers. We'd made the first cut.

And then anxiety hit. Markham rattled off a series of instructions that varied the steps. I filed them in my head, familiar with all of them but unpracticed in putting them all together in a new pattern.

"One, two, three, four . . ."

The music resumed and the girls in the line began to move. I tried to avoid sideways glances, to keep my eyes toward the front. My feet faltered once, twice, and suddenly I was behind. Damn my luck in being in the downstage line.

Markham announced the second cut.

My name was not in the list. My heart sank.

My steps dragged as I returned to my seat.

Damn, damn, and damn.

I sure as hell wasn't going to get to Arizona this way.

In the end, neither Dora nor I were cast, nor was Dora's friend Agnes. Still, I was determined to somehow attach myself to the troupe.

The following morning, I snuck out of the house, intent on my purpose. Just before noon, my heart pounding, I waited outside Markham's office until she exited.

"Miss Markham, I'd like a word. Please."

She turned and stared at me. "You're one of the girls from yesterday."

I shifted and forced confidence into my voice. "Sadie Marcus."

"Cut after the second round."

I met her gaze. "Unfortunately."

"What can I do for you? You must know no amount of pleading will reverse my decision. You're not the first rejected auditionee to turn up at my door. Save your breath if that's what you have in mind." She glanced away, toward the street.

I stepped into her line of sight. "I understand about the role, Mrs. Markham. But I'd like to be part of the show in whatever capacity I can."

"Hmph."

Hellfire. If I didn't win a spot in the troupe, I'd never get to

Johnny. I dug for confidence, like I had back at the brothel. "I know you've heard that before, too. But I'm an experienced stagehand and I'm willing to work hard."

Mrs. Markham sighed. "Look, Sadie . . . I know how desperately you young girls want this but I just can't—"

"I know makeup, hairstyling, props, costuming. I'll understudy any role, no matter how small and the chorus isn't beneath me. You'll get a jack-of-all-trades with me."

"I don't need any additional stagehands. You're wasting both our time."

I'd anticipated this might happen. Though I hadn't whored since leaving Arizona, I'd done what I'd had to. "I also have a recommendation." I proffered the letter I'd secured after spending two hours convincing Lucky to write it on my behalf. We'd both left satisfied, each in our own way.

Pauline Markham broke the seal and skimmed the words. She raised her eyebrows. "You have friends in high places, Sadie."

"I spend a lot of time at Lucky's."

"I'm sure you do." Her words dripped with innuendo.

I shook away the shame of betraying Johnny and told myself he'd understand. I caught Pauline's gaze and held it, so she would have no doubt I held enough of Lucky's interest to impact her career. "I know Lucky would appreciate this as a personal favor to him."

"The implication is clear in what he wrote. I'll create a space. We leave in three days."

The train rocked constantly but I grew more excited with each mile. We'd departed October 21, crossing California by rail through Yuma. From there, we'd go on to Casa Grande, the end of the line. I recalled the horrid trip with Hattie Wells's party and how we'd all come to hate the rough stage travel. Now, the railroad extended further and we'd have just sixty-five miles via stage, the last leg to Tucson. I'd stay with the troupe until we got to Prescott.

Then I'd be in my darling Johnny's arms at last. Lord, I hoped he'd received my note.

Pauline had me learn the role of Hebe, huffing and puffing that she needed to get something out of having me along. Still, she refused to promote me beyond an understudy of the lowest kind. I was not listed as a cast member. Pauline treated me with courtesy, but I read between the lines well enough. I was there because of Lucky's influence and we both knew it.

Had I truly wanted to be an actress, I would have resented it, but it didn't matter. It was nothing but my means to an end. The only thing that caused me heartache was leaving Dora behind. I hoped she'd realize her dreams and not hate me too much.

I brushed the guilt away and concentrated on the town ahead. Yuma appeared as dusty and forlorn as all the other Arizona towns I'd been through, though there was some hustle and bustle generated by those using the crossing over the Colorado River. The train trestle rose high above the river and it shook as we crossed the wide expanse. My breath hitched, then we were safely into Arizona, passing the Territorial Prison and pulling into the red-tiled depot.

"Water stop!" the conductor announced. Passengers sprang from their seats, eager to get out and stretch their legs. Beside me, my seatmate squirmed, her portly arms jostling me as she rose. "Come on, honey. You'd best get out a bit. It'll be a long trek to Casa Grande." She waddled down the narrow aisle.

I exhaled and flung my arms wide.

"Feels good, huh?" the man across the aisle said.

"You have no idea."

"Oh, I do. I sat next to her yesterday."

I flashed a smile at him. "And you had the gall to let me experience her today?" The quip came out flirty and I winced a bit. I'd need to rein that in, once I was with Johnny. "I'm Sadie Marcus." No invented names this time. Rebecca would know exactly where to look for me anyway.

"John P. Clum. Are you with Mrs. Markham's troupe?"

"I am."

"Then I will definitely look forward to seeing the show."

I didn't tell him I wouldn't be taking the stage. Unless, of course, something happened and I was promoted from understudy.

Clum was tall, his hairline receding despite his young age. He couldn't have been past thirty but his pate was already shiny back to the middle of his head. He followed me off the car and we chatted as we walked to the depot. Inside, the tiled floor was unexpectedly clean, given the constant sand in the air.

He seemed familiar and I searched to place him. "Weren't you an Indian Agent?"

"I was, for the San Carlos Apaches. I resigned the position over two years ago. I'm in Tombstone now, publisher of the *Arizona Citizen.*"

"A newspaper man. I'm impressed."

"You're familiar with Arizona, then?"

"I lived here briefly." I held back any further information, guarding my reputation from the newsman. I needed to be on my toes if I was to start a new life here.

The whistle sounded and we reboarded. This time, I sat next to Clum, comfort only a factor in the decision. The man was pleasant and I hoped to gather information. Last time I'd lived here, I'd been naïve, dependent on others. This time, I'd arm myself with knowledge.

"So, tell me about Tombstone. I don't know much beyond hearing silver was discovered there."

"Indeed, two years ago. The town is growing by leaps and bounds, though still rustic by California standards. And wild. I suspect Markham will secure a few performances at the *Bird Cage* there."

"And elsewhere in the territory? What's the news?"

"The Apaches were relocated, Yuma is growing, Prescott will not be reinstated as the territorial capital."

I seized the opportunity. "Prescott . . . I recall the town. Is Behan still in business there?"

"There was just news that he's bought a building in Tip Top, where he intends to open a saloon. No word on his Prescott interests. He's also visited Tombstone several times. Rumor has it he plans to invest there as well."

I stored the news away. With Johnny, forewarned was forearmed. He wasn't always good about sharing details of his life. I'd be able to manage him better if I was aware of all he didn't tell me. I'd learned the hard way that reacting after the fact was not a good route. This time around, I'd take the initiative.

"And do you know Al Seiber?" I asked. I'd thought often of the good-hearted military man who'd helped me get out of the mess I'd been in. I'd never had the chance to thank him.

"He's stationed farther south, now. Engaged with the Apache efforts."

I continued to milk Clum for information, as he did me, and the hours fled by. Before we knew it, the train was slowing for Casa Grande.

"Will you be continuing on the stage, Mr. Clum?" I hoped he would. Our conversation had made the trip so enjoyable that I'd forgotten my worry over arriving at Johnny's door without warning. I'd sent a letter from San Francisco but had no way of knowing if it would reach him. What if he'd already moved to Tip Top?

"I'm afraid not. I have business to take care of before I head south. I hope I catch up with you in Tombstone."

"I would enjoy that."

"Miss Marcus? I'm not sure if I read things correctly but I sensed your interest in Behan went beyond the casual." He paused, as if debating whether to continue. "If you're the same Sadie he was involved with a few years back, you'd best know he hasn't much changed, despite the expanding business interests. I'd stay on my toes if you come into contact again."

He patted my hand as he stood. "Don't trust a word he says."

December 1879

Clum's words haunted me.

Had I once more jumped from the frying pan into the fire?

I wasn't naïve, not like I'd been, but had I been blinded by my dreams?

I fussed with new doubts as the troupe finished its run in Tucson and moved on to Tombstone. Then, we headed to Prescott for a scheduled Christmas Eve performance. My stomach was in knots. In just days, I'd need to decide if I was joining Johnny or remaining with the troupe. Neither option was as pleasing as it had been back in September when the glamour of the stage beckoned and the prize of Johnny Behan had glistened.

Had Johnny really intended to offer for my hand or had that simply been a way to get into my parents' good graces?

Stop it.

Clum knew nothing of the Johnny Behan I knew. Sure, Johnny had his faults and I fully accepted that he could be as much the schemer as I was. But he was a good man, too. Just last week the Prescott paper (which I'd taken to reading whenever I could locate a copy) had reported Johnny had joined a volunteer force led by Al Seiber to protect the area from roving Mexican bandits. He was a tender, passionate man. We had a future together and I *couldn't* let others' opinions of Johnny interfere. Worrying was not productive. I should be planning for a wedding.

And I would be, as soon as the damn stage got to Prescott and I found my Johnny.

The slowing rhythm of the stage broke the edge of slumber. Dark was full upon us and I could barely make out the other passengers as we reined into Prescott.

Pauline was first out of the stage. "I wired ahead for rooms. Get some sleep and be ready for dress rehearsal at noon."

I stared at her, bleary-eyed. "What time is it?"

"Must be two in the morning. It'll be a short night."

Two in the morning? I glanced around. The town was dead. There'd be no finding Johnny tonight.

I stumbled my way into the hotel with the rest of the troupe and accepted the key I was given. Along with my roommate, I found the room and slumped into bed. It was nearly noon when we roused and in the little time I had between rehearsal and the Christmas Eve show, I learned only that my letter to Johnny was unclaimed at the post office and that Johnny was out of town. That meant I wouldn't be leaving Markham's troupe until he returned, and I prayed that happened before the troupe moved on.

I rose early on Christmas Day. My head ached and my eyes were red and puffy but I knew I needed to find out more information. I left the hotel to find the streets empty. There were few businesses open. At the café, no one knew a thing. I drew my coat tight around me and pushed open the door of the liquor dealer, a wiry little man named Jacob Marks. He'd been a regular at Jennie's brothel. If anyone knew about Johnny, it's be him.

Marks looked up as I entered, adjusted his glasses, and grinned.

"Hey there, Miss Sadie."

I winced at his high-pitched voice. And the fact that he recognized me. "Jacob."

"Didn't never expect to see you again."

Dread balled in my gut. I hadn't much thought things through, I realized. I strode in, holding my head high and stopped at the counter. "Let's keep it quiet, about the past. I've cleaned up my life and don't much want word getting out about it."

"Well, now, I don't know . . ."

"Please, Jacob."

"Maybe. Maybe not. You might not be here long anyways."

"What's that supposed to mean?"

"Got a telegram about you nigh unto a month ago. From your brother-in-law. Sent it to me, figuring I'd hear soon enough if you showed up in town. Guess he was right."

The ball in my stomach tightened. *Hellfire.* "What'd he say?"

"Wants you to return back home right away. Says Mrs. Markham will be paid handsomely to accompany you."

"Markham knows?"

"Not as yet."

Thank God. I plunged ahead, determined to learn what I could. "Let's keep it that way." I fished in my pocket for what few coins I had and plunked them on the counter. "And, since you're such a fountain of news, tell me what you know about Johnny Behan."

"Behan . . . well, he ain't around much. He bought himself a saloon up in Tip Top."

"That's toward Phoenix, right?"

"Sleepy little town but he's waking things right up. Got himself five gals working out of the place. Tip Top's first brothel."

Fury burned. A brothel? Johnny hadn't told me he held interest in a fancy house. I'd been as foolish as I'd begun to fear. But I'd be damned if I went back to San Francisco with my tail between my legs. Understudy or not, I'd continue with Markham's troupe and work my way up.

Markham . . . *hellfire.* I glanced at Jacob again.

"What's it going to take to keep you from going to Markham about the telegram?"

Jacob grinned and began to unbutton his trousers.

At the end of January, Pauline Markham left her husband and took the stage for parts unknown. He, in turn, disbanded the troupe and disappeared. Twenty-six of us were abandoned without jobs or the money we were owed.

Or the escape plan I'd planned on.

After a month in Prescott and the growing number of times I'd had to "pay" Jacob to keep his mouth shut, I spent little time mourning her departure. She was gone and if I didn't take control immediately, I'd be a lower whore than I'd ever been.

Damn it to hell and back!

I pinched back my pride and made my way to Jennie Roland's place, knocking on the back door.

Three raps later, it opened. "What?" A woman with kohled eyes and weary lines on her face stood in the doorway.

"Is Jennie here?" I demanded.

"She don't own the place no more."

I huffed out a breath. "Who's in charge?"

"Julia Burton."

Surprise settled my frustration. "Aunt Julia?"

The kohl-eyed woman stared at me, obviously trying to place me. "You one of her girls?"

I shrugged, there was little point in lying. "I used to be."

"Come on in, then." She held the door open wider and left

me standing there. I swallowed and stepped across the familiar stoop. It wasn't what I wanted but I had no choice. I just hoped all record of what I'd owed Jennie and Hattie had long since been written off.

Aunt Julia stepped into the kitchen. Her dark skin had grown saggy, her age catching up to her. "Lord in heaven, Sadie!" She held open her arms and I stumbled into them. "What you doin' here, child? Thought you was long gone."

My resolve slipped. Aunt Julia had been a bright spot in what became a hard life—back when I thought the life would be so glorious, before my heart had to harden. "I thought so, too."

"Yet here you are." She hugged me tight, then drew back, looking me in the face. "You ain't still in the life, are you?"

"You are," I said, not knowing how else to respond.

"Shoot, an old colored woman like me ain't got nothing else. Seems I recall you got free once. What you doin' back?"

I debated, then decided to be honest with her. "I'm stuck, Aunt Julia. Johnny Behan came to San Francisco for me and my sister chased him away. I came as soon as I could, with the Pinafore troupe. And now he's not here and the Markhams just abandoned us without pay."

She *tsked,* then began to bustle around the kitchen. "That leaves you in a fix, for sure. I'll get us some tea and we'll figure out a plan."

I sat, worked out what I wanted to say. "I won't go back to San Francisco again. Not back to my family."

"I never even thought nothing of the sort, child."

"Could I work for you, just until I raise enough to get out on my own?"

She turned her head. "It don't work that way and you know it. By the time I took my cut, it'd take you years. I like you, child, but I can't pull no favors for you in the house. Not if I want to run things smooth with the other girls."

She puttered around, then plunked a cup of tea in front of me and sat down across from me.

"You don't need to be starting back here. That leaves Behan. Since you don't want to end up one of his whores, you need to set your eyes on how to pull the strings." She leaned forward. "I don't see Behan marrying anyone unless he thinks it's his idea. Johnny don't like anyone else making decisions for him. If you want him, you make him want you. My advice? You take my help to go to Tip Top, set yourself up, and reel him in."

I tamped down my nerves and stepped from the buggy I'd rented in Gillette, the closest stage stop to Tip Top. I brushed the dust from my dark green brocade gown and adjusted the matching velvet hat with its black ostrich feathers, then glanced around the town. It wasn't much to speak of. Another mining town.

"Afternoon, ma'am." At the rail, a tattered miner doffed his worn hat. He grinned, his mouth devoid of several teeth. "Can I help ya?"

Pulling confidence I didn't feel, I straightened my shoulders. "There's a livery in town? I was told I could turn in the buggy here, that there was an arrangement with the livery in Gillette."

"Yes'm."

"Good. Deliver it there. Have them register the return under 'Mansfield.' This is Johnny Behan's place, correct?"

He flinched a bit at my clipped tone. "Yes'm."

Encouraged that he had taken the bait, I went on. "Unload my trunks and place them upstairs."

"Them rooms is used, ma'am. By the . . . uh . . . girls."

I huffed, made it a grand gesture. "In Johnny's rooms, you dolt. I am not *one of the girls.* I am *Johnny's* girl."

"Oh, yes, ma'am. Right away."

Emboldened, I tossed the man a coin and marched into the

saloon. "Which stairway to Johnny's rooms?" I demanded of the barkeep. "Outside or interior?"

"Both will get you there." He grinned as if it was the funniest thing in the world.

I rolled my eyes at him. "And once I'm up?"

"Last door."

I tapped my toe, letting him see how impatient I was becoming. "I presume it's locked?"

He stared. " 'Course it's locked."

"The key." I extended my hand.

"Johnny's key?" By now, confusion was pulling at him.

His reaction fed my feigned authority. "Yes, Johnny's key. Don't tell me he failed to inform you I'd be arriving. I'm Sadie Mansfield and those rooms are now mine. The key?"

"I can't just let you in and give you the key!"

I leaned forward, bending over the bar so my ample bosom spilled to the top of my gown. "Oh, honey, yes you can. And you will. Because you don't want to get on Johnny's bad side by refusing me." I drew back and slid my hand to my hip. "And, you most especially don't want to get on *my* bad side. From here on out, honey, you're happy when I'm happy. And when I'm not, you'll have a very miserable day. Now open the damn room."

"Yes, Miss Mansfield. Right away."

I strode away, straight up the stairs, and left him to follow. Just like Aunt Julia had advised.

Within the week, Johnny was back in Tip Top, rapping on the door to his apartment. But it was enough time for me to take control of the bartender and every single one of the girls. And, in the process, to find the hardness I'd once known and would need again.

"Sadie!" he called. "Let me in."

I pulled on a satin wrapper and opened the door. "Well, hello, Johnny," I purred. "Took you long enough."

"What the hell, Sadie?" He stepped into the room and slammed the door shut. "You're the last person I expected to show up here."

I drew my mouth into a pout. "What kind of welcome is that, darling?"

"A shocked one."

"After I managed to get all the way out here?"

"Ah, Sadie. I figured you were lost to me." He pulled me into his arms and took my lips. Not the gentle kiss of a man in love but the savage claim of a man in lust. Then he was pushing the robe from my shoulders. It dropped to the floor, the tie loosening on its own. In seconds, he was lifting my leg and plunging into me. "God, I've missed you."

"Looks that way."

I wiped at a tear, before he could spot it, and realized how much it cost me to lose the dream. Whether I won him or not, it would never be what I'd once imagined. I gathered my clothing while he tucked himself back into his trousers, then I sauntered away, leaving him to follow like an abandoned puppy.

Just like that, I had him.

Chapter Seven: Josephine/Sadie

A cornered woman becomes a calculating woman.

January 1880
Tip Top, Arizona
I adapted to life as Johnny Behan's mistress with great ease.

Oh, I still coveted the security of marriage but I no longer held on to the expectation of love and happily ever after. I'd not get that with Johnny. It had been a fantasy I'd clung to. Once I let go of wanting the love, I enjoyed being his paramour. Though I hadn't the fancy parlor house, I did have the life I'd imagined when I'd ogled the women on Powell Street.

Johnny spoiled me. I had gowns and jewels and was constantly on his arm. All without the mess of being married to him. *My courtesan,* he called me. And I was fine with that.

I had to be.

What I couldn't abide was being left alone while he gallivanted all over the territory. If I couldn't have his love, I wanted his attention.

I worked too hard for it to be otherwise.

"But you're always traveling, Johnny. I get lonely without you." I reached across the bed where we sat and ran my fingers along his thigh.

He drew a breath.

Perfect. I inched my hand a bit closer to his groin. Almost there, but not quite. "Say you'll take me this time."

"You hate stage travel. I've heard you complain about it plenty of times. Tombstone is miles beyond Tucson. You know that. Besides, Tombstone's not much."

My dander rose. It wasn't *Tombstone* I wanted. It was to get out of Tip Top and its endless lonely days of regret. I crawled my fingers a tiny fraction. "I know what Tombstone's like, Johnny. I've been there. There's no need to speak to me as if I'm a child. I'm not, you know." This time, I allowed my touch to brush his swelling cock. It twitched. As I'd anticipated.

"Oh, I know you're not a child."

That was true enough. I'd turned twenty last week and Johnny had honored the occasion by having a professional photograph taken. But that wasn't what he meant and we both knew it. Johnny tensed and I knew diverting my focus from what I'd been doing had cooled the moment.

He brushed my hand away, stood, and closed his trousers. "I won't have any time to socialize. It's a business trip. You'd be in the way."

Anger nipped. "In the way? What the hell is that supposed to mean?"

Johnny crossed the bedroom, stopped at the door. "It means I'm not inclined to explain you to my potential business partners." Then he sauntered into the parlor.

What the hell! Incensed, I grabbed my robe and marched after him. "Why would you have to explain anything?"

He shrugged. "You bring a woman along, it has meaning." He grabbed his boots and sat to yank them on. "There's a rumor the Territorial Legislature is going to carve out a new county out of Pima County the end of this year. And that new county will be rich with mining tax revenue, all of it collected by the county sheriff. I plan to get myself appointed and to do that, I need to appear a family man."

I leaned against the doorframe and jutted my hip. "So,

introduce me as your fiancée."

"You're not my damn fiancée."

"I could be."

He looked up at that. "Why would we want to ruin a good thing?"

The comment stung. I knew he was right, that we weren't suited to be man and wife, but damn if it didn't sting to hear him reject me.

"You told my mother you wanted to marry me." I spat the words out.

"Hell, after the fucking we did at Lucky's, I'd have told them anything to get you back in my life."

Always, it always came back to that. That's really all he wanted.

It was the one thing I happened to be good at. Damn good. I moved away from the wall and approached him. "And what about the fucking you're getting now?"

"I'm already getting it."

"That can be fixed."

"And so can your comfort level."

Threatened, I hissed in a breath. "You bastard."

"Whore."

I slapped his face. Hard.

He winced and his hand flew to his cheek. "Damn, Sadie."

My eyes stung at the thought of being vulnerable. Unsure of how to proceed, craving something tangible, I reached for his arm. "I don't like being threatened."

"And I don't like being pressured." He pulled me onto the arm of the chair. "You live in style, the way you wanted when you pressed me in Prescott. I told you then that my ambitions wouldn't allow me to give you what you were demanding. Well, now you have it. But I still have ambitions and you'll stay put here instead of being on display where it matters."

"What's so damn important about being a lawman?"

"Perks, Sadie. Sheriffs collect taxes. They collect fines. All that comes in cash."

Puzzled, I stared at him. "But you have to pay that to the county."

"The county gives you a percentage for collecting it and with all the mining in that area, that amounts to a lot. Besides, nobody knows how much you're actually collecting."

"Don't you have to do receipts?"

"Who the hell knows how to read?"

My eyes widened. So that was how Johnny had amassed the money he needed to keep me in such style. Only a few businessmen and professionals were educated. The others wouldn't even know to ask for a receipt.

It was perfect.

"All right. That makes sense. You should have explained it that way in the first place."

"And give you something to hold over my head? One tantrum and you'd blather all over town."

"Aw, Johnny, I wouldn't do anything like that."

He patted my leg. "Yes, you would."

I watched him rise and ready his things for the trip. I'd forgotten he was leaving me. Already, I could taste the loneliness, the resentment.

"Johnny?"

He looked up, raised his brows.

"Could we maybe meet in Phoenix on your way home? Tip Top is so dull." I stood and crossed to him, laid my head on his chest, pressed close against him. "I need to go to the theatre, enjoy some fine dining, maybe do a little shopping. Not that I don't *love* your gifts but a girl likes to see the fashions and go out on the town."

He stepped back and leveled his gaze on me. "Will that keep

you satisfied for a while?"

"You know it will, Johnny. It might even inspire me a little." I let my tongue slip between my lips and drew in a heavy breath so my breasts heaved up, the robe sliding.

His eyes narrowed.

"All right, Sadie. You can meet me in Phoenix but I expect no further demands about Tombstone from you. Understood?"

"Of course. I'll be the most content courtesan you ever imagined."

For now.

March 1880
Prescott, Arizona

Replete with a trunk of new dresses, plump from a week of gourmet meals, and exhausted by as much culture as I could pack in, I'd checked out of the Bank Exchange Hotel earlier in the day, bound for Prescott. Throughout the Phoenix visit, Johnny had been attentive, almost to the point of excess. His negotiations for the livery business in Tombstone had gone well and he'd been generous with his money.

We hadn't discussed how I fit into those plans.

Instead, I'd ignored it, determined to enjoy the time in Phoenix instead of wasting it with arguments. But I was equally determined that something needed to change. I grew convinced Johnny planned to abandon me in Tip Top now that he was grounding himself in Tombstone. I'd need to plan carefully if I were to avoid being left alone in such a miserable place.

This morning, Johnny had put me on the stage and promised to see me in Tip Top in a few days, after my side trip to Prescott. I needed to pay Aunt Julia for the money she'd given me. Her advice and her accompanying loan had done the trick. I owed her, no matter that she said the clothes were a gift. I *needed* to pay the debt. I couldn't afford to view it as anything more than a business transaction. No matter her warm feelings for me, I was obligated and being obligated in the skin trade was not a comfortable state.

I stood at Aunt Julia's kitchen door, waiting for someone to answer my knocking.

"She's not home."

I glanced away from the back door to the brothel and into the eyes of a tall, well-dressed woman. Auburn tendrils framed her delicate face and her day dress was modest enough to suggest she was the wife of a local businessman.

"Any idea when she'll be back?"

"She's with the town marshal. It might be a couple hours. They're negotiating her business license." She tipped her head and offered a wry smile. "I'm Kitty."

"Sadie Mansfield."

Kitty eyed me as carefully as I had her, taking in my clothing as well as how I held myself. A habit most of us had. "Well, Sadie, let's you and I find a good cup of tea. I don't think either of us would especially enjoy sitting in Aunt Julia's parlor waiting while the girls stare at us. They don't much care for me." She quirked her head again. "Shall we?"

She took my arm and guided me down the street. The town hadn't changed much in the time I'd been away. It took just a few minutes to get to the teahouse I remembered. The proprietor had married one of the girls and there was always a back room reserved for our use, as long as we didn't flaunt our status to the other customers.

Kitty opened the door and I stepped in, making my way to the rear of the shop.

"You're familiar with Prescott," she said, following me back.

"I worked at the house a few years ago," I told her.

"So what are you doing back here?"

Though I knew it wasn't wise to be open, Kitty failed to stir suspicion. "Paying off a debt," I revealed.

"Wise woman."

We sat, ordered tea, and waited until the waitress poured it and drifted away. "What's your relationship to Julia?" I asked Kitty.

"Now? I live nearby. A few months ago, I was part of the stable."

"Congratulations." I saluted her with my cup.

"I could say the same to you. Looks like we both landed a way out. You're not living in town anymore?"

I took a sip, weighed my response. "I went back to San Francisco a few years ago, made some changes. I live in Tip Top."

Kitty grinned. "You *are* Johnny Behan's girl, then. I thought so."

So, there were rumors. I laughed. Of course, there were rumors. "You know Johnny?"

"Honey, we all know Johnny."

I sucked in a breath. I didn't much like it, even if there was no love lost between Johnny and me. "Were you one of his favorites?"

"Rein it in, dear. He did business with me when I was new and tired of me as quickly as I did him. Then Harry Jones made it clear I was his."

I let the jealousy drift away. Johnny'd had every girl in town, I supposed. I concentrated on what Kitty had said, sure I'd heard the name before. "He's an attorney, isn't he?"

"He is. And now I'm Kitty Jones."

Surprised, I nearly dropped my cup. "He married you?"

"Don't look so shocked. The owner of this tea shop married *his* girl."

I set the tea down. "It's still rare enough to be remarkable."

"Truthfully," she leaned forward, whispering, "Harry hasn't made the leap yet. But he will. In the meantime, I'm testing out the name, getting us both used to it."

"And he's comfortable with that?"

"He doesn't have much say in the matter. I can call myself anything I want. But, yes, he's comfortable with it. He's moving me to Tombstone in a few weeks. When I join him, I'll become Mrs. Ida Jones and no one will link me to Kitty Davenport. Let's just call this my transitional phase."

Envy poked me. "Johnny's talking about Tombstone, too."

"I'd heard. When you introduced yourself, I thought we should get to know each other. It'll stand both of us well if we're friends in Tombstone, protecting one another. Being enemies would serve neither of us well."

But I wouldn't be going to Tombstone. Not if Johnny had his way. "Harry sounds a lot more agreeable to marriage than Johnny."

"Johnny got burned by his marriage to Victoria. He's gun-shy. Harry came to it quick enough but it wasn't without a bit of work on my part."

A tiny spark of hope ignited. If I could soften Johnny toward marriage, I wouldn't have to fear being left in Top Top to whore my way out. "How'd you talk him into it?"

"After he moved me out of the brothel and set me up, I gave him a few months, then just started calling myself Kitty Jones."

"You didn't!"

"I most certainly did. He didn't like it one little bit. Folks started asking him questions he didn't want to deal with. But things changed. People didn't shun me the way they had before and he slowly came to realize that. Once the initial shock wore off, folks learned to accept it. He lost a little business at first but his clients got over it as the gossip settled. To this day, most of the town has no idea whether or not we're legally married. And they quit caring a long time ago. I carry myself like a wife instead of a whore and no one's the wiser. By the time he moves me to Tombstone, he'll be so used to it that making it official will be easy as pie."

I shook my head. "Johnny's not easily manipulated."

"From what I heard about your little trick in Tip Top, he's more malleable than he thinks he is. Didn't you do exactly the same thing in setting yourself up as his mistress?"

Smug, I offered her a smile. "I just marched on into his place like I owned it."

"And it worked like a charm, did it not?"

Had it been anywhere but Tip Top, I wasn't sure it would have worked. "Keeping me was easier than sending me packing, I guess. Plus, he did recognize the benefits."

"Knowing Johnny, I'm sure he did." A snort of laughter poured from her.

Caught unaware, I joined her. Several moments later, we finally sobered. "So just become Mrs. Behan?"

"Once you start using the name, it makes it pretty difficult for him to deny you without casting himself center stage."

I took a sip of tea, then lifted my cup. "Then, here's to Josephine Behan!"

April 1880
Tip Top, Arizona

"What the hell, Sadie!" Johnny slammed the door so hard the windows shook.

Obviously, he'd heard.

"Hello, Johnny. Welcome home."

"Don't you 'welcome home' me. When the hell did you start signing your name as Mrs. Josephine Behan?"

Careful not to rile him, I played the innocent. "I just signed a few letters that way. You know that's how I think of myself."

"Like hell. You think of yourself as Sadie Mansfield every time you twitch that sultry little body of yours and wave your tail at me. Missus doesn't fit you at all, Sadie."

"Seems to me you'd like me being Mrs. Behan. It'll make things a whole lot easier when we move to Tombstone."

"When we move to Tombstone?"

"You've bought into Dexter Stables and you're planning to run for sheriff. That implies a move to Tombstone, does it not?"

"It wasn't the move I was disputing."

Scared as I was, I forced myself to stay calm, not to argue. I'd practiced my words already. Now I just needed to stay on script. "You mean to leave me here and we both know it. I'm done with your decisions leaving me to claw my way up from the bottom. No woman wants to be a whore forever."

He leveled his gaze. "But you're so good at it."

"Bastard," I spat.

"Tsk, tsk, there's no need for name calling."

"I might be your whore, Johnny, but I'm not going to be anyone else's. Not again."

He shrugged. "I could walk out that door right now and be done with you. One less thing for me to worry about."

The words were like a slap. I choked back a flinch and stared at him, cold as he was. "Oh, there's where you're wrong, Johnny. You will worry about me every minute. The closer it gets to election time, the more you'll be looking over your shoulder, praying I don't show up and call you out in front of the whole town."

He laughed. "By the time you have enough money to do that, I'll be in office. Whores left behind don't too often land on their feet."

But he was wrong. Whores left behind always landed on their feet. It was just that some were more nimble than others.

Allie

Mattie's beginnings started before Josie's, her being ten years older and all. But only Mattie ever knew her story. She didn't even say much to me and I reckon I knew her better'n most. There was her sister, Sarah, and there were the years with Wyatt in Illinois and Kansas but she kept the details pretty close. I think there was a lot she didn't want to remember. And what she did tell me, Wyatt and Josie squashed. There was too much that could rise up to haunt Wyatt and James and Virge. And, of course, the less said about Mattie, the better for Josie.

Chapter Eight: Celia/Mattie

A body tends to avoid the truth when the truth hurts. I ought to know.

Fall 1868
Johnson County, Iowa

Celie Blaylock didn't warrant it made one lick of sense, not when she was the one near to nineteen years old. It sure didn't measure out none for her sister, Sarah. Fifteen was way too young for Pa to be considering on marriage.

Zachary Potts had need of a wife, widower that he was. Lord knew those kids of his were running wild with no ma to herd them. It was clear to anyone with eyes that he'd set his sights on Sarah. Being that he was a deacon in the church and all, Pa wasn't likely to refuse him, even if one of those kids had nigh unto two years on her.

"I ain't gonna do it." Sarah's pretty mouth pinched up tight.

Celie pulled her sister close. "Don't blame you one little bit," she said. "He ought not to be looking at you. There's plenty of girls older'n you all but standing in line for a husband." Sour guilt filled up her throat knowing she was jealous of her sister. Her name ought to be offered up first, by her way of thinking. More'n anything, she wanted life like other girls her age had, a family and a man to care about her. Potts wasn't a love match but maybe he'd grow to favor her. Ma said affection grew over time.

Besides, Sarah didn't want nothing to do with him.

Sarah's cornflower eyes rested on Celie, pinning her with unspoken emotion. Yep, Sarah knew it, too—knew that Celie ought to be the one put forward.

Celie swallowed. *Tarnation.* She'd need to talk to Pa. There wasn't much she hated more'n talking to Pa.

"You go on, get ready for the social. I'll talk to Pa."

Sarah's mouth lifted and she hugged Celie tight. "Thank you."

Celie pinched off a second prick of conscience. There was little she wouldn't do for Sarah and it chafed knowing that she wasn't being full honest. She ignored the feeling, telling herself Sarah didn't want Potts anyhow. She'd rightly never even know Celie was allowing a lie. It was all for the best, for both of them.

She didn't have much time and she'd best get it done. Else Potts would get Pa's answer and the betrothal would be sealed. More than likely, Potts was planning to announce the match to the congregation tonight.

Celie smoothed the curl of her ringlets, wishing there was a looking glass in the house. But Pa didn't hold with vanity. One of many sins he eschewed. Tidiness, he admired, though, and she hoped she'd pass muster on that account. She didn't need him finding faults when there was so much at stake.

She didn't need the mirror to remind her she wasn't much to look at, not like Martha and Sarah. Martha was the favored daughter—everybody knew that. Perfect, pious, pretty, Martha was the apple of her pa's eye. Ma's, too. Celie had never lived up to her. She was plain-faced and her auburn hair just didn't catch the eye like Martha's blond tresses. Martha'd married right off and had a family of her own already. But nobody asking for Celie all this time didn't mean she deserved to be an old maid her entire life.

Pa was in the barn, oiling tack. The acrid scent of old oil and leather hung in the small, side room. Celie's mouth fell open so she could draw air.

Bowed over the leather, Pa never even looked up when she entered. Just started a little.

"Pa?"

"What is it, Celia Ann?" he said, using her full name. "I'd have thought you'd be helping your ma rather than neglecting your chores. Ain't you no sense at all?"

Celie winced. Might be she didn't have no sense but did he always have to be reminding her of it?

"My chores are done, Pa. I wanted to talk with you before we went to church."

He looked up at her then, lifting his bushy eyebrows in impatience as he stalled the polishing rag.

"Ma mentioned that Mr. Potts approached you about taking Sarah to wife. I'd like to ask you to offer him my hand instead."

Please, Pa.

"You?"

At least he hadn't laughed. "I'm eighteen. It's time I'm married and the three-year advantage in age would serve well in caring for his children. Sarah's little more than a child herself."

"She's caught his eye." Pa poured more oil onto the rag and returned to his task. Already, the harness shone so Celie couldn't figure why he kept at it. It was dismissive, like her words were worth nothing.

"I'm the more practical choice."

Pa sighed. "You don't think that's a bit forward, advancing yourself so?"

"I don't think Sarah is ready for marriage."

"And you are, with that sharp tongue of yours?"

Celie bit back the retort that would prove him right. She *could* be prickly and opinionated, offering up her views when no one had asked for them. "My tongue can be tamed."

He set the rag down and shook his head. "You are headstrong, Celia, and you haven't a lick of sense in you. No man wants you. Perhaps your role will be to remain at home to care for your parents. I'm half a century old. My dotage is not that far off. Besides if it's tending kids you want, your ma can use a hand with your baby sister and Martha's got them four little ones."

A wave of rebellion swarmed her. She was not going to be a lonely old maid tending her folks and Martha's brood to boot. Besides, she did have sense, she did, even if Pa said otherwise. One way or another, she'd prove it.

"Have you put my name forward?"

"He wants Sarah."

"I'm just asking that you mention it to him."

"There ain't much use in it. A harebrained idea if there ever was one. Like most ideas you have."

It stung, how Pa was always telling her that—how she had no sense and was ugly and sharp-tongued. Stung like a barb even if there was truth to it. There had to be, with no man looking twice at her.

Maybe this wasn't such a good idea.

But lordy, she didn't want to be alone forever. She drew a breath and caught her pa's gaze. "But you'll do it?"

"I'll think on it. That's as much as I can promise. You ought to be up to the house where you belong, helping your ma with the young'un instead of trying to reason things out when you got no understanding of them. Don't you hear Tony May fussing?"

Sarah clutched Celie's hand as they entered the small white-washed church. The fall social was full and the air inside was stuffy with the crowd. Though summer had offered up a round of barn dances, folks were more relaxed, now that harvest had been completed. After prayers of thanks, they'd share dishes of their bounty. Waiting until Thanksgiving itself was too risky, what with the snow and all.

Celie felt the gazes of the hens of the congregation, all ready to predict who would next marry even as they picked apart any less-than-pious behaviors, most *tsking* all the while. Why they weren't outright clucking was a mystery to her.

But this time, she also felt the men looking at her and Sarah. No doubt the rumors were flying, what with Potts setting his eye on a girl less than half his age.

Sarah's palm sweated in hers. She felt it, too, Celie reckoned.

"Pa won't never put you forward. He already made up his mind and there won't be no changing it."

"It'll be all right, you'll see." Celie squeezed Sarah's hand. "I aim to talk to Potts myself."

Sarah's eyes widened. "You wouldn't dare!"

The idea had come to her on the way to the social. Pa wasn't going to do it, she knew that. If she wanted to turn things around, it'd be up to her. A person had to set their own future.

"Don't bother me none if he thinks me forward." He like as not knew it already. It wasn't like it was a secret that she said what she thought. Potts might even dismiss the whole idea as dumb and ill considered, just like Pa said, but she had to try.

Celie ran her hands down her plain brown worsted dress, smoothing any wrinkles that had settled in on the wagon ride. None of the sisters wore bright colors, what with Pa dead set against even the slightest hint of frivolity. They were lucky he let them come to the dances but she figured that was only on account of parents being there keeping their eyes on every move a body made.

She spread a slow stare around the room, meeting the curious gazes of the gawkers one by one, and told herself to ignore them, that it didn't matter what they thought.

When she snagged Zachary Potts's regard, she lifted the corners of her mouth and nodded.

Potts swallowed.

"You go on over with Ma and Martha and the little ones," Celie told her sister.

Sarah drew a breath and crossed the room, Martha plunking a baby into her arms the moment she arrived. Ma, with her own squirming babe, frowned.

Celie took a tentative step toward the opposite corner. *Go on, get it over with.* She forced determination into her stride and met Potts's gaze again. Good heavens, he looked more nervous than she was. Still, he made no move to welcome her. She sighed and closed the distance, through the crowd, avoiding the farmers with the heaviest stench of the week's labor still clinging to them. Like as not, there'd been no time to bathe between chores and the social. She stopped, near toe-to-toe with Potts. His comrades shrank away.

"Mr. Potts, I'd like a word, if I may." The words came out strong, surprising Celie with their force.

Potts grinned at her, blackened teeth and all, and she backed away a half step so the odor of the rot wouldn't hit her so square in the face. "Have you come to advance your sister's cause? Surely you know there isn't any need."

Well, at least he hadn't told her she was stupid. "Do you want to have this talk here?"

"I doubt this will take long, Miss Blaylock. There's no sense setting the gossips to speculating by sneaking off anywhere."

Celie's gaze darted to the crowd around them. "Perhaps just to the corner rather than the center of the room?"

"Spit it out, Celia. I may call you that? We're nearly related, after all."

Shoot . . . he was gonna take come convincing, that was for sure.

"As you wish." She guessed if he wanted to do this in front of everybody, it was his choice.

"Well?"

Just spit it out, Celie.

"You are aware Sarah is just fifteen?"

Potts looked puzzled, then nodded as if he'd figured out some great mystery. "Your father assured me she's reached maturity."

She hadn't meant *that.* "Even so, she's still more a child than woman. She's got a lot of learning to do yet."

"She's young but women play out early. The last thing I want is a woman past her prime. I have children than need caring for and a few good years left to increase my progeny. A young woman will assure my issue take. And my young ones will have an easier time with her. Taking an old biddy will be harder on them."

That he was discussing things with her gave Celie a measure of confidence. He hadn't dismissed the idea itself as if it was some imagined concern. *Keep going.*

"She's still learning her housekeeping skills and has no idea what's expected of her as a marriage partner."

"She's a farm girl. Nothing will surprise her." His chest puffed out like he was a banty rooster.

"She's fifteen," Celie pushed.

"And I like that fact. Byron does so, too."

Well, she hadn't figured on that as an argument. "What's your son got to do with this?"

"He likes the girl, says they'll have things in common. I figure if she can't abide me, having a young man to attend to her will make her more comfortable."

Oh, he was completely missing her point!

"Nothing about this is comfortable for her. Don't you think a more mature girl would be better able to care for your children, keep your house, satisfy your needs? Not an old biddy, but someone a few years older than Sarah."

Potts sighed. "What are you saying, Celia?"

She swallowed and prayed he wouldn't laugh. "I'm of marrying age."

"You?" His voice was full of disdain.

Celie faltered. *Undesirable, just like Pa said.* She should have known better.

"You think I'd want you? A shrew who can't hold her tongue? Known across the county for not recognizing her place? Stubborn, headstrong, and opinionated is not what I had in mind. You're plain of face and your sister is enchanting. Why on earth would I settle?"

But not stupid. At least he hadn't said she was stupid.

She drew a breath. "I would think you'd see the benefits in the offer."

"I don't want you. No one wants you. Why do you think you have no suitors? I'm flattered you desire me so much but you're destined to be an old maid. There's not a man around that's desperate enough to take you on."

"But—"

"Go on with you. People are staring. Where's your sister? I have an announcement to make." He stepped away, turning in a circle, then pointed. "Ah, there she is! Byron has her well in hand."

Celia followed his gesture. Sarah stood against the wall at the edge of the room, Byron Potts in front of her, his arms on either side of her small frame. She was caught by him, her eyes were wide. He leaned toward her and whispered in her ear. Sarah's face grew pale.

Having a young man to attend to her?

Celia's heart stuttered and her desire to marry Potts fled, just like that.

Oh, Sarah . . .

Byron's hand brushed Sarah's face. Then he grasped her elbow and steered her toward the center of the room where his father stood with a beaming smile.

Chapter Nine: Celia/Mattie

Sometimes, the truth of things just slapped a body in the face.

Fall 1868
Johnson County, Iowa

"We ain't never gone, Celie. We ought to, before I'm married off and stuck forever."

The excitement in Sarah's voice sparked a kindred leap in Celie. But it didn't last long. The bright circus handbill Sarah had spotted was tempting but there was no way they'd get to go to such a thing. There wasn't sense in even asking. Besides, Celie needed to figure out how to help Sarah out of the mess she was in.

Seemed to her, neither of them had an ounce of control over their lives. Pa'd made that clear when they tried to tell him about Byron Potts. All they'd got was a good thrashing and an admonishment to stay out of what weren't their business.

"It'll be my last taste of freedom."

No doubt Sarah was right about that. By Christmas, she'd be shut up tight in the Potts house. Zachary Potts had announced their wedding date, giving them just two weeks to sew some new dresses and pack up a hope chest. That didn't leave much time to come up with any sort of plan.

Celie shifted the bundle of cloth in her arms. Ma had warranted a special trip to town to buy the yard goods, but she expected them to return immediately. By tomorrow morning, their fingers would be sore. Young as she was, Sarah didn't yet have much set aside. Most girls hereabouts didn't wed until they were seventeen. There were quilts to be made, tablecloths to embroider, and other practicalities to assemble. Being as Celie was the best seamstress in the family, she supposed the bulk of the sewing would fall to her and there'd be time for little else but the task at hand.

"Almost seems like I should give you what's in my chest. Don't think I'm ever going to need dowry goods with Pa saying I'm set to be the family caretaker." It wasn't going to be much of a future for either of them.

"The circus, Celie . . . you reckon we can find a way to go?" Sarah asked again, pointing out the colorful pictures on the Orton Brothers Circus poster.

Her wistful look near cracked Celie's heart.

"Pa won't let us. Not with them female bareback riders. Heard there's a clown that does a drunk act, too. Pa would have a conniption fit."

Sarah looked back at the handbill one more time, her lower lip jutting forward.

Heavens, there were times she didn't even seem fifteen. Had they babied her that much?

"What if we don't tell Pa? What if we just go without even asking?" Sarah pressed.

It stumped Celie sometimes how Pa said she was the one who had no wits when, to her mind, it was Sarah who fit into that mold more often than not.

"How do you think we'd get away with that? He ain't going to let us come back into town with the circus being there."

"Who's going to tell him? It's October, late for the circus. He won't even suspect it."

"He can see the flyer same as us."

Sarah pondered for a minute, then tore the handbill from the nail holding it to the side of the building. "Not no more."

Celie shook her head. Sarah just didn't see it. "Those are all over town."

"Pa don't go nowhere but the mercantile and church. There ain't no flyer on the church."

"He'll hear about it anyway. He hears about everything. Somebody'll flap their mouth." She turned and started down the block. They'd been away too long.

Sarah's urging rang out from behind. "He ain't heard about it yet and it's day after tomorrow."

Celie kept her pace, her footfalls thudding on the packed dirt. "What about when those circus wagons come into town. Two bits to nothing they'll pass right by our place."

"Have a little faith." Sarah caught up, matched her steps as they drew closer to the wagon.

But it set Celie to thinking.

Seemed like Sarah was entitled to a little fun. She wouldn't have any of it once she moved to the Potts household. She'd be saddled with a passel of kids and would like as not be fighting off the attention of her oldest stepson every spare minute. There was something in Byron's eyes when he looked at her. Either his pa didn't see it, or the old coot was willing to share his wife.

Didn't set well, either way, but there was nothing to be done about it. Pa had decided it was Sarah's lot in life and what Celie thought didn't matter none. Bringing it up to him again would likely set him off on a tirade and he'd ship Sarah off even sooner.

But Celie could think on what to do about preventing it at the circus just as well as at home, couldn't she? And if she didn't figure nothing out, it'd still be the last bit of fun either of them ever had.

"Please. You know neither one of them is going to let me out of their sight." Sarah shivered, her words an echo of Celie's thoughts. She thought about how jumpy Sarah had become, skittering like a bug any time anyone mentioned Zachary or Byron Potts. Didn't like the way either of them looked at her, she said, like she was a shiny new top or something.

Celie didn't blame her none. She ought to still be playing with toys instead of worrying about the marriage bed. Not that Pa had allowed much for playthings in the house. A simple cloth doll for each of the girls, so as they could learn to take care of babies, and a few books. Ma allowed for them to get schooled, up to the eighth grade, despite Pa grousing about it. She said there was no call for to be ignorant when the schoolhouse was so close, and Pa couldn't find nothing in the Bible against females learning, so long as they kept their tongues.

Tarnation.

She guessed Sarah deserved a day at the circus. Maybe they both did. She just needed to figure out how to get them there without Pa finding out.

Celie'd done her best, suggesting a group of girls from church had offered to help with Sarah's trousseau. It was the only thing Celie could come up with. They'd have to take a load of sewing with them. It wasn't a perfect plan, but she and Sarah would get their fun for once.

So they bided their time.

The circus wagons had passed by, day before yesterday. Bright paint adorned the sides proclaiming there were six Egyptian camels, a grand equestrian spectacle, and a female silver cornet band. Pa had herded the family into the house as soon as he realized the troupe was on the road. Celie guessed they must have spent hours setting up tents and getting ready, given the length of the wagon train she'd seen from the window.

"You ready?" Sarah asked from the doorway.

Celie looked up from the wedding dress she was sewing,

practical black so it could be used again. "I reckon."

"Ma's busy running sums with Willy." With the circus in town, school had been cancelled for the day but that didn't stop Ma from holding her son to his studies. Of course, Celie and Sarah, being older, were done with schooling. "I figure we can sneak out the kitchen door."

A prickly feeling crept up Celie's spine. She didn't like changing courses lickety-split. Best to work things out ahead of time. "We ought to stick to what we planned."

"Unless you want to take that wedding dress along, I don't think that's going to work. I ain't toting that dress. Besides, I asked Ma already and she said there weren't no way we were going into town with the circus there."

"What'd you go and do that for?" She wished Sarah had let her do the asking. She might have been able to fool Ma, maybe by saying they'd be headed to another farm instead of town.

Celie sighed. She hadn't been able to figure where they'd stow the dress anyway.

"Are they in the front room or the kitchen?"

"Front room. Ma's nursing Tony May and she's got a pile of laundry to fold."

Celie rose from the rocking chair and laid the dress on the bed, ignoring the unease in her gut. Ma would know they were gone the minute she spied the dress. Celie eyed Sarah, bright and eager before her. There was no way to avoid it, she guessed. Even if she hid the dress, it would gain them nothing. They'd have to take their punishment but at least they'd have a day of fun.

Neither of them had ever seen a circus, but she figured it'd be worth the thrashing. Both their lives were going to be miserable anyways.

"Take your shoes off, else she'll hear us on the stairs," Celie said.

Sarah grinned and plunked herself on the floor, unlacing her plain black shoes. Celie hadn't even put hers on, curled up sewing all day like she'd been. She grabbed her own scuffed pair, pulse pounding. If Ma caught them sneaking down the stairs, she'd know something was afoot. Celie hoped like the devil they all stayed in the front room.

Minutes later, they treaded down the stairs, avoiding the third step from the top—which groaned like a pained cow whenever stepped on—and paused at the bottom of the narrow passage. Celie poked her head around the corner. She could see Willy sitting on the floor of the front room and hoped he wouldn't turn at the sound of the door. The darn thing better not squeak. She wished she'd thought to smear grease on the hinges last night.

She nodded to Sarah and crossed from the stairs to the door. She opened it and slipped out. Mercifully, it was silent. She released her breath and waited for Sarah to exit, then closed the door behind them.

"Where's Pa?" she mouthed.

Sarah pointed to the barn.

Celie glanced across the yard, then sprinted around the corner of the house in her stocking feet. They could put their shoes on once they were out of sight.

At the side of the house, she hunkered down and brushed the dried leaves from her feet. Sarah did the same and Celie was glad she had the sense to keep quiet. Lord but her heart was pounding! Once their shoes were on, she motioned to the grove of trees and they ran across the yard. She cringed as the leaves crunched beneath them but figured the barn was far enough away that Pa wouldn't hear. At least she hoped so.

Once through the grove, they crossed the road and scuttled along the ditch opposite the house, ducking low, just in case Pa came out of the barn. Sarah followed suit without comment.

Celie was glad of it. She didn't want to hear any complaining right now.

A quarter mile down the road, Celie began to breathe easier. Still, she wished they hadn't snuck out the way they did. "This better be worth it because we're going to catch hell when we get home," she muttered.

"Celie!"

"Well, we are. There's no way they won't notice we're gone. We should have thought this out better."

"We've got a few hours. We can come up with something."

Celie doubted it. "As soon as Ma sees we're gone, she's apt to send Pa looking. He'll find us at the circus and we'll get our butts whipped."

"Then we won't let him find us."

"He'll for sure whip us when we get home."

"We'll figure out something," Sarah snapped. "Quit harping on it. What's done is done."

Celie relented. It wasn't the punishment that worried her and she knew it right enough. She just hated not planning things out better. It made her prickly.

They heard the circus long before they came up on the tents and wagons. Loud music sounded as they approached the field where camp had been made. Then, they smelled the animals—a mixture of soiled hay, animal sweat, and strange exotic scents that mingled together in a mix a body couldn't cipher. They passed the penned-up camels with their noses in the air and plodding hooves. It wasn't hard to tell which were male—even the biggest bull on their farm paled in comparison. They must be huge when they hardened up. Celie couldn't even imagine taking in a man's parts without being pained and she felt a bit sorry for the female camels enduring something that big.

"Celie, look!"

Sarah pointed to a crowd of circus folk, bustling around the grounds. Several were painted up like clowns but it was the women in tights and short clothes that caught Celie's eye. Their legs looked bare in their flesh-colored stockings. Short bloomers ended at their thighs and their bodices hugged their middle sections so their breasts stood out in the sequined outfits. Their arms were bare.

"They ain't hardly got clothes on," Sarah whispered.

"I guess a body can't move much with clothes." Celie watched the women approach the horses. They leapt upon their backs with catlike ease. One soft click of their tongues and the horses pranced forward as the women stood tall atop them. What it must be like to have such freedom.

"The show must have started already," Sarah said.

"Seems like."

They headed toward the front of the tent, up a lane of wagons that advertised snake handlers and various "freak shows" for a dime entry fee. At the curtained doorway, a dandified man with fancy clothes and a top hat blocked their way.

"Seventy-five cents, ladies."

Celie's jaw near dropped. "Seventy-five?"

"All to see the greatest acrobatic acts, the English trick horse, Miles Orton and his wild bareback steed, and so much more. You'll be amazed, astounded, and never disappointed." He swept the air with grand gestures, near making Celie's mouth water at the thought of it all.

"But we don't got that much," Sarah protested.

"You'll never see such wonders again, ladies."

Sarah's eyes glistened and Celie swallowed. "We have two bits each," she told the doorman.

He sighed and shook his head. "I can't let you in for that. Maybe take a tour through the sideshows, instead." He pointed to the row of wagons.

Tarnation.

They'd snuck out, wagered on a sure whipping all for nothing. Celie reckoned it was her poor sense that had got them into this. She should have reasoned on it more. But that was done. If they were going to be whipped, at least one of them ought to get something for it.

"Would you let her in, for fifty cents?" she asked the man.

Sarah met his gaze and Celie imagined her big blue eyes filled up with tears. Yeah, the man would let her in.

He took her measure, then nodded.

Celie dropped her quarter into his palm as Sarah drew hers from her dress pocket and handed it over. "I'll wait out over by the animal pens," she told her sister. "You have a good time."

Sarah nodded and disappeared into the big tent.

"There's horses and a tiger and some monkeys over that direction," the man told her, a bit of apology in his voice. "You're a good sister."

Celie strode away. There were times she downright hated being a good sister. Seemed she was always giving up something all for making others happy. But there wasn't much she wouldn't do for Sarah. The two of them had a bond. In all the world, it was Sarah that loved her. Not Pa or Ma or Martha or even Willy. And baby Tony May was too small.

Celie scuffed through the dried grass and bit her lip. She'd be lost for sure, once Sarah was married. What she wouldn't give to have a man ask for her.

"You ain't inside seeing the show?" a child asked, interrupting her thoughts.

She glanced up, saw a young boy watering the animals. From the looks of his damp trousers, he'd spilled as much on himself as he'd managed to provide to the animals.

"Just waiting on my sister is all."

"I'm waiting, too. For my aunts. They do tricks with horses but I'm too little yet."

"So you tend the animals?"

"For now. Once I learn the tricks good enough, I get to be in an act, too."

"How old are you?" Celie asked. They walked the row of wagons, stopping as he sloshed water through the bars and into pans, careful to back away quickly from the pacing tigers and their low growls. The smell of stale hay permeated the air, mingling with the musky scent of wild animals.

"Four."

"My goodness." The kid worked mighty hard for such a little tyke. And seemed mighty grown-up for four.

"Pa says I'm too big for the 'cute baby' acts but not big enough to do my own. Pretty soon, though. I practice every day."

"What do you practice?"

The kid stopped and faced her, puffed out with pride. "It's gonna be a pony act where I ride and do tricks. There's my Aunt 'rene," the boy pointed. "She's a 'questrian."

Celie's gaze followed his gesture. The group of female horse-riders they'd seen earlier was emerging from the back of the tent.

One of the women dismounted and walked to them, leading her decorated horse. She stopped and hugged the boy. "Made a friend, did you?" she asked.

"I did. She's waiting for her sister."

The young woman offered Celie a gracious smile and extended her hand. "I'm Irene Orton. My father owns the circus."

"Celie Blaylock."

"I have to tend to Fairy Bell but you're welcome to come along. You'll be waiting a couple hours yet."

"I don't want to be in anyone's way."

Irene shook her head. "No such thing. Orville, can you help

Julius get ready?"

The boy nodded and sprinted away.

"Julius is one of our clowns," Irene explained. "He's working with Orville on developing a funny act with his pony."

"Isn't four a bit small for a pony act?" Celie wanted to grab the words back lest Irene take offense but Irene just chattered on like she hadn't even noticed how rude Celie'd been.

"It's not really tricks as much as it is humor. He'll learn the trick acts as he grows. For now, it's getting used to the animal and being part of the show. That's how we all grew up and now the little ones are getting their feet wet."

What a way to live, so different from Celie's life. Imagine learning circus tricks instead of cooking three meals a day, digging potatoes, and tending others. "You grew up in the circus?"

"There wasn't much choice. Except for wintering up near Adel, the circus is on the road. Pa's had it since I was just Orville's age or a little more. There's six of us kids and we all grew up this way. Almost all of us do equestrian acts along with a host of other talents."

She led the horse into a corral, made sure it had water and grain, and nodded to a youth Celie hadn't even noticed.

"I'll take her from here, Miss Irene," he said.

"Thanks, Freddie." She turned back to Celie. "I have to change for the Scotch Dance act. You're welcome to come to my wagon with me. We're a friendly bunch here."

Celie hesitated but pushed her discomfort away. There was something about Irene that drew her in. The girl was all sparkle and confidence, not an ounce of self-doubt about her. Celie should have envied her but it all but suckered her. Lordy, to be like that, all independent and carefree. It was something she'd never even thought on.

They ducked into one of the painted wagons. Inside, brightly colored clothes were strewn about along with feathered headpieces and assorted boas.

"Oh, the look on your face!" Irene said. "They're not all mine! Some of it belongs to my sisters, Celeste and Hattie. We share the wagon and have about a dozen different acts among us, different costumes for each."

"That's still a lot of clothes. What's for one of you is more than I own for everyday and church both."

Irene laughed, a soft lilting tinkle. "A circus is as much about what you wear as the acts you do. It's all shine and amazement."

"It must be some life."

"When we were small, Ma made sure we got our lessons done and we tended the animals until we started learning tricks. That's the way of it. It's one big family. Most of us are related but even those who aren't are part of it. Some come and go. Others stay with us for years."

Celie fingered the silks and taffetas, trying to picture it all. "And you just travel around?"

"Our circuit runs from the Midwest all the way down to Texas. We spend summers on the road and winter here in Iowa."

"Imagine getting to see that much of the world!"

"It's mostly the same, everywhere you go. We don't get to go anywhere exciting like New York City."

"Oh, I can't hardly think what that would be like. Just getting out of Johnson County would be more than I ever done."

"Most who are of a mind to join the circus have a desire to wander, I guess. Performers, animal tenders, even those who help with the sideshows or sew costumes—I suppose all of us want to experience more than life in the same spot forever." She added a perky bow to her hair and turned to Celie. "I'm ready. Come on along and I'll sneak you in the back way. No sense you missing out on the rest of the show. You can hunt up your sister when it's done."

They left the wagon and crossed the grounds, Celie's mind tumbling. The sky had filled with clouds, hinting of an early dusk. Yep, it'd be darker sooner than later. Celie hoped it wouldn't rain before they walked the few miles to the farm.

"Celie!" Sarah's panicked voice broke Celie's pondering.

Sarah stood in the shade of a wagon, nearly trembling. "Where you been? We gotta go."

"Go?" Celie reached for Sarah's hands.

"What is it?" Irene asked.

"Byron's here. He was coming for me but I snuck out. We gotta go."

They'd stayed in Irene's wagon for nigh unto three hours, long after the show ended. Irene had directed them there, advising to wait things out. Little Orville had kept an eye out and reported the lingering man had finally departed. That was an hour ago.

When it was full dark, they started for home. They walked in silence most of the way, clutching their shawls tight against the chill, their footsteps a quiet thud on the packed dirt road.

"What am I gonna do, Celie?" Sarah's voice was plaintive in the still air.

Celie wished she had an answer but there wasn't a way around it that she could figure. "I don't rightly know. Daughters don't have much say, especially when they're young as you. I don't see a way out of it. Maybe we're just imagining things when it comes to Byron."

"Irene thought we was right."

"I know, but maybe we're twisting it up in our minds."

"He means to take me like a husband would. I ain't making that up. He said it to me clear as day, that he'd place his hands anywhere he wants and there won't be a thing I can do about it. Anywhere, anytime, and his pa ain't gonna worry none about it."

"He told you that?"

"That's word for word, Celie." Sarah stopped dead in the middle of the road. "I should have told you before, but I couldn't say it out loud. I just couldn't. There ain't no way I can wed Potts. I ain't gonna be used like that. I ain't."

Celie paused alongside her. "Then what are you going to do? Once you're married off, Potts will own you. If he looks the other way, how are you going to fight it? Byron's strong enough to force you. You got no choice in it. Women got no choice in anything."

"I'm running, Celie. I'm gonna pack up my things and as soon as Pa falls asleep, I'm running."

"You're barely fifteen. How do you expect to survive?"

"I'm set on it."

Celie pinched her eyes shut. Either way, Sarah's life was ruined. She didn't have a lick of sense about her, not about life. Ma had sheltered her too much. Pa would find her in a day or so and everything would be worse.

The minutes dragged. Life was going to be hell if she stayed. Byron's paws on her, always at unexpected times. It'd destroy Sarah's spirit as well as her body, fighting him or not.

Tears filled Celie's eyes. *Tarnation.*

"If you're running, you'd best do it now. There's no sense going home to a whupping first."

"I'll miss you, Celie. I ain't told you in a long time but I love you." Sarah threw her arms around Celie and they stood in the dark, squeezing each other as if life depended on it. "G'bye, Celie." She slipped away and shuffled down the road, back toward town.

Celie watched, tears filling her eyes.

Tarnation!

Celie drew a breath and strode after her sister.

Chapter Ten: Celia/Mattie

When it came to survival, hiding the truth was just pure unavoidable.

1868

Johnson County, Iowa

Worry prickled at Celie. The circus camp bustled with activity and Sarah had peeked out the window more than a few times to watch.

"Close the curtain, Sarah."

"Did you see that woman with the beard? She's as hairy as an ape!"

"Close the curtain!" Why her pa said *she* was the one without a lick of sense plumb puzzled Celie.

"You don't need to snap at me!" Sarah's voice quivered.

Celie forced up a measure of calm. "I'm not trying to be snappy but this won't work if folks know we're in here." She'd come up with the only plan she could. If they were running away, joining up with the circus seemed the easiest way to do it. They wouldn't be out on the road where folks could see them and they'd get a whole lot farther than they could on foot.

At least it was a plan.

"But Irene and her sisters know. And they gotta tell their pa."

That much was true. Celie and Sarah had arrived near unto bedtime, drenched from rain and muddy as pigs, but Irene had opened the door to her wagon all the same. Her sisters had mixed feelings about it and had determined they'd have to tell their father once morning came.

Celie figured that was part of why she was so edgy. She hoped they'd be able to convince Hiram Orton to let them stay. Her stomach had been turning at how to do it. Orton would either agree or turn them out and there wasn't a lick she could do about it if she didn't lay out a good case to him. She'd spent the night coming up with as many reasons as possible.

She had to convince him of it. Last night had been the final show of the season. The troupe would be on their way to Adel, where they wintered on land a few miles out of town. If they weren't kicked out, she and Sarah would at least get to Adel. If her idea worked, they'd spend the winter with the circus and maybe even travel with them next season.

"Should we lie, tell them we ain't the Blaylock girls?"

Celie rolled her eyes. She didn't want to start things out that way. Besides, Irene and Celeste and Hattie already know who they were. "Lying's just going to complicate things. In all my life, I never once told a lie that didn't mess things up more in the end."

"I ain't going back, not as long as there's even the smallest chance of Potts laying his hands on me. And if I gotta lie for that to happen, I'll do it."

"I didn't say you were going back, now did I? I said I didn't want to lie. Besides, I bet Pa won't even look for us. He's more likely just to shut us out like the Amish shun those who leave. He talks about that Amish colony all the time."

"That ain't right." Sarah's lower lip quivered.

Celie shook her head. For herself, she wouldn't care if Pa shunned them forever. They weren't going back anyway.

Sunlight spilled into the wagon as the door jerked open. Irene's sister stood there, an older man with her.

"That them?" he asked. At the girl's nod, he climbed into the wagon and closed the door.

The knot in Celie's gut tightened up. The future would depend on the next few minutes.

"My daughter tells me you've run away. That true?" The man gazed from one of them to the other.

"We ain't done no such thing," Sarah sputtered. "We're orphaned."

"Sarah!" Celie cast a stern look in her sister's direction, then faced the man directly. His face was weathered but his eyes held a softness to them.

"You ready to tell me what you're doing here so I can figure out what to do with you?" he said.

Celie swallowed and found her voice. "I'm Celie Blaylock and this is Sarah. We ran away last night on account of our pa wanting to marry Sarah off to a widower. The man's grown son made it plain to her that he plans to share Sarah." Celie's face heated, but it was best to lay it all out from the start. She reckoned that was the only chance they had.

Hiram glanced at a beet-red Sarah. "You know this for a fact?"

"He put his hands on me and said it plain as day."

"Does your pa know this?"

"Pa don't believe it," Celie said. "He thinks Sarah's trying to get out of being married off so young."

"I'm sure if he knew the details—"

"Pa ain't the kind to believe it possible and I don't think he much cares. Women don't count for much and the widower's a deacon in the church. We already tried telling him," Sarah told him.

Orton held her gaze, then shifted it to Celie. "That accounts for Sarah. What about you?"

"Sarah's fifteen. What's she going to do on her own? I can't let her marry Potts, but I can't let her strike out on her own, neither."

"And if I let you stay, you'd earn your keep?"

"I'm a good seamstress." She gestured to the pile of show clothes still scattered on the floor of the wagon. "I reckon another set of hands would help some on the repairs to all those costumes and sewing up new ones."

Orton turned his attention back to Sarah. "And you?"

"I can teach sums and do other schooling. Ma always said I was a born teacher. And I'm a fair cook. If need be, I can help with the stock. And I'm a natural with horses, if you've a mind to add another trick act."

Celie bit her tongue at the outright lies. It wasn't right, telling them, but if she said anything, he might not let them stay. She'd planned to suggest Sarah could tend children—there were a bunch of them and it'd be a valuable skill.

"You'd do the chores assigned? Stay out of trouble? And no romancing with the young men. I've enough to worry about with my own daughters."

"We will," Sarah said.

"There's not much choice but to bring you along, given the circumstances. I'll need to tell my wife and the boys—this show is as much theirs as mine—but I see no reason to share details about the situation with anyone else. The girls will keep quiet. I'd advise you both to do the same. The fewer folks who know about you, the better."

"You need help with things now?" Celie asked. Best to prove their worth from the start.

"No, you stay inside until we reach Adel. That way, no one knows you joined us here. Once we settle at the winter camp, we can put the word out that you're distant cousins or something; no one needs to know your last name." He offered them a smile. "You're safe here."

"Thank you," Celie told him as he exited.

Then she turned to Sarah. "A born teacher? Fair cook? Natural with horses? Sarah Blaylock, what are you about?"

"He wasn't about to keep me on if I'd been honest and told him I wasn't skilled at anything, now was he?"

"You lied."

"Yeah, I lied. I figure we're both gonna lie a lot from now on."

Celie figured she was right but couldn't shake the feeling that the falsehoods would create problems later. Despite being allowed to stay, her gut still wouldn't unclench itself.

Summer 1869 (six months later)
Texas—on the circus circuit

Celie fisted, then released her fingers. Her hands ached from constant sewing. So far, there wasn't nothing great about Orton Brothers Great American Circus. But it was a roof over their heads and she wasn't about to complain. She was earning their way and after a few years, she'd have enough of a nest egg tucked away to start a life somewhere, a normal life like she'd always imagined. That was her plan and it seemed to her it was a smart one.

She just needed to get Sarah to settle in and behave herself.

At first, Sarah had been excited, getting to know the circus folk and helping settle the outfit into its winter quarters. But that hadn't lasted. The work turned routine and the newness had worn off. Sarah groused about everything. Celie guessed she didn't much like circus work.

It hadn't taken long for Orton to learn Sarah had no cooking skills, couldn't milk a cow nor pitch hay. She'd been next to useless with teaching and acted scared of the trick horses when they started prancing around. She'd been relegated one chore after another along with the youngsters, mostly feeding and watering the caged animals.

In time, she'd worked her way into tending the toddlers and that seemed a better fit than most other things—she handled them better'n the older kids. Now that the circus was back on the road, parents were performing and there was a need for someone to tend the young ones. Maybe she'd finally found a place she fit. It was what Celie'd imagined her doing all along and she wished Sarah'd let her advance that route from the beginning. It would have made a smoother path.

All these months, Celie'd had to earn keep for both of them and it soured her that the burden was all on her.

"That's fine work, Celie," Irene told her. "I don't know how you can stitch so small."

"Ma insisted on it," she said.

"You're going to work yourself out of a job if you aren't careful. With seams like that, there won't be any repairs to make."

"The way you move around on that trick horse, you keep ripping them out, no matter how fine the sewing."

Lord knew there was more than enough sewing to be done, with all the costumes and such. And she kept the Orton sisters' wagon tidy, too—or at least she tried. With three of them plus her and Sarah sharing the small space, it wasn't an easy task.

"Sarah's off with Manny," Irene said.

Celie's stomach tightened. Sarah trailing after that boy wasn't something she had figured on.

These last few weeks, Sarah had spent the better part of her free time with the young juggler and acrobat, despite Celie's fussing. Another worry to deal with, especially since Orton had told them Sarah ought not to be encouraging the advances of one like him.

"Mooning over boys isn't good. I'll talk to her. Again."

Irene pranced to the mirror, holding up the new costumes

Celie had sewn. "Have you ever mooned over a boy?"

Celie laughed. "Lord, no. My folks don't much believe in allowing any chance of that."

"But, still . . ."

A pang of longing shifted through her. She pushed it away. "I reckon having a beau isn't in the cards for me, no matter how much I want it. I'm a homely girl and it doesn't help none that I'm prickly."

"You're not homely. And Sarah's prickly—that doesn't seem to limit her."

Celie wasn't so sure about that, with that mirror showing her as much all the time. She couldn't figure why she'd ever wanted to have a looking glass, now that she did.

"Sarah tends to be spiteful if crossed and sasses some. Me? I can't stop my tongue from butting in with opinions and there aren't many men who'll put up with that." She'd always hoped there was one out there that liked a woman who expressed herself but she sure hadn't found him yet.

Irene turned from the mirror, her expression disbelieving. "You've never been smitten?"

"Not once." Celie tied off the thread and held the finished garment up. It looked good, more than good.

Smitten?

Nope. It didn't matter none how much she pined for somebody to notice her for more than her sewing or how she yearned for a family. At the rate things were going, that empty space wasn't going to get filled. Not in her estimation. She'd end up having to settle for being part of Sarah's family, when she had one. But that . . . well, she needed to make sure that was a ways down the road. Sarah wasn't ready for a man at all.

Celie handed the costume to Irene. "All fixed and ready for tonight."

Irene sat next to Celie, reached for her arm. "You know I'm

not trying to fault Sarah. She's young and Manny's a flirt. Papa plans to talk to him, too. But it'd be best if Sarah resisted his attention a bit more."

"She doesn't too often see beyond the moment she's in. She's never had a boy chase after her and it puts her in a pickle. I reckon maybe she was coddled some. Now, she's having to grow up faster'n she ought. I'll be more firm with her."

What a hoot—me offering advice on how to resist a boy!

Celie rose, stretching her aching fingers again and feeling the hours of sitting in her legs. She needed to get out and about, get some exercise. "You mind if I head outside for a bit?"

"Go. You might as well take some time for yourself."

Celie left the wagon, the hot summer air outside almost as cloying as it had been inside the wagon. Not a breeze stirred. She guessed all she'd heard about Texas was true. Next week, they'd head north, into Kansas, but it wasn't likely to cool down there.

She brushed at the bangs that stuck to her forehead and strode toward the animal pens. She enjoyed watching their antics most days and knew most of the performers would be busy preparing for the evening. The gates would open up soon and the grounds would be swamped.

As she neared the camel pen, Sarah's voice sounded from behind the tiger wagon. Sharp and angry.

Tarnation. Now what?

"I saw you plain as day, Manny, so don't you dare deny it?"

"I'm not denying anything. You don't own me."

"But I let you kiss me. You ain't got no call to be kissing anybody else."

Celie drew in a sharp breath. It'd gone farther than she'd thought. She ought to march right around that wagon and have words with both of them. But she stalled, waiting to hear more so she'd know just how far the dalliance had gone.

"Kisses are a dime a dozen, sweetheart." Manny sounded cocky, like he did most of the time. "I take them where they're offered."

"But I thought you cared about me." And Sarah sounded whiny, like the child she still was.

"I made no promises and I'm not looking for any. You were quick enough to kiss me back."

"I love you."

Oh, good heavens. Celie needed to nip this in the bud.

"Love? You barely know me and what you're feeling isn't love. It's lust, pure and simple, the same as what I'm feeling."

"Lust?" The sound of a slap, sharp and biting, filled the air.

Celie rounded the wagon and grabbed Sarah's arm. "That's enough."

Manny at least had the good grace to lower his head while he rubbed at his reddened cheek.

"You," Celie told him, "take yourself off to get ready for the show." She waited until the young man disappeared, then dropped Sarah's arm. "And you? What in heaven's name are you doing?"

Tears filled her sister's cornflower eyes. "He took advantage. Called me wanton."

"*Did* you kiss him?"

"You heard?"

Celie bit back the tirade pushing up on her tongue. She needed to choose her words, and her tone, careful-like. "You have no business kissing a boy, most especially one like that."

"But . . ."

"But nothing."

"He's been so sweet, doting on me."

"You aren't used to boys and all their ways. He's been toying with you. You think he doesn't know how innocent you are? If we were at home, Pa would be watching over to make sure no one did such a thing." Celie paused, waiting for Sarah to digest what she'd said. "You can't be going off alone with boys. Orton especially said there was to be no romancing. That's because he knows what'll happen."

Sarah sniffled, then nodded.

Regretting her tone, Celie reached out, stroked Sarah's arm. "Ma said there's some boys that will use all sorts of sugary words, then press their way. If they mean to respect you, they'll court you proper, with chaperones and the permission of your pa and brother."

"But I ain't got no male family now."

"You got me. I guess I'm having to take this on, too." She hadn't meant to sound sharp.

Sarah's eyes heated, the cornflower blue darkening. "What's that supposed to mean?"

She didn't see it? "It means I'm putting food in your belly and a roof over your head, such as it is. All while you're off on a lark encouraging the advances of one like him. I wasn't expecting to be safeguarding your virtue on top of it all. Fact is, I wasn't expecting to be earning both our keeps."

"I didn't ask you to come along."

"No, you were just bound to run off all on your own. Where'd you plan on running to?"

Sarah shrugged.

"You just go all willy-nilly, not thinking about what'll happen next. We done the right thing, leaving home, but we jumped from the fry pan into the fire and we best tread around the coals the best we can. That means you need to take more care and start thinking about the future."

"You can't make me do nothing." Sarah turned away, stomping across the circus grounds.

Celie shut her mouth tight to keep more words from spilling out. She'd known Sarah was a handful, but this rebellion was unexpected. Somehow, she needed to teach her sister how to think long and hard about her actions. And she'd need to come up with some way that didn't set things off worse than they already were.

Late summer 1869
Fort Scott, Kansas

The town was full to the brim with cowboys and soldiers. Celie reckoned there was more activity here that any place they'd visited all summer. Sarah'd been wide-eyed ever since they set up camp, just itching to see the sites.

"You gonna let me go?"

Celie'd been expecting her to ask. The Orton sisters had been babbling on and on about the town, especially the dressmakers and millinery shops. And truth be told, Celie wouldn't mind seeing them herself. Johnson County, Iowa, didn't offer up such fancy stores, even if Pa would have allowed the family to visit them. The circus *had* stopped in a few other cities but Celie had steadfastly kept Sarah from straying from the camp. But, my, was this town calling to her.

She figured on her and Sarah going together, spending a few hours just the two of them, talking about how best to navigate the future. The end of the circus season would be coming up before they knew it and Celie wanted to get Sarah's commitment to buckle down and be productive for the winter. If they could both manage to put away savings, they might have enough to settle somewhere by this time next year. But that all hinged on Sarah contributing more than she had been.

"You got your chores finished?"

Sarah held up the pile of costumes she'd been stitching.

She wasn't as good as Celie, not by any means, but the sewing kept her under her sister's watch and that had been a godsend these past weeks. In another year, she might be able to make a living with it—it'd take both of them, Celie knew.

"My fingers are raw but I finished it."

Celie rolled her eyes. "Your fingers aren't raw. They might be achy but you're not bleeding."

"Can I go?"

"I reckon we could both take some time."

"I'll be good, Celie. I guess I'm tired of fighting."

Relief flooded her. It was about time. Sarah'd been pouty for weeks, snappy and mean-spirited. Her sour mood had lasted far too long.

Celie smiled back. "Me, too. I wasn't trying to make your life difficult."

"I know. You were doing what needed to be done, filling in for Pa."

That was a good sign, her recognizing Celie's motives. "I don't like being strict with you. We've always been friends and being a parent doesn't set well with me. Not any better than it does with you." She finished up her seam and tied off the thread.

Sarah was already packing up her sewing basket. "I know Manny was trying to trick me. I didn't want to see it on account it made me feel a fool."

Celie patted Sarah's arm. "You're not a fool, just young is all. Not wise to the world." She laid the freshly repaired costume on the bench seat. Sarah's project lay in a heap. Celie straightened it and laid it next to the one she'd worked on.

"I forgave you a long time ago but didn't want to let go of being angry," Sarah said, behind her.

Celie turned. "Sometimes, Sarah, you cut off your nose to spite your face."

"Yeah, I know. But it takes hold of me."

Always had. Sarah held grudges; Celie couldn't hold her tongue. They were quite a pair. "You forgave Manny?" she asked.

Sarah's eyes stormed. "Hah! That cur's still on my list."

Rancor did no one any good. "You'd best let go of that, too."

"We going or not?"

"We're going but don't be setting your eye on buying anything. We need all we've set aside." She stowed her wicker sewing basket on the shelf at the top of the wagon, dropping it over the raised edge so it would stay secure when the wagon moved. There was no need for a wrap, not as hot and sticky as it was. She debated taking the reticule Irene had given her, then decided against it. No sense tempting temptation.

Minutes later, they'd crossed the half mile from the circus grounds to the newly laid railroad tracks just south of the town. They stepped over the still shiny rails and headed to Main Street. Celie reckoned that's where the shops would be.

The town was indeed as busy as the Orton sisters had claimed. Celie's eyes widened at the number of dark-skinned folks about. Back in small-town Iowa, there wasn't a one of them. She'd seen a few since, in the cities on the circuit. Irene had told her the town had been a haven for escaped slaves during the War Between the States. She'd heard there'd been lots of fighting between free-staters and pro-slavers in other parts of Kansas but the soldiers at the fort here had spared Fort Dodge that fate.

"Look," Sarah pointed across the street, drawing Celie's attention to the town itself. "There's a whole row of stores."

Bright signs announced dress shops and hatmakers, mercantiles and bakeries and cafés. The city was bursting with activity. Women poured in and out of the stores, some with packages under their arms and well-tailored dresses to proclaim their wealth. Others wore duller plaids and everyday calicos, the working half of Fort Dodge, most at the mercantile rather than the specialty shops.

Sarah grabbed Celie's hand and hauled her across the street

toward the largest dressmaker. Bright gowns decorated the windows, shimmering satins and damask silks—evening gowns such as Celie figured she and Sarah would never have occasion to own. They stopped to ogle the display.

Celie figured it was as good a time as any to get things rolling on what she wanted to discuss. "I'm thinking maybe next year, you and me could take jobs at a place like this."

Footsteps sounded on the boardwalk and Celie glanced to the side. A woman stood next to them, bright red kid-leather shoes on her feet.

Sarah gasped and Celie jabbed her in the ribs. So much for talking about the future.

Bright red shoes! Well, now, didn't that beat all? Celie didn't even know there was such a thing.

Sarah leaned toward her and whispered in her ear. "My gracious! You think that's one of them fallen women?"

"Shhh."

The woman shifted at the sound, stared straight at them. "What's the matter, girls? Never seen a working girl before?"

Sarah blushed, deep red, and the woman laughed.

"Innocents," she said before she disappeared into the shop.

"Let's move on." Celie reached for Sarah's arm. If the establishment was catering to women like that, she and Sarah shouldn't be here. She pulled at Sarah, but the girl didn't move. She stood, her gaze on a couple exiting the store.

A gawdy woman hung on Manny's arm, gushing about the purchase he'd just made. He pulled her close, his hand tight against her side. Then he spotted Sarah.

"What are you staring at?" he asked. "If you'd have played along, I'd be buying for you."

Sarah's face reddened again, but her eyes blazed with anger this time rather than embarrassment.

Celie tightened her grasp, trying to turn Sarah away.

Manny laughed, his hand drifting to the woman's derriere. He pinched her, obvious in the action. She giggled as they turned away.

Sarah stomped her foot. "That low-down, son of a—"

"Sarah! Stop it this minute." Lordy, the whole adventure had gone south.

"I'll get even with him if it's the last thing I do."

"For what? He didn't do anything but stir you up."

"He made me into a fool all over again." Tears streamed down her cheeks. "He took a good day and spoiled it. He gave to her what could have been mine." She jerked out of Celie's grasp and marched away, toward the tracks and the campground beyond.

Celie sighed. Now, she'd have to endure another damn month of spitefulness before she could talk to Sarah about their future.

Celie's gut wouldn't settle. Only two days and already Sarah had quit slamming things around. She was even humming. It wasn't normal and Celie didn't know what to make of it. She guessed she should be glad and let the worry go.

She closed the door to the wagon and hiked toward the circus tent. She'd asked if she and Sarah could watch the show, saying she needed to get a better idea of why the sleeve-set of Irene's costume wasn't quite right. But she aimed to talk with Sarah about buckling down, putting the effort into really learning her stitching over the next few months. That way, they'd be ready come next fall.

At the doorway, Frank nodded to her, even doffing his beaver hat. "Afternoon, Miss Celie." His fine brocaded vest shown gold in the sunlight.

"Mr. Frank."

"Miss Sarah is here, too. Delightful to have you both in the tent." He bent with a flourish.

"Oh, posh." Celie offered him a smile, warmed by his attention, even if it was pure showmanship. "Did you see where she's sitting?"

Frank pointed to a bench near the center ring. "Best get in before the seats get filled."

Even now, at the end of the run in Fort Scott, the tent was filled to capacity every day. Celie reckoned Orton had made a pretty penny in Kansas. She edged past gossiping girls and made her way to Sarah.

"You feeling better?" she asked as she settled onto the bench.

"One hundred percent."

"That's a good thing. We need to have a talk about what we're going to do in life. I reckon we won't be with the circus forever and I've got an idea I want to share with you."

The show began then, the grand march interrupting the moment with a cacophony of sound. Cornets announced all the entertainers in their finery as they paraded into the tent. Camels plodded by along with cheering clowns. Horses pranced and wild animal cages rumbled past. Acrobats tumbled alongside the bearded lady and the tattooed man and the snake charmer, the crowd cheering for each in turn. The female cornet band marched at the rear, a few musicians short since some were filling other roles.

When the acrobats passed, Manny flashed Sarah a sour look. She glared back.

So, it wasn't all done with.

When the show began in earnest, Celie brushed the pings of anxiety away. Once the clown act finished, the laughter would lessen and she'd be able to talk to Sarah again.

Then, Manny and his act took the ring and Sarah tensed.

Celie flashed her a look.

Sarah blew out a breath and relaxed her shoulders but Celie wasn't fooled. There was still resentment in her. Her jaw remained tighter than was normal.

A clown circled with a wheelbarrow full of clubs. One of the children appeared with a set of balls, cascading them from one hand to another. Manny reached for them, perfecting the cascade. The clown pitched two more balls to the child. Those, too, Manny grabbed away, adding them to his collection and began a complicated pattern in the air, both hands flashing. He caught them, one by one, and passed them to the child before reaching into the wheelbarrow. The kid stowed the balls and returned to feed Manny more clubs.

Sarah moved to the edge of her seat, her attention focused on the juggler.

Manny tossed the clubs. One, two, three, four in the air. As he threw them higher, a body could hear them slap against his hands. But it sounded different from the way it usually did, more of a thud, Celie thought. Seconds later, the clubs cracked and Manny faltered as splintered pieces flew into the air and rained down uncontrollably.

Sarah cackled.

Manny's eyes darkened. He focused on Sarah, whose laughter prompted the crowd. He stalked forward, the remaining pieces of the clubs forgotten in the air. The last hit him in the head within the first two steps and he crumpled to the ground.

Beside Celie, Sarah doubled over in laughter as a hush settled over the rest of the audience.

Lord, Sarah, what did you do?

Chapter Eleven: Celia/Mattie

When desperation comes calling, deception greets it.

1869

Fort Scott, Kansas

"You were seen switching out the clubs so don't try to deny your role in this!" Hiram Orton paced back and forth. "What in heaven's name were you thinking?"

Beside Celie, Sarah swallowed and hung her head lower.

Celie nudged her in the ribs. She'd already asked her the same thing three times with no answer. But she reckoned she knew. Getting even with Manny. That was the root of it.

This wasn't good, not good at all. She just hoped she could find a way to keep it from ruining everything she had planned for getting their lives back on track.

"Answer me, girl," Orton shouted.

Both Celie and Sarah flinched.

"He made me out a fool. I was letting him know what it feels like to be laughed at." Sarah's voice was small, childlike, and full of guilt.

"Those clubs could have killed someone, coming apart in the air like that. One of our people or one of the crowd. They were in that scrapbox for a reason. Cracked clubs are dangerous."

"I figured they'd be wobbly. I didn't know they'd break apart like that."

"One of my best acrobats is injured and you made the Orton

Brothers Circus look a fool. The newspaper is having a heyday. We may never be invited back to Fort Scott again, a city that's always made us a profit."

"I didn't mean for all that."

"But there's the end of it. Your childish impulses, this little attempt to 'get even' has ricocheted."

"I'm sorry, Mr. Orton. Real sorry."

"Of course, you are. But you've caused a great number of problems. I told you when you signed on that I didn't want problems." This time, he looked at Celie.

She met his eyes, hoping she could reassure him. "I had no idea she was going to do this. Had I known, it wouldn't have happened."

Orton shook his head, calmer, but anger still gleamed in his eyes. "I let you girls stay against my better judgment, given the dire straits you were in. You, I've had no problems with. You keep to yourself and do your job well. She," he said, shifting his gaze to Sarah, "has had to be reassigned from one task to another because she either can't or won't complete them. I've had words with her twice about keeping her distance from Manny."

He had? Sarah hadn't said a thing.

"I didn't know," Celie told him.

"I talked to him, too." Orton sighed. "Neither paid me any heed. Manny's got talent, though. He brings in money and has been with us for years. I can't afford to lose Manny. Sarah is expendable."

"You mean to fire her?" Celie bit back her panic. She had to stay calm. Orton's reaction was understandable. Sarah was at fault here.

"I'm afraid so," he said.

"You'd leave her here where there's no one? How do you expect her to survive?"

"That isn't my problem."

"That's not right." No matter how stupid Sarah had been, it was wrong to leave her.

Orton's expression softened but stayed firm enough. "It's a business decision."

"You can't just dump her. She's won't survive on her own. Give her another chance. I'll watch her more closely, keep her with me."

He moved toward the door of the wagon. "I gave her chances, Celie, far more than I normally give anyone. I warned her the last time we spoke that I wasn't going to tolerate anything further."

Celie looked at Sarah. "That true?"

Sarah hung her head further and sniffled.

"Sarah Blaylock, you answer me this minute. Did Mr. Orton already warn you?"

Sarah nodded.

Her pulse thundering, Celie glanced back to Orton. "Even if I watch her like a hawk?"

"I'm sorry, my mind is firm. She's old enough to take responsibility for her actions. My own girls, at that age, were wise to the world, not acting like ten-year-old children. There's no reason to think it would turn out any differently if I gave her another chance."

Celie closed her eyes and drew a deep breath. There wasn't much she could say, not if he'd already given Sarah a warning. He'd taken them in when he hadn't needed to, and her mind told her he was speaking the truth.

But a girl like Sarah on her own in Fort Scott? Celie shuddered.

"We leave town day after tomorrow," Mr. Orton said, reaching for the door. "She can stay until then, but make no mistake. When we leave, we won't be taking Sarah with us."

The door shut with a quiet click.

"What do you aim to do?" Sarah asked.

Celie stared at her sister. *Good God Almighty!* What was *she* going to do?

"I ought to just let you make your own way."

"You'd leave me?"

She was tired of taking care of Sarah, tired of rescuing her from being a child. "You should have thought about that before. What possessed you to get into those clubs that way?"

"All I wanted was to make folks laugh at him, the way some were laughing at me. I figured they'd juggle funny, not break apart."

"Nobody was laughing at you."

"Yeah, they were. I let him kiss me and all and he went and told everybody."

Celie's hands flew to her mouth. She'd thought she'd nipped all that. "Kiss you and *all*? What's that mean, Sarah? You let him do more than kiss?"

"Some." Sarah's voice quivered.

"You let him have a poke?" It was a question she didn't really want to ask, but she needed to know just how much trouble Sarah might be in.

"No! I swear I didn't. I stopped him and he said I was a prude."

Celie drew a heavy breath. She'd failed her sister. She should have talked to her about this. Ma had said boys did things like that if a girl allowed it. "Did you let him touch you? In places only a husband should?"

"A few." Tears crept down Sarah's face.

Celie swore out loud. "Into your drawers?"

"No!"

"Under your bodice?"

Sarah hung her head, nodded. "And under my skirt. Just the

skirt, though. Not under the petticoat. But he made fun of me. Told the other acrobats and they all laughed at me."

Celie crossed the wagon and pulled Sarah into her arms, letting her cry out her shame. Seemed to Celie there was no going back and no way to change what was to come. All she could do now was help Sarah find a way to deal with it.

"I wanted to make him feel what it felt to be laughed at, too."

"And now you have to pay the price for it."

Sarah pulled back. "What am I gonna do?"

Celie shrugged. "I guess *I* don't know."

"You think I can find work?"

"Don't see you have much choice. You'll have to figure out what." It broke her heart to think of Sarah making her way through this but it was past time she stood on her own two feet.

"Maybe I can wait tables at a café? Help in the kitchen? I can't cook but I could peel vegetables and such, like I done at home. I know I could set plates and bring food."

"I reckon if it was me, I'd head into town and start looking while I still had a place to lay my head at night."

"Now?"

"Yes, now. There isn't much point waiting around until you get left, now is there?"

Sarah stared at her. "You ain't coming with me?"

"I've got a job. You're the one who got fired. Pick yourself up and get into town and find a job. It isn't going to find you."

"I ain't never been on my own."

"Only when you're getting into trouble. It's long past time you learn to do for yourself, Sarah. You've got a day and a half. You'd best make use of them. Seems to me suppertime would be good for asking at restaurants."

Sarah shuffled to the door while Celie's heart shattered, just like their future already had.

★ ★ ★ ★ ★

Evening was full set by the time Sarah made her way back to the wagon, tearful and worn-out. Celie didn't have much sympathy for her. Onc snap decision had changed the course of both their lives. Again.

Here she'd been imagining they'd make their way together, get things back on track and eventually settle down into family life. She wasn't too sure that was going to happen the way she'd planned, not with each of them being on their own.

Sarah stomped in and slammed the door behind her. "I washed dishes at two different places. You satisfied?"

Irene and her sisters looked at one another, then headed out the door, no doubt anxious to be out of the tenseness that hung thick in the air.

Celie waited until they left, then turned to Sarah. She'd plopped herself on the bench and sat with her head in her hands.

"Washed dishes? For the day or did you get a job?"

Sarah jerked her head up, stared at Celie. "I made two bits, each place."

It was a start, Celie guessed. "Either one want you to come back?"

"The first one was shorthanded for the night. The other one said I should come back tomorrow."

That wasn't what Celie meant. How had they failed Sarah so badly? "They'll hire you on?" she asked.

"They'll pay me for the day. Four bits." Her eyes sparked with defiance. "I did what you said, now let me be. I'm tired."

"Every day?" Celie pressed, forcing herself to stay calm. She couldn't go setting Sarah off, not when there was so much to get settled.

Sarah's shoulders slumped. "If they need me."

"And they said fifty cents? For the whole day or for every meal?"

"The day." With that, her lips trembled a bit and Celie knew she was beginning to work it out.

Celie sat down next to her, took her hand. "That's not much, Sarah."

"How am I supposed to know what's much and what ain't?" The words snapped out but there was no anger behind them. Her voice held an edge of desperation.

"Did you think to stop at any of the rooming houses and ask how much room and board is?"

"No. You told me to look for a job. I looked for a job. You didn't say anything about rooming houses."

Celie frowned. Of course, Sarah hadn't done anything more. It wouldn't have occurred to her. Just like it hadn't occurred to her to ask about positions rather than day labor.

Celie reckoned fifty cents for a whole day's work wasn't much, not if the circus could charge folks seventy-five cents in some places. If she had to guess, she figured most folks must make at least a dollar a day, maybe two. She wasn't sure . . . she'd never known anyone who worked a job before. All she knew were farmers. Orton was paying her seventy-five cents a day for her sewing, but room and board came with that. Sarah should have been paid at least that much.

It was clear as day Sarah wasn't going to figure this out on her own. Celie'd need to go into town with her tomorrow.

Her mind whirled, trying to cipher it out. There wasn't much Sarah was able to do. She hadn't perfected her sewing and washing dishes didn't pay a good deal. Celie hoped there were other jobs that would pay enough to survive.

"Celie? What am I gonna do? I don't know how to do any of this."

"You're going to have to learn."

"What if I can't get a job? What if room and board costs more than I get paid?"

Celie pulled Sarah into a hug. Sarah'd finally seen it for what it was. But Celie wasn't sure her sister understood the full measure of it, how it expanded full across both their lives. The likelihood that Sarah would make it on her own was slim to none. And that meant Celie would be staying in Fort Scott, too.

Whether she wanted to or not.

1870 (about six months later)
Fort Scott, Kansas

Bone weary, Celie dusted the snow from her shawl. The flakes drifted to the bare wooden floor of the rooming house and she realized they'd melt and need mopping. She was dead tired but Sarah wasn't back from her job at the café and there was little else to it but do it herself. But she'd be damned if she was going back downstairs to fetch the mop. She bent and sopped the mess up with the hem of her dress. It was soiled anyways. What was a little more grime?

The dress would bear washing before long. If she kept showing up at the dress shop with it this dirty, the owner would have words with her, even if she spent all her time in the back room, stitching at a table.

Celie sighed. Laundry was one more expense they couldn't afford.

They were hanging on by the hair of their chins and she knew it. Knew it deep down in the pit of her stomach and the depths of her heart. And she knew it wasn't going to get any easier, given how quiet the town had grown since fall and the end of the cattle season. She had to figure a way out of it, a way to get their lives back on track. The weight of that wore on her more than the endless labor.

Though how anything could possibly throb more than her body was a mystery to her.

Celie rubbed her eyes. They ached almost more than her fingers did. Her back pained, too, hunched as she was over the table for near twelve hours today. All of it working on some rich girl's wedding trousseau. More dresses than Celie'd owned in her entire life and underthings like she'd never imaged.

She stretched, fingers wide open and her back arched, and winced at the agonizing pulsing that came with it. It'd go away some in a minute. She closed her fist, then opened it wide again and straightened up.

She fumbled with the fasteners on her homemade bodice—hooks because they were cheaper than buttons and far easier than buttonholes—then removed the garment and hung it on the wall hook. The skirt followed. Celie eyed her tattered cotton underclothing, a far cry from the silks she'd been stitching on all day.

There sure was no fairness in the world.

The door squeaked open and Sarah slipped in. "You going to bed already?"

"I'm tired. Reckon you are, too." Celie buttoned her thin nightgown and slipped into bed. "We don't have much kerosene left anyway."

Sarah glanced at the lamp. "Guess you're right about that." She fingered her food-stained clothes, then gave up and began to undress. "Gonna have to wash soon."

Celie winced at the reminder. "I was hoping we could hold out until the end of the week."

"I'll see if I can get a Mother Hubbard apron tomorrow, cover up the stains." The restaurant's full aprons were always in scarce supply and Sarah seldom got to work early enough to grab one before they were gone.

"You'd best be early, then," Celie mumbled. She shifted. The damn pillow had a lump.

Sarah flashed Celie a stinging glance and Celie reckoned

she'd said enough. Time to change the subject. "How was your day?"

"My day was rotten, as usual. Yours?"

"The same." Celie punched at the pillow, trying to break up the lump, then gave up. "I figure one more day and we'll have the order all finished. Then, the days won't be so long."

"There's more work waiting?"

"Enough." But even as she said the word, Celie knew that might not be the case. Fear had been stewing inside her all day, once she realized the wedding trousseau was almost complete. Last time the shop had finished up a big order like this, the owner hadn't had enough business to keep her on and Celie'd spent two weeks picking up odd jobs until she'd been asked to return.

"In the dead of winter?" Sarah's voice was full of doubt. Somewhere, these last few weeks, she'd caught on.

"How am I supposed to know." Celie snapped the words, tired of pretending. It wasn't like Sarah didn't know.

Sarah swallowed. "There ain't as many folks at the café, either. After lunch one of the girls got let go."

The future, such as it was, hung there between them in the cold air.

"You're shivering," Celie finally said. "Best finish getting ready for bed."

Sarah pulled on her nightgown, turned out the lamp, and slid into bed next to Celie. Her feet were like ice. Just like they'd been when they were kids.

"Where's your socks?"

"On the chair. They're wet from the holes in my shoes." Sarah huddled close, pulling the quilt around their shoulders.

"You want a pair of mine?"

"They clean?"

That brought Celie back to the present. At home, there'd

always been clean clothes. "Clean enough for bed, I reckon."

"Stinky?"

Celie sighed. "They ain't stinky. I aired 'em out. You want to be picky or you want to be warm?"

"I want to go home."

"Go, then."

Sarah turned in the bed, telling Celie what she thought about that idea.

But it got Celie thinking. Surely, Old Man Potts was married to someone else by now. No way he would have waited two years, not with all those little ones.

Maybe, it was time Sarah *did* go home.

If she could figure out a way to pay for it.

Five weeks later, Celie and Sarah stood at the kitchen door of Rose Hart's brothel.

It shamed Celie to be here and she reckoned they'd sunk pretty low to be knocking on the back door of such a place, but they'd exhausted every respectable option in the city. They were cold and wet and hungry and she reckoned there wasn't much more to be done.

Their meager savings had lasted but three weeks after she'd lost her job. Sarah'd been unemployed for a month. For the past few nights, they'd slept in an alley, eating scraps from garbage pails. Last night, they'd been approached twice by drunken men. That's when she'd known there wasn't any other way.

But she'd be damned if she'd service men in an alley.

Celie fought tears and told herself it wouldn't be forever. If this was the only way left, she'd earn what it took to get Sarah back home. She shivered and clutched Sarah's hand.

A dark-skinned woman opened the door and gave them the once-over. "What you girls want?" she asked.

"We're looking for work," Sarah announced.

Celie winced. "We were hoping for kitchen work. Washing dishes, helping cook." She'd told Sarah that's what they were doing. If luck was with her, maybe they would be hired as domestics and all her worry would be for naught.

"I'm the cook and I've got all the help I need. Unless you're talking about 'keeping house,' there's no work here."

"Keeping house. Yes, we'd do that," Sarah piped in. Eagerness shown in her eyes, bright for the first time in a week.

Celie bit her lip. Sarah didn't know the term meant prostitution. It wasn't what she aimed for Sarah to be doing.

"Well, that you gotta talk to Miz Rose about. Come on in. You're letting a draft into my kitchen." She motioned toward the table as she shut the door. "Go on. Sit if you want. I'll see if Miz Rose is about." She disappeared through a swinging door.

The kitchen was toasty warm, such a welcome change from the days outside. It was a wonder neither of them had caught pneumonia. She and Sarah clustered in front of the large cookstove and held their hands over the heat. Celie wanted to say something but she didn't know what. Might be the less Sarah knew, the better. She didn't need any arguments about what she'd decided. Not when she was as shaky about it as she was. Nope, the less said the better.

The door swung open and Miss Rose entered. Her dark hair hung loose about her shoulders and she wore a dressing robe. Tired lines etched her face. Celie guessed she was about thirty but it was tough to tell. She might be as old as fifty.

"Martha says you're looking for work," she said.

Sarah nodded. "We are, ma'am. We were wondering about keeping house."

Rose met Celie's gaze. "You two ever do that type of work before?"

"No, ma'am," Sarah said. "But I reckon we'd catch on quick.

We done plenty of housework back at home, before we come to Fort Scott."

"Oh, lordy." Rose waved her hand. "How old are you girls and where are you from?"

This time, Celie jumped in. "I'm twenty this year and Sarah just turned seventeen. We grew up on a farm in Iowa, before we ran away."

"You been in Fort Scott long?"

"A few months," Celie said.

"We need work bad, ma'am. The jobs we had dried up and there ain't no money left and we've been out on the street for the past four days."

Celie pinched Sarah's arm, silencing her.

Rose's eyes narrowed. "Keeping house might not be what you're expecting."

"I reckon I got an idea," Celie told her. "Could the two of us talk in the other room? Leave Sarah here in the kitchen?"

Rose wrinkled her brow and offered up a gesture to indicate she didn't care. "Come on into the parlor, then, and I'll run through how we operate."

"You stay here," Celie told Sarah. Then she followed Rose.

"Your sister?" Rose asked, once the door swung shut.

"Yes. I'd rather keep her out of this." Celie'd thought long and hard about it. She didn't want Sarah involved in this, not if there was a way around it. She reckoned that would take some negotiating.

"I'm not sure I'd want just the one of you. She's mighty pretty, fresh as a daisy."

"You need girls, you'll settle for one of us." The words came out strong, a whole lot more certain than Celie felt.

"She can't stay if she's not working."

"Why don't we talk about that later? Once you tell me what's what and we work out the details of *me* working here?" She needed time, to get Rose's measure, to be certain how things operated. This wasn't a dressmaker's shop or a restaurant where a person got paid regular-like. That much she could guess.

Rose blew out a breath, clearly not pleased. "This is the gathering area. It isn't fancy, like the bigger parlor houses, but it's a step up from street-walking. I assume that's what you're trying to avoid."

Celie eyed the tattered wallpaper and dirty carpets. The room was lined with mismatched chairs and a roughly made bar stood in the corner, planks atop a pair of barrels.

"It'll do. It's better than an alley."

Rose laughed. It was a raspy sound, not at all like Irene's tinkling amusement. Thick and low like it didn't happen too often. Almost harsh.

Like what the life would be.

Celie swallowed.

"You'd have a room upstairs. Your sister, too, if I take her on. I run things simple. We don't have a menu. I work same as the girls so it's easier to charge everyone the same. The johns pay the bartender and he gives them a token. One token gets a straight poke, or a swallow if that's their inclination. Two buys them something extra and they work out the details with the girl. First girl free takes the first john in line; no special requests."

Celie nodded, her eyes stinging.

Rose peered straight at her. "You understand? You know what this is all about?"

"I understand."

"That's more than I expected. Innocent as you look, I thought I'd need to explain it all."

In truth, Celie wasn't sure of the strange terms. But she knew what a poke was and she expected she'd learn the rest. "I've seen farm animals do it and Ma said married folks did the same. I heard gossip there was places a man could pay to do it."

"You have the sense of it, then. It's a little more complicated than the barnyard but you'll find the way of it. You had a man yet?"

Celie shivered. "No," she whispered.

"Aside from seeing cows and pigs, you know what's involved?"

"Sort of. I know his . . . his . . . man-part . . . gets put inside a woman."

Rose laughed again. "It's a cock, honey. Or a prick. You know where it goes?"

"Inside." This time, Celie made sure she didn't whisper. She wasn't going to lie about her experience, but she'd be damned if she'd let Rose see any more of her fear.

"You know where?"

"Not exactly."

This time, Rose slapped her on the arm. Slapped her like they were old friends but didn't volunteer any explanations.

"The men will love you. You know anything at all?"

"Just that Ma said not to let a man inside your drawers."

"Aw, honey, you got a lot to learn." Rose *tsked* but offered nothing more.

Celie reckoned that would be the way of it, then. She'd be going in blind, learning by way of experience.

Tarnation. Her eyes stung like hell.

It's only for a little while. Just to get Sarah home. Just to get back on my feet. It doesn't mean my dream is gone. It doesn't.

"What will I get paid?"

"Room and board and two bits for every token you turn in."

Celie ciphered it out. "That don't seem like much."

"It isn't. But I don't make much either, not after I buy you clothes and underthings. You do well, we can talk about more."

At two bits a poke, it'd take four pokes a night to earn a dollar—about half what a tailor made in a day, even with room and board. Course, a seamstress never got a tailor's wages anyhow.

It wasn't much at all but Celie reckoned it was about right for someone just starting out. Like Rose said, she could ask for more once she got practiced in doing it.

"Now, about your sister?" Rose said.

Celie looked her in the eye. "I don't want her doing this."

The madam's mouth dropped open. "What's she going to do? Live on the street?"

This was it. This was the crux of it. Where Celie had to be strongest. She stood full tall and drew a breath.

"I'm thinking we can strike a bargain, maybe. You pay me up front, enough for me to send her back to Iowa, and I work for you without pay until I pay off the debt."

"Advance you money?" Rose shook her head. "The other girls would have my hide."

"The other girls don't need to know." Hating that she was doing it, Celie played the only hand open. "I'll turn in the chips same as they do but you don't give me anything back."

"I don't know about that," Rose said but Celie saw the sparkle of greed in her eyes.

She sweetened the pot. "I'll pay back extra."

"Interest?" Now Rose was hooked.

"If that's what it's called."

"You'll sign a paper?"

Celie nodded. "I'll do whatever it takes to keep her safe."

Including selling my soul.

Chapter Twelve: Celia/Mattie

It all happens little by little, the lying. Especially when it's lying to yourself.

1870
Fort Scott

Two days later, her heart in shreds, Celie sent Sarah home, along with the fancy photograph Celie had bargained for.

Sarah hadn't been too happy about going, but there was nothing to be done. Even if things turned out bad back in Iowa, Celie reckoned it'd go a lot better for Sarah there than lying under strange men several times a night.

At least Sarah would have the remembrance of her.

Rose had sent Celie to be photographed, insisting the best parlor houses attracted clients that way—teasers to get them interested. The photographer had posed Celie leaning up against a pedestal in nothing but her chemise, her bare legs showing and her nipples dark under the thin cotton. She'd brokered direct with him to take a proper photo, too, and he'd decked her out in a demure plaid dress with ruffles at the hem.

She'd paid for the extra photo by allowing him to finger her.

Celie told herself the shame of it was worth it in the end. She'd learned a bit more of what would be expected of her in her new career and reckoned Sarah could look at the photo and remember how Celie had been before becoming a fallen woman.

This morning, she'd given the proper photo to Sarah, hugged

her, and sent her away on the train. Tears had streamed down her face as the cars disappeared into the dark coal smoke that hung over the tracks. Sarah'd been full sobbing.

That was pretty near what Celie wanted to do. Then and now both.

She just needed to get through the night. After that, it'd come easier.

Miss Rose had opened up some ten minutes earlier and men had started drifting in. None of them were too respectable looking. Of course, if they were respectable, they wouldn't be at a place like this. The respectable men, if a body wanted to call them that, would be at one of the fancy parlor houses where all the pretty women were, the ones with more class than Celie had. The houses like Rose's catered to a lower-class clientele and Celie dreaded the hours to come.

She was drenched in sweat despite the chill that hung in the room. Rose rationed the coal for the small stove, saying the men would warm the place up in no time. Celie tugged on the low-cut chemise peeking above the tight corset Rose had laced her into. Celie reckoned it had once been white but it was faded to a dull cream. She'd also been given a gawdy scarlet dress but Rose said there was no need to bother with wearing it, not tonight anyway.

Being half-naked like that was plumb shameful, but Celie figured it was nothing like what would come later and she'd best push it out of her mind. She wished the corset didn't thrust her breasts up so high. It pinched at her and they were near hanging out. A bit of powder came off on her hand when she mussed with the corset and she sneezed.

Rose turned her head and stared. So did the five men at the bar. Their lusty gazes drifted across the tired room. They all grinned, one after the other, as they eyed Celie and the other girls lined up in a row at the edge of the room.

Celie near retched.

One of the other girls elbowed her in the ribs. "Buck up."

Celie swallowed.

"There's the girls. First time tonight you'll get a pick," Rose announced. "Them three and me. Down your drinks, boys! We're ready for you."

The men shot down their whiskeys.

"Oh, and the redhead is new. And I do mean new." Rose paused for effect as the men ogled Celie like she was a piece of meat. "First to have her will need to fork up extra tokens."

"She unused?" one of them asked.

"Pure as the driven snow and completely inexperienced! She goes for four times the usual price, boys."

The men searched their pockets while Celie trembled. Damn if her knees weren't shaking. For the first time since the photograph had been taken, she was glad she'd allowed the liberties at the studio. At least she now knew where the damn cock would go.

Then, there were whoops and the men were congratulating a burly bear of a man.

She sucked in a breath. *Good Lord, he's huge.* He towered near a foot more than Celie, well over six feet, she guessed.

The man strode toward her as the others purchased their tokens from the bartender. He lurched enough to tell her he'd been at the bar awhile. Either that or he had a gimpy leg but Celie didn't think so. He reeked of alcohol, among other things. She doubted he'd bathed in close to a month.

Celie turned away and drew another breath of air.

"Good luck," the girl next to her said. "Better you than me." The girl shoved a glass of whiskey into her hand.

Celie choked back the bile in her throat, her hand to her mouth as she swallowed it down. The bitter taste lingered. She rinsed it away with the whiskey. The burn scorched all the way down into her chest.

"Let's go, sugar." The man grabbed her bare arm and jerked her across the room. "You ain't much to look at, but I'll take fresh pussy any time I can get it."

Celie nearly stumbled on the stairs. She wished he'd slow down. Once they reached the hallway, he shoved her into the first room and slammed the door. It wasn't even her room! She staggered a step in the small space, then hit the bed.

Lurch was already shucking his suspenders from his shoulders. Underneath, his grayed undershirt was grease-stained down the front and near-black under the arms.

"What are you waiting for?" he demanded.

She shook, hating that she did, unable to move beyond that. She had no idea what he wanted her to do.

He was near enough that she could smell his foul breath. Onions maybe, along with the whiskey.

"Hell, you *are* an innocent." He grabbed at the yellowed chemise and yanked her breasts out, fondling them roughly as his onion breath heated her face. Calloused fingers squeezed at her like she was bread dough. She shut her eyes, fighting the discomfort, trying not to think of it.

Don't think about any of it. Think about spring flowers and sunshine and . . .

He dropped her breasts and tugged her close, his hands grabbing at her bottom. His man parts stabbed at her. He ground against her and pulled her even closer. His sour mouth crashed down on hers.

"Shit. Open your damn lips."

Celie did as she was told. That had been the sole piece of advice Rose had offered. *Do as you're told.*

Lurch's tongue forced itself between her lips, into her mouth. "Open, damn it."

Celie forced her jaw to relax, not to fight against the intrusion.

"Damn, girl. You don't know a thing!" He pushed her away and jerked open his trousers. His man-part—cock, she corrected—sprang out.

Lord a'mighty! Images of the circus camels flashed through her mind.

"Let's teach you what to do with that mouth."

Celie stared at him. Now what did he want of her?

"On your knees." He shoved her down until she was eye level with the thing. "Put it in your mouth."

Tears filled Celie's eyes.

"You hear me?"

Do as you're told.

She opened her mouth and moved toward his cock. Stale sweat and urine clung to it and she tried not to think of what might be crawling in the wiry black hair around its base. She took him into her mouth, praying the smell would dissipate once she did. But he still reeked and the taste of him was all salt and foulness.

He pushed on the back of her head, forcing more of his cock inside. "Suck on it."

She closed her stinging eyes and tried, gagging.

He pumped his hips forward, forcing more of it into her as he shoved her head forward.

And then she retched, bile erupting up her throat and into her mouth.

"You bitch," he yelled, stumbling away from her. His hand snaked out and slapped her cheek. "You goddamned good-for-nothing whore. Look what you done to me."

Celie opened her eyes. Vomit dripped from his cock and had splashed into the coarse hair; it oozed from her mouth, onto her chest. The sting of the puke filled her nostrils as it dribbled out of them.

He yanked her to her feet and slammed his fist into her nose.

She reeled from the pain, fighting to stay conscious as she fell back onto the bed, blood spurting everywhere.

Swearing, he pawed at her corset and ripped it away, the hooks flying across the room. Then he shoved her legs apart and plunged into her.

The last thing she remembered was screaming as she tore.

Summer 1871 (a year and a half later)
Fort Scott

Celie learned real quick just how important Rose's instructions had been. She also learned what Rose hadn't told her—that a body had to ignore pain and pretend to enjoy what was being done to it. The other girls told her later that Rose had kept her ignorant on purpose, since most men who paid for innocents wanted to control the events and got more excited when the girl didn't know what was happening.

It had been her misfortune to vomit on Lurch.

Her nose had healed a bit crooked from the break and she'd been off the line for a few nights until she could take a man in without reopening the injury down below and bleeding all over. At first, Rose had thought to use that to trick customers into believing she was a virgin but one look at the scabs had convinced her that wouldn't be possible. Instead, she'd added extra onto Celie's debt for the nights off.

All that did was to make Celie more determined to learn all she could. The faster she made money, the sooner she'd get past all this and on to the life she wanted.

In the months since, Celie had learned to control her gagging and make a man think she was enjoying herself, if that's what he wanted. If he wanted to exercise his power, she could play along with that, too. If a body cried out in pain at the right point, there was a chance to avoid getting bloodied. Sometimes there *was* no avoiding it since a few men simply beat a girl up more, hating it when she didn't cry out, and working themselves into a frenzy when she did. Those times, she just held her breath and tried to find a way down the middle of things.

There was a water stain on the wall. Looking at it now, Celie saw it'd grown bigger, spreading brown across the faded flowers that a body could hardly see anymore. Not a lot bigger, but larger all the same. Or was it all in her mind? The john on top of her groaned as he spent his seed and collapsed with a sigh. She let out a little gasp and shuddered her body so he'd feel good about his performance. Then she pasted a contented smile on her face so he'd see it when he pulled out of her. Sometimes, when they thought they'd satisfied her, they left an extra coin or two. Sometimes.

He rose.

She let the smile spread and stretched like a cat. "You going to come back again, cowboy?"

"Count on it," he said. He pulled on his clothes, grinned at her again, and tossed her a half-dollar.

Once he was gone, she dragged her aching body from the bed, poured a measure of water into the basin, and splashed it on her privates. It dripped some on the floor but she didn't care none. The water cooled her, cleaned the stickiness away. She eyed the token on the commode, next to the basin, thankful for it in addition to the extra tip. Last week, one of the johns had pocketed the token on the way out, stiffing her. When she'd told Rose, the madam had called her stupid and told her to put the tokens in a drawer.

The only problem was that the drawer was stuck. Never mind that Celie had been complaining about it for nigh unto a year now. Now, she moved the tokens behind the basin so they wouldn't be so easy to palm.

Celie squatted, legs spread wide, and splashed a little more water on herself. Then she dipped her finger into the bowl of butter on the nightstand and smeared it inside to make things easier with the next man in line. She redressed in the thin chemise and hooked the corset around her middle, plumped her breasts up, and checked in the mirror to make sure her hair was presentable. Her stockings and boots were still on. A lot of times, the corset and chemise were, too—just pushed all willy-nilly. This john liked his girls bare.

Funny how that made her feel a little less used.

She glanced again at the mirror, spied Sarah's letter wedged in between the glass and the wood framing around it.

Thank God it wasn't all for naught.

Sarah had written twice now—once to say she was safely returned and that Celie'd been right. Both Potts men were married up and Sarah hadn't been shunned. She'd sent a second letter with the news that their older brother had passed on before the end of the year, his war injuries finally taking their toll. Pa still called her soiled goods but was willing to tolerate having her tend the house and help care for Tony May. She'd even thanked Celie for what she'd done.

Seeing the letter, remembering that Sarah appreciated her, made Celie smile a bit before she left the room and headed back downstairs.

There was time for one more customer, assuming there was one here this late.

Halfway down the stairs, she noticed him. He'd been there before, though Celie hadn't had him. She remembered his hair—how clean and soft it looked. He leaned against the bar, easy and relaxed. Probably not too demanding. A good way to close up the night.

"You waiting on somebody?" she purred.

"Waiting on you, I suppose."

"Then it's a good thing I'm here. You still nursing that whiskey?" She nodded to the half-full glass of amber liquid in his hand. "I'd join you, if you've a mind to share."

She sidled up to the bar. She wasn't one to buy her own whiskey, not out of the pittance she made, but she sure wouldn't mind a drink if he was buying. She'd learned real quick that whiskey made the night easier. On the tough nights, she might even coax a john into buying a bottle and bringing it to the room. She could wash down the lies she was forced to act out. Them and the ones she told herself about how easy her life was.

The man signaled for another glass and Celie drained it.

He saluted her and took a sip of his own, then set it on the wooden plank.

"You got a name?" he asked, when they were halfway up the stairs.

The question took her by surprise, warmed her. Johns only asked for her name once in a blue moon. "Celie."

"I'm Wyatt."

That, too, came as a shock. Men almost never gave their names. Made this Wyatt more real, having him introduce himself. A gentleman, even.

"Good to meet you," she told him. "You thinking we need to shake hands or something?"

He laughed, a solid hearty sound from deep inside. "I'll take the 'or something.' Which room, Celie?"

She pointed and he opened the door with a flourish. "Ma'am."

She laughed then, at how ludicrous it was. Lord, she hadn't laughed for a long time. She reckoned this Wyatt fellow might be different.

A genuine smile crossed her face this time. "You tickle me,

you do," she told him.

"Glad to hear it. I aim to please."

"I bet you do."

He reached for her then, an easy grasp that gave her room to back out, if she had a mind to. Felt odd. He pulled her into an embrace and his gaze met hers, gentle, undemanding. Then, he bent his face toward hers and kissed her.

She didn't much like kissing customers and didn't ever kiss them back. Not for real—just the semblance of it, enough to give them what they wanted without putting any feeling into it. It was part of the job, a deception. But Wyatt's kiss was so different, it pulled her in. Before she even realized it, she was responding, her tongue meeting his.

A surge of desire spurted through her, tingling her skin from the inside out.

Lord in heaven, if she wasn't careful, this man would be the death of her.

Then she kissed him deeper.

In the weeks since meeting Wyatt Earp, Celie'd come to reckon he was the sort of man she'd imagined in her girlhood dreams. He had a certain energy about him that drew folks in, her especially. And it was for certain he was handsome, with all that soft dark-blond hair and mustache. But it was his story that grabbed at her—she knew that the minute he told her, tears glistening in his blue eyes.

Wyatt wasn't a wild bachelor or tired cowpoke. He was a widower, his wife of nine months—Urilla had been her name—dead and their baby along with her, a few short months ago. Afterwards, he'd lost his temper and gotten into a fight with her brothers, while doing his duty as Lamar's town constable by helping the sheriff raid their still. Not his fault the Sutherlands had gotten all het up about it. No wonder he was running from it all.

Seemed most folks were running from something, in her estimation. Her, too, in a way.

Wyatt had gotten under her skin for sure, reminding her of what she'd used to dream of, back before life had taken such a turn. He was the sort of man a body could spend a lifetime with, the kind who would be devoted to a wife and family.

The kind she'd always wanted.

And now, he was in her bed most nights, finishing up at the bar only when she became available. She couldn't stop mooning over him when he wasn't there. It was like she was floating on air, always thinking about the tender words between them. He said he needed her and that was a boon she'd never expected to experience. He was the first man she'd ever had that made her feel cherished—that was a word she'd never thought to be using. And them together was something she'd never imagined, either. From that first night, he'd made her body react in ways she'd never known: sweet, quivering waves of release that made her want a man for the first time ever.

Her heart had gotten all wrapped around him and maybe, just maybe, they'd find a way into a life together. That's what she was aiming for, leastwise.

She'd made her mind up of it.

Wyatt shifted next to her, still groggy. "Crap. I fell asleep, darlin'. How much time we got left?"

He'd taken to buying two tokens, to allow them more time together, but Celie knew she risked Rose's wrath those times when they were so sated that sleep came upon them.

"It's near midnight."

"I'll pay her extra." He rolled over, pulled her into the crook of his arm. "I hate this, Celie. There's not another girl like you and settling for a quick poke and going on my way doesn't set well. It's not fair to either of us. Not when we care about each other the way we do."

He'd hit the nail on the head there. She despised every second of serving other men. At times, it near made her die, having them on top of her. More and more, she counted cracks on the ceiling while they done their business.

"Long as I'm a working girl, there's no way around it."

"You ever think of leaving?"

Celie's heart raced like a demon on fire. "Leaving?"

Don't read too much into it. Don't.

But she did. Lord a'mighty, she wanted nothing more than for Wyatt to take her out of this life and settle down with her.

"You don't belong here. This isn't the life you were meant for."

"There's been none other to jump to." There, she'd put it out there.

"Do you owe Rose?"

That was what kept most girls bound to houses, paying off debt. Then, after that, existing until a body could save up enough to leave.

Unless someone offered for her.

"Not anymore, but after I pay for room and board, there isn't much left for saving up none."

"But you'd be free to leave?"

Tarnation, the man beat around the bush. Best to meet it head-on, she reckoned. "What are you getting at?"

"Have you ever thought of striking out on your own?"

Whore on her own? Disappointment filled her, despite having told herself not to set up expectations.

It must have shown on her face because Wyatt pulled her in close. "Now don't look like that."

Celie fought the tears that stung at her eyes. "I'm no street-walker."

He stroked her shoulder, kissed the top of her head, then wiped at the corners of her eyes. His smile was soft, reassuring. "I know that I was thinking you ought to have your own house, or at least be working with someone who pays you your fair share. What's Rose pay you?"

"Two bits a poke." It sounded paltry. Hell, it *was* paltry. She knew it, but Rose hadn't been willing to raise the share and Celie'd been too timid to push any harder.

"Two bits? A dollar a night?" He sounded disbelieving.

"Two if business is good or someone pays for extras."

"That's shit. You know how much it costs us for a token? I pay her a dollar for my time with you, two if I want extra. If you had your own place or partnered with someone who treated you fairly, you'd be making four times what you do, maybe more."

Celie sat up and stared at him. "That much?" She'd had no idea. That showed how stupid she was. She sat with her bareness exposed, trying to process it all.

Wyatt remained on his back, his hands under his head. "You have a lot to learn. There's ways to get rich in this trade and I could help you get there."

Celie wasn't too sure a man could have any way of knowing such things. "How's a farmer like you come to know so much about this business?" She crossed her legs and pulled the sheet over them so she wasn't gaping open down below.

Wyatt offered a sideways twitch of his lips. "I spent some years on the road. I learned."

"Learned about prostituting?" She didn't believe him.

He sobered, stalled. "Doesn't matter. Let's just leave it that I've been around. I know how things work." He shifted, rose to sitting, and shoved her pillow on top of his to bolster him further. "If you're in on the management of things, there are a lot more ways to make money. Look at how much Rose makes off you girls. That's where you need to be, at the top . . . or at least in on it."

Celie shook her head. "It takes years to work up to having a house, Wyatt. You have to have money to open a house."

"There's ways to get that." He punctuated the comment with a gesture. "But we'd have to work together."

Celie leaned in. "And how would *you* make money off the flesh trade?"

"The bigger brothels have managers. They're mostly to bounce out the rowdy customers, but they also recruit business. There's money exchanged here and there. And, like the bartender here, they handle customer payments. But there are no rules, no regulations, no bookkeeping. No one really knows what comes in before it's handed over to the madam. And in some houses, they also run gambling tables—there's a lot to be made there." His voice had become spirited.

Managers. Folks that told others what to do, she thought. Not so different from being with Rose to her mind. "So, you want me to move to another house where you'd *manage* me?"

"I'd manage the *house*. The advantage for you is that I'd make sure you weren't gypped of your fair share and that you serviced only the best customers."

Anger churned. That wasn't what she had planned. More of the same, to her way of thinking, even if the clientele was better. It was still crawling under strange men every night.

Men who weren't Wyatt.

"You sound like you have this all planned out." The words came out in a huff and hung there between them.

Wyatt blew out a blast of air. "I don't plan to stay in Fort Scott. I'm thinking of heading north, toward Chicago. I hauled logs up that direction a few years back and my brother Virgil lived in Peoria, Illinois, for a while. Peoria's a town with opportunities, a thriving flesh-trade business. Virge gave me a few names and Morgan, one of my younger brothers, and me have a mind to see what we can make of it." He reached for her hands. "I don't want to leave you here."

Celie swallowed. "You're asking me to come along?"

"I think we'd do well together."

Pull up stakes and move somewhere she didn't know. She'd done that before, jumped without looking. It hadn't landed her in a good spot.

"That'd be a mighty big chance I'd be taking. What would stop you from just dumping me when you tire of me?"

"I'm not going to tire of you. We have something together." He smiled that lopsided way of his and her heart stuttered.

She stifled it. He wanted her to whore, not marry him. "But only so far as business goes?"

"Hell, Celie. I care about you." His head fell back, frustration in the action.

"Care about me, yet willing to have me service other men?" She fought to keep her voice from shrinking, from shaking.

Wyatt met her gaze. "I figure it's a job with nothing personal involved. It has nothing to do with what's between us."

And *that* was something they hadn't talked about. "What is between us?"

"I don't know."

It was an honest answer. She reckoned she didn't much know either. But she guessed the last few minutes had told her what they felt wasn't balanced out none. "You love me, Wyatt?"

"Aw, don't ask me that." He turned, swung his legs over the side of the bed. "I'm not ready for love again. I loved 'Rilla and she got taken from me. If I love somebody else, I might get my heart broken again. You saw how I was when we met. I can't go through that again."

Celie crawled from the bed, grabbed her wrapper from the floor, and pulled it on. She jerked the belt tight, knotted it. Inside, hot anger and disappointment warred with understanding in a confusing jumble.

Tarnation.

She walked around the bed and stood before him. "So you expect me to go with you, on account of you caring for me, so you can manage me in a brothel and pimp me so men can use me?"

"It sounds bad when you put it that way."

"Of course it does. You don't pimp out a woman you care about."

"It's a damn living. You think men enjoy everything they do to make a living? It wouldn't be part of *us.*"

"So, sleeping together is a business arrangement, pure and simple? If that's all you think about it, you'd best not come to my bed no more."

"That's not what I'm saying at all! Goddamn it! You don't see it clear. What's special between two people is separate from how those two people act with others. It's the special feelings that make sleeping together an act of love. Without those feelings, it's just an act, just a poke. You don't know how it is in the world. Back where you came from, where it was all families and church, there was nothing but couples and farming was their way of living. You're in the big world, now, and things are different. In the city, couples do what they have to in order to survive and get ahead. If that means a woman shares her body with other men, so be it. It isn't like you're sharing your heart. Grow up, Celie. Sometimes you don't have a lick of sense."

A lick of sense. Celie near doubled over at the words. Had she truly not learned anything these past three years?

Damn him for bringing that into her mind.

But, she wasn't simple-minded. Look at how she'd figured out how to get Sarah's life back on track, even after the punch Fate had thrown them.

Wyatt stood and pulled her into his arms. "Aw, hell. Don't

you worry about it. Trust me. I've been out in the world and I know how it works. You went from being sheltered at home to being taken advantage of by Rose. If we team up, you'll be making your own decisions, with me to guide you. A few years and you can leave the trade behind you and it'll just be us."

She wanted to believe him. She reckoned she could stomach it, if there was an end to it . . . an end she wanted. And . . . he'd called what was between them an act of love. That said something, didn't it?

"This wouldn't be your life forever." He kissed her atop her head. "We can milk this for all we can get, then move on to a respectable life. Don't you see, that's what I want more than anything? Being respected would be a wonderful thing. We just have to get from here to there."

Was he right? She hankered for that, too, but didn't figure it could ever be within her reach. And maybe, by then, he'd be ready to love again. Still, it was a huge risk.

"What's to stop you from taking advantage of me once I leave here? Or even after we go into business together? Can you guarantee I won't be left in the lurch?"

"What do you want, a damned contract?"

She could see his grin in her mind, even standing there being held. Maybe he didn't love her but he did care, probably as much as any man ever would, given all the faults she had. She supposed she could weather a few years in the business, long as she knew there was more to it. That there was a future beyond it. But she had to be sure. She didn't want to make any more mistakes.

"I don't need no paper contract." She pulled back so she could catch his gaze. "But if you want me to leave here and partner with you on this, you have to bind yourself to me in some way."

He did grin then. "Whatever you want."

Celie drew a breath. "I'm not leaving with you unless you marry me."

Late fall 1871
Near Aullville, Missouri

Celie strode across Ma and Pa Earp's farmyard. She and Wyatt had been here less than a day when Wyatt's ma had spilled the beans about the mess Wyatt had gotten into after 'Rilla had died.

Wanted! No wonder he'd been wound up so tight the whole time across Missouri.

Damn him to hell and back for not telling her before. If she'd known he was a wanted man, she might never have married up with him and she sure wouldn't have agreed so readily to staking her future alongside his. Made her wonder what else he hadn't told her.

She wasn't going to Peoria only to have him land in jail and her end up whoring forever. She needed to get to the truth of things and she needed to do it now.

"Wyatt Earp, you in there?"

"Finishing up the chores," he called from the barn.

She stomped her foot. "I got a bone to pick with you."

Wyatt ambled out of the barn like he hadn't a care in the world. His blond hair was messed up, making her want to smooth it down. He made her insides quiver, even when she was mad as a hornet.

"What's got you all in a bother?"

"You! Your ma just opened up and told me all about what happened before you came to Fort Scott." She crossed her arms in front of her hammering heart, as if doing so might somehow quiet it.

Wyatt scowled and circled his head around. "Everything?"

"Enough so I know there was more than a fight with Urilla's brothers that sent you running."

"Ma ought not to have done that."

Celie was mighty glad she had. "I guess she figured it was the type of thing a wife would already know about. You didn't think to tell me you were an outlaw before we up and married?"

"Simmer down. They never even filed charges in Lamar and they dropped the charges in Fort Smith. There was nothing to tell." He turned back toward the barn door.

She'd learned that was the way with him but she'd be damned if she was going to let him avoid talking this time. She shot out an arm to stop him. "They couldn't find you to charge you, your Ma said."

"No sense sticking around." He shrugged like it was a small thing and Celie's pulse thundered.

"And Fort Smith? You jumped bail. Ran away and left your pa holding the bag?"

"I didn't want to get tangled up with the two that really stole the horse. They stood trial for it."

Tarnation. He was avoiding fessing up, she was sure of it. "Your ma said you was in on it."

Wyatt sighed. "There wasn't any way I could know they didn't get a bill of sale. I figured it was all aboveboard. I wasn't about to get hanged for making a mistake just because I was with them."

It sounded logical. She'd heard of juries being too hasty to consider all the facts, but still . . . his own ma talked like he'd done it. Even if what he said was true, it could still raise up and cause problems.

"They could still haul you in," she said. "That's why you've been looking over your shoulder the whole time we've been in Missouri. When we stopped at your brother Newton's place, his wife fussed and said you was bound for trouble again. Now I know what she didn't say. You ain't planning on stealing horses in Peoria, too, are you?"

"You already know what we'll be doing in Peoria."

Her gut clenched. "I'm not so sure I want to go with you. You're a loose cannon. What if you get into trouble in Peoria? Old trouble or new, it'll still drag me down when it comes."

"So don't go. I don't care."

The comment stung like a slap. He wasn't even going to fight for her?

But she nipped the sting and pressed on. There were things she needed to know. "Did you steal the money from the city like they said?"

"Lamar? Hell, that's how collecting taxes works. The constable collects taxes and skims some for himself. Pa always did that when he had the job. How was I to know the city treasurer was such a stickler? Pa should have told me to collect extra. I wouldn't have got caught if I'd understood the system."

"So you did steal that tax money?"

He shrugged. "The city treasurer said I failed to turn it in. Who says it wasn't the treasurer?"

"You didn't think to tell me any of this? You didn't think about how this might affect me?"

"Lamar never even filed charges for it. There wasn't enough evidence. As to the horse incident, yeah, I jumped bail, but I sure didn't want to stick around and risk my neck for something I didn't do."

She settled her anger. A lot of folks might have done the same, she guessed. She wasn't in a place to judge and that wasn't what was nettling her anyway. "I don't like it that you hid things from me. I'm your wife. I expect to be told of things that could impact me. I expect to have choices."

"Life don't give us many choices, Celie. We work with what we have."

"But you should have told me."

He leveled his gaze straight on her. "Would you have come with me if I had?"

Doubt crept in and she avoided looking him in the eye. "I don't know."

"Yes, you do. I was your ticket out of that place. You know it as well as I do. Well, you're out now. You coming with me to Peoria, or do I leave you here?"

June 16, 1872 (more than a half year later)
Near Aullville, Missouri

Celie was damn glad she'd listened to her gut and stayed put at the farm. Plans went awry from the minute Wyatt and Morgan got to Peoria, both of them arrested over and over. It was time Wyatt quit this plan of his and she aimed to make sure he was done with it.

If he ever got back to the farm.

"I reckon that's prodding enough, girl. Something on your mind?" Wyatt's ma, Jenny, said from the other side of the kitchen.

Celie stalled, her hands still in the dough and stared at her mother-in-law. "How long was I kneading?"

"Long past what was necessary. We'll be lucky those rolls don't turn out hard as a rock. I'll roll them out and put them in the pan. If I let them rise on the back of the stove 'til morning, maybe we can undo it."

"I'm sorry, Jenny."

"Fussing about Wyatt?"

Celie set the dough in the bowl and wiped her hands on a wet towel. "Guess I was. He and Morgan should have been here by now." They were a day late and she worried they'd gotten into even more trouble.

Jenny put the dough in a pan and set it on the stove. "They'll get here when they get here. I expect they were delayed and didn't think to send word. Wyatt don't do too much thinking beyond himself."

Celie knew that for sure. She'd figured Wyatt was a grown man, one who'd learned from his past. She hadn't reckoned on him being just as needy of a caretaker as her sister had been.

The brothers had left the farm determined to hire on with their friend George. Together, they planned to manage Jane Haspel's brothel. When Wyatt and Morgan got to town, they found Jane and her daughter had caught the attention of local law by opening a fancy new place. She'd been raided and lost nearly everything paying the fines. George was partial to one of her girls and figured Jane needed help rebuilding the business. He'd talked Wyatt and Morgan into partnering with him instead.

"Of all my boys, Wyatt's the one who always charges ahead. Not a bit of patience in him. That's what got him into trouble in Missouri."

Fresh anger heated Celie's innards and she near broke the bowl, slamming it into the sink. "They shouldn't have put all they had on the line."

"Dreaming of bringing in more girls and shaking down rowdy customers, I suspect."

"He should have talked to me about it. I could have told him it was a bad idea. Brothel keepers take all the risk. And hiring extra girls alerted the law just as much as Jane's fancy new house did."

"Snowballed on 'em, it did."

Celie let out her breath in a huff.

Jenny patted Celie's arm. "I reckon all my boys got their faults. Wyatt plunges into things, Morgan's a hothead, Virgil hesitates, James takes the easy route. And they've all been led astray more'n once. Newton stays out of trouble. I gotta give credit to Newton's ma for that. She done a good job raising him, afore she passed. And the war grew him up good." Jenny scrubbed at the dough on the wooden table, pushing scraps of it and leftover flour into her hand. "My boys, well, let's just say too much of their pa rubbed off on them."

Celie stared at her mother-in-law. "Nicholas doesn't seem a lawbreaker."

Jenny snorted. "You don't know the man well enough."

"I've been here six months."

"I've been holding things pretty close to the vest, I guess, after Wyatt got so mad at me back when you first arrived. Besides, I try to shelter Adelia. She's too young to know most of what the Earp men do."

Celie reckoned keeping the youngster in the dark was a good thing, to a certain point. But given how the girl idolized her brothers, she'd be in for a rude awakening when she discovered they weren't the saints she thought they were.

Jenny nodded at the table. "You're part of the family now and I guess you got a right to know the way of it, whether Wyatt wants you to or not. Better you know. It'll help you deal with him, knowing how he was raised and all." She sat.

Celie pulled out a wooden chair and joined her. She reckoned Jenny was right about learning all she could. Wyatt was a complicated man, to her way of thinking, and she'd get further in trying to persuade him to settle down to farming if she had more information. It was already clear she was going to have her hands full.

"Nicholas ain't no saint, no more'n the boys are, but he's sensible. That what my boys ain't learned yet. Nicholas knows not to be too greedy. He ain't a law-abiding man, but he don't upset the system and he don't draw attention to hisself. What money finds its way into his pocket comes there careful. What Wyatt tried to do—back in Lamar—he learned from his daddy.

The law overlooks a bit of extra tax collection as the town gets what it's owed and long as a body don't over-collect from the wrong folks. A little extra here and there don't even get noticed."

"Nicholas takes extra tax from people and lines his own pockets with it?"

"Maybe a dollar here and a dollar there, raising up business licenses a little, things like that. Don't really hurt no one."

Celie struggled to grasp the reasoning that it was acceptable. Her own pa would have strung up any town official that done such a thing. Stealing was against the commandments. "But that's not right."

"It's done by everybody in office—constables, justices of the peace, judges. Nobody cares unless greed comes into play. I hear some places even allow for tax collectors to keep a parcel of it. Wyatt got greedy, wasn't patient enough to take his time."

Greed, impatience . . . she could see it. And she guessed she'd seen a fair number of town constables and judges who seemed to live on the better side of life. Could be Jenny was right in skimming being a common thing. Besides, the commandments were followed selectively. Even by her pa, she reckoned. She sure hadn't kept true to them.

Celie nodded at her mother-in-law. "Well, I guess that explains a whole lot."

"Them boys got big ideas. They took on too much without planning and it cost 'em."

"It near broke my heart when they wrote they had to serve a jail sentence this last time. Thirty days is a long time. That they didn't even have the money to pay the fine tells me things aren't going well up there. Somebody's got to talk some sense into them." At least they'd had the sense to agree to sell out their shares and come home once they were released.

"I reckon that's what wives are for."

"Wyatt and Morgan are coming!" Wyatt's younger sister,

Adelia, shouted from the yard.

"Speak of the devil and there he is." Jenny stood, shed her apron, and bustled out the door.

Celie rose and untied her own apron, laid it across a chair, then followed Jenny.

At the edge of the yard, the two brothers stood near their horses, unloading heavy packs. They looked tired and unkept.

Jail hadn't been kind.

"What you got?" Adelia asked, edging close enough to peak into a saddle pack.

Wyatt pushed her away. "Get on back, birthday girl. You'll see soon enough."

Adelia pranced, her braids bouncing and her impatience evident. At eleven, she still got excited about such milestones. Celie hardly even cared about her birthdays anymore.

"You brung a lot," Adelia said.

Morgan ruffled his sister's head. "We were hunting buffalo. Made a lot of money selling hides."

"That's why Morg stinks so much," Wyatt jested.

The lies slipped off their tongues so smoothly they would have convinced Celie, had she not known the truth of it.

Morgan grinned at his brother. "You smell pretty ripe, too."

"Boys, you gonna greet the womenfolk or is it just kids and bickering that gets your attention?" Jenny asked.

Celie was glad of it and gladder still that Morgan and Wyatt had the grace to look ashamed at the reminder.

"Hey, Ma!" Morgan crossed the yard, escorted by Adelia, and enfolded Jenny in an embrace.

"Celie, I didn't even see you." Wyatt flashed her a grin and held open his arms.

She went. Of course. Trying to hide that it hurt he hadn't come straight to her but feeling the need for him all the same.

"Hello, darlin'," he whispered.

"Wyatt." It came out sharp, not like she'd intended.

"Aw, you're mad."

It wasn't the way to start things. "I was worried," she explained with a squeeze.

Wyatt hugged her close. "We got hung up. Selling our share of the business took longer than we thought."

Celie pulled back. "You really did it then? You're done with brothels?"

"Shhh . . . not in front of Adelia. She doesn't need to know." Wyatt pulled a few more items off the horse, speaking low. "We're done partnering with George. Too much trouble and not what what we're planning this time."

"What's that mean?"

"I'll tell you tonight. Let's get the horses unloaded and presents opened first." And like that, he was done and on to other things.

Celie bit back the spike of anger. But she stewed all through unpacking and finishing up supper and the brothers presenting Adelia with her gifts—a package of new clothes that the child had chattered on about the whole time Jenny was getting her off to bed.

There'd even been a package for Celie. A pretty new dress with lace at the wrists and collar. It warmed her, realizing she'd been in his mind after all.

"Thank you, Wyatt," she said. They all sat in the kitchen, only Jenny and Adelia missing. She'd give Wyatt a proper thanks later, in private. There was an ache in her ever since she'd seen him standing there in the yard.

"I missed you, Celie," he said, his voice holding its own promise. He balanced his chair on its back legs, boyish in the act.

She grinned, caught up in him. "I wasn't sure, you living in a whorehouse."

"There wasn't a girl there like you."

Wyatt's teasing warmed Celie. Lord, she'd missed that.

Morgan shattered the moment with a snicker. "You sure had your eye on Sarah, though."

Wyatt's chair banged to the floor. "Shut up, Morg."

Celie glanced from one brother to another. Morgan's expression was teasing but held something more.

"Who's Sarah?" Celie asked, not sure she wanted to know.

"Nobody," Wyatt said, punctuating his answer with a toss of his fork on to the table.

Morgan pressed on, egging his brother. "The madam's daughter."

Celie thudded back against the chair and sighed. "Your favorite, given I wasn't there?" Her gaze bore into Wyatt. It'd been too much to hope he'd given her a second thought.

"She was a whore in a brothel," Wyatt said.

"As I recall, you somewhat like whores in brothels," Nicholas said.

Morgan chuckled.

Celie's face heated.

"You didn't tell me Jane Haspel had a daughter," she finally said. He'd told her about Jane, of course, but his letters had been sparse, mostly short mentions of the all-too-frequent fines.

"Reckon you boys had best tell us what went on up there," Nicholas prompted from across the table. His interest had clearly risen up a notch.

Celie flashed the father-in-law a sharp look. She wasn't much interested in *all* the details, just those that concerned Sarah Haspel. His probing was going to derail her learning what she wanted to know. Any time Nicholas probed, the boys balked.

"So you can lecture us?" Wyatt's voice rose, as Celie had expected.

"So I can get a feel for what you got yourselves tied up in."

Wyatt shifted in his chair. "We got ourselves out."

"What exactly did you find when you got up there?"

"It was like George wrote us when he asked us to come. It was Jane and her daughter and a girl named Carric, but Jane moved them into that big house. The law normally raided every six month, but the move must have triggered their attention."

"That makes sense. But you jumping right on in as partners?" Nicholas shook his head.

Celie couldn't hold back her tongue any longer. "You should have weighed out the risks of tying up our money."

Morgan looked down. "We had no idea on the fines."

Nicholas shook his head. "You boys should have talked with me about that. Brothel keepers pay twice the fine as those who work there."

"We found that out in January," Wyatt drew out the words, no longer arguing.

"We got raided all the time. I think when we hired the extra girls, the law got concerned."

Celie looked from one to the other as the words spilled out of them. Thank goodness she hadn't been part of all that. It sounded like a nightmare from start to finish. The two were still going on about it.

"Not to mention the prosecutor—"

"Sixty brothels in the town and our places were the ones getting raided all the time."

"Jane was drunk half the time and Jennie Green over at the McClellan Institute didn't know shit about the business. The whole thing was a mess from start to finish."

"You know what they called Wyatt? The 'Peoria Bummer.' He was in the paper so many times it wasn't even funny."

Nicholas pounded his fist on the table, interrupting their exchange. "You boys never learn. You just keep charging into things. There's a big difference between keeping a house and pimping for it."

"Quit nagging, Pa," Wyatt said. "It was supposed to be different. We never counted on the police raiding so much. That wasn't part of the plan."

Celie'd finally had enough. "There wasn't a plan and you two had no business trying to run a brothel. I hope you've learned a lesson."

Wyatt expelled a heavy breath. "What I learned is not to partner and lose control. George's girl testified against us, can you believe it? Shook her up so bad she killed herself. If you want to keep charge, you run things yourself and keep out of entanglements like George had. You steer clear of drunks like Jane and inexperience like Jennie Green. And, most important, you stay out of Peoria's jurisdiction."

"Seems to me it'd just be easier to stay out of the business altogether," Celie mumbled.

"The girl's right. Time to move on, boys. You got your investment back and you should count yourselves lucky."

Wyatt glanced up. "We got the damn investment back because we tolerated thirty days in that stinking rot of a jail instead of paying the city every penny we had."

"Next time you venture into something, put more thought into what you've planned."

"That's exactly what we're doing, Pa." Wyatt's words were innocent enough but Celie recognized the excitement in his voice. A shiver flashed up her spine. "Wyatt Earp, what the hell are you planning now?"

"Simmer down, Celie."

"We're gonna buy a retired gunboat," Morgan announced. "Have a floating brothel on the river where we can't be arrested."

Wyatt grinned like the cat that ate the mouse. "It'll be just us and we got the best girls in town lined up to work for us with Jane's daughter, Sarah, to manage them."

Chapter Thirteen: Celia/Mattie

Sometimes, it's a heap more comfortable to believe things are something they're not.

Early summer 1873 (the next year)
Rice County, Kansas

Celie lay under Wyatt as he finished with her. She choked back the tears at her body's betrayal. It wasn't the same no more. Hadn't been in the whole nine months since he returned from his second run in Peoria.

Wyatt rolled off and stretched out beside her. "Night."

Her eyes burned. Tonight, he didn't even pull her into his arms afterwards. The sting of it bit at her.

She cursed Peoria and all it had cost her. She'd tried to hold him back, but he'd been bound and determined to pursue the brothel on the Beardstown Gunboat, sure that their new partner, John Walton, was leading him straight when he said the Wesley Bend cove was outside the city limits. So much for not relying on others! That she-devil Sarah Haspel recruited some girls and they went into business. Things had gone south right away.

"That it?" she asked him. She wasn't too pleased about the bitter tone in her voice, but she'd be damned if he was simply going to use her and roll off like she was no more than the whore she'd been.

"What do you want, Celie? I'm tired."

"Too tired to spend a few minutes loving your wife?"

"Damn it, I work all day like a horse. Farming ground that resists me every step of the way. I don't have the energy to hold you and whisper sweet nothings. I'm dead tired and morning will be here quicker than I want it to be. This is our life now, the one you insisted on. Quit your harping and go to sleep."

Celie huffed and rolled to her side, her back to Wyatt so he wouldn't see her tears.

It wasn't her fault. Coming out to Kansas was the only way to get Wyatt out of getting back into trouble. Peoria near broke them. That Walton fellow had turned out just like all the others Wyatt was tangled up with. Walton's map had been wrong and the police were there waiting, the very night Wyatt opened up the damned gunboat brothel. By the time he'd paid the fine this time, there was nothing left.

She'd figured it was worth it, though, since it got Wyatt away from Sarah Haspel, who'd taken to calling herself Wyatt's wife.

Wyatt never said a word about the madam. Celie'd learned it all from Morg and the news clipping he gave her, including that Wyatt had paid the whore's fine in addition to his own. Oh, she had no doubt what Wyatt had been doing. She should have had more sense than to let him go off alone. A man like that wasn't made for staying true, despite his vows, and the only way to keep him in *her* bed was to keep him away from whorehouses.

So Celie turned him into a farmer and their relations had gone downhill ever since. Wyatt never took time to make it good for her no more. He just took his due and pumped into her like she didn't matter.

A small part of her had wanted to believe Wyatt had come back to her because his gunboat madam had gotten too attached and he cared too much about Celie to put up with it. But she knew deep down that Wyatt had come home because there was nothing left. Like as not, he'd also been warned by the judge to clear out and never come back.

"You blame me that much for making you come out here?" she finally asked.

"What?" he murmured.

Celie turned, looked at his shuttered eyes. "You blame me that much for turning you into a farmer?"

"I don't blame you. I'm tired."

"You been pulling away from me bit by bit for the entire nine months we've been here. It's time we talk about it."

Wyatt sighed. "Nighttime's not the best for it."

"It's the only time I see you and it's stuck in my craw. You just rolled off me like I was nothing to you. So, we're going to have it out. The whole damn mess of it."

"Speak your piece then."

Celie scooted to sitting, her proper-embroidered white cotton nightgown tangling about her. "You mad about me making you come out here? About farming?"

"I saw your point in leaving. Peoria was a mistake. And with Pa on my back, I sure didn't want to stay around Aullville."

"I figured living near a town called Peace might bring us some of it."

"Might be it's a little too peaceful. I enjoy towns, Celie. Places to get away. Sure, I like living close to my brother. It seemed a good choice, following Newton out here to Rice County, but there are times I can't abide his wife lecturing me. She's as bad as Pa. All in all, I'd rather have the excitement of a city. I like gambling, meeting people, trying new ventures."

Celie chose her tone carefully. She didn't need to rile him. "But you're not good at gambling and you don't think your ventures through. You just keep finding trouble head-on."

"There is that."

"I don't like the work, neither. I got a taste for more than sewing clothes and cooking and cleaning. But you're not in jail and we finally got our heads above water."

"So this is our life now? Dullness and never-ending tiredness?"

Celie sighed, thought about his words. "It's a heap better than sleeping with strange men every night and living life on the edge. You got no talent for grand plans. You don't much like me running our lives but at least we're on an even keel."

"I don't want to do this forever."

She didn't either, she reckoned, but there was a heap more to it than being overworked. "Are you resenting me for it?"

"No, not so much. But I am tired. I guess I don't pay you the attention you deserve."

"And that's all there is to it? I don't like feeling I don't matter none, like I'm here just for you to have your release and be done."

He didn't respond and Celie's heart stalled.

"Wyatt? You done with me? Done caring about me?"

"Things aren't the same."

"True. We're living respectable instead of you visiting me in a brothel."

"Look at us. You in your frilly nightgown. You spent the winter in flannel. You look like my ma."

Confused, she fussed at the fabric. "Isn't this what respectable women wear to bed?"

"What if I don't want you to be respectable in bed? What if I want to see you in garters and stockings with a lacy corset pushing up your breasts? What if I like you saying suggestive things?"

She gulped. "You want a whore in your bed?"

"Maybe I do."

"I thought you'd want someone like Urilla was. You said you loved her."

"You aren't Urilla and I don't want you to be. I like wanton women. If I'm honest, that's part of what draws me to brothels.

It excites me."

"And now that I'm not a whore, you don't want me?"

"I want you to look like one. I want you to act like one."

"And if I did, you wouldn't treat me like one, like you're doing now? That don't make sense."

"I need to be excited." He paused. "Truth be told, it even aroused me that there were other men."

Shock chilled her. "What?"

"Knowing they wanted you. Even if they had you, I was the only one who got your full participation, the only one you kissed back, the only one you came with. That stirred me up."

"I don't warrant I understand that one bit. But if you want a woman who dresses like a slut and does all those things that nice women aren't supposed to do, I reckon I can do that. I don't understand it, but I'm tired of laying here looking at the wall."

Early summer 1873 (a week later)
Rice County, Kansas

Celie hummed as she fussed in the kitchen. Life . . . well, at least nightlife . . . had improved this past week, ever since Wyatt had come home from town with them fancy new underthings. They weren't like the tired ones she'd worn back in Fort Dodge, but they sure were effective.

Wyatt hadn't groused once about faming life in days. She hoped like hell James and his new bride being here didn't mess with it.

They'd settled into a good compromise. Living wild at night and being farmers by day. She didn't want James upsetting the balance by luring Wyatt into something. James was attracted to the wrong side of the law and Celie was half scared of what might happen during his brother's visit. This was the first time things were good between her and Wyatt in months and she wanted it to stay that way.

She'd need to keep a firm hand on those two during the visit.

She crossed her fingers on it and finished up with the cake she was frosting. It was lopsided but the icing was sweet as could be. Sort of like life was becoming, now that she had Wyatt back again.

Celie dropped the knife into the sink, where it clattered as it bounced against the porcelain.

Tarnation. Stay calm, for Pete's sake.

She set the empty icing bowl into the sink, careful this time, and ran her finger around the edge. Yep, sweet as could be. She pumped water into the bowl, glad for the convenience of not having to run outside for buckets of water, then smoothed her dress. It was almost time.

She'd met James a couple times now. He had a bit more sense than Wyatt, but not much. After the last time she'd seen him, James had headed to Kansas City. Now, he'd hitched himself to a woman and they were thinking about settling nearby.

It gave Celie's stomach the whirlies. She hoped his woman had some good sense to help balance out the menfolk they'd tied themselves to.

"They're here, Celie," Wyatt called out.

Celie took a quick peak in the mirror, stuck out her tongue, and headed outside. The screen door bounced behind her and she ambled over to the wagon where Wyatt stood with his brother. James was older, his left arm crippled up from the war, but it didn't seem to hold him back. A woman sat in the wagon, not pretty in any sense but far from ugly. She was thin and had a ready smile. Two children, a boy and a girl, bounced in the back of the wagon.

Kids . . . nobody'd mentioned Bessie had kids. That ought to help keep James wrangled.

James spotted Celie and pecked her on the cheek.

"This here's Bessie and the kids, Frank and Hettie."

"Good to meet you," Celie said. "Welcome to Kansas. Wyatt says you traveled from Illinois."

"It's good to be here. James and I met in Kansas City, but the kids were with my relatives back in Illinois. We fetched them, then headed on out." She climbed down and nodded to the children, who scrambled to the ground. "Say hello to your new aunt and uncle."

The kids offered shy greetings.

By Celie's reckoning, they looked to be either side of ten. She smiled at them, hoping to make them comfortable.

Wyatt ruffled their heads and told them to explore the place. "There's new kittens in the hayloft."

The two disappeared into the barn before the adults reached the house.

Wyatt opened the door for Celie and Bessie, then nodded toward the field. "I'm going to show James what I have planned, talk about how we can get his planting done."

And grumble about farm life, she expected.

She led the way inside. The parlor wasn't much, just a few chairs, but it'd have to do.

Bessie took a seat. "Well, here we are." She seemed about as nervous as Celie felt.

"It isn't fancy," Celie said, taking the chair next to her.

"It'll do. I'm not used to fancy."

They stared at each other a few moments, strangers. Then Celie figured that was enough of that. "How did you and James meet?"

Bessie paled. Then sighed. "I guess there's little point to beating around the bush. Morgan knows the truth, which means everyone in the family will know soon enough. I was a working girl. We met in a brothel."

That didn't surprise Celie. Whorehouses were a common factor for the Earp brothers. Besides, the admission would make her own easier. "Me and Wyatt, too."

"James already said as much. No secrets among the Earps."

Celie smiled at her. There was something in her manner that Celie liked. She wasn't uppity and she seemed to see things for what they were. "Not among the brothers. The wives . . . let's just say we are the last to know some things."

"Hah!" Bessie slapped her leg. "That isn't too difficult to imagine."

"How'd you end up there?" Celie asked, hoping she wasn't prying into things too much. But she reckoned that there wasn't much that counted as secret between two women who just admitted to being whores.

"My husband died. I tried to provide for the kids but couldn't. I finally sent them east."

"I was trying to support my sister."

For both of them, the simple explanations stirred memories. Celie could see it on Bessie's face, a sort of sadness that settled into acceptance. For herself, there were flashes of her sister and Potts and the circus. Then the reckoning after.

"Life does throw a punch in women's faces, doesn't it?" Bessie said.

Celie signaled her agreement, fiddled with a thread on her pocket. "So you're going to farm?"

"James will give it a try. He tried last year near Pineville, east of where Nicholas and Jenny are. I think that was just after you and Wyatt left." Bessie closed her eyes, then looked at Celie. "The man has wanderlust and I suspect he may never settle in one place. He's been talking about Wichita. He's bound and determined he can make a living gambling."

"Don't that sound like an Earp." Celie laughed.

But Bessie's serious expression sobered her.

Oh, hell.

"You might as well know. He's set on Wyatt joining him."

Celie thought on it almost all through the night, restless at the thought of what it would lead to even after Wyatt's loving. No way in hell she was staying put on the farm alone if Wyatt had it in his mind to go to Wichita. And there wasn't a question about what he had in mind.

Not after he and James had talked about it all evening. Keno and faro, James operating one game and Wyatt the other. James already had the lay of the land and a job offer to deal at Keno Hall, a well-established saloon.

She knew Wyatt would be itching to join him. Celie figured he'd stick out the summer, bring in the crops he'd already planted, but she reckoned that'd be it. By fall, there'd be a move to Wichita and she didn't have much time to work out a plan for managing Wyatt.

She rose from the bed and padded out of the bedroom to the parlor.

In the dark shadows, Bessie paced the floor.

"Can't sleep?" Celie whispered.

"You got that right. Every word those two said to each other rattled you. I feel so bad. James is leading Wyatt to something I don't think you want."

Celie shrugged. "That's the way of being married to Wyatt."

"You feel like talking? We could sit outside. There's a full moon and it's hot as the dickens."

Celie nodded. Bessie was right. There wouldn't even be need of wrappers. She grabbed a bottle of whiskey and a couple glasses, then they slipped out the door and sat on the stoop. Crickets chirped in the silvery glow. A cow mooed, as if its sleep had been interrupted by something or another, then quieted.

"James think out his plan?" Celie asked as she poured a measure into a glass and handed it to Bessie.

"Except for their pa and maybe Newton, there isn't one of them that thinks out anything."

"So what are the chances they'll make a living, let alone a fortune?"

As soon as the words were out of her mouth, Celie knew it was a dumb question. They'd make some money, she figured, but they'd find trouble, too. It would be a matter of which won out in the end. And, knowing Wyatt, it would likely be trouble unless he'd learned more than she thought he had. He wasn't too good at gambling. She poured a glass for herself. It went down warm and she was glad of it—there was a chill in her that didn't belong, given the summer heat.

"Wichita's a cow town," Bessie said. "There's a lot of gambling that goes on during the summers, when the cattle drives come in. The rest of the year, money will be more scarce. The bets will be lower, the profits along with them."

"Does James know that?"

"I told him. He thinks he knows better."

Two peas in a pod. Good thing Morgan wasn't around or there'd be three of them to rein in. "He sounds like Wyatt."

"They'd be better off to pick a place with more wealth, maybe someplace with mining, but he's got his craw stuck on Wichita."

Bessie seemed practical, a woman after Celie's heart. One who reasoned things out. Too bad they both had impulsive husbands to tend to.

"Do gamblers get arrested?" she asked. She hadn't much knowledge in that area, though she was plumb near a genius on the perils of prostitution by now.

"Not when they work for the saloons and gambling halls. But that also means the house gets a share of the winnings." Bessie drained her glass and poured herself another.

"They'll be looking for ways to skim extra, then."

"In more than one way."

Celie swallowed her own whiskey and dispensed herself another. Something told her she was going to need it. "How so?"

"Most places like that have upstairs girls. I can see it already, James pressuring me to return to the trade." Bessie propped her elbows on her knees and stared into the yard.

Just like Wyatt had pushed at her to go to Peoria. Seemed the brothers were of a mind on that, too—sharing their women as long as it was business. It didn't surprise her none. That she wasn't surprised was more a wonder. She'd changed a lot, she reckoned, from what she used to be. Hardened.

"He ask you to behave like one when you're in the bedroom?" Celie felt the heat creep into her face and was glad the night hid it.

"Says he likes it. Of course, we are newly married."

"If he says he likes it, it won't change. You want to keep his interest, you'll be shameless, just like he wants."

"He doesn't seem to mind me servicing other men. I think it even excites him a little." This time it was Bessie who looked like she might be blushing.

"Wyatt, too. I can't figure it."

"I expected to settle down to a respectable life. Not to be turning tricks again."

"And if Wyatt follows him—"

"He will."

"—he'll expect me to do the same."

"I don't see any way that doesn't happen if the two of us go with them."

Celie didn't like it, but pondered on it anyway. Clear as day, they'd both been promised respectability. She figured they were both lying to themselves if they thought they were going to get it this easy. Not with the men they had. Life had a funny way of being complicated.

She'd stayed behind before while Wyatt floundered in Peoria without a lick of sense. He'd floundered and he'd strayed. She didn't want either of those things to happen again. She poured a third glass of whiskey, drained it, and plunked the glass on the stoop.

"Well, I don't aim to let Wyatt go off on his own, that's for sure. I did that before and he got in no end of trouble. Tangled up with the law and with other women. One of them was even calling herself his wife."

"If we go with them, they'll want us back in the business. The only way around that will be to leave them."

A pang hit Celie, one filled with the memory of being on the street with her sister, unable to support herself, let alone both of them. "Leave them and we'll end up whoring anyway."

"So, what do we do?"

"If that's going to be our life, we figure out how to do it so we come out on top. And so it doesn't lead to trouble with the law."

They stared at each other as the words settled, then burst out in laughter.

Bessie slapped her leg. "Running a house? Doesn't that mean we pay more in fines?"

Celie thought on it. "Not if we do it right. I spent time talking with Ma Earp, listening to what she said about Nicholas. She said Pa always ran for constable or justice of the peace. Constables collect taxes and skim off the top. Justices of the peace collect fines and do the same. Long as they're smart about only taking a little and being careful who they take from, they don't get in no trouble. One of our men needs to do something like that."

"That doesn't seem to be what James and Wyatt are looking for."

"But maybe being a lawman would be." Celie paused, hoping she'd figured on it right. "Don't lawmen decide which brothels to raid? Long as they're careful, like Pa Earp says you need to be about siphoning taxes, they could raid certain places less often, maybe tip off the madams when they're coming."

"Well, shoot girl! The lawmen also collect license fees. I bet some pad those a bit, too. Who's going to complain? That could go right into somebody's pocket, as long as they stay smart enough to not charge too much extra or overcharge the more influential places."

"And I bet some of the places pay out to avoid raids, too."

"So we talk them into being lawmen? We get back in the business?"

"Whether I go with Wyatt or leave him, I end up in the business anyway. Better we control what happens than leaving it in the hands of these men of ours. We just need to get them to see the benefit of staying out of brothel management and at least one of them pinning on a badge. They could even run card games in their time off. Lots of lawmen do that."

"Hell, Celie, you got more sense than James said you did."

Celie didn't know if that was true, but she figured she was smart enough to learn from her elders, even if Wyatt wasn't. She just hoped she could get Wyatt to dance to the same tune without knowing it was Nicholas who had taught it to her.

December 1873 (that winter)
Wichita, Kansas

Celie gave the house on Douglas Avenue the once-over. It looked to be roomy and in good repair. Bessie'd chosen well. Given the short spurt they'd had to plan things, Celie reckoned she had to be satisfied with the step-by-step approach they'd been forced to take. Didn't matter none. With her and Bessie being on the same page, they'd manage the Earp brothers just fine.

"Well, look who's finally here," Bessie called from the doorway.

Celie turned to the driver and told him to unload things at the back, then strode inside. The place was clean. Not fancy by any means but far from shabby. At least the wallpaper wasn't peeling off and the paint looked to be fresh. Given what she'd heard about their landlord, she hadn't been too sure.

"Took a bit to get the farm lease settled on someone else," Celie explained. "Wyatt behaving himself?"

"He's still working the faro game. I told him I didn't want him involved here until you arrived. Surprised he listened, but I guess he don't know me well enough to risk crossing me."

"We had the same words before he left the farm. Now that I'm here, I'll work on keeping him at the gambling table and aiming for a badge."

"You think he'll do it? I've been keeping my eye on how things work. Found out lawmen also have to keep sidewalks swept and repaired and maintain city property. It'll mean hard work besides the excitement."

"It'll be less work than farming and the excitement will win out."

Bessie led Celie into the kitchen, warmer by far than the unheated parlor. Bessie had good sense, not wasting the fuel when they had no customers. The kitchen was well-stocked and as clean as the front room, even homey. Celie smiled and nodded at Bessie. Then, Bessie led her back into the hall and they headed away toward the bedrooms.

"So, tell me about the place." Celie figured the hallway could do with a few rugs but dismissed the thought. They'd just need to be beat too often with so many people. It wouldn't be like tending a real household.

"I had to give up a room for Wood and his wife, Meg, but I figured with the girls they already had working here, it was worth it. They're willing to stay out of management and with four girls it seemed a safe arrangement. You and I won't need to take on too many ourselves. Wood steps in if we need a hand with rowdy johns."

"Is there a lease or just his word?" Celie peered into one of the bedrooms. Like the parlor, they were worn but not threadbare. Not a parlor house but definitely a place that would have some class.

Bessie laughed. "With Wood's reputation, I hired a lawyer and put it in writing."

Smart. Celie reckoned they'd be good partners.

"We've got four girls then?"

"Meg, Georgie, Laura, and Kate. I just hired her. I left it up to them if they want to register under their own names or use 'Earp.' "

"Long as they don't claim to be married to Wyatt, I don't care."

"Georgie used Wood's name before so I think she'll switch over for sure." Bessie pointed out the bedrooms in the back she'd reserved for them, then they headed back to the kitchen.

"City registration of all sporting women?" Celie asked, ticking off another of her concerns.

"Yep, with a licensing."

"Any chance on the men moving into the law any time soon?" To Celie, that seemed like it would be the hardest step in the plan. She'd need to start working on Wyatt right away.

"Right now, it's all locked up by a fellow named Meagher. He's tackled a lot of the violence and the townfolk like him. But he's also willing to work with the rest of us. He ignores the saloons as long as the gambling games are honest and there's no violence. As to brothels, there's a token arrest at each house monthly and a preset fine. Us taking over Wood's house made us part of that agreement. Otherwise, we'd have been escorted out of town."

Celie breathed a bit easier, it seeming like she had a bit of time then. "Good decision, then. Any whiff of that changing?"

"Not so as I can tell. Wyatt and James both sidled up to him, just like we suggested, and he calls them both friends."

"That works for now. He'll be more likely to hire them on as deputies if he knows them." Celie paused. "Are you on record as madam?"

"There isn't any sign saying so, but the whole town calls it 'Bessie's Whorehouse' so no getting around it. I didn't register that way but it doesn't matter as long as Meagher's system continues. You'll need to register with the city, though. Just list yourself as a sporting girl, too. It'll be less in fines."

They entered the kitchen to find a pretty blond sitting at the table.

"This her?" the blond asked.

Celie fought back a stab of jealousy at the woman's tumbling blond hair. She'd need to keep Wyatt from this one, that was for sure.

"I'm Celie, if that's what you're asking."

"I figured as much. I'm Kate Fisher."

Kate had a sophistication about her, a way of carrying herself. She didn't seem to fit in a house like this. Celie pictured her in a fancy parlor house, speaking French and singing for the customers. Or maybe in a saloon, sidling up to customers and plying drinks. Exactly the type of woman Wyatt would like. Good thing she was here where Celie could keep an eye on her and not at his gambling table.

"Do you plan to work the house or just sit back and let the

rest of us handle it?" Kate asked. "Where are you from, anyway? That's quite an accent."

Direct, too. And full of questions, with an accent of her own that Celie couldn't quite place. She'd bear some watching, this one would. Celie reckoned she could be meddlesome as well as catching Wyatt's eye.

"Iowa. I'll see on taking customers. Where you from?" There, she could be just as direct.

"Sheathe your claws, Sallie. No need to hiss at me."

"Celie."

"Not the way it tumbles from your mouth." Kate laughed.

Celie bit her lip. She'd be damned if she let Kate see any more of her temper. If she was going to be madam here, she needed to stay in control. "Reckon you didn't answer me," she reminded Kate.

"I *reckon* you're right. Hungary. Not that you have a clue where that is."

They stared at one another until Bessie cleared her throat.

"I know where it is," Celie said, but she didn't and Kate knew that, sure as shooting.

"Gracious, you look sour," Kate finally said, flipping her tresses. "I'm no threat, Sallie."

"Celie."

"Kate's been a big help getting things going," Bessie said before Kate could get in another quip. "She's helped me decorate and get the house in order."

Celie nodded and said nothing more. She wasn't too happy about having a Hungarian princess in the house, but she reckoned Kate brought in business.

And she'd much rather have her here than at Wyatt's saloon, that was for damn sure.

★ ★ ★ ★ ★

June 3, 1874 (six months later)
Wichita, Kansas

Celie tried to focus. Some damn fool was pounding on the door. It wasn't even noon yet. She rolled over in bed and shook Wyatt awake. "Something's not right."

"Hell, let me sleep."

The pounding stopped and footsteps sounded in the hall.

Unease snaked through her. "I think we need to get up. Somebody's in the house."

Wyatt swung out of bed as the door burst open.

"Sallie Earp?" City Marshal Bill Smith stood in the doorway. "I have a warrant for your arrest."

Celie reckoned there wasn't no way to claim otherwise and she'd have to accept there was yet another fine coming her way. Ever since Meagher had resigned in April, Smith had been targeting her. She'd paid fourteen fines so far. She'd heard he was just responding to the local reformers, but she suspected he and Wyatt had gotten into it at some point. Of all the brothels in town, this was the one that got raided the most.

"Give me time to get dressed," she told him. Damn idiot. Her careful planning had run into a rut when Meagher quit. It was clear Smith didn't like Wyatt, seeing how he ignored his repeated applications to serve as a deputy.

"Hurry it up." Smith stood, watching her.

Bastard.

Wyatt crossed the room, naked, took the warrant, and peered at it. "It's legal," he told her, then turned back to Smith. "Aren't you getting tired of this?"

"Voters are tired of the loose morals in this town. Whores have gotten away with far too much. Time to get things under control."

Celie grabbed a silk robe from the headboard and pulled it over her own nudity. Then she rose and shrugged into a housedress. Smith's gaze was still on her, like he had a mind to see her naked and she wanted none of it, whore or no whore.

She took her time, making him wait on her. If he was going to inconvenience her, she was going to do the same right back at him.

"Enough!" he said and grabbed her arm before the dress was fully buttoned.

Celie fought the urge to stick out her tongue like a child. Wouldn't do her an ounce of good. Smith was het up this time, unlike other raids. It sent a chill up her spine.

Smith escorted her into the hallway. Bessie stood there in the grasp of a deputy. "Time to go, *ladies.* Justice Mitchell is waiting."

Wyatt and James spoke from behind them. "We'll be there."

Celie sure as hell hoped so. This wasn't the regular practice at all. There was usually a fine charged and those charged showed up at court to pay. This was the first time they'd been hauled in and it scared her. Deep down inside, her heart pounded.

The lawmen pulled them outside and loaded them into a paddy wagon.

"Damn raids are getting annoying," Bessie whispered. "Expensive, too. Hell, we don't even have any customers in the house."

"I got a bad feeling on this one. They've never showed up with a warrant in the morning like this instead of raiding at night." Celie's stomach knotted. This was exactly why they needed a lawman on their side.

Bessie's eyes widened a bit, like she was just now waking up and considering it. "Oh," she mouthed.

They pondered on it as the wagon lurched the few blocks to

the jailhouse. Once it rolled to a stop, Smith and the deputy pulled them out and tugged them into the jail. Then the bars clanged shut.

"Home sweet home," Celie joked, though it wasn't funny.

"At least they could have changed the bedding, given us fresh lice."

Neither of them laughed.

Instead, they grew quiet. Avoiding the narrow cots, they paced the cell, Celie growing more tense as the minutes ticked on. Judge Mitchell was a moralist, religious like her pa had been. He wasn't going to be easy on them. It would be an expensive arrest.

Within the hour, they were in Mitchell's courtroom with another crusader, prosecutor Sam Martin, smirking from across the aisle.

"Shit," Bessie whispered. "Where are James and Wyatt?"

The bailiff stepped forward and read the charges. Once again, the court had messed up their names—Sallie and Betsey Erp—but it mattered little. It was the charges that were important. This time, they were being charged as madams, keepers of a house of prostitution. The fines would be double or triple. Celie reckoned that would be the way of it from here on. Marshal Smith had stepped up the game.

Celie glanced sideways at Bessie. There wasn't much they could do. "Guilty?" she whispered.

Bessie sighed and nodded.

"How do you plead?" Mitchell asked.

"Guilty," they chorused. As soon as Wyatt and James got here, they'd pay the fine and it'd be over.

Judge Mitchell stared at them from the bench. "I refuse to accept that plea."

What the hell?

"I hereby order a plea of not guilty be entered for each of

you and that you be remanded to custody until trial. Take them away."

"Goddamn it to hell," Wyatt shouted once they were outside the jail. "Put it in your hands, you said. Let you and Bessie run things. So much for that!"

Celie cringed. It had taken five hundred dollars each to bail them out. Wyatt was fit to be tied.

"That's every ounce of money I have. All my faro money. My seed money for bets, Celie. What do you expect me to do?"

She wanted to swear back at him. It wasn't all his money and he knew it. Some of it had come from her stash. Instead, she leveled her voice and tried to keep calm. "You'll get it back."

He just strode off down the street, ranting. "Not for sixteen damn weeks I won't. Mitchell set that court date with the intent to break me, sure as hell."

Celie marched after him and grabbed his arm, pulling him to a stop. "Mitchel set the date and the bail both. What are you so mad at *me* for?"

He ran his hand through his hair, mussing it. "For getting yourselves arrested."

Celie sighed. He knew the risks in what she did. If he'd done like she told him, they wouldn't be in this pickle. "I've been after you for months to get a job on the police force." She started back on to the house, Wyatt keeping pace.

"I've tried, you know. Smith won't hire me."

"You should have done it before Meagher resigned."

"I didn't think it mattered so much. Meagher's system worked just fine and it would have been extra work that wasn't necessary."

"Maybe you ought to fix whatever the problem is between you and Smith or this is going to be the story of our lives."

He flashed her a sharp look. "If you were better at what you do, it wouldn't be happening. You don't have a lick of sense sometimes."

Celie recoiled from the sting of it. "Don't you *dare* say that to me," she told him, her words slow and measured.

"Or what? Are you going to leave me?"

He said that every time they argued. She guessed he knew she wouldn't do that. When it came down to it, she figured he wouldn't leave her, neither. They were two peas in a pod—suited to one another—and that wasn't going to change. He needed her. Without her, he'd go off half-cocked and run himself into even more trouble and he knew it.

"It'll be me bringing in money these next few months," she reminded him. "Money enough to support your gambling. Don't you forget that. Think about it a minute. Mitchell didn't ban us from turning tricks, just running the house."

Wyatt stopped dead in his tracks. "And who's going to run the house? You can't and the girls'll drive it into the ground. There isn't one of them that could handle it."

Celie shook her head. "I reckon somebody else'll have to take it on. While you've been having a tantrum about your money, Bessie and I have been making plans."

"Don't tell me Kate's going to take over!"

"Kate won't be doing anything more than grumbling about leaving for Dodge City or thereabouts. Me and Bessie are turning the house over to Mattie Bradford."

September 15, 1874
Wichita, Kansas
Celie sat at the courtroom table with Bessie and their attorney, William Baldwin. An extra chair sat empty, as if waiting for Mattie Bradford.

Their plan better work.

Celie's pulse pounded. She could feel it in her fingertips but she kept her hands folded in front of her and pretended otherwise. The case had been elevated to district court, with a jail term of six to twelve months now a real possibility. The holy trio of Wichita had laid the groundwork, setting this as a test case that would drive forward their efforts to shut down all of Wichita's vice. Smith and his cronies aimed to put them away for sure.

Bessie shifted in her chair. Sweat dotted her face.

This better work.

She and Bessie had initiated things back in June, laying the groundwork for Baldwin's defense. He'd been in on it, filing "Mattie's" registration with the city and paying for her license. There'd been four raids on the house since then, regular raids—probably to check on her and Bessie. Just like usual, the girls had all given their names and identified the madam of the house. The policemen had filed the paperwork and Baldwin had appeared to pay the fines on their behalf. Mattie had never actually been seen, but she sure was on record.

Celie had come up with the name, a slap to her older sister Martha. Martha had derided Celie until the day she up and died, according to all her younger sister had written. Martha had always been uppity, even above using a nickname like "Mattie." It was spiteful of Celie to give the name to the pretend madam, but it somehow pleased her to do so.

She hoped it would be enough to establish that someone other than Bessie or Celie ran the house.

Lawyer Baldwin would lay out a case that Celie and Bessie had pleaded guilty out of fear and that Mattie was the true madam of the house.

"All rise," the bailiff ordered, despite the fact that the prosecuting attorney had not yet arrived. That didn't look too good for him, getting there late.

They stood, waiting until Judge Campbell entered and was seated. He stared at the empty prosecutor's table.

Lawyer Baldwin looked like he'd just been handed his Christmas stocking. He grinned at Bessie and Celie, then stood. "Motion to dismiss!"

Up front, Judge Campbell shrugged. "I can't try a case when the prosecutor's not here. Motion granted."

It was all over, just that quick. Baldwin hadn't even had to argue.

"He didn't even show!" Bessie gushed.

"We laid the case well, ladies. I'm sure he didn't want losing the case on his record. It was a wonderful idea."

"This it, then?" Celie asked, still in a bit of shock at how fast it had happened. She guessed maybe a bottle of whiskey to celebrate was due. Maybe they'd have whiskey on the house tonight.

"This is it," Baldwin confirmed. "The bail money will be refunded and you're both free to go with no restrictions. Resume your previous roles or keep Mattie on if you prefer." He shoved his papers into his case and headed toward the door. Then he turned and grinned at them again. "You did well."

Celie warmed. Not a lick of sense, indeed!

April 2, 1876 (a year and a half later)
Wichita, Kansas

"God, Mattie, but that was good." Wyatt swatted Celie's butt as he pulled out of her, then bent to nip her rear.

Celie'd taken to calling herself Mattie full-time now, ever since the raids quit. When it came down to it, she liked being Mattie more than she did Celie. Wyatt liked it especially well.

"You're my favorite," she said. "You know that, don't you?"

"I do, Mattie girl. And you're mine. Turn around and give

me a kiss, before I head to work."

She turned, folded into his arms, and felt his cock stir again. "Another? You know that'll cost you extra."

He kissed her, hard and deep, then backed away. "I wish I could. Come to the saloon later?"

"I'll be there." She cupped him with her hand, slid it up and down his length. "We'll handle this problem later, too."

He grinned at her, then dressed and strode out the door.

Celie . . . no, *Mattie* watched him go, still tingling from their coupling. She reckoned she'd be anybody he wanted as long as it left her feeling like this. His choice of positions sometimes cheapened her, but she sure did like the time he took to leave her as sated as he was.

Of course, having life run smooth was a boon, too.

Oh, right after the trial they'd been raided a few times and "Celie" was fined as one of the girls, but there'd been no trips to jail, just the regular charge and pay system. She reckoned it was because Wyatt had finally seen a way into law enforcement. He'd taken on volunteering right after Celie and Bessie got released and had come to know several officers on the force. Some folks in town even called him "Officer Earp." Last April Meagher had returned as marshal, with Wyatt being appointed policeman the same week. That's when the raids stopped.

They'd stayed out of hot water for more'n a year now and she'd become Mattie somewhere along the line. Folks didn't bungle up the name, not like "Celie," and there was no getting around how aroused Wyatt got by being the lawman who was having his way with the madam.

Mattie pawed through her closet, chose a midnight blue dress that set off her figure to its best. She reckoned her curves were more pleasing than she'd realized back when she was growing up. Old Potts hadn't known what he was missing when he called her ugly. Her face was nothing to brag about, but her body was and she was glad she finally knew it.

The indigo dress would thrust up her breasts the way Wyatt liked, but wasn't whorish. In public, she took care not to cross the line too far. She didn't want to hurt Wyatt's career, now that he had one.

Wyatt was surprisingly good at being a policeman. He was calm and even had earned himself a few commendations. The city was growing and he worked the job year-round now. He balked a bit at all the work included, repairing sidewalks and such, but he'd stayed with it. Even when Morgan showed up last September and took a job tending bar over on Third Street. Still, Morg managed to get himself in a couple pickles with an arrest at Ida May's brothel and another at a house of ill-repute with Nellie Spaulding, his woman of the week. But he'd stayed out of the brothel business and Wyatt had kept his nose clean.

Just like Mattie'd planned. She was good at that, too, as it turned out.

She tossed on her underthings and fastened up the dress, then headed out to join Wyatt. They didn't often have time to just enjoy being out in public together.

The time was coming when she and Bessie aimed to make some changes. They didn't often take on customers, forcing their minds to shut out the johns they did see. Truth was, they both wanted to hire a couple more girls and ease out of the line. As long as they kept enough lure for their men, they figured they could cut back some. One day they'd stop whoring for good. But more girls meant they'd need to add on some rooms or move to a bigger house. She'd need Wyatt to talk to Meagher about it, so they could find a way around city restrictions.

Mattie entered the saloon and spotted Wyatt right off. He was waiting right where he'd promised—at the bar. It wasn't a fancy place, but it was one of the few saloons that allowed women, and the higher-class restaurants didn't tolerate sporting girls. She reckoned it'd have to do, until she could take that last step to respectability. Moving off the line would take her closer.

She sidled up to the bar and took a swig of Wyatt's whiskey. He ordered a bottle for her, grabbed an extra glass, and escorted her to a table like she was a fine lady. The floor wasn't sticky. She felt better—about herself—when the place wasn't dirty.

One day, she'd be somewhere with a fine tablecloth and matching china. It was time to get moving in that direction.

Wyatt pecked her on the cheek. "Hello, darlin'."

"Sweet talker."

He pulled out her chair, seated her, then sat across from her. After pouring them drinks, he corked the bottle and glanced around the near-empty room before settling his gaze on her. "Sorry it isn't fancier."

"It's all right, Wyatt. We'll get there."

"We're a damn sight closer than we were two years ago." He lifted his glass in a toast. "I like feeling folks' respect." He paused. "You always said I would."

"Here's to respectability." Mattie clanked her glass against his and drank. It was bad luck not to drink when a person made a toast. But she didn't drain the glass.

Wyatt didn't take much more'n a sip. He never did. But he sure did notice she wasn't drinking. He cocked a questioning eyebrow.

"I wanted to talk," she said.

"I figured, you asking to meet outside the house. That doesn't usually happen unless you want to avoid the girls overhearing. Problems?"

"No, nothing like that. I got a new plan."

He laughed. "Don't know what I'd do without your foresight, Mattie-girl. Even if I do complain about it."

The recognition of her intellect warmed her, as did the pet name. Wyatt's charm always melted her. But she wasn't here to get all mushy. "Remember when you lit out for Peoria? You said you were aiming to get to a respectable life."

"I wouldn't have thought staying on the right side of the law would be rewarding but ever since I turned in that five-hundred dollars I found on that drunk instead of pocketing it, folks look at me different. Peoria is a long ways back and I like feeling like this."

"I reckon that's a pretty good thing, having folks think well of you."

"It is indeed."

She drew a breath, chose her words. "I'm glad you've gotten what you were aiming for . . . but I sure as hell would like to be there with you."

He stared at her, as if it hadn't occurred to him until just this moment that she hadn't shared his new reputation.

"You aren't being fined anymore, haven't had your name in the paper for a year."

Frustration crept in. She'd need to spell it out for him. "I'm still in the business and long as I am, I'll never be respectable. You know that well enough," she said, and watched him ponder it.

"I guess I do."

"Then I reckon maybe we need to talk about me. You promised we'd both be respectable someday. That being in the business would only be temporary."

He puckered his brow. "Did I say that?"

"You sure enough did and you know it."

"But the money . . ."

Lord, was it always the money? "There is that. But you know as well as I do that success can slip away any time. Whoring is a young woman's trade. We need to start making plans for me to get out of the brothel business."

"We can't live like we do on a policeman's salary."

"I reckon not." She shifted in her chair. "It's not like I aim to up and quit tomorrow. There's other things we'd miss, too." She winked at him and he grinned. "I don't want to lose the fire between us, but I figure there's ways to keep that alive, even in a respectable life."

"That's good because I don't want to lose that, either."

"I'm thinking there's some changes to set up me being able to leave it down the road, though. Sort of a gradual pulling back and building up our savings. If we don't think ahead, I won't ever get out."

"Okay. I'm listening."

Mattie exhaled her relief. He hadn't dismissed her right off. "First, I figure maybe Bessie and me can expand a bit. She doesn't want to do this forever, either. If we take on a couple more girls, we got more money coming in. We could start setting more of it aside. I've already been tucking some away."

The wheels in Wyatt's head seemed to spin in his eyes. His brow creased again. "I don't think we can, not without being in violation of the law. Meagher would have to run us out of town for expanding."

"Can you talk to him, find a way around that?"

"I don't think there is a way around it. I'm learning how it all plays together. As long as he doesn't let the trade expand, the city council will let him continue the system he has in place. But if he lets it grow, they'll come down on him."

Mattie sighed and took a drink. There had to be a way around it. They'd need to put their heads together.

A fuss sounded from the doorway, drawing both of their attention. Bill Smith and a bunch of his cronies entered and approached the bar.

"That's the biggest reason we need to be careful. If Meagher loses the election to Smith, that bastard will fire me and the raids on the house will start again."

Mattie shuddered. "Could he do that, with the public support you have?"

Wyatt shrugged. "Let's go. I should get back to patrolling the street anyway." He stood and pulled Mattie's chair out.

They were halfway to the door when Smith spotted them and wound his way through the room. "Well, well, well, if it isn't Officer Earp and his *lady*. Hello, *Sally*."

Mattie bit back a retort and pasted a smile on her face.

Smith sneered at Wyatt. "Heard you and Meagher are plotting."

Oh, hell! Wyatt was up to something. Something he hadn't consulted her about and that was usually trouble.

She had that feeling, the one that prickled whenever there was a hint of something going wrong. She tugged at Wyatt's arm.

He pulled away from her and turned to Smith. "None of your business what's between Meagher and me."

Smith smirked. "Rumor's true then? You can't seriously think to get away with him hiring your brothers to the force!"

Oh, Wyatt. Of all the stupid ideas to pursue before an election, that had to take the cake.

Wyatt puffed up. "James and Morgan are qualified and you're a son of a bitch to think otherwise."

"Is Meagher buying in on brothels now? Is he becoming a pimp?" Smith stepped closer, lowered his voice. "I heard all about you, Earp. What was the name? *Peoria bu—*"

Wyatt's arm shot out, his fist catching Smith on the jaw.

Twelve days later

It had taken four men to pull them apart. Smith was near beat to hell. Most folks lost fistfights with Wyatt. But it nearly cost Meagher the election and there'd been no avoiding him having to arrest Wyatt for assault. Tonight, the city commission was deciding whether Wyatt would retain his job. Mattie reckoned life was turning on her again and it was best she and Bessie were prepared.

Bessie came into the kitchen, offered a smile that fell short.

"What'd you decide?" Mattie asked. She guessed she knew even without Bessie saying anything.

"James filed on forty acres near Troy."

Mattie nodded. It was at least 150 miles away, near Leavenworth. Closer to Bessie's old Kansas City stomping grounds but still rural. A safe spot to raise a family.

"I figured you'd be on your way," Mattie said, wiping down the table. They'd closed the house again, as they had every few nights since the night of the fight. Any whiff of a raid and they'd shut things down. With Wyatt suspended, they were fair game again. She figured their time in Wichita was at an end.

Bessie grabbed a plate from the drainboard of the sink and dried it with a flour-sack towel. "I'm done with being hauled into court, paying fines. I'm done with whoring, if we can swing it."

"We were so close." Mattie felt like weeping, but she'd be damned if she would let Wyatt's rash stupidity bring her to tears.

"Close don't count when Wyatt's lack of control takes over."

How the man could be so calm on the job but so careless in his own life was something Mattie couldn't cipher. "No, I guess it don't."

They laughed but the sound was brittle.

Lord, Mattie would miss this. It had been a boon, discussing her thoughts with Bessie, mapping out plans. It was something she hadn't much been able to do with Wyatt—the man didn't think things out like she did. A body had to have a plan already made when she started talking with him.

"You decide what you're going to do?" Bessie asked.

"Depends on what happens tonight. If they keep him on, we'll stay, but I aim to give up the business one way or another. Eyes are going to be on me. I'm guessing he'll end up with a fine. Lawyer Baldwin will do his best but there's no way around the fact that he hit Smith. If they fire him tonight, I'm going to push him to leave, same as you and James are doing. I don't need him and Morgan getting into trouble and Meagher won't be able to protect me without losing his job, too."

"You staying with Wyatt?"

Mattie's eyes stung. "I reckon so," she said. "I love him." She did . . . all his charm and flirting ways melted her into pudding and she was plumb proud of how he did his job. She just wished he could find a way to braid his way of being responsible on the job with all that carefree appeal. There were times he seemed like two different men.

Bessie hung up the towel and pulled Mattie close. "You just keep him moving the right direction."

"I will."

"And don't you dare let that man turn you back to what we've been doing. This is our chance, both of us. Seize that respectable life he promised."

Mattie's chin quivered before she set her jaw. "I plan to, Bessie. I won't go back. I won't."

Chapter Fourteen: Celia/Mattie

1876–1879

Pa always said lies of omission were lies nonetheless.

December 1876 (that winter)
Atchison, Kansas
"Any news?" Mattie asked from the farmhouse as Bessie reined the wagon to a stop. Mattie pulled her shawl tight against the wind and squinted into the sun, hoping to see Bessie's face clear.

They'd been alone since the brothers had headed out back in October, right after she, Wyatt, and Morg had arrived from Dodge City. The men had hatched up a plan to hunt buffalo like James had done a few times before with a couple of local men. But they had been gone two months now with nary a word.

Mattie reckoned they ought not to have let them go. *Damn foolish boys.*

Bessie sighed and climbed down. A body could see the gloom in her movements.

That meant they'd need to talk about things Mattie would just as well leave buried. They wouldn't make it through the winter otherwise.

She bit back her resentment. If she had her way, they'd hog-tie those men of theirs. 'Cept they had no idea where they were.

She stomped out to help Bessie unload the wagon.

Bessie's son was already unhitching the horses, her daughter lifting a box from the wagon. To Mattie's way of thinking, the box looked awful light.

Bessie waited until Hettie entered the house, then turned to Mattie. "The store cut off our credit."

That sure enough explained it. They'd been worried about the food stock, too. With James out hunting buffalo most of the summer, harvest had been small—just what Bessie and the kids could manage on their own.

"We still got meat from the last hog. But with four of us, it won't last much longer."

"There ain't too much in the root cellar, either."

Mattie pulled Bessie into her arms. "We never should have come." A wave of guilt washed over her for suggesting that they come to the farm for the winter. But with Wyatt's assistant marshal position in Dodge City being just for the summer, it seemed a way for them to save the little money they had.

Bessie drew back and waved her hand, dismissing the idea. "You had no way of knowing things were so bad here."

"We could have written before we showed up. We could have stayed in Dodge City, even." But Mattie had known that wouldn't work. Wyatt was a better gambler than he had been, but not skilled enough to get them through the winter. A few nights' bad luck and they'd have been broke.

"Why those men can't be satisfied with a regular job is beyond me." Bessie put both their thoughts into words. "Wyatt had a good position on the police force and still he was at the faro tables. Am I right? You didn't have anything saved back."

Mattie shrugged, not wanting to lay blame out loud. "It's his nature. Like always moving on is part of James being James. As to Morgan, he's just having a good time."

"Well, they damn well better start thinking about their families."

Grabbing the remaining box, Bessie headed for the house,

Mattie matching her stride. Halfway there, they passed Hettie. On her way to the barn, Mattie guessed, to help her brother.

They were going to have to talk about it. The money was gone and there was only one way for a woman to feed a family. Mattie's jaw tightened.

The farm had been such a respite from Dodge City when they'd first got here. Mattie'd hated the unrelenting stench of cow manure and rotting buffalo hides that hung over the town like a cloud. Here, there were no loud saloons on Front Street, tempting Wyatt to gamble, and no more arguing with Morgan, who'd followed right along when she and Wyatt moved to Dodge. Morg had settled into spending his time at saloons and brothels right off and had hounded Wyatt.

The farm was supposed to have been a peaceful place to regroup. Instead, the men had left for God knows where, with no thought of how their women and children were to survive.

Mattie entered the kitchen, the screen door slamming behind her. For good measure, she shoved the heavy wooden door shut with a bang.

Bessie stood at the table, unpacking the boxes. "Guess there's no doubt how you're feeling."

"Where do you reckon they are so long?"

"Hell if I know. Somehow, after two months, I doubt they're still hunting buffalo. They'd need to bring the hides in by now."

"Dealing cards somewhere?" Mattie figured she already knew the answer. "One of us could go get them."

"Hell, Mattie, they could be anywhere. Leavenworth is closest, but there are cattle towns stretched all along the railroad. And there was gold discovered in the Black Hills, out in Dakota Territory. They could have lit out for there."

"Then it's up to us, I guess."

"I'm not bringing any men into this house, not with the kids here."

"Then I guess I'll need to go into town for a while." Mattie didn't need to say why. They both knew it right enough. Best for her to go, with Bessie and the kids living here permanent.

She'd seen the brothels, by the railroad tracks, when they'd passed through Troy and she knew there were plenty in Ellsworth. She didn't much want to sign on with any of them. Maybe, she could find a spot at a saloon where she could attract less attention. She'd need to figure out a name to use—she'd be damned if she left a trail this time.

A hard lump sat in her stomach at the prospect of it. *Damn the Earps to hell and back.*

Wyatt had promised her. But promises made between them weren't worth much.

She ought to have known better.

July 1877 (eight months later)
Dodge City, Kansas

Mattie stepped off the train, her carpet satchel in her hand, and drew a breath before wishing she hadn't.

Dodge City *stank*! Didn't matter that she and Wyatt had lived there the past two summers. A body never got used to the uncured hides and the thousands of cows. She avoided the nearest pile of hides, flies buzzing over the rotting meat still attached to them, and headed toward the depot.

Inside, stuffy as it was, she finally drew a clean breath.

It was good to be shed of Iowa, and she realized now, she'd have been better not to visit at all. Sarah had been right. There'd been no welcome for her back at home, and it had been useless to try to mend things. Ma had grown hard since Pa had died; she'd blamed Mattie for bringing shame to the family and sending him to his grave. Ma's words had been bitter and Mattie reckoned she'd never return home again. Beyond Sarah's occasional letters, it was a part of her life best cut off.

But Ma's spite sure did make her crave good news from Wyatt. The whoring she'd done to get through the winter had left a bitter taste, and Ma's lecture had made her feel worse. It was far past time she and Wyatt settled into respectable living.

When she'd departed for Iowa, they'd been waiting word on his rehire to the position of assistant sheriff, delayed because he'd taken off to Deadwood in the spring at Morgan's behest. Thank heavens Morg hadn't come back to Dodge with Wyatt. The Earp brothers were best apart. James was back on the farm, Morg on the way to Montana, and Wyatt at home in Dodge. He'd been dealing faro, but his luck had held and, hopefully, he had been awarded the job.

She was halfway through the depot when she spied James Masterson, one of the other deputies, outside the front door.

Mattie rushed to catch him.

"Hey, Mattie! Welcome back to town."

"Wyatt get rehired?"

"He did, despite the fight."

"Fight?" *Oh, dear lord, now what?*

"The night you left, there was a big hullabaloo over at the Dodge House. Frankie Bell was shooting her mouth off and Wyatt told her to leave the faro table. She started calling him names . . . she's about the most uppity whore in town . . . and he slapped her right there in the saloon."

Mattie hissed in a breath. "And they hired him anyway"

"Plenty of witnesses said he tried to handle it peaceably. We had to fine Wyatt, but it was just a dollar. We threw Frankie in jail."

"So Wyatt's back on the force? Away from the faro tables? Settling town disputes instead of flirting with saloon girls?"

Jim's face reddened.

Her temper flared, a hot flash boiling up through her bones.

When it reached her empty hand, she knotted it into a fist. "James Masterson, you tell me straight up. What kind of trouble did he get into?"

"Lily Beck's been all over him."

"Dutch Lil?"

Jim nodded. "The one and only. I'm sorry, Mattie. I don't think there's anything more to it, honest."

"There better not be." She was sure Wyatt hadn't done much to discourage the saloon girl. He never did. "Thanks, Jim."

She shifted her satchel and strode away. Their little house wasn't far, just a couple blocks. She'd be there within minutes. Once she dropped off the carpetbag, she'd head out to find Wyatt and they'd have a little talk about his straying eye. He knew damned well she wouldn't tolerate that.

Mattie stepped onto the porch, opened the front door, and slipped inside.

Right off, she heard feminine laughter. Didn't take more'n a second to realize it was coming from the bedroom and the woman wasn't alone.

Fall 1877 (a few months later)
Fort Griffin, Texas

Mattie wasn't too fond of Texas but she reckoned it was better than Oklahoma. The dust, worse with the fall winds, was enough to choke a body at times. Besides, she ought not to complain. She was here by her own choice. Dust or no dust, she'd be damned if she let Wyatt out of her sight again.

She clicked her tongue and slapped her heals against the sides of the horse. Riding was new to her and her thighs ached toward the end of each day. And, there were the nights camped out on the prairie. All in all, it put whoring in a new light. The discomfort was different but not so very much more.

Wyatt was on the ground ahead of her, peering at tracks. He'd taken on bounty work since the end of his seasonal assistant deputy position. It wasn't official work, since it was all on his own, and he wasn't working at it especially hard, but he said he'd make money on every outlaw brought in. They were tracking a train robber. Sort of. In between the stops where Wyatt would spend the nights at the faro tables.

She reckoned she'd let him be, as long as they had money enough. He was getting better at it but luck could be fickle. She'd hidden some back, just in case. She didn't want a repeat of last year.

She pulled alongside Wyatt and reined in her horse. "It him?"

"Looks to be. I'm guessing he headed to Fort Griffin. It's not far and it would be a good spot for him to blend in."

"I thought it was a fort." Mattie didn't know much about Texas, except for the areas Orton's circus had visited all those years ago. Lord, she'd learned a heap about life since then, if not geography. Whoring had schooled her in more than one way, she reckoned.

"It is," Wyatt said, "but there's a town, too. Used to have a bunch of different names: *Hide Town* on account of all the buffalo hunters or *the Bottom* or *the Flat* because it's below the fort. Anyway, they finally officially named it after the fort. It's a pretty wild place, a lot of saloons and people."

A place for a little more gambling, she reckoned. "You think we'll find him there."

"Good chance. If he's there, you're staying out of the way. Bringing you along was a harebrained idea. You should have stayed in Dodge or gone to Fort Worth to stay with Bessie again."

"We've been through this. I can't trust you. You stranded me last winter without the money to survive. The minute I left for Iowa you were tangled up with Dutch Lil. Near every time you're on your own, there's either trouble or a woman. I'm not letting you out of my sight."

She'd dealt with Wyatt and that woman, and she'd done it without beating her to a pulp. And she'd made damn sure he knew she was the only one entitled to lie in his bed. He might get heated up by her lying with other men but she wasn't going to stand for sharing him.

"They don't mean anything, Mattie."

She blew out a breath. She'd heard the same words before, more'n once. "They do to me."

She knew that was a repeat, too, but it didn't hurt Wyatt none to hear it again.

"You slow me down and you're going to get in the way."

"Oh, for Pete's sake. You aren't working that hard at it and you know it. All you've done so far is gamble."

Wyatt ignored her. "Let's get into town. See if he's there."

And see if there are any open faro games. She didn't really expect much to come from the bounty hunting. "I could use a whiskey. My tooth is paining something awful again."

"You ought to get the damn thing pulled out."

She'd seen whores with missing teeth. She didn't want to look like that. "I ain't having a hole in my mouth." It'd feel better, after the alcohol kicked in. Always did.

"It's not going to get any better."

"Whiskey helps."

They settled into silence, not much more to be said, and rode toward where the fort was supposed to be.

The land was scrub, mostly. Rolling hills that stretched between the forks of the Brazos River. Back before the military had established itself, the Kiowa and Comanche had battled with settlers over the land here. Mattie reckoned it was the water that made the area worth fighting for. She sure didn't see much else to recommend it.

They topped a hill and spotted the fort. Built atop a bluff, it overlooked Clear Fork. The town below it was a hodgepodge of log houses, tents, frame buildings, and a few stone buildings. It was big, like Mattie'd heard, and a body could hear it from miles away. The streets thronged with soldiers, buffalo hunters, and drovers, and reminded Mattie of Dodge City with all its bustle. The stench was an all-too-familiar mix of rotting meats on uncleaned hides and cow shit. Along the central area, saloons and merchants lined the street. Mattie reckoned there was no end of prostitutes there, as well.

Wyatt slowed his horse in front of an unpainted frame building. Sounds poured from its open front door: piano, off-key singing, laugher. Not even four in the afternoon, the place was already packed. "John Shanssey's Cattle Exchange Saloon. Best place in town to gather information."

He slid from his horse and eased Mattie down. His hands were gentle and he seemed to have a fair idea of how her body ached. All in all, he hadn't grumbled more'n a handful of times about her insisting on coming with him. He knew the truth of what she'd said. He had a straying nature that almost always led to pokes and he knew the wrongness of it, too.

She wobbled a bit, once on the ground, and straightened her skirt. She'd abandoned proper petticoats for the bother they were on the horse, and the skirt hung large now that she wasn't sitting with it bunched up underneath her. She reckoned it didn't matter much. This wasn't a fancy place.

They strode into the saloon. Wyatt approached the bar and shook hands with the barkeep. She waited, letting her eyes adjust, until he returned with two bottles and two glasses.

"Got your whiskey. Shanssey says I'll get the most news over at the faro table. Makes sense."

What a surprise, a card game. Mattie clipped off the thought. It was what it was. She didn't mind it so much, as long as it didn't lead to being without a penny or whoring.

He led her across the room and made spots for them at the table. Two players sat across from the dealer. Wyatt spoke to them, handed them one of the bottles, and waited until they left. Then he turned to the dealer.

"Wyatt Earp, my wife, Mattie."

"Pleased to meet your acquaintance, ma'am. John Holliday—Doc to my friends." He tipped his head at Mattie with a flourish, all charm offered up in a southern drawl. He offered Wyatt his hand. "Something tells me you're not here to play faro. Most players don't buy a bottle to send people away."

Wyatt laughed. "Maybe later, Doc. Let's start with business. I'm looking for news on a train robber. He'd have been in during the last day or so, plenty of money." Wyatt pulled a wanted poster from his back pocket, unfolded it, and handed it to the dealer.

Doc took it and shook his head. "Never seen the man."

Wyatt sighed. "I'll wager no one has. Trails always seem to grow cold in places like this."

Most times Wyatt moved on to the next bounty, rather than chase leads that didn't seem firm. Mattie reckoned this would end up the same.

She poured a glass of whiskey and drained it. It stung when it swished past the tooth.

"Well, well, well, look what the cat dragged in. Hello, *Sally.*"

Mattie turned at the voice, all purr and uppity foreign accent. "Kate Fisher," she said, then added, "It's Mattie now."

Kate frowned, a sassy little moue. "Too bad. I liked *Sally.*"

Mattie glared at her.

Kate winked and sidled up to Doc. She hadn't changed much. A little worse for the wear, tired lines starting to etch across her face, but still with her pretty blond hair. "As long as we're making corrections, it's Kate Elder for me."

"Elder? Saloonkeeper in Great Bend?" Wyatt asked.

"The very one. I spent a few months there after I left Wichita, worked his place, liked the name. Good man, Elder."

"What brought you to Fort Griffin?" Mattie asked. She could see plain as day that it was the same old thing for Kate. Her gawdy dress gave it away right off.

"A wagon." Kate laughed. Still the same throaty sound that made men look twice. "I spent some time in Dodge City—Elder said it had opportunity—working at Sherman's Saloon as a dancer. Sherman sold out in '75 and a bunch of us girls went with him to Sweetwater, Texas. He had a tent saloon there for a while. Now, we're here."

Wyatt smiled at her. "We've been in Dodge City, too. The past year or so."

"You like Dodge?" Doc asked. "Kate said they had a moral crusade when she was there."

"Short-lived."

Time to step in, Mattie reckoned. "Wyatt's on the police force. In the summers."

Kate's eyes widened. "You don't say? That could be of benefit."

Mattie bit back an urge to remind Kate the idea had been all Mattie's, way back in Wichita. She reckoned Kate knew that well enough. The woman was playing, batting her big blue eyes at Wyatt even while she was standing behind Doc with her hands all over his shoulders.

"You still in the business?" Mattie asked instead.

Kate glowered and made her way around the table.

Wyatt edged closer to Doc and the two men bent their heads in conversation about Dodge City.

Kate stood next to Mattie, leaning against a pillar so her generous bosom thrust upward. "I generally work saloons now, part of Sherman's dance troupe. Unless we get caught dead to rights with a john, there's nothing to say we're doing anything otherwise."

Kate had a point. Mattie had followed the same strategy last winter when the Earp brothers had abandoned their women. She rubbed her jaw. Damn that tooth hurt. She poured another glass of whiskey and took a gulp.

"Are you saying you aren't?" Kate asked.

"Not since Bessie and I gave up the house in Wichita." There was no need to tell her anything more.

"Well, isn't that nice. Wyatt just brings you along to hunt outlaws?"

"I stayed with Bessie last winter. This year, Wyatt and I wanted to stay together."

"How sweet."

"Your tooth hurt, darlin'?" Doc asked from across the table.

Mattie quit rubbing her face. She hadn't even realized she was doing it again.

Kate smirked. "Doc's a dentist. If it's rotten, he could pull it for you."

"No, it's fine. Just an ache is all. A little whiskey'll chase it right away."

Doc's expression softened. "You let me know if you want me to look at it."

"I'm sure it will be fine."

"Wyatt's been telling me nothing but good about Dodge. Maybe next summer Kate and I will wind our way up that direction. If it's still paining you, I'll take a look then."

"Oh, wouldn't that be something. Kate and Sally . . . oops, I mean Mattie . . . in the same town again. Maybe you'd like to go back in the business?"

Wyatt smiled as he rounded the table. "What d'ya say, Mattie? You and Kate? Kate's a fine asset." He slapped Kate on the butt and grinned.

August 18, 1878 (a year later)
Dodge City, Kansas

Mattie held Wyatt's arm as they stepped into the Comique Theatre, glad of the night out. She didn't get him all to herself often, and she was looking forward to the evening—a chance for them to make up after their most recent argument over whether or not to join James and Bessie in Fort Worth this winter. After a gambling jaunt into New Mexico, they'd spent some time with them last year. But with James dealing keno full-time and Bessie back to brothel work, Mattie figured it was best to avoid Fort Worth.

These days, she did her best to keep Wyatt focused on supporting her hard-won respectability, such that it was, given the folks they tended to socialize with. Still, it was a step in the right direction and for that she was mighty thankful. With Wyatt working as a lawman again, he seemed more supportive of her being retired from the business, as long as she still played the role of a whore in the bedroom.

The grand foyer of the theatre was full of people—men in brocaded vests under suit jackets and women in silks and chiffons. Almost every female carried a fan. With this many people, it would be stifling and they'd all be fighting sweat.

From the saloon across the hall, Bat Masterson tipped his bowler hat and another man nodded to them. Bat's brother, Jim, still served on the police force with Wyatt, and Bat was a sometimes lawman.

Mattie fought a stab of anxiety. She didn't want Bat pulling Wyatt away from her and into the saloon. She snuggled tighter against Wyatt and said, "We'd best get in and find our seats."

Wyatt raised a hand toward Bat, then turned toward the theatre doors. He and Bat weren't friends so much as two men with things in common. Mostly, Mattie and Wyatt saw Bat when they had dinner with Doc Holliday and Kate Elder, the pair having shown up in Dodge in May. Every few weeks, Doc and Kate rounded up a group of gamblers, saloon owners, and their wives and mistresses for dinner or a show. They'd invited Wyatt and Mattie a few times.

To Wyatt's credit, he'd made no further suggestions about Mattie and Kate going into business together. Mattie reckoned he didn't dare, after the fuss she'd raised. He kept his distance from Kate, at least in Mattie's presence, and she'd heard no rumors. To keep things peaceable, she and Kate had stopped baiting each other and reached a truce.

Their seats were toward the rear of the theatre. They settled in and the lights began to dim.

"Wyatt! Wyatt Earp . . . there's trouble in the saloon." The man who had been with Bat earlier stood at the end of the aisle.

Tarnation.

Mattie clenched her fist. She ought to hold Wyatt back and let the man find whoever was on duty. Instead, she resigned herself to the situation and followed Wyatt out of the theatre and into the main hallway

"What's going on?" he asked the man.

"James Kenedy and a bunch of his ranch hands are drunk. They started a fight and Kenedy's arguing with the barkeep. Bat left so I figured I'd get you."

Halfway across the foyer, gunfire sounded from inside the saloon.

Mattie cringed but Wyatt charged into the room, his gun drawn. She slipped in behind him, careful to sidle along the wall, out of firing range. She saw a crowd of cowboys, each one rowdy as all get-out. Mean drunks, one and all, it looked like. A couple had their guns out, bent on shooting up the place.

"Settle on down, boys," Wyatt called out. "No need to let things get out of control."

"Go to hell, Earp. We're just havin' some fun."

"I want you all out," the barkeep shouted.

One of the cowboys turned his gun toward the bar. Two others advanced on Wyatt.

Mattie stepped forward, stopped in her tracks by a pair of restraining hands. "He don't need to worry about you, too," the stranger said.

At the back of the room, Doc Holliday rose from the faro table—his usual nighttime occupation after spending his days doing dental work—and pulled a weapon, said something to a man at the table. In seconds, he had that man's gun in his other hand. He rounded the table like a streak of lightning.

"That'll do, boys. I have two barrels on you and I'm a far better shot than Wyatt. Why don't you put your guns away?"

The three cowboys glanced at one another, then holstered their weapons. Doc had a reputation.

Jim Masterson and Marshal Bassett rushed in through the door at the same time and Mattie breathed easier. Arrests would be made and she and Wyatt would be able to return to their night together.

She glanced toward Wyatt.

He stood in the middle of the room, embracing Doc, both of them slapping one another on the back. Then Doc said something to Wyatt and pulled him toward the faro table. Wyatt laughed and nodded.

The two headed away from her, thick as fleas.

Mattie stood forgotten at the edge of the room.

★ ★ ★ ★ ★

January 1879 (six months later)
Fort Worth, Texas
In the back bedroom Bessie had loaned them, Mattie rifled through the dresser drawer.

Where the hell was the money?

Damn it to hell! It had been here yesterday! Gone . . . all gone. How the hell were they going to get through the rest of the winter without a cent?

"Wyatt Stapp Earp!"

He poked his head into the doorway, a lopsided grin on his face. "You call me, honey?"

"I sure as hell did. Where is it?"

"You mean your stash?"

Mattie stared at him. This last stretch of bad luck had hit hard and she had a bad feeling about it, just like her gut knotting up about the two of them. She figured he'd been straying again, likely with some saloon whore. He'd not touched her in a week.

"Yes, I mean my stash. Where is it?"

"I used it."

Mattie reached for the glass on the bureau and threw it at him. Narrowly missing his head, it crashed against the wall of the hallway.

"Christ, Mattie." He wasn't grinning anymore.

"That was meant to get us through the winter."

"It looked to me like it was you hoarding my hard-earned money. If I'd known you had cash, we would have stayed in Dodge."

Frustration welled up. "Your luck ran out in Dodge. The landlord evicted us!"

"There was enough in that drawer to pay two months' rent."

"Not if we planned to eat."

"So, pull out one of your other stashes. I'm sure you have more somewhere."

She sighed. It was near always the same, every winter. Without a job to carry him through the season, Wyatt lost all focus. Even after all this time, he still didn't think ahead. "There is no more. Damn you to hell, Wyatt. We shouldn't have stayed that extra time in Dodge."

"Doc and I were doing good."

"Doc was doing good. He was dealing. You were running on luck and luck doesn't run forever. Three months of you spending our money to stake one game after another."

Wyatt shrugged and offered her his lopsided smile. "I was bound to win soon. Besides, Doc would have seen to it we didn't want for anything."

Resentment pinched at her. Doc, always Doc. Ever since the man had stepped up and saved Wyatt, Wyatt spent all his time with the man. "Doc was too busy coughing up his lungs," she said, bitterness in her tone.

Damn she needed a drink. Her tooth hurt like hell.

"That isn't nice, Mattie."

It wasn't, but she didn't much care anymore. It was plain as day Doc had consumption and it was bringing him down in more than one way. "He couldn't even hold the deck anymore. He was losing money as fast as you and taking the house with him. Why the hell do you think he kept getting fired? As sick as he was when they left, Kate's probably buried him by now."

"She said she'd get him to a higher climate, nurse him back to health."

"And no matter what Doc promised, she isn't going to let him send for you, not the way she hates you." The way Kate resented Wyatt, Mattie reckoned she and Kate were of one mind about their men spending all their time together.

"Jealous is all. She doesn't like not being the center of his world." Wyatt's mouth took on that smile again. "Come on, Mattie, pull out some more of what you tucked away. You don't need to give me all of it. Just enough to get me into a game."

She softened a bit and blew out a breath. "There isn't any more. That was it."

"How am I going to get into a game?"

"You should've thought about that before you gambled the whole thing away."

"I thought you were smart enough to scatter it around at least."

That prickled her right back up. Smart enough? She was the only smart one between them. She'd had to be. "This is my fault? Because I didn't hide it well enough?"

"You're my keeper." He crossed the room, took her in his arms. "You know I depend on you. I always have." He kissed her on the head, let his hands roam her body. "You bring that red dress of yours?"

Damn, he was smooth. "I did."

"Will you put it on?"

"In the middle of the day?" She slapped at him, playing. "You are a devil, Wyatt Earp. Here I was thinking you had your eye on someone over at the saloon. Or one of Bessie's girls."

"I've just been worried, with the games going sour. I should have come to you before now. You're the one with the skills to get our heads above water again. In that dress, men would line up for you."

Mattie stiffened. "You want me to put that red dress on and take johns?"

"It's a way out, Mattie. Besides, you know how it drives me wild, knowing how you stir them up but they can't call you theirs." He nipped her on the neck, drew her flush against his rigid cock.

"Damn you, Wyatt."

His hands roamed her body and her nipples hardened. Lord, she'd missed his touch.

"James won't stake me anymore. We owe for groceries and the extra coal it takes to heat up this part of the house. He already asked twice today. I don't have a cent." He nipped at her again.

Damn you.

Resentment warred with the lust he was stirring inside her. She'd had enough of being Wyatt's whore. If she didn't love him, she'd leave him to find his own way through it. Tears burned her eyes.

"I love you, Mattie. You know I do."

Her heart clambered. In all this time, he'd never said the words.

Never.

He inched her dress up, found the slit in her drawers. His hands brushed her, fingers nimble, tempting. He slid one into her and damned if her body didn't betray her.

Then he entered her, his cock dancing as she bucked against him.

She knew she'd do whatever he wanted.

September 1879 (that fall)
Dodge City

She'd whored in Texas for three months, Wyatt attentive and gambling better. He hadn't said the words again but she'd clung to them all the same. Still did, even now that they were back in Dodge and living respectable again.

She held tight to what he'd said, telling herself he *did* love her, that it wasn't the money she brought in whoring.

Wyatt loved her. Saying it wasn't his nature.

Maybe Wyatt got as much satisfaction from being respected for doing right as he did from being married to the woman other men wanted. She didn't cipher that, either, but Wyatt was like a different man now that they were back in Dodge. It was like he was feeding off the admiration of the townfolk. There'd been all them write-ups in the newspaper about him and he fairly strutted with the pride of it. Law keeping seemed a fit for him, despite all his history of breaking laws.

To Mattie's way of thinking, Dodge City was changing, too. Seemed it was settling down, more businesses coming in and more folks civilizing things. There was even word they might start keeping the assistant marshal on year-round. The way folks liked Wyatt, she expected he could run for town marshal and win the job hands down. She wondered if he ever thought on it.

Wouldn't it be something if they could make a life of it, permanent-like?

She hummed as she finished up the dishes. With the night being so nice, she figured on joining Wyatt out on the front porch. Having him home of an evening was something she'd come to enjoy and she didn't want to waste the time with him when she had it. Mattie stacked the plates on the shelf, hung up the flour-sack towel, and headed for the porch.

At the mirror, she tidied her hair. Though her body still had its curves, they were filling in with a bit of pudge. But her face, never much to look at anyways, was beginning to show her age. She'd be thirty, come the new year, and there were lines that hadn't been there before and that sore tooth had blackened some, up along the top. She reckoned she should have had Doc pull it out after all.

Wyatt was settled on the porch, his feet propped on an empty whiskey box. "Aren't your feet cold?" Mattie asked, taking the chair at a right angle to his. It was warm for fall, but there was a chill in the evening air.

"Too sore to care. Needed to get those boots off."

She took his feet in her hands, swung them into her lap, then began to knead.

Wyatt sighed. "Oh, that feels good. Thank you, Mattie."

She rubbed, looking for the right words to start. "You hear anything more about putting a deputy on year-round?"

"Just idle gossip, I'm guessing."

She sighed and dug her fingers into the arch of his foot. "The town's settling."

"Less wild, true." He groaned and leaned back in his chair. "Feels good."

"More families and business folk coming in."

"Growing but they won't put on a full-time force. It's not big enough for that yet."

Well, leastwise he'd gotten around to her question. "You ever think on running for marshal?"

Wyatt's eyes popped open. "Against Bassett? I wouldn't stand a chance. He's got the job locked up, as long as he wants it." He cocked his head at her. "Why?"

The way he said the word made her skin prickle.

"I was thinking it'd be good to stay here and give up the constant moving around in the winters. We do well with you having a regular job. The summer's been good. Especially with Doc not being here to tempt you to the faro tables."

He shifted his feet, putting the second one in her hands. "We've managed."

She breathed a bit easier. He hadn't snapped when she mentioned Doc being gone. "I think you ought to put yourself up for that year-round job. Folks like you here and you like being on the police force."

He pulled his feet off her lap and leaned forward. "I used to like it but it isn't the same as it was in years past. The way I see it, Dodge is drying up, leastwise for a man like me. Theatres and restaurants and factories are springing up. But saloons are closing, gambling is dying out. Hell, there isn't even anybody to arrest some days."

Mattie was baffled. "Isn't that the way it's supposed to be when a town gets more respectable?"

"I'm not sure I like *that* much respectability."

She stared at him. "That's what you wanted."

Wyatt plopped against the chair back and blew out a gust of air. "I guess maybe I was off a bit. Working a respectable job in a respectable town is damn boring. More and more so every day. I like having the wild edge to things."

"Your wild edge always comes down to you drifting across the line of respectability and taking me with you. What happens when that doens't work out like it has before? I'm not getting any younger. I'll soon get passed by for the younger girls."

She reckoned that hadn't occurred to him, that she wouldn't always be his ace in the hole.

"I guess I like having people's respect but that doesn't necessarily mean I like respectability."

Mattie's heart stuttered. "And here I am wanting respectability."

"You can have respectability other places. It doesn't need to be in Dodge."

"Well, neither of us is going to find it wandering all over the place, gambling and whoring."

Silence stretched. "True enough," he conceded.

"So why not try to stay in Dodge this winter in that year-round job?"

Wyatt stood and began to pace the porch. "I need to be where there's excitement, where I'm mastering chance, taking charge of danger. If Dodge doesn't offer that anymore, I have to find that elsewhere. Otherwise, I'll shrivel up. Besides, you aren't so fond of Dodge, are you?"

"I like the stench of cattle a whole lot more than being a whore for other men."

He stopped and caught her gaze. "I'm not staying in Dodge this winter."

A chill shuddered through her. "But—"

"In fact, when the season ends, we're moving on for good."

She rose to her feet. "Moving on?"

"I've been hearing a lot about the silver strikes out in Arizona Territory. There's a town called Tombstone, formed this year. Lots of ways to strike it rich."

She didn't much care for the stubborn set of his chin and she sure as hell didn't like the idea of pulling up stakes for a boomtown. There'd be no end to the trouble to be had in a place like that.

Tarnation. "We need to think this through."

Wyatt put up his hands, almost like she was aiming a gun at him. "Nothing to think about. It's already decided. I wrote James and Bessie and they're coming. Morgan and his new wife, too. They'll head down from Butte and join us there."

James and Morg both? "Hell, Wyatt."

"Think of it. We can take over the town. I can see it now. The Earps can run a game in every saloon . . . at least three anyway . . . and we can all find a way into law enforcement, getting in this early. There'd be plenty of excitement in a town like that."

Her head throbbed.

"It's an opportunity like no other, Mattie. The Earps are going to rule the place."

Chapter Fifteen: Celia/Mattie

1879–1880

Not facing the truth wasn't really a lie, was it?

October 18, 1879 (the following month)
Las Vegas, New Mexico Territory

Mattie and Bessie trailed behind the men. Bessie's sixteen-year-old daughter, Hettie, wandered ahead, drawn by the lively music pouring from across the way. The Las Vegas plaza was a busy place. Mattie remembered liking it when they'd passed through a few years back during one of their winter gambling seasons. Bright bunches of red peppers hung from the wooden porticos that covered the sidewalks opposite the square and women were selling tortillas with spicy fillings from baskets. Saloons and restaurants were getting busy but the warmth of the fall day still hung about them, not yet fading off to evening chill.

"You figure we got a chance?" she asked Bessie.

"It's worth a shot."

They'd met up a few weeks ago, joining their wagons into a small train and following the Santa Fe Trail. Wyatt and James were of a mind to pass through Prescott, where their brother Virgil and his wife, Allie, had settled.

But Mattie and Bessie were of a different mind. If they could sway the men, the Earps would show up in Tombstone all set to run a stage business, or leastwise some freighting. They reckoned a growing town would have need of such support and it would be a good solid living. One that didn't risk their savings on a constant basis.

"You think we ought to look at wagons here or in Prescott?" Bessie asked.

Mattie laughed. "That'll pretty much depend on money. I reckon we'd do best to bring up the idea while their luck is running good."

"Then we'd best catch them before they head into that saloon."

Mattie glanced up, noticed Wyatt and James had changed direction.

"Well, I'll be damned!" Wyatt rushed forward and Mattie's gaze followed him.

Doc and Kate stood at the corner of the plaza.

Tarnation.

Kate didn't look too pleased to see them, either.

"Well, Wyatt Earp. I surely did not expect to see you here," Doc said.

The rest of the party caught up, Bessie signaling Hettie to join them. Wyatt made introductions.

"Whatever brings you all to our little town?" Doc asked.

"Silver," Wyatt told him. "We're headed to Tombstone, in Arizona. Town's starting to boom, along with the mines, and we're planning to get in while things are on the upswing."

"I didn't think I'd ever see you leave Dodge."

"Bigger and better things, Doc. What are you doing here?"

"I had that bout with the consumption. Kate nursed me through it and I bought a saloon here, The Holliday Saloon—isn't that catchy? Kate divides her time between here and Santa Fe."

"Still in the business, Kate?" Mattie asked, unable to stop herself.

Kate glared. "Part and parcel of being married to a gambler, it seems." She leveled her gaze on Mattie, then on Bessie. "You two know that, I'm sure."

Mattie drew a breath and nodded.

"Why don't you two come on out to our camp? Share supper with us," Wyatt said.

Kate hugged Doc's arm. "We have business to tend to."

"You're more than welcome at the saloon," Doc offered.

Bessie shook her head. "We have Hettie with us. I'd prefer to keep her out of saloons."

They all headed back out of town, Kate sullen. Moments later, they neared the wagons.

"Those are mighty nice horses you got staked there, Wyatt. You steal them?" Kate asked.

Wyatt's face paled.

Mattie knew the comment was like a slap, given what had happened back before they met. She suspected Kate had heard about it. She had a smug satisfied look about her.

"You have a big nose, Kate," Wyatt said. "Best to keep it out of my business."

The evening continued on a par, with Kate baiting Wyatt. Mattie figured she did it just to needle him, but Kate had always been full of questions. The men had taken themselves off to the edge of camp to talk for a bit, then Doc and Kate headed back to town.

Mattie and Bessie approached Wyatt and Jim with coffee in hand.

"We've a mind to talk a bit," Mattie said. "Bessie and me have been thinking."

"That's not always good," Jim said.

Bessie slapped at him, playful. "If you think on it, it most usually is and you know it."

Mattie glanced at Wyatt. "We've been looking at your run of luck these last few years. It's been up and down."

Jim chuckled. "Luck usually is."

Bessie glared at him. "The thing is, maybe we shouldn't be putting all our eggs into one basket."

"What do you mean?" Wyatt asked.

"Something neither of you have talked about," Mattie said. "Maybe you ought to look at opening a business in Tombstone, something that would bring in steady income ."

"We figure on getting hired on as lawmen." Wyatt's standard answer.

Mattie bit her lip, drew a breath. "What if the law jobs are filled when we get there?"

"They'll open up soon enough."

Bessie raised her hand, stopping the exchange between Mattie and Wyatt. "Enough. But while you're waiting, why not have some money coming in?"

"I'll tend bar. Deal cards," Jim said. "I planned on that, anyhow, along with mining."

"What if you don't strike it rich? What if the silver run drops? There won't be as many folks gambling. Or, what if there are no dealer positions when we get there?"

"We're good dealers," Wyatt said. "We'll get them bumped."

Mattie put her hand on his arm and caught his gaze. "And if there's a run of bad luck?"

"We weather it."

Mattie shook her head while Bessie snorted.

"We did just fine the last time Mattie and me offered up an idea, didn't we?"

They all sat quiet for a minute, then Jim said, "All right, what are you thinking?"

"What if we invest in a wagon, set up a freight company to bring in goods? Or even transportation?"

"We can't afford a stage." Wyatt waved the idea away.

Mattie blew out a breath. Damned argumentative fool. "It doesn't need to be a stage. If the town is growing as fast as you say, there'll be need to get places, be it in a stage or a wagon."

"It isn't a half-bad idea. A wagon, some horses, and a driver." Jim swallowed his coffee.

"We figure it'd be a good hedge," Bessie said. She faced Wyatt. "Folks would get to know you. Folks beyond the saloons. You'll need the townfolk to support you if you have to run for any of the law positions."

Jim stood, hugged Bessie. "We could use one of the wagons we already have. Shouldn't take too much to convert it over."

"So you agree?" Mattie said. "We'll plan on a freight business?"

Wyatt nodded. "All right. Long as we can follow all the other opportunities as well."

"Things are falling together just fine," Jim said. "We'll have the whole town wrapped up. Did Kate tell you the news before she left?"

Mattie glanced from Jim to Wyatt, already not liking it. "News?"

Wyatt drew a breath. "Doc and Kate are coming along, too. With Doc's card skills and Kate's side business, we'll make a fortune. Hell, we might not even need the freight business."

November 1879 (a few weeks later)
Prescott, Arizona Territory

The leg of travel to Prescott had been full of bickering. Mostly about what they'd focus on first. Wyatt argued a stage business would be dull; lit up with excitement when he spoke of running a gambling enterprise with Doc. Jim went back and forth. Mattie and Bessie stewed. Then, when they got close, it came out that Wyatt and James had been plotting all along to get Virgil and Allie in on the move. It wasn't going to be three brothers in Tombstone but four.

Thank goodness Wyatt and Jim had already agreed to pursue the stage and freight business or the bunch of them would unravel everything. Mattie figured they'd best hightail it south before the brothers pulled the plan apart entirely.

"We'd best get things loaded," she said.

Allie frowned at her. "Don't see what the hurry is."

Mattie'd gleaned right off that the idea of leaving Prescott at all wasn't too high on Allie's list. She and Virge had been pecking at each other ever since the brothers had put it all together. She'd fussed the whole time they were pulling the household belongings out to the yard.

"We spent two years building up this place, don't know what that man is thinking about."

"We've started over before and it all worked out." Virge bussed her on the cheek and drew out a smile.

Allie turned her gaze on Wyatt. "I ought to hog-tie you for putting this idea in his head."

Wyatt marched to a box of kitchen items. "We'll be sharing a house for a while. We only need one set of pots and plates and such." He set the box aside.

Allie stalked to the box and pulled out a rolling pin. "This here is made of fine hardwood, handmade."

The arguments continued, debates on near everything. Mattie figured it was a good thing Doc and Kate had taken a liking to Prescott. The pair was set to stay put rather than come the rest of the way with the Earps. Mattie was pleased. At least she had a chance to keep Wyatt from jumping into heavy gambling now.

"We don't need the sewing machine, either. That cabinet will take more space than we can spare."

"Virge gave me that!"

Virge pulled Allie into his arms and held her. "They're just things."

Mattie felt bad for her. She'd never had much in the way of things herself but it sure enough seemed to be a hurtful thing for Allie to part with it all.

Maybe if Allie knew how important it was, she'd take it less personal. "It's just that the sooner we get there, the sooner we can set up the stage and freight business."

Virge looked up, sharp-like, at his brothers. "A freight business? There's already a Wells Fargo line, a second line coming in, too. There's not going to be room for a third."

A lead ball settled in Mattie's stomach.

"It's a new town. Jim can tend bar and I'll take up the law, like we were planning in the first place."

"It's not as simple as that, Wyatt," Virge said. "Tombstone doesn't have a police force like Dodge City did. County sheriff is elected. Town marshal is appointed. You're going to need to be in town a while to get known enough for that to happen."

"Lots of gold at the faro tables," Jim said.

Bessie glowered at him. "Neither one of you has a good record with cards. Unless you're running the table, your luck won't hold our heads above water. Mattie and I are going to be respectable. You both agreed."

"Settle down. I didn't say anything about whoring."

But Mattie saw the lie in his eyes. She could tell Bessie saw it, too, because her jaw set up tight and her mouth pinched into a thin line.

Mattie just stared at the men, the sting of tears behind her eyes.

December 1879 (the next month)
Tombstone

Wyatt had been right that there'd be opportunity in Tombstone. Mattie noticed it right off, when they saw the tents and adobe and frame buildings all scattered across the slope of the hill. Mostly it was the tents that caught her attention, but it was good the place was busy, with folks working on all those new buildings. Once they pulled in, the sounds of hammers and saws mingled with catcalls and piano music. There were dance halls and saloons near everywhere and the scents of whiskey and tobacco drifted from one to the next.

Mattie winced as a gust sent dirt into her eyes, then rubbed at them with her fist. So, it'd be dust and dirt here instead of rank odors. There was a steady wind that had been blowing for the last few days.

The wives had settled what to do on the trip from Prescott. Cards, saloons, law, and prospecting would have to suffice, but to stretch the money they'd combine households for a spell. Meanwhile, the three women would find a respectable trade. Everyone just needed to pull their weight and hold to their promises.

They rolled the wagon down Allen Street, looking for Kinnear's stage office. They'd determined the first order of business was to sell off their outfit. They reckoned to get out from under their wagon instead of trying to compete.

Pulling to a stop, the entire bunch clambered out to stretch. They all had jobs to do. Bessie's daughter would purchase supplies, Wyatt headed to the stage office. Jim crossed over to the nearest saloon to inquire about bartender jobs. Virge, who'd had the good sense to check with his connections in Prescott before they left, strode down the street in search of the U.S. Marshal's office with his shiny new Deputy U.S. Marshal badge. Appointed to the position before they got to Tombstone, he'd have his foot in the door of the town's convoluted law system.

As she watched the three men walk away, Mattie marveled again at how much they resembled one another. Wyatt and Virge were near identical, with their tall, lanky frames and blond hair.

Jim was shorter, darker, but still, one could see they were brothers. Especially when they were coming at you with them mustaches twitching.

Mattie pushed the thought away and glanced at Allie and Bessie. "What d'ya think?" she asked.

"Ain't much," Allie said. "But it looks like they're building fast."

Bessie nodded. "I heard there's near nine hundred here already."

"Not too many women, yet, though. I'm not sure that sewing machine you worked so hard to talk Wyatt into bringing will do much good. I don't see a single dressmaker."

They walked the street, clutching hats against the wind. There were lots of restaurants among the gambling parlors. She hoped Wyatt found work. He was better at gambling than he used to be, but she'd long since learned it was best for him to deal for the house than against it. He would need to work for a concession.

They passed mercantiles with rotted fruit and thin supplies of vegetables on display. "Looks like we're going to need to put in our own garden," Bessie said.

"If we can raise a good crop, we can sell it," Allie agreed.

A freight wagon rolled past, filled with lumber. Mattie wondered if they ought to take a second think on running freight, but she reckoned it was too late. The men had made a decision to sell and she doubted they'd change their minds.

"No dressmakers, not even a tailor," Mattie said, eyeing the street.

"We toted that sewing machine all the way here and left my rocking chair behind for it."

"Hush up, Bessie," said Allie. "You seen all I had to leave."

Mattie stopped in her tracks. "Stop bickering. Are we going to leave this all to the men?" The words came out a bit harsher than she intended. Her tooth was aching something horrid and she needed a drink.

"We don't have much choice," Bessie said. "Unless some Chinese laundryman wants to hire us to do repairs."

"Don't hurt to check." Allie, with her usual direct ways, marched straight up to a ponytailed man in a white coat and started talking. The man chattered back, waving his arms. He didn't look none too happy. Allie came back, shaking her head. "Well, shoot!"

The three scanned the street, looking for other laundries, then each strode away in a different direction. With all the dirt in the air, Mattie reckoned the laundries did brisk business but most folks didn't appear to take things in to be washed all that often.

A half hour and four refusals later, she headed back up Allen Street. En route, Virge came out a door and smiled at her. That Virge . . . of all the brothers, he was the one that took law the most seriously. For Wyatt, it was a means to an end that he enjoyed but Virge . . . well, Virge just plain liked justice, she figured.

"Settled?" Mattie asked him.

"I'll take over in the morning. There's a desk waiting but not much more than a closet for a cell."

"Prisoners all go to Tucson then?" she asked.

"The county prisoners do. I'll handle all the federal offenses like stagecoach and mail robberies."

"There much crime?"

"Worse than Dodge City at its wildest, from what I hear. There's the usual drunkenness and a gang of ex-cowhands turned rustlers and stage robbers. Folks call them the Cowboys. They wouldn't be too hard to handle except the small ranchers buy the cattle cheap and the rustled cattle supply meat to the merchants in town. City marshal doesn't do much about their rowdiness in town and the county sheriff doesn't do much about the crime in the county."

"Any chance of Wyatt getting hired on?"

"Well, it'll take some time. The city marshal is elected so Wyatt will need to make himself known and run in the next election. The county sheriff is elected, too, but he appoints the deputy sheriff, so that's a possibility, if it ever comes open. Meanwhile, I can hire him on if I need a special deputy federal marshal, but that's only for special situations. His best bet would be to hire on with Wells Fargo to ride shotgun if he aims for law work. It'd be the best way to attract attention for future election or appointment."

"I'll tell him."

Virge put a hand on her arm. "I'll tell him, Mattie. He'll listen to me more."

They returned to the wagon, found Bessie and Allie gathered with Wyatt and Jim.

"Jim found a job and we rented two houses, over on Fremont Street, next door to each other," Wyatt told them. "We'll be crowded but it's a start. I used the money from selling the wagons. We need to unload, then get them back here."

"And," Jim said, "we got leads on a couple mines in the area. I'm headed out to take a look. If it seems a good bet, we're filing on them."

Bessie rolled her eyes. "You sure that's wise?"

Not even in town two hours and they were already looking at mines. Mattie bit back her pique. When the hell would their men take responsibility seriously? She hoped Jim would work enough hours at the saloon and leave the prospecting for his spare time.

Wyatt patted her arm. "Easy, Mattie. I can see the steam coming out. It'll be fine. People are striking silver all over. Jim and I are getting in while we can. We'll have time to work the mines while we're getting settled."

"We agreed on this, girls," Jim reminded them. "Part of the compromise for our promise to you."

Mattie drew a breath. She didn't think the men were going to like what she had to say, but she'd had the thought when they'd come into town. It'd taken her a while to work it out and it wasn't the best answer but it was one more way to keep them afloat. She caught Wyatt's gaze and plunged ahead with saying it.

"You three aren't going nowhere near the mining district until you unload that sewing machine and spread the word around town that we're sewing and repairing tents."

★ ★ ★ ★ ★

Part Two: A Tainted Taste

TOMBSTONE 1880–1881

★ ★ ★ ★ ★

Allie

Them two years in Tombstone changed everything and the story got told all kinds of different ways afterward. Wyatt come out a hero and making sure he stayed one became the focus of Josie's life. Mattie and the other Earp wives and even his brothers disappeared into Wyatt's shadow and the truth vanished into the darkness, too.

Chapter Sixteen: Josephine/Sadie

And then there are the lies others tell.

May 12, 1880 (a month after the Earps arrived; two months after Kitty's advice to Sadie)
Tombstone

I signed the register of the Cosmopolitan Hotel and turned the revolving book back to the innkeeper. The hotel was richly appointed, with warm woods and rich fabrics—quite a feat given the infancy of the town. I'd anticipated less. If the rest of the town proved this nice, I'd settle in here just fine.

"Ah, Miss J. Marcus, is it?"

I glanced at the curious little man across the counter. "It is." I'd left Sadie Mansfield behind, but decided against taking on Behan as my name. I'd let Johnny adjust gradually. "I'm Mr. Behan's fiancée."

"I didn't even realize he was betrothed. My congratulations. He has fine taste, if you don't mind me saying so." The surprise on his face confirmed Johnny hadn't mentioned my existence. I'd been right to come.

I dipped my head as if a bit embarrassed but too cultured to say so. A bit of groundwork laid early, just like Mama always advised. A pang of loneliness hit me like a gust of wind. I hadn't thought of Mama in months. I'd write, that's what I'd do, just as soon as I finished establishing my new identity.

I lifted my head and found him still staring at me. "I don't mind in the least, Mister?" A lady would expect an introduction without having to ask and I let my voice convey my discontent over having to ask for one.

"Pettis. Ernest Pettis. Are you relocating, then, Miss Marcus?"

"Johnny thought it would be good for me to visit, see the town. It all depends on whether Johnny has everything settled with the stables." I kept my answer vague. If all went well, the townsfolk would talk me into staying and there'd be a wedding in a few weeks. "He said I should just check in when I arrive since he and Mr. Dunbar could get quite busy."

A cloud of confusion darted across the innkeeper's face, quickly replaced by an ingratiating smile. The little ferret was hiding something.

Obviously, he wasn't going to spit out the secret, whatever it was. I'd need to do some digging. "Is there something I should know about the partnership, Mr. Pettis?" I widened my eyes.

His Adam's apple rippled. "Nope. I'm sure Mr. Behan will fill you in on everything."

Fine. I'd milk the information elsewhere. I extended my hand. "My room?"

"Oh, my apologies, Miss Marcus." He handed me a key from a hook behind the counter. "Number seven, top of the stairs."

Perfect! In direct view of the innkeeper, Johnny wouldn't dare risk a private argument in my room. It would imply a rendezvous and *that* would damage my . . . and therefore his . . . reputation. Let him lust a few days without his customary relief.

"Could you tell me where I can find the Dunbars' house? I'd like to pay a call to Mrs. Dunbar so we can get acquainted. With our men being in business, we'll likely spend time together."

His eyes shifted and he sighed. "Yes, ma'am. Let me draw you a map." He tore a page from the rear of the register book and sketched out a diagram. "Right there at the end of Allen Street, just down from the stables."

"Very good, thank you. This helps me more than you can know." I flashed him my brightest smile, tempered with a hint of innocence. It was a thin line I planned to tread—confident but not worldly. "I hope I won't take her too much by surprise." I nibbled on my lower lip, then turned away.

I felt him watch me as I ascended the stairs and knew he was hooked. Thirty minutes later, he was waiting expectantly for my return.

"I hope you don't mind, Miss Marcus. I took the liberty of sending a note over to Mrs. Dunbar. She'll be expecting you."

"How thoughtful, Mr. Pettis. You are so kind. I wonder if you'd send a note to Mr. Behan to let him know I've arrived safely. I thought he might have checked on me by now." I drew my mouth into a moue, then let it drift away. "No hurry, though. I don't want him to feel obligated to sashay me about. His business must come first."

"I'll send someone by shortly."

"Very good. Thank you for taking such good care of me."

I left him blushing and strolled out the front door, following the route on the map. It didn't take long to cross the few blocks. I rapped on the plain wooden door of the dwelling marked with an X.

The door opened and a tall woman peered out, curiosity filling her faded blue eyes. "Miss Marcus? I'm Rachel Dunbar. Come in."

"I hope I'm not imposing. I know you weren't expecting me. I hope Johnny at least mentioned I was coming to town."

She shook her head. "I suspect Mr. Dunbar didn't see fit to pass the news on to me. Typical of a man to not realize we'd want to get acquainted. But then, Johnny's not too often at the stable these days, what with tending bar and all." She paused.

"Has Johnny shown you the town?"

Aha! Tending bar and all? So that was what Pettis was afraid to mention. I filed the information away for later, something to explore directly with Johnny. I had other things to accomplish with Rachel Dunbar.

"My Johnny is a busy man." I let my mouth turn downward just a bit, wistful. "I've only seen from the Cosmopolitan to here. Is there much more?"

All sympathy at my deserted plight, she patted me on the arm. "Not much. I'll walk with you and point out the landmarks."

I pressed my palms together, the perfect picture of a lady. "That would be wonderful, so I get my bearings. I want to know all about my future home."

"You aren't staying?"

"Oh, not this trip. I'll move in a few months."

"Where are you from then?"

"San Francisco. My father is a well-established merchant there." The lie rolled off easily. A bit of regret rolled with it at how different my life might have been had Papa actually had a bit of ambition.

"And family?" Rachel continued. "You must tell me all about yourself. However did you and Johnny meet?"

I launched into a description of being introduced by Lucky Baldwin, leaving out a few critical details, of course. Within the hour, we were on a first-name basis and Rachel knew everything there was to know about Josephine Marcus, daughter of a wealthy Jewish merchant, lover of the theatre, and recently engaged fiancée.

She never knew what hit her.

By the end of the afternoon, Rachel had introduced me around town, sharing information about my past with those we encountered. Everyone knew how Johnny and I had met, how my sheltering family had resisted his initial proposal. I avoided entering the saloon she'd pointed out, telling her I didn't want to bother Johnny at work. The Grand Hotel, one of the better places in town, from the looks of it. Instead, I'd urged Rachel on, sealing our friendship with eager interest in her family. I returned to the hotel spent, hoping I'd be able to keep track of what I'd told whom.

"Ah, Josephine. There you are, my pet. Did you enjoy your afternoon?"

"Johnny!" I rushed across the lobby into his arms. He was stiff as a board and this time, it had nothing to do with desire.

He lowered his mouth to my ear. "What the hell are you doing here?"

"Johnny . . . Mr. Pettis is just over there." The note of suggestion in my voice was enough to stall him.

"Damnation." He spit out the curse, then took my arm in his, his lips thin. "I hope you aren't too tired to stroll a bit more."

"I am a bit weary."

"Let's go." He pulled me out into the sunlight with Mr. Pettis frowning at his uncouth behavior.

Once outside, my ire surfaced. "Stop man-handling me."

"I'll handle you any way I want." He grasped my arm tighter and steered me down the boardwalk.

"You'll handle me as a gentleman would. Eyes are watching. The whole town knows your fiancée has arrived in town and you didn't see fit to meet her stage or escort her about. Word is you're quite the oaf leaving such a charming young woman on her own all day. You'll need to make amends."

"Damn you, Sadie."

"Josephine. Josie if you must. I decided to leave Sadie behind." I lowered my voice to a whisper. "She has a reputation, you know."

He glared at me. "I'm in no mood for this shit."

Oh, Johnny, you foolish man.

"I told you I was smart, Johnny. You wanted to play hardball. Now you'll have to deal with it. I suggest, for the sake of your political ambitions, that you play it right this time. Things have changed."

"You damned little whore."

"Shhh, Johnny. Not in front of the townspeople."

He clammed up then, didn't say another word for the length of the block.

"I heard you're a bartender, just a silent partner at the stable. More your style, I guess."

"I never said I planned otherwise."

"Saloon work is hardly the respectability you were gushing about back in Tip Top."

"Being a business owner is respectable enough to count even if I'm not there daily. Tending bar lets me get to know those who live here. Saloon work is accepted and every voter in town knows me now." He stopped at the door to the Grand Hotel bar. "Come on in, meet my friends. Seems you've already met everyone else in town."

He pulled me in and I pasted a shocked expression on my face. "It's a bar, Johnny," I squeaked out.

"You've seen them before."

I stalled. "Josephine doesn't enter saloons."

"Oh, stop it, will you?" He led me into the darkened room. It was fancy but it stunk like stale beer all the same. "Hey, everybody, meet my gal Sa—"

"I'm so pleased to meet you all. I'm Josephine Marcus, Johnny's fiancée."

Cheers and congratulations filled the room, all of them echoing surprise.

"John, you never said a word!"

"Ain't a missus gonna tie you down?"

"She's a looker."

Johnny's jaw tightened, twitched.

"Now boys, don't tease so." The crowd was an assortment of miners and businessmen, a few gamblers. One of them flashed me a smile, its energy hitting me like lightning. I shivered.

"Staying long, Josephine?" the man asked.

"I—"

"Josie's here for the day. Nothing for you to stick your nose into, Wyatt. First thing tomorrow, she's headed back to Tip Top."

"But—"

"One of us has to close up my businesses there and I can't leave." Johnny's eyes glistened with triumph. "My little turtledove is all set to take care of things for me. Selfless as she is, she's promised to stay there until the saloon sells, no matter how long it takes."

He grinned then, all pride and adoration to his customers but I saw the victorious spite clear as day. He'd regret that.

May 1880 (the same week)
Prescott, Arizona

I marched toward Kitty's house, praying her husband was still at the office. Our scheme hadn't taken this scenario into consideration and I needed her advice.

There was no way in hell I was going to be stuck in Tip Top for months. I'd planned on Johnny and I being married by June and I wasn't about to let the bastard put a wrench in everything I'd worked for. He'd handed me into the stage in Tombstone, still smug, and told me to enjoy Tip Top. I shut the door on his hand.

I'd finish up his business all right. I'd sell the saloon to the lowest bidder and be rid of it, then head straight back to Tombstone and throw it in his face. But I'd need Kitty to help me make it work.

I rapped on her door and stewed.

"Well, look who's here!" she chirped. "How's the future Mrs. Behan?"

I strode in and plopped into the nearest chair. "I need some help."

Kitty arched her eyebrows. "You look like you need a drink, too."

"Oh, God, yes." The words spewed out, revealing I was still a whore underneath the façade I'd pasted on in Tombstone. A hardened one once again.

She poured a healthy measure of brandy for each of us, handed one glass to me and watched me down it in a gulp. Then she sniggered.

I slammed the glass onto the side table. "It isn't funny." But her laughter lightened me a bit and I let go of some of the bitterness. It wasn't helping matters anyway.

"Tombstone not to your liking?" Kitty asked.

I sighed. "Tombstone suited me. Johnny, not so much."

"Oh, our Johnny can definitely be a tough man to put up with. Is he balking?"

"He's got his feet dug in and sent me back to Tip Top via a public declaration I couldn't refute without the whole town knowing there was a problem between us."

Kitty rolled her eyes, then peered at me. "You sure you want him?"

"Well, he can be damn exciting when he's not insufferable!" But her question gave me pause. He had the respectability, the status I'd yearned for all these years. I didn't think I was going to find that within my grasp again. "Our goals mesh, Kitty. We want the same things from life. And when I'm away from him, I long for him."

"You love him?"

I doubted it, knew it even, but it didn't matter the way it had once. "I don't even know what love is."

"Will he make you happy?"

Hell, I didn't know what happy was either. Had I ever been happy? "I'll be a whole lot happier being a wife than a whore, that's for sure. And I sure don't want to live out my life as a dutiful daughter under the thumb of my family."

"The lesser of multiple evils, then."

Maybe so but when things were good with Johnny, they were damn good. "He's the only man I've never faked it with."

"Well, that does say something, doesn't it?" She whisked her hands together to dismiss the topic. "What do you need from me?"

"Absence tends to make Johnny's heart grow fonder. But I'm not inclined to let it stretch for months. Are you and Harry still planning to move to Tombstone at the end of the month?"

"We are."

"Would you be willing to prime things a bit? Drop my name? To Johnny and to the society ladies?"

She snorted. "Society ladies! That's a hoot."

"Well, Tombstone's upper crust, anyway."

Her mouth stretched into a grin. "Honey, I can talk you up plenty. Make that man wish you were by his side. And in his bed."

"Perfect."

Kitty eyed me for a minute. "You just going to wait in Tip Top for him?"

"He said he was sending me back to sell the business for him." Spite drifted through me. "I'd like to sell it for the first nickel offered. It'd serve him right."

"It isn't worth much, anyway. If it were, he wouldn't have chanced suggesting it. He likes money too much. He's banking on you being trapped there or it taking you a good long while to get rid of it."

"Maybe I'll just leave it." I sank back into the chair and let out a heavy breath.

"I'll pass word around. He has upstairs rooms, right? There ought to be somebody desperate to strike out on her own. You might not sell it to a saloonkeeper but market the place as a brothel and you might be surprised."

It was what I'd been hoping she'd suggest and I'd not had to push our friendship by asking the favor. "Sounds good."

"What's more, Johnny won't like it if word got out in Tombstone that he sold his nice 'respectable' business to a madam. You can always use that to your advantage, should you need."

"I like the way you think."

"A woman can't be too prepared." She set down her glass. Then her face lit. "Oh, even better! Sign agency to sell the place over to me, go pack up everything of value to take with you, and head back home to San Francisco."

I stared at her. "You have got to be joking!"

"I'm dead serious. In a month or so, I'll have Johnny all talked into coming to get you. Better it's his idea than you turning back up in Tombstone on your own."

A couple months in San Francisco would sure as hell be better than in Tip Top. I didn't see Rebecca having the same sway as she had the last time and I supposed I could tolerate Mama's fussing. As long as it was temporary. I glanced at Kitty. "And if he doesn't come?"

"Oh, he will," Kitty assured. "And when he does, you make sure you play it to your advantage. I'm guessing you have about six weeks to figure out how to do that."

Chapter Seventeen: Celia/Mattie

It wasn't really lying, just hiding the truth a bit.

June 1880 (one month after Josie's visit to Tombstone)
Tombstone

Mattie rubbed her jaw and headed down Fremont Street. Tombstone wasn't all that big and she reckoned she could find what she needed without too much fuss. At least she hoped so. She didn't want to be asking around, but if she didn't figure a way to fight this damn tooth pain, she was going to lose Wyatt. He already spent most of his time away from her.

Hell, it hurt to even kiss him and he'd grown tired of accomodating her.

One of the miners who brought in his canvas trousers for repairs had mentioned she ought to try laudanum for the pain. It was plain the whiskey wasn't enough anymore. Not unless she drank herself under the table.

She walked the five blocks to 6th Street and turned right.

In the half year they'd been in town, she'd stayed away from the Red-Light District but she figured it was the best bet for finding what she needed.

She'd stayed away from most places in town. All three of the Earp women had. Their canvas repair business kept fingers busy during the lighted hours and there weren't too many places for respectable women to go after dark. She reckoned she missed that most of all. They weren't society ladies, frequenting the fancy theatres, and they weren't the type who could visit saloons.

It was part of being respectable that she hadn't expected.

It was a dull life and sometimes it made her wonder why she'd wanted it so bad.

Disappointment flickered at the thought. There wasn't much in her life that had turned out the way she'd wanted. She reckoned loving a man was about the only thing she had to hold on to and she didn't aim to lose Wyatt over a damn tooth. If it took laudanum to fight the pain enough to make love again, so be it.

The sun baked down on her and she hadn't been able to abide the thought of covering up with a shawl. She hoped she didn't meet anyone who'd recognize her. But, then, she didn't know anybody so who would?

Still, she didn't work her way too far down the block. Just like the towns she'd whored in, the brothels off the main streets blended into the neighborhood and she headed for those. She chose a plain house, well maintained but not too fancy, and slipped into the side yard. At the rear door, she knocked. It was afternoon and she expected the women would be up by now, though not yet ready for the night's business. Late enough so they wouldn't be cranky at her interruption.

She knew the routine, much as she'd tried to forget it.

A woman in a plain housedress opened the door and raised her eyebrows. "You lost?"

"I know where I am."

The woman straightened, defensive. "Your husband, whoever he is, isn't here. We're not open yet."

Mattie laughed. "I'm not looking for a husband so settle your feathers. I need to buy some laudanum. Any advice?"

"You're direct."

She shrugged. "No sense beating around the bush."

"Most folks buy from the Orientals," the woman told her.

"Any one in particular? I don't want to run all over town asking." The fewer people who knew she was using liquid opium, the better. Wyatt hated the stuff.

"You want to step inside? I'll have to run and get Lorna. Or you want to wait outside where folks can see you?"

"I'll come in."

Mattie entered the kitchen and a sharp memory sliced through her. She could see it plain, her and Sarah all desperate, waiting in the kitchen back in Fort Scott, that picture-man fiddling her the day she sent Sarah home on the train, her spewing vomit all over her first john and how his reaction had learned her to pay attention and do what she had to do. Her eyes stung and she pinched off the thoughts.

It was just a brothel kitchen and she was shed of all that. The room was clean but not sparkling, the heart of the house when the girls weren't working or asleep. The woman left her standing and slipped up the backstairs, returning a few minutes later. A stout woman in a red dress followed. To Mattie's way of thinking, she looked like a trussed-up hen.

"You want laudanum, I hear. On the sly."

Mattie nodded. She'd thought about going to the druggist but she reckoned Wyatt would hear about it sure. He'd be mad and there was the chance of the druggist starting gossip. Folks tended to frown on opium, whatever form it took, and she didn't want to damage his chance of getting that deputy position Sheriff Shibell had been dangling.

"Just tell me where I can get it," she told the woman.

Lorna stared at her, intense. "Do I know you, honey?"

Mattie held her tongue. Best to leave things anonymous. "I don't think so."

"You're one of those Earp women."

"Doesn't matter who I am," Mattie finally said, neither denying nor admitting.

"No, I guess it don't." Lorna scratched her head. "Those men of yours are damn attractive."

Right there, that was part of the problem, too. The Earp men spent their time in saloons, right in the midst of women like this. Might be Wyatt had even been here. If she didn't get her pain under control, she'd lose him to one of them.

"You going to tell me what I was asking about? If not, I'll be on my way."

"Stop fussing. I'm not a threat. Curious is all. You got busy husbands, with their hands in everything. Whole town knows them but there's nary a word on the wives. Except for seeing you in the mercantile, no one knows a thing about you."

Lorna was fishing, that was for sure. Information was valuable in her world. Lord, Mattie knew *that.* Especially information about lawmen. "We're private. Busy."

Lorna's smile stretched. "And the menfolk like it that way, I'm sure. Quiet and out of their business."

Mattie gestured, her hands opening. "The laudanum?"

"What's it for?" Lorna pressed.

"Does it matter?"

"No, I guess it don't. But you answer a few questions and I'll set you up, save you from walking all over town."

"Why?"

"Because it seems a fair trade, information for what you want. I learn a little more about the intriguing Earp men. Satisfies my curiosity and it might come in handy for me to know it. Which one is yours?"

Mattie stiffened. "I reckon that's my business."

"You want the opium or not?"

Oh, she wanted it. Needed it. "Wyatt."

"That the marshal or the one who tends bar at Vogan's or the one that rides shotgun for Wells Fargo?"

Mattie's heart raced. She knew the game, had played it

herself. She reckoned too much information would put her in the madam's debt but if she wanted to ease the pain, she'd need to play.

"Wells Fargo."

Lorna grinned. "Ah! The handsome one."

"Are we done here? Did you learn what you wanted?"

"Almost. What do you want it for?"

"Toothache."

"Damn, that ain't too exciting. That don't scratch my itch much."

"It isn't an itch, Lorna. You're gaining leverage and we both know it. You got what you want?"

"You're a smart woman. It helps to have a bit of information. After all, if he does get appointed as deputy, it might come in handy to know a few secrets."

Mattie didn't figure how her having a toothache would be of value. Best that was all she revealed, though. "I think that's enough for today. How much do I owe you?"

Ignoring her sense of unease, Mattie drew out her pocket reticule and opened it.

August 1880 (two months later)

"Mattie? Mattie, wake up! Wyatt's on his way down the street."

Mattie forced her eyelids open and tried to focus. Was that Bessie at the door? She sighed and pulled herself to a sitting position. Whoever it had been was gone. What had she said? Somebody was coming?

Wyatt. Wyatt was on his way home.

Mattie rose and poured water into the basin, splashed it on her face, flinched as she touched her face.

Tarnation. How long had she been out? If Wyatt was coming, it must be late in the day. She didn't remember anything since morning.

She felt like she was moving in a fog.

The laudanum did that to her. Made her sleepy and forgetful. She tried not to use much but part of a tooth had fallen out this morning, a blackened chunk, and the gum was ungodly swollen where the rest of the tooth remained. She was going to have to get it pulled. Her mouth tasted like blood again and she knew the pain would return as soon as the laudanum wore off.

The door slammed out in the parlor.

Wyatt. Damn, she'd forgot Wyatt was coming home.

She tidied her hair and moved toward the door, fighting not to stagger. She couldn't let Wyatt see her this way.

She opened up the bedroom door and moved down the hallway. Was that Morg he was talking to? The younger brother had joined them a week or so back, taking on Wyatt's role as shotgun rider with Wells Fargo when Wyatt'd been hired on as temporary deputy. Morg had come alone, his new wife, Louisa, to follow once Morgan got established.

Mattie neared the front room, making out both Morg and Wyatt talking.

"You actually arrested Judge Reilly? That's a hoot. I bet he was fit to be tied, being arrested in his own courtroom."

What the hell? That wouldn't help Wyatt with getting the official appointment to the job.

"The man tried to throw me in jail for contempt just because I let Harry Jones out on his own recognizance instead of taking him all the way up to Tucson for one night in jail. Where's Mattie?"

"She was passed out in her room, last I saw her."

Mattie cringed and drew a sharp breath. Morg had a big mouth.

"Mattie!"

Time to face the music, she reckoned. "I'm here." Pulse racing, she rounded the corner. Morg took one look at her and left the room.

"You look like hell," Wyatt said, his voice full of accusation.

Mattie scrambled for an excuse. "I guess I had a little too much whiskey. The tooth came out."

"Quit playing games with me. Lorna tried to blackmail me today! On top of the shit day I was having already."

Hell. Mattie plopped into a chair. *Hell.*

"I can't have this right now. Do you know how much it cost me to pay her to keep quiet?"

"Who's gonna believe her?" The words slurred more than Mattie wanted.

"It doesn't matter who actually believes her. What matters is the gossip." He ran his hand through his russet-blond hair. "How long you been taking that stuff? How often?"

Mattie dropped her head. She'd been afraid of this happening. Every bottle she bought fraught her nerves tight. She shouldn't have trusted Lorna. She'd have been better to see a doctor.

"Jus' a few weeks, when the tooth is awful," she said. There was no way she was going to tell him she'd been going through a bottle a week. "I can't stand it otherwise."

"Opium is nothing to play with. I've seen it wrap around folks and suck them under."

She knew that right enough. It took more and more to get the same result. Or else it was the tooth itself. "I don't take it too much."

"You shouldn't take it at all."

Hot anger spurred her to her feet. "You seen my mouth, Wyatt? You even notice how bad it is? Look here!" She hooked a finger inside her mouth and stretched it open.

Of course, he hadn't noticed. He was never home.

"Good God, what a mess." He backed away from her. "It stinks, Mattie. You need to see Doc when he gets to town."

"If you'd kissed me lately, you mighta noticed."

"You haven't wanted to kiss me for months."

Tears sprang into her eyes, stinging as she tried to fight them. "It hurts, Wyatt. Especially when we play your games and you ain't so tender. It hurts like hell."

"We haven't played games since we got to Tombstone. You've been passed out when I get home and asleep all day to boot."

"Jus' since it got so bad."

"Damn it, why didn't you say anything?" His voice softened and for a minute, Mattie heard the old Wyatt. Lord, she'd missed that side of him.

The tears sprang up fresh.

"You make sure you stay put in the house instead of stumbling around town like this."

"You care more about who sees me than how much pain I'm in?"

"Of course, I care about the pain, Mattie. But you're not too sharp when you're like this. That politicking you've always been so worried about? Well, there's more politics in this damn town than I've ever seen. The McLaurys and the Clantons stealing mules, bar fights that should get prosecuted, murders with no convictions . . . far too many people getting off because of who they know. Add in the messed-up overlap of jurisdictions and it's a mess. Trying to navigate it is hard enough without people talking about my looped-up wife."

"I don't go nowhere."

"You go out to buy it. You stagger six blocks to do it."

"You think I don't know to go when I'm clearheaded? Why the hell do you think I bought from Lorna in the first place? I been tryin' to keep it hid. And doin' a fine job of it, too, since you ain't heard one bit until now and that come from the damn whore."

"No more, Mattie. If I hear one whiff of gossip about you, I'll tan your hide."

Mattie shook, anger more than fear. "You won't touch me and you know it."

"I swear, Mattie, you stay put until we get through the election. Shibell plans to appoint me officially in a couple months. Then, when he runs for Cochise County sheriff, he'll bring me along. That's ten percent of the taxes, split up between us. Do you know how wealthy this area is? We'll be rich, even with splitting it with Shibell. Don't you dare ruin that for us."

She sank back into the chair and buried her head in her hands, the dammed-up tears overflowing. "It jus' hurts. It hurts like hell."

Wyatt squatted in front of her, finally spent. His hand stroked her arm. "Doc Holliday will be setting up here next month. I want you in his office first thing."

"I don't want a mouth full of holes."

"You prefer a mouth full of black teeth and swollen gums while you wander around in a stupor?"

"I ain't doin' it on purpose."

"Then fix it. This isn't any way to live, fighting pain every day." He kissed her on the top of the head and rose to his feet.

"I've had enough, Mattie. If you don't fix this, I'll leave you."

Chapter Eighteen: Josephine/Sadie

A few white lies here and there never hurt a flea.

June 1880 (a month after her trip to visit Kitty)
San Francisco

"The mail came," Rebecca said, her voice full of taunting. "Nothing for you. Again."

I bit the retort off before it flew from my mouth. Things were not turning out as Kitty and I had anticipated and frustration baited me. Johnny'd written only once, cool and distant, and it grated on me that he'd not come for me yet.

My sister knew it and she milked it for all it was worth.

I shrugged as if it didn't matter.

"You'll be waiting forever. That man isn't coming for you and you know it."

"He'll come. He's just so busy with the new businesses in Tombstone. It made more sense for me to wait here, rather than in some boardinghouse there." I dredged up a smile. "He knew how much I was missing all of you."

"Oh, please, I'm not an idiot, Josie." She drew the name out, mocking.

As far as Mama was concerned, Johnny was a knight in shiny armor, one who'd rescued me when Markham dissolved the Pinafore troupe. Mama had been drawn in straightaway but Rebecca rolled her eyes at my tale of theatre adventure and Johnny's heroism. And she still didn't believe a bit of my story.

"Josie! Too grown up to be the Sadie you've always been."

"There's too much bad history with that name. I've put that behind me."

"You'll never put it behind you. Aaron and I keep digging into our pockets to rescue you and you keep running back to it. Good lord, do you know how hard it is to maintain your reputation when you do that? I had to talk the census taker into adding your name to the household so we could continue the story that you were on an extended trip. He didn't believe a bit of it."

"Then why bother?"

I was sure she thought it looked better to have me represented here than in Tip Top as a "courtesan," but I didn't much care. The barkeep had probably listed me in Tip Top, too, since I hadn't bothered to tell any of the staff I wasn't returning. The whole lot of them was likely damn surprised when the new owner turned them out on their asses.

I winced at how harsh my thoughts were. It happened far too often and I didn't much like it. Was it just the impatience waiting for Johnny or was I truly becoming that much of a shrew?

"You still think that rogue is going to make an honest woman of you?"

"Will you stop!" She thought she was so high and mighty just because she'd had the good fortune to marry. She and Aaron probably laughed at night about how we all had to live with them because Papa couldn't support his own family.

She shook her head and strode from the room.

I stuck my tongue out at her retreating back. Damn her for begrudging me my chance to seize the brass ring. I'd show her, I'd already had adventure and far more experience than Rebecca would ever have. And when Johnny sent for me, I'd go to Tombstone as one of the finest ladies in the town. And at night, I'd be as wanton as I wanted to be, shameless in the bed of my well-satisfied husband.

Luck . . . adventure . . . being a fine lady on John Behan's arm . . . I picked up Rebecca's favorite teacup and threw it at the wall.

It shattered like my dreams always seemed to do.

It was another month before Johnny sent word he was coming for me. An exasperatingly long month in which my bitterness brewed. I wanted to make him pay for making me wait so long, but my heart sang that he'd arrive today. I despised him for the delay, but my body craved his touch. My emotions were a damn pendulum.

I smoothed my sprigged lawn dress, straightening the demure bodice. It wasn't much to my taste, but it kept Mama and Rebecca off my back. I'd have donned a red corset underneath, just to tease Johnny, but it would have shown through.

Instead, I removed my drawers. That would get his juices going. And mine. When he arrived, I'd glide down the stairs to heighten his anticipation.

"Josephine?" Mama's voice broke into my reverie. "Mr. Behan is here."

I didn't even hear the knock. I *was* discombobulated. My heart pounded as I headed toward the stairway. I'd wanted to be in control and it flustered me further that I was so nervous.

It's just Johnny. You can manage Johnny. Except I felt like everything was topsy-turvy.

There he was, standing at the bottom, waiting like a gentleman. God, he looked good. I took a step, nearly stumbled, and drew a breath.

Stop it.

"Johnny!" In a snap, I abandoned the cool descent I'd planned and flew down the stairs and into his arms. "I missed you so!"

My father cleared his throat and Johnny gently set me back a step. A small smirk lingered just behind his polite smile. Same Johnny as always.

"I missed you, too, Josephine." My respectable name sounded foreign on his tongue.

"Shall we?" Mama said. "We should sit in the parlor, *ja*?"

I sighed. Could she sound any more Polish? But then, Johnny likely had no idea of the social striations between Germans and Poles. To him, she was a colorful immigrant, nothing more. I focused on slowing my heartbeat and followed the others into the parlor. Rebecca and Aaron had joined us, of course.

"Welcome back to our home, Mr. Behan." This time, Mama remembered to control her accent. "I am so glad we knew you were coming this time. So Mr. Marcuse could be here."

Johnny raised an eyebrow at the pronunciation but didn't comment on it. "I'm pleased you opened your home to me." He glanced at Rebecca and Aaron, a small dig at Rebecca for having thrown him out last time, but well-disguised.

"Your business is doing well?" Papa, direct, got to the heart of the matter. "You are ready to bring Josephine to Tombstone?"

"Perhaps we should have tea?" Rebecca jumped her feet.

We'd be here forever and my body hummed with lust for him. I glanced at Papa, pleading for him to quiet Rebecca's delaying tactics.

He caught my glance, caught the impatience within it. "Sit down, daughter. There is no need to fuss with tea."

"Papa . . ."

"Sit."

Rebecca plopped down, her mouth drawn into a pout.

"Excuse me," I interjected into the pause. "Mr. Behan is my guest and I would very much like at least a little time alone with him. We've not seen each other for months. Could we take a walk in the yard for a few moments and then talk together?"

My entire family stared at me as if I'd asked to have them

butcher a pig first. I tamped my rapid breathing, told my body to relax before it betrayed me.

"I don't know if that—"

Mama patted Papa's arm. "Oh, *ja,* we should let the lovebirds have a few minutes."

They stared at one another, then Papa nodded. "Just a few. Stay in the yard."

I lowered my head, shy, and reached for Johnny's hand. "This way." I pulled him toward the back door.

"They should stay in the front," Rebecca advised.

"Let them be." Mama beamed at us, overjoyed my Johnny had come at last.

My pulse racing, I led Johnny through the kitchen and out into the bright sun.

"Good God, Sadie. I feel like a schoolboy."

"How do you think I feel? Come on." Suddenly adventurous and carefree again, I skirted behind the shed, Johnny following. As soon as we were out of sight, I turned and pulled him into a kiss. My tongue darted into his mouth and he responded. Flush against him, my hands went to his chest, under his fancy vest. As close as I could get to his skin without tearing open his white shirt.

"Settle down, we haven't much time."

My heart pounded at how much I'd missed him, how much I craved him.

He cupped my butt with his hands and my leg crept upward, circling his, pulling him closer. He was *so* hard against me. I reached for him and he slid a hand under my skirt.

"You minx!" He ran his fingers across my bare skin, then dipped inside.

Wet already, I moved with him, my release coming nearly immediately. "Take me," I told him. I might not love Johnny but I loved what he did to me.

He loosened his button fly, lifted me, and plunged.

I circled him with my legs and rode him hard. It didn't take him long, either.

"Oh, God, I am going to be so happy to have you back with me."

It stung that it came down to the sex but I knew it was true. For both of us. "We're a pair, Johnny, you know that. A pair."

"Josephine? Johnny?" Mama's voice rang out. "It is time to come back in."

"Coming!" I fought a giggle at the unintentional double entendre. "Let me down."

He settled me on my feet and we hastened to right our clothing, slow our breathing. I led him from behind the building, knowing we were being watched, but lingered with a stroll as we returned. Enough to let our pulses ebb.

Mama beamed at us, none the wiser.

Once inside, we took our places in the parlor, but Johnny kept my hand in his.

"Now, to business," Papa prompted.

"Mr. Marcus, I'd like to ask for Josie's hand."

I let out a breath. Until that moment, I hadn't been sure if Kitty's plan would pan out in its entirety.

"Your business is solid? You can care for her?" Papa probed. "You will treat her well?"

"Yes."

At Papa's curt nod, Johnny turned to me and pulled out a small box from his jacket pocket. "Josie, will you marry me?" He opened the box to reveal a glittering diamond nestled in a cushion of black velvet.

I stared at the ring. *Finally.*

The resentment raised its head. *Months you made me wait. Months.* I opened my mouth. Shut it. Drew a breath.

"I don't know, Johnny. You took so long to come for me, how

can I be sure?"

Johnny's eyes clouded, then grew dark.

"Perhaps I should think about it."

July 1880 (two weeks later)
San Francisco

"Good lord, what *were* you thinking?" Kitty paced my sister's parlor. She'd arrived not long before, responding to my desperate telegram, dispatched less than an hour after Johnny'd marched out of the house in a blaze of fury. "It took me a week to undo the damage. The man was outraged."

"I know." I'd regretted my words the moment they poured out, but the damage had been done and he'd stormed away despite my attempt to recall them.

Kitty glared at me. "Wasn't having him propose the entire goal? Whatever got into you?"

"I was mad." The words sounded weak.

"Mad? He said you two mated like rabbits less than five minutes before you turned him away!"

"We did. And it was glorious, but I was still raw from him waiting so damn long in the first place. Do you have any idea how hard it was to live with Rebecca harping at me every day? I got catty with him. I didn't really mean to turn him down."

"Catty doesn't work well with Johnny. You ought to know that by now." She stared at me. "You still want to marry him?"

"Yes."

"Then I'm here to haul you back. He refused to come himself and have you turn him away again."

"I figured I'd pretty much lost any chance. Thank you."

"You need to know he's pretty much taking you back only because all the ladies in town keep asking about you. Johnny wants to be sheriff of the new county, once it's formed, and community support is important. Having the women on his side is to his benefit, providing they sway their husbands. Of a sudden, you've become a political asset instead of a threat."

"Thanks to you, no doubt." Kitty Jones did have her skills. "Who's the competition?"

"A few folks are talking about Wyatt Earp but nothing solid. He showed up in December with his brothers and their wives. Virgil is the new federal marshal. James is a bartender. Wyatt works several jobs; dealing faro, serving as deputy to Virgil when needed, and riding with Wells Fargo. The wives are making and repairing canvas tents."

"Enterprising family. That won't help matters any."

"I wouldn't worry. Johnny has friends in high places. You coming back with me or not?"

"I'll come." There'd been no doubt of it and we both knew it. I wanted the life Johnny was offering and I wanted him in my bed.

Kitty snorted at my feigned reluctance. "When your family gets back, introduce me as Ida Jones. I left 'Kitty' in Prescott. Harry thought it'd be better to shed the name with my old life, just in case. I'm here as Johnny's ambassador. Guess I'm coming up in the world."

We chatted, Kitty—Ida—catching me up on events in Tombstone. There was a new theatre being built and Clum had his new newspaper up and running. *The Epitaph,* he called it. Fitting for Tombstone. A group of rustlers had established itself and was plaguing the local ranchers. Within the hour, we heard the back door and my parents' chatter from the kitchen.

I rose and went to the back of the house. "We have a guest," I told them from the hallway.

Mama bustled out, brushing her skirts. "Who is here?"

"Ida Jones, from Tombstone. She's married to an attorney there."

"Mrs. Jones," Mama said as she led the way to the parlor, "what brings you all this long way?"

"I've come on behalf of Mr. Behan, as his ambassador, if you will."

Mama beamed at Kitty's words. "An ambassador. *Ach,* that is a fancy title."

"Mr. Behan sent me in hope that I can persuade Josephine to change her mind and accept his proposal. He wasn't sure it would be wise to come himself, given Josie's state of mind during his last visit."

"And you know my daughter?" The question hung for a moment.

Kitty smiled. "Josie and I became acquainted when she visited Tombstone. She's a fine young lady and all of us ladies have been looking so forward to having her among us. There are so few quality women. A good deal of upstanding common folk, mind you. But we'd welcome Josephine into the cream of the crop, so to say."

Kitty had found Mama's soft spot. Mama shone at the thought of me being among society's best.

"She should have never sent him away."

"Mama, you know I wasn't sure."

"*Ach,* you've been moping like a sick dog ever since. You should be thankful he is a persistent man."

Kitty patted my hand. "What do you think, Josie? Will you change your mind, come back to Tombstone with me to be wed?"

Mama's smile faltered. "She will not be wed here?"

"I'm afraid that won't be possible, Mrs. Marcus. Johnny can't leave the business. He'd hoped to marry Josie while he was here. Her refusal put a wrench in those plans."

"Oh, and I wanted a grand wedding for her."

Kitty shifted to Mama, took her hands, and leaned forward.

"I would most certainly be willing to take on the mother-of-the-bride role for you, Mrs. Marcus. I'll see to it we plan a wonderful wedding for her. I can take on all the organization and you can travel out for the ceremony itself."

"You would do that?" Tears glistened in Mama's eyes.

Kitty sat back, the matter settled. "It would be my honor. I'm collecting Miss Marietta Duarte while I'm here. She's betrothed to Peter Spencer, another of our finer citizens. Her parents have placed her under my charge."

"I think our Josephine should go with you," Mama said, as if none of us had yet thought of the idea.

"Mama . . ." I let the sentence die out. She would relish convincing me.

"*Ach,* you know this is what you've wanted."

I glanced in Kitty's direction. "And if I go, what happens when I get there?"

"Johnny is setting up a home for you. If he delays, you will stay with me and Mr. Jones. When I left, Johnny was looking at a house on Allen Street, just across from us."

"Oh, wouldn't that be fine?" Mama said. "Of course, she will go."

"You'll see, Josie. Everything will be as Johnny promised you."

A wave of doubt swept through me. I'd learned a long time ago that Johnny wasn't so good at keeping promises.

Mama turned to me. "You will have a handsome man who dotes on you, a fancy home, be among the most respected women in town. Finally, you will have everything we ever dreamed of."

"All right," I said.

Mama beamed. Ida looked triumphant. I wasn't quite so sure.

If John Behan reneged on me this time, I'd make him regret it.

August 1880
Outside Tombstone

Mercifully, the train had extended tracks all the way to Benson since my last trip to Tombstone. We'd taken the train from San Francisco to the end of the line. But I loathed stage travel and this last leg from the railroad to Tombstone had been full of nonstop dust, unbearable heat, and overall discomfort.

I loosened another button and pulled my bodice open further. I blew into the gap to dry the sweat dripping between my breasts.

Marietta—Maria—Duarte, Kitty's other charge, sniggered but her own bodice gaped just as widely. She rocked in the seat across from me, her Spanish heritage evident in her dark complexion and wide brown eyes. Like I'd done since a child, she disguised an accent and preferred an Americanized version of her foreign name, Marietta. I wasn't quite sure how Kitty (I just couldn't think of her as Ida) knew her, but suspected they'd worked together at one brothel or another.

I guess we were all coming up in the world, even if we were sweaty as pigs.

Glancing upward, toward the front of the coach, I asked about the Wells Fargo guard.

Marietta had ogled the man, chatting with him before he took his place next to the driver, but had said little. We'd been sharing Marietta's lemon drops and had been lulled into silence these last miles. Now, my thoughts returned to the attractive guard. He looked familiar but I couldn't place having met him before.

Marietta leaned closer, bouncing with the sway of the vehicle. "Morgan Earp. New to town, younger brother of Wyatt, who was appointed as the deputy sheriff a couple days ago. He took on Wyatt's duties guarding for Wells Fargo."

Deputy sheriff? What the hell? My stomach dropped. "Wyatt, is he the one you mentioned?" I asked Kitty.

"He is, but deputy sheriff is something new," Kitty chimed in. "I bet Johnny's stewing."

Oh, he'd be stewing all right. And he'd be boiling over onto me.

Kitty glanced at Marietta. "What else did Morgan say? You milked him for information long enough to get the whole story, I'm sure."

We hit a bump and our shoulders banged against one another.

Marietta grabbed at her seat. "Don't I always?" She grinned as if savoring the moment of knowing more than we did.

"Out with it," I prodded.

Marietta sat back and drew a breath. "According to Morgan, Shibell decided he needed a deputy to handle this part of the county while Shibell is in Tucson. Johnny balked at taking the new slot, said his plate is too full, tried to push Shibell into waiting until fall. Shibell wouldn't wait."

"Damn." I looked at Kitty, trying to sort it out. "So what happens when the new county is formed? Will Earp get the sheriff appointment then? Oh, Johnny's going to be a bear to deal with!"

Kitty shrugged. "As far as I knew when I came to fetch you, Shibell promised the Cochise County sheriff position to Johnny, once they carve Cochise County out of Pima County early next year. Whoever is the Pima County Sheriff then will appoint law officers for the new county. Since it's certain Shibell will get elected again, it'll be his decision."

"But if it turns out Shibell likes this Earp fellow . . ." I let the words trail off, not wanting to think about it. Johnny wanted the appointment and he wanted it bad. He'd said he'd make money hand over fist. Not from the salary, of course, but from the ten percent of the taxes and fees he would collect. The mining success would make it a lucrative position indeed.

"Oh, I wouldn't worry your pretty little head about it. Shibell likes Johnny and he'll have to pick someone the legislature will approve and Johnny's got the connections to assure it."

I knew Johnny had the influence. He had served in the legislature himself and still had friends there, including his business partner Dunbar. Johnny would already be lobbying hard.

I hated politics and I was barely part of it. "You said in San Francisco you have Johnny convinced he needs me to sway the townswomen?"

"Public appearances! All the connections in the world won't matter if he can't maintain his image of an upright family man. The divorce up in Prescott did him a lot of damage and he won't risk that again. I reminded him how much the women liked you when you visited."

"Josephine Marcus *was* quite a hit."

"And she will continue to be as long as no one connects her to Sadie Mansfield, the woman at the root of his divorce to Victoria. If anyone so much as breathes a word of your history, it could ruin everything for him. As long as he remains respectable, he'll be appointed with no problem, Deputy Earp or no Deputy Earp. Johnny's got the whole town eating out of his hand. He does that well, winning folks over."

I pinched my brow. "Yeah, Johnny bullshits well. But the politics of it seems complicated."

"That's why I don't care a whit about politics," Marietta said. She passed more lemon drops around and popped one into her own mouth.

Tired of them myself, I pointed to the front of the stage again. "That Morgan Earp . . . he's a looker."

Both ladies laughed.

"They all are, the Earps," Kitty said. "The whole lot of them are handsome. Each a bit different, but all hard to tear your eyes away from."

The stage gave another lurch as we rounded a bend and all three of us slid to one side, giggling. Marietta's lemon drop popped out of her mouth and clattered around the floor. Then the vehicle slowed.

"Thank God," Kitty said. "I hate this ride."

I nodded and assembled my things. Moments later, the door opened and Morgan Earp stood there with a cheeky grin on his face. "Ladies?" he said. "I'm at your service." He handed each one of us down. Not only handsome but charming.

I wondered if the deputy sheriff was as engaging but didn't have time to linger on the thought.

Johnny stepped forward, drawing me into his arms. "Josie, I'm so glad you're here." He kissed me, more chastely than he normally did but deeply enough to start the crowd cheering.

I pulled away, put a hand over my mouth. "John!"

There were a few titters. Enough to tell me the ruse worked. I let my eyes wander over the crowd. At the edge, a tall, slender man grinned. The tin star on his chest told me who he was, that and his resemblance to Morgan.

Oh, my!

My heart pattered as our gazes met. The man I'd seen in the Grand Hotel in May. Just as charming as his brother for sure. And even more attractive.

Johnny was going to have his plate full. A town full of brothers, all involved in some facet of law or saloon business. And likely all just as appealing. Everyone in town would know the Earp name.

I peeled my gaze away and took Johnny's arm.

I hoped like hell Wyatt Earp was not going to come up as an

alternative candidate for sheriff of the new county or we'd all be in a fine mess.

Chapter Nineteen: Celia/Mattie

It was all appearances; not really lies.

September 1880 (a few weeks after the argument with Wyatt)
Tombstone

Mattie headed down the street, looking for Doc's sign. She reckoned the time had come. She couldn't keep on in the fog she was in most of the time—even with rationing the occasional bottles Wyatt had allowed her until Doc arrived. She'd lose him if she didn't get the tooth attended to. She'd need to have Doc look in her mouth and do what he had to do.

Resentment stabbed at her, making things worse. For all Wyatt had sounded off about not wanting her to draw attention by stumbling around town, he didn't seem to worry none about coming under scrutiny for his own behavior. His friend Bob Paul was running against Shibell for sheriff and both candidates had pledged they'd support Wyatt's appointment when the new county was formed. But now that Doc had arrived, Wyatt had been finding trouble. The latest was getting involved in an argument between Doc and Milt Joyce, the owner of the Oriental Saloon. Now Joyce was mad at the Earps and ready to shut down Wyatt's gambling concession at the Oriental. Folks were talking about it all over town and it made her plumb mad how Wyatt kept harping on her about damaging his reputation. He barked at her all the time, it seemed.

But, then, Wyatt never did look at his own self too much and it didn't much matter to him what she thought of it.

Anger set her jaw tight and Mattie winced at the sharp pain. *Tarnation.* Damn Allie for taking away her laudanum.

Mattie hadn't figured she was that dependent on the stuff. The nausea and shakes and cold sweats had been awful. Today, she felt weak and peevish and she figured the worst of it was over. She was sober so there was no sense putting off the appointment any longer. Her mouth hurt like hell.

There it was, *Doc Holliday, Dentist.* She opened the door and made her way up the narrow stairs. She didn't want to do this. Not at all.

It wasn't pulling the tooth that ate at her but the thought of a hole in her mouth and how her face would sink in where the tooth was gone like some old granny. Or a used-up whore.

At the top of the stairs, she pushed open the door and stepped in.

"Well, look who the cat dragged in," Doc said.

It never failed to surprise her how he always seemed so chipper. "You that happy to see me or just pleased you might get to pull teeth?"

"Both, maybe. Come on in and let me have a look." He gestured toward the chair in the center of the room. "Have a seat. Wyatt says you're suffering."

"My teeth are rotten. Have been for years, I expect." She eyed the chair. It was fancy-looking with brown velvet upholstery and tassels hanging off the bottom like a parlor chair. She wasn't too sure about the odd-shaped foot rest, though, or putting the back of her head against the floppy thing up above.

"It won't bite you."

She climbed into the chair and was surprised when it laid out near flat right underneath her.

"Open up and let me take a look." Doc turned his head, coughed to the side, and peered into her mouth. He tilted his head and opened her mouth wider. Then he backed away. "They aren't good, you're right about that. You got two more abscesses perking and it looks like a few teeth I might be able to save. I'll have to drill out the rotten areas and fill the holes with gold foil or amalgam."

Mattie's pulse raced and she sat straight up. "Drill out? Won't that hurt?"

Doc offered up what passed as a sympathetic smile. "I can give you nitrous oxide to help."

"Night-what?"

"Nitrous oxide. It's a gas you can breathe in so you feel less pain."

"But you still have to drill?" The thought of it made her sick . . . a drill poking into her.

"If you want the cavities filled. Or, we leave them and they get worse. Right now, we'd best pull those two bad ones. Up to you on the other three. Drill and fill or wait until they rot and pull them."

An even bigger sinkhole. She pinched her eyes shut, then glanced at Doc. "You're going to pull two teeth?"

"They're bad, Mattie. They'll pain you something fierce while they rot through. Just like the one you had problems with a few weeks back. There's still a little chunk of that one in there. You want to live with that every day?"

"No."

"Then let me treat you."

"Then I won't have no more problems?"

Doc sighed. "Your gums are bad, your teeth are bad. I can slow things down, but you're always going to have problems."

"I'm not even that old." But she knew that wasn't true. The life she had lived had aged her. She reckoned all that whiskey she'd downed to keep herself numb while she laid under all those men hadn't helped any.

"You clean your teeth regularly? With a toothbrush and baking soda? Or paste . . . they make cleaning paste for teeth now."

"I used to rinse my mouth, when I was a kid. Just get it over with," she told him. "Whatever you got to do. Else I'm going to be drinking my way to a grave."

"Alcohol isn't all bad. Helps clean your mouth."

"It's the laudanum I was referring to."

"I'll do what I can, Mattie."

He leaned her back, shifted some strange looking machines into place, and put a mask over her face. Seconds later, she relaxed.

Too bad a body couldn't have that stuff every day. Maybe what was going on between her and Wyatt wouldn't hurt so damn bad.

At least she'd be able to stop takin' the laudanum and get him back.

October 27, 1880 (two months later)

Mattie was fed up and the temptation of doing something fun was more than she could resist. Tonight, she and the other Earp women were having a night on the town. Except for the visit to Doc, she'd been cooped up in the house for close to two months and she was sick of it. Sick and tired and more than a little peeved at Wyatt. Now a permanent deputy sheriff, he was seldom home, with Sheriff Shibell saying he was looking for Wyatt to prove himself these next few months.

The reconciliation Mattie'd hoped for hadn't come.

Despite her quitting the laudanum and sacrificing teeth.

All three of them were tired of being homebodies, Mattie and Bessie especially. Jim was always at Vogan's tending bar and Wyatt just plain never came home. Virge was more attentive, but then he and Allie didn't have the sort of past the other four did. They'd planned the night out for days, ever since they'd got wind of the open rehearsal for the upcoming recital. The Presbyterian Church wasn't the Tombstone Social Club, but that was just fine. So far, no one even seemed to notice them. Besides, them being at church wouldn't mess up Wyatt getting appointed as sheriff when the new county was formed.

Mattie shifted in the pew. She hadn't been in a church since running off with the circus back in Iowa all them years ago. A pang of longing surfaced, then faded.

Up front, the Peake Sisters finished their last song, "Amazing Grace," and the whole collection of folks clapped, then started shuffling out. Mattie sat still, thinking how the night had stirred something inside her, filled up her soul a bit. She'd missed this without even knowing.

"You ready?" Allie asked.

"Sorry. Just recollecting."

"I did that, too. A long time past but good memories all the same." Bessie patted Mattie's shoulder. "Good to recall them again."

Mattie nodded and gained her feet. Her teeth had felt better since the visit to Doc. Well, at least since the *recovery* from the visit to Doc. She had a few holes in her mouth but hadn't had need for laudanum for near on a month.

"You two feel like a stop for a whiskey?" Bessie asked.

Mattie's stomach tumbled at the thought. If Wyatt caught her in a bar, she figured they'd be done for. "It's nine at night. We'd best scoot on home before Wyatt or Virge stumbles on us during their rounds."

"They don't make rounds 'til later. This time of night Virge is holed up in his office unless there's trouble, and Wyatt's likely playing cards somewhere. I'd guess Morg is half drunk." Bessie looked eager. But then, she didn't have near so much at stake.

"I don't know, Bessie," Allie said.

"Let's treat ourselves to something to eat, at least. What about the Melrose Restaurant? Or the Palace Chophouse? We could get a drink with our meal at the Palace."

Mattie's mouth watered. She hadn't had a drink for a long time. "I guess as long as it's not a saloon . . ."

Bessie strode out of the church and toward the business district, Allie and Mattie on her heels. Mattie pushed the worry from her mind. It'd be all right. As long as they picked a respectable place and stayed in the dining room.

They navigated side streets, avoiding busier routes where they'd be most likely to encounter any of the Earp brothers. A half block off the busy Allen Street, the Palace dining room wasn't too crowded.

Mattie blew out a breath and told herself things would be just fine.

Despite the Palace's reputation for serving meals at all hours, it took a long time to get waited on and even longer for the food to come. By then, they'd all had a couple whiskeys. Mattie reckoned it was their due. By 11:30, they figured it was time to head home.

The street was busy now and Mattie shrank close to the building. "Let's keep to the shadows. There's lots of folks out."

Bessie waved her off. "They're all drunk. They won't notice us."

"Still, Wyatt'll have a fit if someone sees us."

"You worry too much about Wyatt," Allie said. The last drink had loosened her up.

Mattie stood, unsure, then said, "Wyatt's already visiting brothels. Heard that the last time I bought laudanum."

"A body can't keep Wyatt from straying. It's in his nature."

Bessie's words were true enough, but it didn't make knowing any more tolerable.

They hadn't taken but a handful of steps when shots rang

out. At the second shot, a shiver ran up Mattie's spine.

"What the hell is that all about?" Bessie strode away toward Allen Street, leaving Allie and Mattie behind.

"Two shots means the law's gonna be called." Allie's gaze followed Bessie.

Mattie stalled. "It doesn't concern us. Let's go home. It's just shooting. Most likely the Cowboys are shooting up the saloons again."

"Our men could be in the middle of whatever's going on," Allie said and marched away.

Mattie's gut lurched. What if Allie was right? She dashed toward the gathering crowd, catching up to Bessie and Allie. They rounded the corner and clustered under an overhang. In the street, Curly Bill Brocious was firing his pistol at the sky, falling-down drunk. Several other men stood around him, encouraging him.

"You were right," Allie whispered. "Just the Cowboys shooting up the town."

City Marshal Fred White strode into the street, headed toward Curly Bill. "I'm an officer. Give me your pistol!"

Wyatt ran down the street along with Morgan and another man. Mattie's heart near stalled. Where was Wyatt's gun?

White was tussling with Curly Bill, trying to grab at his gun. "You goddamn son of a bitch, give up that pistol." The man with Wyatt handed him a gun and Wyatt launched into the fray, grabbed at Curly Bill. A shot sounded, white-hot light flashed, and White shrieked. He crumpled to the ground, his trousers on fire from the close shot. Wyatt slammed the pistol against Curly Bill's head and the Cowboy landed on the ground next to White.

Mattie launched forward, while Wyatt yelled something about Curly Bill having a date with a noose.

An instant later, she was pulled back into the shadow by Allie. "It's all done. Let's get home. If he hasn't seen us yet, he soon will."

November 12, 1880 (about two weeks later)

Mattie plunged her hands into the sink and scoured hard at the cast-iron pan. If only she could scrub away Wyatt's recklessness. If he kept up with his snap reactions, he was going to mess up all the progress he'd made toward becoming a lawman like they'd planned.

The Earp women had staked their future on that plan and she'd be damned if she'd let Wyatt toss it away. Sewing tents wouldn't provide earnings forever, not with more and more permanent buildings going up.

Two weeks of nothing but trouble, first about Fred White's killing, then the election. Wyatt had been a loose cannon through it all. When White died, there was a big fuss with some saying Wyatt's grab for Curly Bill's gun had forced him into firing it. Sheriff Shibell had words with Wyatt. It'd taken two days for her to calm Wyatt down. Then, damned if Wyatt had up and quit his job when Shibell won the election.

The next day, he'd gone one step further, one that was going to cause more problems.

Water sloshed from the sink and Mattie stilled her hands. She had to think on it instead of getting so upset. It was up to her to help Wyatt find his way out of the mess. Wyatt sure didn't think anything through on his own.

She figured he could've fixed things up with Shibell if he hadn't started shooting his mouth off that Shibell had rigged the election. Sure, Wyatt's friend Bob Paul had lost to him and it might be there was fraud like Bob was saying, but Wyatt taking Bob's side was only pulling Wyatt in deeper. He ought to stay out of it, let Bob challenge the election if he wanted. If he stayed on both men's good sides, he'd be able to walk a line down the middle and get appointed whatever the final outcome.

Thank goodness Virge was holding tight to the family goal of law-keeping. Already a federal marshal, Wyatt's brother had been appointed to fill the town marshal position, too. Today's special election would confirm the appointment. Tomorrow, Virge would hire Wyatt as his town deputy and Wyatt would finally quit stewing about it all.

Mattie sighed and dried the pan. She just couldn't get Wyatt to wrap his damn head around the fact that it was better to work up plans before a body went off half-cocked. You'd think he would have learned by now.

The front door slammed. "Goddamn it all," Wyatt shouted.

Mattie's stomach knotted. *What now?*

She tossed the dishcloth on the table and went into the front room.

"It's all coming apart," Wyatt said, sinking into a chair. "Virge lost the special election."

Her mouth gaped open. "He lost?" They'd thought Virgil would be a shoe-in.

"By fifty votes."

"That other fellow has no experience."

"Could be somebody rigged that election, too."

"Maybe you ought not to have resigned." The words spilled out and Mattie winced. But they were out and she might as well keep on with what was on her mind. "It just seems to me that it might have been better to stay on the job. Now Shibell's mad at you and Behan's got an inroad."

Wyatt glared at her. "Quit harping, Mattie. Shibell was mad when I fired off about him."

"Maybe you should have thought twice afore you did that, too."

"Well, I couldn't keep on serving under Shibell when I called him a cheat. Half the town heard me and everyone knows I support Bob. Hell, we're good friends and it's clear as day Shibell is cheating him. Bob will win in the end and I'll have the job back."

"Half the town didn't need to hear it. You could have supported Bob without saying all that about Shibell. You act without thinking whenever you get mad. You need to slow down."

"I'm handling it!"

"How are you handling it?" She took the chair next to him. "Seems to me you keep announcing one crisis after another instead of making plans."

"It'll be fine. Quit harping on it." He sank his head into his hands. "I'm just frustrated. If Virge had won, we'd be looking at having the entirety of Tombstone's law in Earp hands. Federal, county, town, all of it. Just like we talked about on the way out here."

"If Virge had won, you'd have two offices in Earp hands. The county position went up in smoke when you resigned in a fit of temper and now John Behan has Shibell's support."

"As soon as Bob wins the challenge and finally gets named sheriff, I'll have the job back. Bob'll appoint me as Cochise County sheriff in February, as soon as the new county is formed."

"And you're dead sure that's going to happen? What if Bob Paul doesn't win?"

Wyatt jerked his head back up.

Mattie caught his gaze. "Allie says them Cowboys are wrapped up in the fraud. They hate you with a passion, all of you. You testified against Curly Bill and Virge went after the bunch of 'em for stealing them Army mules. Shibell's in thick with them and has friends in high places."

"Bob will win out."

"You need to be thinking on all the possibilities, Wyatt. Not just what you want to happen or what's right. If you don't think on it, you could end up the odd man out."

"Don't you think I know that?"

"You aren't acting like you know it. You're acting like you're not thinking at all."

"I am thinking. Me and Behan together. We've talked all about it."

"That squirrelly little varmint?"

"I like him, Mattie. He's been nothing but decent and friendly, even if he supports Shibell. We worked out a deal."

"He's oily. You don't see it but it's plain as day to me. He's got the soul of a politician and you aren't good at politics."

"It'll be fine. I trust him."

Mattie's skin went cold. "What kind of deal, Wyatt?"

"If I drop my run for Cochise County sheriff and defer to him, he'll appoint me as undersheriff, just as soon as he gets in."

Mattie stared at him.

Had he lost his mind?

Chapter Twenty: Josephine/Sadie

Politics and lies, one was just like the other.

November 1, 1880 (the day before election day)
Tombstone

I slammed my tortoiseshell hairbrush on the dresser and shoved a pin into my hair. I was going to have to talk to Johnny about the wedding again. It had been three months since I arrived in Tombstone and Johnny was still stalling.

I wasn't going to stand for it much longer. Until he actually married me, I was no more secure than I'd been in Tip Top. I'd need to drop a few hints to the ladies at the election rally today and Johnny'd be mad as hell at me.

It was my own damn fault for not insisting on getting married right away, but the wily bastard had tied my hands by spreading it around that we'd married quietly in San Francisco. I'd had little choice but to move in or set tongues wagging. I countered by letting everyone know there was a large ceremony planned since we'd had only a civil service.

But months later, there was still no ceremony looming. I picked up a bottle of toilet water, spritzed it, and threw it against the wall.

"What the hell?" Johnny yelled from the parlor.

I drew a breath, let it out, drew another. All I had to do was get through tomorrow's election. Johnny would be less on edge and I'd be able to pin down a wedding date with him.

He poked his head into the room, raised his eyes at the broken bottle. "Drop something?"

"Yeah, way over there against the wall." The words were catty. No sense trying to hide my frustration.

"You about ready?" Spite fueled his tone as well. Ever the happy couple.

"Will you relax? We have plenty of time. You'll make more of an impact arriving 'just on time' than you will waiting for everyone."

"It's not an afternoon social, Josie. It's a political rally. Let's go. I sent Albert on ahead."

I'd had no idea that Johnny's son was going to be living with us until I stepped off the stage and there he was, waiting to greet me. It wasn't that I disliked the boy. Now eight and the spitting image of his handsome father, he was a quiet boy in his deafness. A good kid when it came down to it, and he was chipping away at my heart, but I'd not planned on being an instant mother and it'd taken me a bit to adjust. Johnny, of course, was beyond delighted to have a live-in caretaker.

"You're such a family man," I snapped.

"Stop it, Josie. I've had enough of your tongue." He guided me out the bedroom door.

"Maybe you should take better care of me, then."

"You don't want for a thing and you know it."

Except his attention. He came home after tending bar, usually in the wee hours of the morning, and rolled into bed. On the nights he did come home early, he did nothing but grumble. His mood grew more ever more sour as the election neared.

Much like mine.

We left the house in silence.

"Look," he finally said, "just be on your best today. The rally is important. Help turn this election and you'll have the big house you've been whining about."

I slowed my step. A bigger house would be nice. The three of us were cramped here.

"Is Shibell's election in danger?" I asked. Johnny's appointment as sheriff of the new county depended upon Shibell being in office to put his name forward.

"No, he should win. Couple of the Clanton gang are serving as election officials out in the Charleston precinct. Here in town, we still have folks to finesse. This rally, and your efforts there, are important. The businessmen will support the party ticket, but the other folks, they're back and forth, some falling for whomever Earp backs."

I pictured the handsome deputy. Good thing women didn't vote or racing pulses would get him elected. A small knot formed in my stomach. Shibell had already appointed Earp over Johnny once.

"How do you know Shibell won't renege on his promise and choose Wyatt again?"

Johnny's smile became smug. "Too much has happened, with Wyatt showing himself for Paul. Shibell feels betrayed. And Wyatt won't be a problem. He won't even try to get the appointment. I've laid contingency plans."

"Oh?"

"Wyatt's likable, a bit gullible, and totally naïve of politicking. I've been working on him for months. We've got a deal. He doesn't like administrative duties, prefers to be on the street. Should Shibell break his promise, Wyatt will refuse and defer to me. In return, I'll appoint him as deputy. I told him we'd split the income. Not evenly, of course, but he'll get a share. And, he'll be the one handling arrests and public problems. I won't even have to get my hands messy."

I bristled again. "I don't like you offering him a share of your percentage."

"It's worth it. Town's been a mess. Might as well let Wyatt

deal with the trouble. It's already gained him plenty of enemies. A lot of the businessmen that buy the rustled beef from the Clanton gang have had their fill of the Earp lawmen coming down on the Cowboys. I just wish Wyatt wasn't so vocal in his support for Shibell's competition."

"The whole town knows he supports Bob Paul. They're friends."

"But here's the issue. The townsfolk who love law and order follow the Earps like sheep. They'll vote for Bob Paul because the Earps support him."

"And the rally today will somehow change that?"

"It's a formal event, with voters bringing their wives. Women could be key. They admire you. You've charmed them, Josie. Your presence at the rally demonstrates support for Shibell. In the end, all those admiring women will go home and speak their minds to their husbands. Respectable family folk support Shibell, they'll say. They'll point out that it was Shibell who appointed Earp to keep the law and Earp isn't even supporting his boss. That's what I need you to tell the women today."

I sighed. So much for spending the afternoon spreading "news" about wedding plans.

Still, worry clenched. "And if Wyatt's playing you like you're playing him?"

"He isn't. He isn't smart enough. We're almost there. Pull out your charm and put on a smile. Everything will work out perfectly for all of us."

We rounded the corner and waved as we approached the last rally of the election. I doubted this was going to be as easy as he anticipated.

Nothing ever was when it came to Johnny.

★ ★ ★ ★ ★

December 1880 (a month after the election)
Tombstone

The mercantile was busy but that didn't stop the whole kit and caboodle of the women inside from clamming up in unison when I entered.

The snub hit me like a slap.

How dare they!

But I knew how they dared. The little plan to sway the election had backfired when Bob Paul contested the results and accused precinct officials of coercing registered voters to change votes and certifying nearly nine times more votes than there should have been.

I wasn't sure if they'd come up with the idea themselves, or if it all came from Shibell. I didn't want to think about how deeply Johnny might be involved.

But the rumors were flying and I was no longer welcome, being Johnny's "wife" and all.

The dumb son of a bitch.

I hadn't felt this way since I'd quit whoring.

I raised my gaze and met their hostility head-on. "Hello, ladies. Gossiping, are we?" I glanced around, spied two of the Earp women—I wasn't sure which of them.

"Mrs. Earp and Mrs. Earp! How's Wyatt these days? Has he found a new job?"

"You ain't worried about it none so quit pretending," one of them said. Allie?

"John and Wyatt were friends, I hope they still are. I was concerned when Wyatt resigned. He was a good deputy and I don't want John to lose his friendship."

"Wyatt's doing just fine," the other said. Wyatt's wife, I figured.

"I'm sorry he felt he had to resign."

"Could hardly stay on when he's in the thick of the recall fight. Wouldn't be right when he's all but accused his boss of election fraud."

"He's an honorable man. I'm sorry he felt caught in the middle." The words were difficult but I spit them out all the same, and with a smile on my face.

"And how's Mr. Behan enjoying being appointed in his place?" It was the first one again. She liked to needle, that one.

I held my smile steady. "John takes the position seriously. He's been a lawman before so he's aware of all it entails."

"Yep, up in Prescott, I believe. Ain't that where the two of you met?"

I leveled my gaze on her, tired of the taunting. "We met at Lucky Baldwin's theatre in San Francisco."

"I could've sworn I heard you was in business in Prescott. Tip Top, too."

In business. Josie's neck heated. It was just another term for whoring and she was sure the she-devil knew it. "I'm sure you're mistaken. I never lived there. I did travel to Tip Top to close up Johnny's business there. Perhaps that's what you're thinking of."

The first one tipped her head. "Seems like there was more to it."

"Well, you know how gossip feeds on lies." This time, a hint of derision crept into my voice.

"Oh, I know all about lies. Lots of folks lie."

"Perhaps," I said, and shifted to turn away. "At any rate, do give our best to Wyatt. I hope his mining ventures are going well, now that he has more time for them."

"They are doing just fine and—"

"Allie," the other woman interrupted, "let's be getting on home. Missus Behan doesn't need to hear our business."

"Sorry, Mattie."

Allie gave a nasty smile and slipped out the door. The other one, Mattie, shrugged and followed. That one *was* Wyatt's wife—I recognized her name. The other was married to Virgil. The elections hadn't gone well for him, either. He'd lost his bid for city marshal.

Allie and Mattie knew a whole lot more of my past than anyone here needed to know.

They'd damn well better keep their mouths shut.

The Earp woman's chirping stayed with me all day, fueling my anger. I paced the house, waiting for Johnny to get home. He'd been gone for days, on some sort of official business, but I'd seen his horse in front of the sheriff's office on my way home.

I had a bone to pick with him. It was long past time we were married properly. There were too many rumors circulating about my past and that gossip would fuel itself into an inferno without notice. Once it did, Johnny would never marry me and I'd lose all the security I worked so hard to win. He'd commit to a date and he'd commit today.

"You're wearing a hole in the floor," Albert said from his place in the parlor. He sat with a schoolbook on his lap, his face drawn into a frown. School was difficult for him. Even sitting in the front with the primary students, he had a difficult time hearing the teacher.

I crossed, kissed the top of his head, and mouthed, "Sorry."

Albert gave me a small smile. Poor kid had a tough time of it.

The door squeaked open and Johnny entered, slamming the door behind him.

Hellfire. That didn't bode well for me.

Albert took one look at him and scuttled into his room.

"What now?" I asked.

"Damn Earp brothers. I think the Earps tried to tip off Ike

Clanton about the subpoena I was serving on him. They just keep stirring things up."

Johnny's news was confusing. "The Earps don't even like the Clantons."

"No, but Ike not testifying would mess up the voter fraud case. The election would be overturned, and Bob Paul would appoint Wyatt as sheriff."

And there it was, the heart of the matter. "I thought you had an arrangement with Wyatt."

"I don't think it's in play anymore. In any case, I delivered the damn thing and Ike has to testify."

"So what are you so all-fired upset about?" These days, it was one problem after another. I wasn't even sure I cared about Johnny anymore, but the lure of the wealth and prestige remained strong.

Johnny glanced at me as if I was daft. "I'm upset that the Earps stuck their noses into it. Ike says they've been threatening him."

"Have they?"

His shoulders dropped. "Hell, I don't know. It's about as big a mess as it can be. Wyatt's horse got stolen a while back and now he says somebody saw the horse over in Charleston. He claims he and Doc Holliday rode out there to get it and Billy Clanton tried to make off with it and they telegraphed Virgil to bring the ownership records. Instead of anyone coming to me, as county deputy, Virgil sent a posse to arrest Clanton for horse theft. Only then did they turn it all over to my office to deal with. Ike claims the Earps are trying to force him to into lying about the election. If Ike admits there was election fraud, Earp will drop the horse theft charge against Billy." Johnny paused, took a breath. "And, there's word Wyatt offered to testify that Curly Bill Brocius didn't murder Marshal White back in October, that the gun went off accidentally, just like Curly Bill claims. But only if Ike and Ringo confess they rigged the voting."

It was so complicated it made my head ache. "Why would Ike and Ringo confess to that? They'll be arrested for fraud."

"Hell, they likely won't even serve time." Johnny sank his head into his hands. "What's more, if Wyatt testifies that Curly Bill didn't kill White on purpose, he'll go free instead of the sure hanging he's headed for."

I sorted through it again. A web of charges and trial testimony that all came back to the election. My pulse pounded. All our plans gone. "Bob Paul would be certified as sheriff instead of Shibell?"

"If Ike and Ringo get pressured into lying."

I remembered Johnny's assurance that Shibell had the election *all taken care of.* "Lying or telling the truth?"

"What the hell, Josie! I wasn't there. I don't know what the truth is."

I stared at him. "Are you neck deep in this mess?"

"Of course not." He flashed me a hard glance, then stood and walked away from me. "Nothing links it to me. I just have to deal with the shit. And the Earps meddling in it might throw the whole election."

"John Behan, I know you." There might not be proof, but Johnny'd had his hand in it. I'd bet my life on it.

Oh, Johnny, what did you do?

"I'm just trying to do my job. The damn rumors and interference are driving me mad. That's all."

I held my tongue. He'd spent his anger and my probing further would only stir it up again. The last thing I needed was to push him into defending himself. I might bet my life on his involvement but not my future.

And I wouldn't get it if I turned on him. "You shouldn't be facing all this on your own, Johnny. Let me help you."

"I didn't think you believed me."

I steadied myself. "If you say you had nothing to do with it, you had nothing to do with it." I crossed to him and put my hand on his face, drawing his gaze to mine. "But you're losing sight of the entire picture, Johnny. You need to settle down. Let things play out without anyone seeing you've taken sides."

"Everybody knows I support Shibell." Johnny's eyes darkened. "I'm not turning on him and throwing to Paul!"

The whole town viewed him as part of this mess. It was time to turn public opinion around . . . on several fronts. I caught his hand and led him into the parlor, giving myself enough time to cast a plan. If I played it well, I could save his appointment and prod him into marriage at the same time. I pushed him gently into a chair, then sat down across from him, my strategy forming a step at a time.

"Rumors are flying, Johnny, and they have to be nipped before they get out of control."

"What have you heard? That I'm part of the fraud?"

I had his attention. Finally. "You already know they're saying that. You told me yourself. The only way to counter it is to take a neutral stand. Quit implicating yourself. You don't have to support Paul, but you do have to quit defending Shibell. Distance yourself." I let my words sink in. "You need to start thinking like a politician again."

"I can do that."

"Shibell will understand. He's a politician, too. Say you had nothing to do with the election. You have no idea what arrangements Shibell did or did not make. You just want to be a good deputy sheriff and hope you'll be selected to serve the new county."

"You're right." He reached for my hand and squeezed it. "How did I not see that?"

"You're in the middle of it. Sometimes, it's easier to see from the outside." I squeezed back, ready to push my next point. "But you've missed the other gossip. I was at the store today and heard things I hadn't realized were being said."

"There's more?"

"They are saying you're not the respectable family man you claimed to be, that you brought me here under false pretenses. Some are saying that we are living in sin."

He bristled. "I call you Mrs. Behan. Who the hell knows otherwise?"

I sank back into the chair. "Someone knows because there are rumors we're not really married. Today, I heard two ladies in the mercantile suggest I might have a past. An unsavory past."

"It was bound to happen."

"Bound to happen? You let things slip when you drink, enough to get people talking. If it continues, it will get worse. It will ruin my new reputation, and coupled with the fraud problem, it will ruin yours. You won't stand a chance in hell at winning that appointment."

"But we told the whole town we were married in San Francisco." He stared at me, the truth dawning on him bit by bit.

"We also said we were planning a big ceremony, which was enough to silence those who weren't too sure. That didn't happen and now they're doubting our story. We need to move forward with the wedding. Plan a big ceremony, invite the whole town."

"I don't see how a ceremony is going to silence them."

"There would be nothing left to gossip about. Bring in my family from San Francisco. Marry Josephine Marcus with the Marcus family all right there. If they believe you'd live in sin, with a soiled dove to boot, they'll have no problem believing you capable of actively engaging in election fraud. Gossip feeds on itself."

"Aw, Josie. I intended for us to be married by now. I really did. Married with you all set up in a brand-new house. I even picked out the lot. You deserve that before you take my name."

Unease prickled me. The answer was too quick, too smooth. "Is that what the delay has been about? A house?"

"I promised your parents I'd have the money to support you in style. I didn't want to tell you. There isn't any money, Josie."

I didn't believe him. "No money? How can there be no money?"

"I'll get it back. In a few months. I just made a couple bad investments. Once I'm sheriff, it'll work out just fine. We'll get married then."

"You won't *get* appointed if we let the rumors build. Then we'll *both* be out in the cold."

His expression fell at the realization that our futures were tied together.

Once it did, I knew I had him. I tugged at the diamond engagement ring, twisting at it until it slid from my finger.

Johnny's eyes widened in panic.

I plunked the ring on the table. "There. Take it."

He stared at me. "You're leaving?"

"I'm solving a problem. Pawn it if you have to. I'd rather have the marriage than the ring." *The marriage and the future that went with it.* "I also have some money. I'll have Papa withdraw it and send it."

No more excuses, Johnny, no more.

"You have money? Where'd you get money?"

"Just what I've saved up all these years." I wasn't about to tell him it was his money, that I'd tucked away the profit I'd brokered with the sale of his place in Tip Top. He didn't need to know I'd made a dime more than what I'd given him. "Consider it my dowry. I'll telegraph Papa today."

February 10, 1881 (less than two months later)

I couldn't erase my smile. Finally, all I'd dreamed of was within my grasp.

Cochise County had been officially established ten days earlier with Johnny's appointment as sheriff approved by the legislature today, despite the battle between Shibell and Paul remaining unsettled. Harry and Kitty organized a party and their home was packed to the gills with well-wishers and supporters.

And next week, Johnny and I would finally be married.

I'd reluctantly agreed to the delay in return for Johnny's promise to put the new house in both our names. A fair trade. Then Kitty and I had set to work with announcements in the paper, involving the townswomen in the planning and showing 'round the grand designs for a dress. Nearly everyone had received an invitation. The massive show of planning seemed to turn the gossip and Johnny had regained public trust.

"You ready?" Kitty poked her head into the room. "I swear the entire town is crammed in here."

I took one more look in the mirror and turned to join her. "Johnny must be floating on air." I sure was.

"He looks pleased as punch. So do you."

We entered the parlor. True to Kitty's proclamation, it was full. People clustered. A person couldn't tell who was with whom, they were so close to one another.

"I'm going to get them moving outside. It's warm enough, I think. We'll just round them back up when you and Johnny are ready. He wants to toast your future after he thanks everyone.

He said to give him about a half hour. I don't think everyone is here yet."

I spied the handsome Earp brothers in the library, all of them in attendance. Likely anticipating Johnny's announcement of his new deputy. The wives were in the corner. I swallowed, knowing I'd need to mend fences with them.

I waved to Johnny and the mayor, then sidled up to Wyatt. Now that he'd be working for Johnny, we'd all need to become fast friends.

"I've never seen you in a suit before." It looked good on him, damned good. Black serge with a deep blue brocade vest. My pulse quickened.

He turned and smiled, taking my breath away. Mattie Earp was a lucky woman. "Don't too often wear one."

"New?"

"I splurged. My mines have been doing well. Figured I might have need of it."

I nodded. Word had gotten round that there'd been silver strikes among his holdings. He'd sold one of the mines in December. Likely one of the reasons he'd been agreeable to sharing with Johnny rather than seeking the office for himself.

"It looks good on you, Wyatt. A man that looks like you is made to wear suits. You should do so more often."

He laughed. "I like wearing one, but law enforcement in Tombstone is a dusty job, Josie. My suit will likely languish."

"Too bad." I glanced across the room and caught Mattie staring. "Your wife?"

"The one with the auburn hair, Mattie. Named one of the mines after her." He turned his smile on her and lifted his glass of champagne.

I nodded to her and lifted mine. "Lucky woman."

Wyatt sipped, then glanced my direction. "What draws a woman like you to a man like Behan, Josie? I've never quite seen the two of you as a fit."

"That's a pretty personal question."

"Did I offend you?"

"No."

"Figured as much. Polite convention doesn't seem your preference. You've a wild streak in there somewhere, I suspect."

I laughed, despite the ripple of discomfort at how well he understood me. "You read people well."

"Kindred spirits, maybe."

Silence stretched. "Might be," I finally said. "I think Mattie is trying to get your attention. I'd best be on my way."

"I enjoyed our conversation, Josie." He turned and headed toward his wife. His broad shoulders were emphasized by the draw of the suit jacket. It fit well, hugging his muscles, leaving little about his form to the imagination. Mattie was indeed fortunate, to have that body all to herself.

"Ladies and gentlemen, please gather in the parlor." Kitty floated around the house, gathering folks together.

I smoothed my skirts and made my way to the room.

"Miss Marcus?" a strange man said.

"Yes?"

He handed me a folded paper. "Will you give this to Mr. Behan for me? I can't even get close to him."

I lifted my brow.

"The paperwork for the new house," he said.

My house! I took the paper and the man drifted away. Odd . . . I would have expected Kitty's husband to handle the legal matters on the house. He handled all our other matters. A slow burn gnawed at me. I slid my finger under the seal and lifted the pages apart, skimmed the document as applause erupted from the parlor.

Son of a bitch!

If that scoundrel thought he could take my money and put

the house in his name only, he was sadly mistaken. I marched toward the parlor, my jaw tightening with each step.

"Thank you," Johnny was saying. "I am honored to accept the appointment. I know many of you are here to share in the personal announcement Josie and I will be making, but first I want to take my very first official action as sheriff of Cochise County. Please help me welcome my new deputy sheriff, Harry Woods."

Across the room, Wyatt Earp's face registered shock.

Who the hell was Harry Woods? Johnny had never even mentioned the name.

I should have been just as stunned, but I felt only numbness. John Behan was never going to marry me, no matter what he announced to the good citizens of Tombstone. He couldn't tell the truth if his life depended on it.

I clutched the document in my fist and followed Wyatt out of the house.

Chapter Twenty-One: Celia/Mattie

Games weren't lies, were they?

February 1881 (a couple weeks after the announcement)
Tombstone

Mattie pulled the trunk from under the stairway and sighed. Her whore clothes. She hadn't figured on ever having to pull these things out again. But it was all she could think of.

Wyatt was slipping away. He had been, ever since they'd come to Tombstone and he'd been honoring his pledge that she'd remain out of the brothel business. She wasn't sure if it was the laudanum that drove them apart or if it was all Wyatt was going through, but either way he didn't come to her bed no more. Maybe respectability was taking its toll on his spirit.

Oh, he hadn't said a word about her whoring again and she expected he'd stay true to his promise. They didn't need the money. He'd taken on assignments with Wells Fargo again, sold off the town lots he'd bought last year, as well as some of his mining shares. They'd kept their heads above water.

But his eyes were drifting. That whole time at the Behan house, before Johnny'd stabbed him in the back, Wyatt had been watching the women there. Behan's wife had especially caught his eye. No wonder—Allie said she'd been a whore once. Mattie hadn't liked it then and she didn't like it now. But as long as Wyatt just looked, it wasn't a problem. Wandering eyes never hurt too much.

What pained her was him letting his body stray. Her heart ached at the thought of him touching another woman and she reckoned she'd need to do something more than just hurting about it.

He'd bought into a gambling franchise at the Oriental and spent all his time there now. He was following whores up the stairs and bedding them before he came home to her. Mattie could smell them on him—cheap perfume and the musky scent of sex. No one steady, from what she'd heard, so it had to be he was tired of the quiet life and looking for thrills. Without the excitement of being a lawman, he was scratching his itches in other ways.

The only thing she could figure to get him back was to get out the whore clothes she'd long since packed away. If it meant playing his bedroom games again, she'd do it.

Her heart heavy, she tugged at the handle, pulled the trunk down the hallway and into her bedroom. Opening the lid, she saw it was all there. The fancy corsets in gawdy colors, the red dress with the low neckline—she didn't even know if she could fit into it again—and all the silk stockings and underthings that always made her feel so cheap and ill-used.

A shiver ran down her spine.

It'd be worth it, even if she had to pretend it didn't hurt that he only wanted her when she was shameful. That he reached his satisfaction even while she relived all those other men rutting on her. If she did it right, it wouldn't be forever and he'd get tender with her again, like he'd been in their early days. When she was his special one again, it would be worth it.

If she could get him back, keep him happy, they'd be solid again. Once Wyatt beat Behan out of office in November, he'd be fulfilled again. It was only a few months. She could tolerate anything for a few months.

★ ★ ★ ★ ★

March 1881

Mattie and Allie made their way down Allen Street, Mattie's feet leaden. She ought to sew up something herself, but Allie'd scoffed at the idea of trying to get the measurements right so here they were. It was this or looking all trussed up like a turkey trying to stuff her now-plump body into the sinful clothes she'd pulled from her trunk. Now that they were here, Mattie'd lost her nerve.

"You ain't gonna die of it. Let's go." Allie opened the door to the establishment and Mattie had no choice but to step inside or look the fool.

"Hello, ladies," the proprietor gushed as she crossed the store. "What may I help you with?" She eyed them. "Ribbons, perhaps?"

An insult. Mattie knew it for what it was, but it hurt all the same. The seamstress she had worked for back in Fort Scott had done the same. One gander at customers and they were sized up for their spending.

"We'd like to see your unmentionables," Allie announced.

Tarnation. Mattie's face heated.

"Fancy ones," Allie said.

"I have a few serviceable ready-mades."

Mattie drew a breath and approached the woman. "I'm looking for something my husband would like. Silk. A negligee, a bodice and drawers set . . ." She paused. "Something that will please him."

The seamstress nodded. She opened a drawer, lifted a few items out, and laid them out. Lace-trimmed silk, white as snow. The sort of thing a bride might include in her trousseau.

Allie looked over Mattie's shoulder, up on her toes so she could see. "Got something with more color?" she asked.

"Something like the girls on 6th Street might buy?"

The woman gasped.

Mattie cringed at Allie's words No way to dance around delicate-like with Allie along. "Just show me the collection you save for those girls." She reckoned they'd be tucked away somewhere special.

The woman led them to the back of the shop, closed a curtain, and gestured toward two wardrobes. "In there. Gowns in the closet, underclothing in the drawers. Smaller sizes at top. You seem to know what you're looking for. Let me know when you find it and I'll figure the cost."

She stuck her nose in the air and returned to the main part of the shop.

"You're not much help," Mattie hissed to Allie.

"Hell, you'd still be pussyfooting around. Ooh, look at that one." Allie pointed to a pale peach gown, edged in all the right places with black lace. "It ain't red but it sure does scream its intent."

Mattie sure enough figured it did. She held it up to herself. Peach wasn't too often her color, what with her auburn hair, but this shade was near perfect. And the size was damn close. She'd need to let seams out, if there was enough allowance, but it'd fit right enough once she did. There was a black one, too, edged with red, its neckline so low she'd spill out. She selected silk underthings, some garters, and two embroidered corsets, red and black. It'd take all she had, but she'd be the whore in them without a doubt.

The woman totaled the items, packaged them, and handed them to Mattie. "I hope these do the trick."

Outside, on the boardwalk, they giggled like schoolgirls.

Morg found them there. "You two are having a good time," he drawled.

"We plumb are," Allie said. "Guess we've got spring fever."

"Have you finished up your shopping?"

Mattie nodded, a hint of shame nipping at her. "I reckon so. We'd best be getting back home."

"Aw, now, what's the hurry. You never get out. Let me treat you to a glass of wine. Just like the elegant ladies of town."

"Morgan Earp, you know we're not supposed to be out and about more'n just shopping." The Earp men didn't stand for their respectable wives in saloons.

"Mattie, girl, I have never been one to follow rules and I am not about to begin now. Besides, I need a drink. We'll go someplace nice, so quit worrying." He offered an arm to each and ushered them down the sidewalk and into one of the fanciest establishments in town.

The place was full of women in tailored walking-dresses. There wasn't a faded housedress in sight. But Mattie held her head high and told herself she was as good as anyone else.

Morg secured a table, seated them, and ordered champagne all around.

"Ain't we highfaluting?" Allie observed.

They clinked their glasses together, toasting spring. Morg ordered finger foods with some strange French name and they all sipped again. The bubbles tickled Mattie's nose and danced all the way down her throat.

"Mattie, look! It's her."

Mattie lifted her head, following the tip of Allie's head. Josephine Behan. She was at a table with Harry Jones's wife and Marietta Spencer. All three were decked out like society ladies.

A stab of jealousy poked at her. Wyatt'd told her they wouldn't be welcomed in a place like this, that common housewives wouldn't fit in. Well, the three of them were about as common as anybody. Spencer was little more than a former cowhand, ran around with the Clantons. Jones was a lawyer and Behan a businessman, but it was plain as day that all three women had been whores.

Might be no one else knew for sure, but Mattie did. She could see it in the way they tried too hard. Whores always knew another whore.

Josephine stared back at her, a glint in her eyes.

Mattie drained her glass and handed it to Morg. "Pour me another," she said. "I've got a sour taste in my mouth."

April 1881 (a month later)

Mattie dipped her hand into the bath, testing the water. Hot, but tolerable. As it needed to be so it wouldn't grow chill. She slipped off her housedress and laid it on the bed, shed her underthings, and stepped into the tub.

Lord but that felt good.

She settled into the water, let it surround her, and percolated a bit.

Wyatt hadn't been home much these past few weeks and that made it difficult for Mattie to put her plan to rekindle their loving into action. Ever since that attempted stagecoach robbery, he'd parked himself in the saloon every night. Some said Doc Holliday, and maybe even the Earps, had been involved with the robbery.

Mattie didn't believe it. Wyatt's friend Bob Paul nearly got killed and Wyatt wouldn't have shot him. She figured it was the bunch that supported Shibell, trying to silence Bob, who still wasn't letting go of the election fraud claim. But the gossip spread like wildfire and Wyatt kept to the saloons where he could fight the rumors head-on. If things had been bad with Johnny Behan before, Mattie reckoned they were a jumbled-up mess now.

The same as things between her and Wyatt. She'd asked him to come home tonight, special, so she could get him back in her bed where he belonged.

Back when she was whoring, she'd loved baths. They hadn't been too common but they washed off some of the filth, even what couldn't be seen.

She sat, breathed in the heavy rose-scented soap she'd bought. Then she lathered her body, let her skin tingle a bit, and rinsed. The soap floated on the water and she used the leftover suds to wash her hair, then stood and rinsed with the clean water she'd saved back in the ewer.

The shame she was already feeling about playing the whore didn't rinse away, though, but she had no choice, not if she wanted to keep her man.

After drying, Mattie eyed the clothes she'd spread on the bed. She'd chosen the peach gown, the one with the black lace. Bessie'd dug up a sheer silk chemise that a body could near see through. Mattie reckoned she'd pair it with the black corset and stockings.

Halfway into trussing herself into the clothes, she needed a whiskey.

The silk caressed her skin, almost like Wyatt's touch when he had a mind to spend the time. Light, feathery. It didn't feel like the rough hands of the other men who'd had her, but it reminded her of them all the same. Like things were crawling on her.

Wyatt wasn't like that and it confused her that she felt shameful over what she was doing.

She downed the whiskey and let it drown out the shivering as she finished dressing. Then she fixed up her hair, dotted her face with a bit of rouge, poured herself another drink, and settled atop the bed.

Sounds of the door being shut with a quiet click edged around her, waking her. Wyatt. Lord, what time was it? She opened drowsy eyes, looking through the darkness. "You can turn up the lamp," she told him.

"I didn't mean to wake you. You didn't go to bed?"

"I was waiting on you. Fell asleep. What time is it?"

"Late."

She snuffed her resentment, fighting a yawn as she stood. Late or not, he was home and it was time. She crossed to the lamp. Wyatt had left it barely lit, undressing in the near-dark. She turned it up, just a soft glow, then moseyed to where he was removing his boots. "Let me," she said.

His gaze lifted. His eyes were tired above his mustache but her stomach tumbled all the same, the way it always did when he looked at her straight on. His mouth stretched into a smile.

"Well, what do we have here?"

"Thought you might like something special to bring up your spirits."

His gaze roamed down her body. "Look at you! You're pretty as a present."

"Unwrap me?"

He kicked off the second boot and reached for her, kissed the tops of her breasts where they nearly spilled from the dress. His hands roamed her body, found the hooks that held the dress shut, and parted it. The straps slid from her shoulders and the gown tumbled to the floor.

Wyatt sucked in his breath.

Mattie stepped out of the gown and began to work his clothing loose, sliding buttons, peeling off his shirt, opening his trousers. She caressed him, bold, teasing, firing him up but not fulfilling the promise. Then she walked away, sat on the bed, and pulled up her chemise, just enough to slide her hand beneath it.

She let him watch her lean back, knowng he could see her hand beneath the thin fabric as she fingered herself. Like she'd done for so many other men.

And he watched. Like she knew he would. He'd been excited already, when she'd stripped him, but his cock jumped up more.

"Like this, darlin'?" she asked, throaty and suggestive.

"You know I do."

"Come here. I got an itch for something else." She shifted, waited for him to near, then moved to take him in her mouth.

Her throat tightened. *Don't think on it.*

But the memory of Lurch, her first demanding john, crawled up on her anyway. She gagged, then shifted.

Just don't hit that one spot in your mouth and it'll be fine. It was the reminder she gave herself every time since that first time. She squeezed her eyes tight but the memories didn't fade none.

Wyatt pulled from her mouth. Had he remembered how difficult it was for her to do that? Wyatt tumbled her onto the bed, pulled up the chemise, and entered her. His hands cradled her hips, moving her in concert, creating that glorious friction she'd near forgot. He came, with her an instant behind.

Oh, Wyatt.

"Damn good, Mattie. Damn good."

Then he pulled out, turned away, and fell asleep, leaving her as alone as she'd been before he returned home.

Chapter Twenty-Two: Josephine/Sadie

There were times I hated the lies. Mostly while I was living them.

May 1881 (three months after Johnny became sheriff)
Tombstone

I strolled back to the house on Safford Street, replete from a quiet café dinner. I'd moved into the new house immediately, sure that Johnny would do the right thing and sign the house over to me now that he had his sheriff income. He hadn't, of course.

I couldn't believe I'd been so stupid as to blindly turn over my money to him and trust him to record the house in both our names. It was my own fault and I knew it.

Moving into the house had been my only choice. My money was gone. Besides, I'd paid for the house and it was mine!

There'd been little Johnny could do, not unless he wanted to toss me out on the street. It was enough of an embarrassment that I'd postponed the wedding ceremony. Johnny continued to live in the tiny house on Allen Street and Albert floated between us, spending more time with me than with Johnny.

Light from the window lit the front porch and I stalled. I hadn't left a lamp burning.

I marched up the front steps and flung open the door.

Crates filled the front hall. In the parlor, Johnny sat in his favorite chair, his feet propped on an ottoman and a glass of whiskey in his hand.

I stared at him. "You can't possibly think you're going to live here."

"And why not? It is my house."

"The hell it is." This was my house and I'd be damned if I was going to share it with him.

"Legally, my dear, it's all mine." He slurred the words, more than a little drunk.

I strode into the room. "We were doing just fine as we were."

"With me paying for two houses? I gave you time to get over your little tizzy. Now it's time to reconcile."

Stunned, I just stood there. "You stole my money," I finally spit out.

Johnny shook his head. "I didn't steal anything. You gave me the money."

"For our house." I gestured helplessly, still not able to believe he was here.

"And I spent it on our house."

"Which you put it in *your* name."

"Property always goes in the man's name." He lifted his glass and peered at the amber liquid. "Wives don't own property in their own right."

"I'm not your wife!" I shouted.

Johnny smirked and drained the last of the whiskey. Then he hefted himself from the chair and stumbled in my direction. "You made damn sure the entire town thinks you are."

Pride in that accomplishment was no longer as appealing as it had been. "It's not your house, Johnny."

"You made a point of insisting we were married. That means it's my house. Part of the marriage contract and all. If you don't like it, move out."

"The hell I will."

"Matter of fact, Josie, darling, you've been woefully inadequate in keeping up with your wifely duties." He took another step forward.

Bile churned in my stomach. "You have got to be kidding."

"I've missed you, wife."

I snorted, loud so he wouldn't miss it. "I'm not your wife."

"As long as you insist on living in this house, you are." Johnny reached for me, his breath as sour as the drunks who frequented the brothel back in Prescott. The stench made me gag. He'd obviously been drinking for hours.

"Get out."

"Haven't you missed me, Josie? It's always better when we've missed each other."

His arm snaked around me and he grabbed my butt, pulled me flush against him. "Time to kiss and make up."

My skinned crawled at the thought of it, all desire for him long gone. "Over my dead body."

"Whatsamatter, Sadie? Forget where you came from?"

"Let me go," I struggled.

"Once a whore, always a whore."

The sting of the words worked its way through me. A whore I might be, but I would no longer be his. "Let go!"

"You want to live in my house, pretend you're my wife, then by God you'll do your duty. Or you can put out like a whore. I don't care which. I get you either way."

"You will not! I'm not your whore anymore and I sure as hell am not your wife. Take your hands off me."

He grabbed at my bodice with his other hand, caught the edge, and ripped it downward.

I struggled, lifted my knee, and shoved it into his crotch.

He buckled and crumpled to the floor.

I left him there and rushed down the block, my shawl

clutched over my torn dress. If it took becoming a whore again to avoid being Johnny's wife, so be it.

July 1881 (two months later)

I swallowed my pride and moved into a room above the Oriental Saloon, bitter hatred for Johnny Behan brewing stronger each time I lay beneath a john. Vindictive, Johnny made sure the entire town knew Josie Marcus Behan and Sadie Mansfield were one and the same. Most of the time I answered to whichever name they used. There was little point in trying to keep up pretenses.

Once Johnny revealed we'd never been married, I took my revenge and claimed the house. It had taken an affidavit from my father stating the funds had been his in order to get the money back. Except it had been returned to Papa, which was of no help to me. The occasional wires Papa sent were hardly enough to support me, but at least Johnny didn't get the house.

So I was once again a whore. At least I'd spent enough time in the right circles to attract a higher-class clientele, most of whom delighted in having Johnny Behan's girl. They paid better, saving me from having to suffer an endless stream of men every night, but they sweated and grunted just like their lower-class counterparts.

Though I called myself a courtesan, it held no appeal. My thirst for adventure and long-ago optimism had faded. That cynicism I'd hated in Ella had become part of me.

I took to spending time downstairs, in the Oriental, watching Wyatt Earp deal faro. He owned a part interest in the saloon and divided his time among dealing cards there, serving as a part-time federal deputy marshal under Virgil, and managing his mines.

"You all right, Josie?" Wyatt asked.

I smiled from my place at the bar. "As expected, Wyatt." It was now an old routine between us, a pat question and answer.

I glided across the room, my drink in hand. Wyatt sat at the faro table, nursing his own whiskey. The glass was still full. I'd never seen him sip more than a bit in all the nights I'd watched him play. It was a policy, he said, borne from experience. He'd learned the hard way that drinking influenced the game; the glass was an illusion.

And I understood illusions.

The table wasn't crowded. It was a quiet night. I took a stool near Wyatt's side, a little back from the table rather than joining the two strangers across from him.

"Not playing, miss?" one of them asked.

"Cards are not my forte."

The other man sniggered.

My chest tightened but the shame never crossed my face. I simply smiled and let a small laugh tinkle out. "You play your game, I'll play mine."

Wyatt turned his head and winked at me, then dealt the next hand.

The shame shifted and I relished the increase in my pulse. Wyatt Earp was a desirable man and I'd missed that rush far too much. I crossed my leg and leaned my foot on his thigh.

His mouth parted and his shoulders rose. Enough that I saw it, but not so much as to attract any attention from the men across the table.

I shifted my foot, pressing it harder against his leg.

I'd been a fool, betting it all on Johnny. Too much history, too much lust, too much blind faith. There were other paths to the life I'd imagined. I just hadn't seen them.

The hand ended and Wyatt stretched. He yawned and moved the arm closest to me under the table, stroking my ankle with the lightest touch. His fingers were nimble and I shivered.

Then he was back to shuffling the deck, those fingers flying.

God, he'd be good in bed.

If he touched me like he touched those cards, I'd come in seconds.

"I'm out," one of the customers said as he pushed his chair away from the table.

Wyatt raised his brow at the other man.

"Guess I'll call it a night, too." He glanced at me. "You working?"

"Sorry. I've played my last hand, too." I yawned, daintily, for effect. I wouldn't have bedded him anyway. I had my standards, after all. Besides, I hadn't folded with the dealer yet.

Wyatt pushed his chair and relaxed in it as the two men collected their things and sauntered out the door of the saloon.

I shifted on the stool, faced him, and slid my foot into the vee of his crotch. Time to up the ante.

His lips stretched into a half smile and he spread his legs further.

"You want to switch games?" I asked, my voice husky. "Play a round with me?"

He chuckled under his breath. "You aren't shy about things, are you?"

"Being shy gets a girl nowhere."

He grinned. "I like that. Upstairs?"

Skin tingling, I nodded. "Number five."

I reached the second floor and started down the hall. I heard Wyatt's footfalls quicken. He was behind me before I got the door open.

We tumbled into the room and he slammed the door closed. His hands roamed my breasts, then one drifted lower and he cupped me, tugged me close. "You are a temptress, Sadie. But you know that already."

"I want you, Wyatt."

"You say that to everyone?"

Oh, I'd said it often, that was true, but I'd only ever wanted Johnny and that lust was long in the past. But I itched for Wyatt, craved him. "Saying something and meaning it are two entirely different things."

"Which is it this time?"

I shifted, turning in his arms, and looked straight into his eyes. The blue was dark, smoldering. I let out a ragged breath.

"I couldn't fake this." I laid his palm over my thundering chest, watched his eyes widen.

"Slow or fast?" he asked, giving me the choice.

Women like me didn't often get a choice. *God, I was panting.* "First one, then the other," I told him.

He pulled at my dress, sending hooks flying. "I'll buy you another. I just need to see you, feel you against me. Flipping dresses is for pokes that mean nothing."

I stepped back, stripped off the dress, parted my corset, and let everything drop.

His eyes never left me.

"You'll do the same?" I asked. "A man that takes me with his pants still on is just a john."

He shed his clothing.

My eyes never left him.

He was magnificent, strong, erect, and standing at the perfect angle.

I swallowed and dropped my chemise.

Then he was there, his fingers teasing, as light and skillful as I'd known they would be. He grinned as he encountered my wetness. "You did want me."

"No deception between us, Wyatt." I clamped around his fingers.

He lifted me and slid into me, holding me as I rode him, both of us bucking until Wyatt stiffened and plunged, tumbling us onto the bed.

I shrieked as I came, the sound choking on the gasp that flooded out with it.

September 1881 (two months later)

It didn't take long for me to realize Wyatt was all I'd been looking for.

He was attentive, offering far more to our relationship than Johnny had even given. The lust I'd experienced with Johnny, along with my girlish dreams, had tricked me into believing I'd loved him. I'd been so naïve.

Wyatt spent time learning about me, my hopes and dreams along with what I craved in the bedroom. He expected nothing more than return of the same. We were equals. He never saw me as a tool, to his sexual satisfaction nor his political aims.

Not that he didn't have aims. Wyatt saw the potential the office of sheriff held. The tax percentage, combined with what he was making from his mines and his interests in several gambling concessions and saloon partnerships, would make him a wealthy man. But he didn't aim to win the next election for the office via political maneuvering. He'd win it through his dedication to law and order.

That suited me just fine.

In a few weeks, he'd toss his name in as a candidate in the November election. By that time, I aimed to solidify our relationship. Already he spent more time with me than he did Mattie. For me, it was a sign that the marriage had failed. That he'd soon leave her was never a question in my mind.

I just needed to make him realize it.

We'd skirted around the issue of him doing so, but it was time to push a little harder, get a commitment from him.

"You're tense," I whispered. I kneeled behind him on the

bed, massaging his shoulder muscles.

"Whole damn town is tense."

"With the heat, the drought, the fire, and now the flooding from all the rain, it's to be expected. You can't fix any of that, Wyatt. Quit worrying so much."

"It isn't the weather that concerns me. It's those damn Cowboys."

The Cowboys. Again. Always the Cowboys. I was tired of the endless problems the damn ragtag rabble-rousers caused. And the amount of attention it drew from Wyatt.

"Can't we just forget about them? Talk about us? I thought Virgil had that all under control. Hardly anyone shoots up the town anymore."

In July, there'd been an uproar about all the gunplay and violence, not just in Tombstone, but in the entire county. Rustling was rampant and there was fighting along the Mexican border. The town marshal was run out of office and Virgil appointed in his place—in addition to his federal marshal office—and given the fancy new title of police chief. Virgil had cracked down hard.

He'd had no choice, Wyatt said. Not with the governor advocating for Virgil's job to be assumed by the new vigilante group known as the Tombstone Rangers. Word was that unless order was maintained, the Tombstone Rangers would be empowered to take over. That hadn't set well with Virgil. He'd hired on nine deputies, enforced the new law forcing surrender of weapons unless licensed to carry them within town, and made arrests for even the smallest violations of the law.

And Virgil had pulled it off. The town had quieted and he'd cut his police force back to two. The renamed Safety Committee still rode his back, but at least there wasn't constant trouble to address. Not in town, anyway. Virgil struggled to maintain an even keel between the demands of the local Safety Committee, who continued to pry into everything Virgil did, and common sense. It was one thing to keep law and order and something else entirely to overreact when simple negotiation could address the issue.

I leaned my head on Wyatt's shoulder, where I'd been kneading. "Wyatt? You know the Cowboys are Virgil's problem. Can't you let it be? It's been forever since you relaxed. Maybe we could take a few days to ourselves, take a holiday together somewhere and make some plans?"

He shifted, faced me. "I can't. Not with all the rumors flying around. When Virge and Morg and I brought Stilwell and Spencer in for that last stage robbery, it should have put all that to rest."

"You did what you had to. I don't see why there's gossip."

Wyatt drew a breath. "When the damn judge dismissed the case, it reunited all the old gossip."

Old gossip? The rumor that Johnny Behan himself had helped instigate—that the Earps and Doc Holliday had committed the Benson robbery last spring. "About March?"

Wyatt nodded. "I don't like losing respect. What's more, I'm not going to get elected if we don't get past that."

I sat back, frustration brewing. "Even more reason to get away, decide how to handle things with Mattie."

"Every time I think I'm getting somewhere, that I have an opportunity to prove my dedication to the law, some damn mess occurs. I can't make plans to leave Mattie for you until November election is past. I can't stir up any more fodder for the rumor mill. I can't. I'm risking enough seeing you as much as I am."

White hot anger surged. Was there no man exempt from political plotting? And did every bit of it have to impact what I wanted?

I blew out my exasperation in a whoosh of air and reminded

myself that Wyatt was a man with noble goals. Respectability didn't come easily—I knew that. "Behan has connections. Deep connections. If messes are occurring, you can lay that at his feet."

In fact, I wouldn't have been surprised if Johnny and Shibell hadn't been at the root of the March murder—paying the Cowboys to commit the crime and make it look like a foiled robbery. After all, the victim had been sitting in Bob Paul's usual place and the robbery itself forsaken. The lucrative tax percentage was a hell of a motive for getting rid of the competition and the election had still not been ratified.

But that angle had never been pursued. Johnny had immediately claimed he'd been informed that either the Earps or Doc had committed the crime. There'd been no proof but the rumor lingered.

And Wyatt hated it.

I stood and started to dress. There was no way I'd make any progress on Wyatt divorcing Mattie. Not today. For now, I'd need to do what I could to support him and help squash those rumors he so feared.

"You know Ike Clanton?" he asked.

I turned. "I know of him. He and his brothers run with the Cowboys and his name pops up everywhere. Drinks a lot and isn't too smart."

Wyatt ran his hand through his hair, mussing it. "Back in June I offered to pay him my share of the bounty for bringing in the Cowboys responsible for what happened on the Benson stage."

"Good lord, Wyatt, that was $1200 each!" I swallowed, calculating how much it added up to.

"It would have been worth it to bring them in. All Ike needed to do was lure them to the McLaury ranch on a pretext of another robbery. I'd swoop in with a posse and get the arrest, and Ike would get the reward."

"Obviously it didn't happen."

"Ike balked. Said he was scared the reward wouldn't be paid if they got killed in the arrest. I had to have the Wells Fargo agent telegraph the main office for approval to make it a 'dead or alive' reward. But the whole thing unraveled when two of them ended up dead before we could pull off the ambush." Wyatt shifted, defeat filling his eyes.

I wasn't sure what to do, how I could help. *If* I could help, even. "And that's what has you all tense?"

"It just keeps rearing its head. Every time I think I have it tied up. Now Ike's all twitchy, saying I blabbed about the secret deal." He lifted his gaze, caught mine. "Honest to God, you're the first person I've told."

His words gave me pause and a slow chill crept up my spine. "But somebody knew."

"The Wells Fargo agent who sent the telegraph. He got drunk one night with Ike and mentioned something about it. Ike got it in his head that I was telling people to get Ike killed and he won't let it be. Hell, Ike's told enough people in the last week that it's not going to die off."

"Is Ike really that dumb? Why would you do something that hurts you?"

"Ike *is* that dumb. And he gets lit up easily. If I didn't know better, I'd think someone was egging him on."

I shivered. *Johnny.* Would Johnny actually stoop to doing something like that?

I had no idea if he had or not, but I had little doubt he was capable of it. Johnny Behan was capable of just about anything when his goals were threatened. Wyatt Earp gaining any ounce of respect was something Johnny was not going to stand for.

And he'd use any weapon he could to make sure of it. There wasn't a thing Johnny wouldn't stoop to. The shiver grew icy.

Johnny would use my relationship with Wyatt as yet another weapon. I knew it with rock-hard certainty.

If I didn't pull away from Wyatt now, if I wanted any chance of a future with Wyatt, I'd need to stay away from him until after the election.

I kissed him, full and hot, then turned and walked out the door.

October 26, 1881 (the next month, around 2:30 p.m.)

In the end, we couldn't keep our hands off one another for more than a couple weeks. Wyatt had rented me a little house so our trysts would remain private. He came only in the wee hours and we barely acknowledged one another in public. A few visits to a whore was one thing, but an affair while married was another entirely.

Wyatt craved respect and I couldn't foil that for him, no matter how cheap I felt being kept on the side.

It'd been nearly a week since he'd been able to drop by. I had planned a romantic dinner and had laid out a new dress that showed every curve I had. I might be short, but I'd been blessed with full breasts, ample hips, and a tiny waist between them.

Early in the afternoon, rapid knocking sounded on the front door. Insistent rapping. Enough to make my heart patter.

I opened the door to find Marietta Spencer—who'd come from San Francisco with me—on the stoop, panting.

"Heavens, Marietta, what's going on?"

She rushed into the house and drew a few breaths, her dark hair a tumbling mess. Then she lifted her gaze to mine. "Trouble's brewing."

My heart stalled. "For me?"

"For the Earps," she said, her accent thick in her excitement. "Ike Clanton and Doc Holliday fought at the Alhambra early this morning . . . a little after midnight, Pete said. Ike was drunk and spouting off about Wyatt. Doc got word of it."

"Oh, lovely." An angry drunk and a confrontational consumptive.

"Doc called him a son of a bitch and told him to get his gun so they could have it out."

I tensed. "He didn't, did he?"

Marietta shook her head. "Ike didn't have a gun."

Worry deepened. "Doc does."

"Morgan Earp sauntered over and got into it."

Morg was a hothead. And if both Morg and Doc were involved, Wyatt would be, too. Impatience bubbled and I took Marietta by the arms. "Wyatt?" I asked.

She shook her head. "Not then. Virgil broke it up. But Ike has been all over town saying he plans to have it out with all of them."

"Wyatt won't get drawn into that," I said, but anxiety lingered.

"Ike said he was going to get his gun. Virgil and Wyatt both tried to calm him down."

I blew out a breath. "Get to the point, Marietta!"

"Ike got his gun. Virgil arrested him, but he paid his fine and now he's back out on the street saying he's going to kill them all. His brother, Billy, and Frank and Tom McLaury are with him. Bill Claiborne, too."

"Tom McLaury is usually levelheaded. He'll get Ike out of town before anything happens." But even as I said the words, I didn't believe them.

"There's more. Wyatt saw McLaury with a gun and pistol-whipped him."

Oh, Wyatt.

"And Virgil hit Ike in the head, too. The Cowboys were headed to the O.K. Corral for their horses, but the Safety Committee ordered Virgil to disarm them and he's gone to get a shotgun. I don't like this. I feel something bad in the air."

My heart raced. I felt it, too. "I should go. Maybe I can calm Wyatt down." I flung my shawl over my shoulders and turned toward the door.

And heard the shots begin.

Chapter Twenty-Three: Celia/Mattie

Sometimes, there was no ignoring the truth of it.

October 26, 1881 (a little before Marietta visited Josie)
Tombstone

Uneasy, Mattie shoved a large needle through the section of canvas on her lap and glanced at Allie. "You reckon we ought to be worried?"

Allie turned from the window where she'd been staring out on Fremont Street. "Something is brewing. I just seen a bunch of folks headed toward town."

Her nerves all prickly, Mattie set the canvas down and joined Allie at the window. "Should we go?" The business district was just two blocks off.

"It's probably nothing," Allie said.

Mattie wasn't so sure. "Ned Boyle woke us up to tell Wyatt Ike had a pistol and planned to shoot it out. Boyle said there was a tenseness about Ike that bothered him. Wyatt went back to sleep but it kept me up. It doesn't feel right."

"Virge said Ike's been drunk since early yesterday, staggering all over town, saying he wanted to fight it out. Virge and Wyatt dealt with it all night, even took Ike's gun away from him. Virge didn't get home 'til near eight. Officer Bronk showed up two hours later to say Ike was still at it. Virge like as not has got it settled by now."

The news did little to quiet Mattie's worry. Wyatt had said

nothing, just crawled into bed. Like he near always done now. Gambled all night, slept all morning, then left again with hardly a word to her in between.

It didn't bode well, the conflict going on for so long. Ike riled Wyatt up more'n anybody she knew of.

"Come on, it ain't nothing." Allie steered Mattie back toward the chairs. "Them fancy new clothes do the trick?"

Mattie bit her lip. "Got him excited but didn't bring back the loving. He takes me like a whore and turns away. He used to hold me close, make me feel special. I feel cheap. Used."

"Ah, Mattie. That ain't good."

"He's spending time with Behan's throwaway. It's never been like this, not with all the women he's had over the years. I worry I'm losing him. If I hadn't insisted on being respectable, I'd have been with him more. If Wyatt leaves me, I'll have no way to survive."

"Virge would step in. I know he would."

"It isn't Virge's problem. It's mine. I've got to find a way around it, if the worst happens."

Shots rang out, shattering the afternoon, and Mattie jumped. Not a single wild shot, but a series of them. Twenty or thirty of them.

Her heart stuttered and she glanced at Allie.

Her sister-in-law had paled.

"Allie?"

"A ghost just crossed my path."

"What?"

"A shiver, a feeling in my gut. Something's happened."

Mattie threw down her sewing and rushed to the door. She flew from the house, down Fremont. Half the town seemed to be doing the same. She neared 4th Street, where the crowd had stalled. Unable to muscle through, she asked someone what had happened.

"Shoot out. The Clantons were coming from the O.K. Corral and the Earps were going to arrest them."

"There's been trouble back and forth all afternoon," someone else said. "There's blood and bodies all over."

Mattie stumbled and pushed her way through the throng. When she saw the wagon headed in her direction, she stopped. Her heart pounded as she waited, knowing.

Then she lifted her gaze and saw Wyatt, walking behind the wagon.

As the wagon neared, she spied Virge and Morg in its bed, bloodied but alive. James trailed a block behind, running to catch up. Wyatt approached, took her in his arms.

"It's all gone to hell, Mattie. Frank McLaury's dead and his brother, Tom, soon will be. Billy Clanton won't make it, either, not the way they're shot up." He pulled away, his face full of regret. "We didn't mean it to go that far, but they wouldn't let it be."

"But you're all right? Virge and Morg?"

"There's going to be hell to pay, Mattie. Life as we know it is done for."

October 30, 1881 (four days later)

Mattie's heart was in shock. She glanced across the kitchen at Allie, whose mouth was set into a thin line, same as Mattie's.

First degree murder was nothing to mess with and they'd best all be thinking together. Like usual, the Earp brothers figured on taking on the decision themselves instead of letting their practical wives help with the matter.

Up to the gunfight with the Clanton gang, Mattie'd figured the worst that was coming was Wyatt leaving her. She never reckoned on having to think how to save Wyatt from hanging. But, the two conditions were pretty much the same in how they'd end. If there wasn't a way to save Wyatt, she'd be on her own anyway. Except there wouldn't be the family safety net because they'd all hang together. Whatever the men decided would affect them all.

"If they so much as hint we need to leave, I'll throw a fit," Mattie whispered. "Damn idiots."

Allie stood with a dishrag in hand. "You got that right." She wrung it out and draped it over the sink while Mattie folded the towel. Then they crept closer to the open doorway, watching from the shadows. Bessie and Louisa, Morg's wife, drifted closer from their spot in the hallway.

The men sat in Allie's front room together, talking where Virge and Morg could join in. Both were stretched out on settees, healing from their wounds.

"This is all a formality," Doc's attorney, T.J. Drum, said. "Spicer will look at the testimony from the inquest, rule that a public offense occurred, and send it to the grand jury. There's nothing we can do at this point."

"But there was no offense," Wyatt insisted.

Virge glanced up from the settee. "I deputized everyone before we went up there. We were acting in our legal capacity to disarm the Cowboys. The Safety Committee pretty much ordered me to do so. Otherwise, there'd have been vigilantes involved, too."

Mattie looked at Allie and rolled her eyes. Like everything in Tombstone, it wasn't that simple. Too many threats had been traded in the hours before. When the coroner left the cause of death as "gunshot" instead of a result of lawful action, Ike Clanton pressed for murder charges. The little ferret Behan had been happy to oblige, arresting the Earps and Doc straight off.

Tom Fitch, the lawyer the Earps had hired, stood and paced the room. Mattie liked him. He had a keen mind. She hoped he'd offer some sensible advice to their stubborn husbands.

"It's not that easy, gentlemen. Not with the witness from the hat store saying she heard Doc making threats and Behan backing the witness up."

"That son of a bitch is a backstabbing liar," Wyatt roared.

Mattie cringed at his tone. They would get nowhere if Wyatt and Morg got their tempers going. She stepped into the front room and settled her hands on Wyatt's shoulders. "He's a liar but that makes no difference. Settle down and find a way around it."

Fitch smiled at her. "You have a smart wife there, Wyatt."

The words warmed her. She'd figured out a long time ago that Pa had been all wrong about her not having any sense, but it still felt good to have someone say it. She gave Fitch a smile, for once not even caring about the holes where her teeth had been.

Wyatt sat back, but his shoulders remained tense beneath her hands. He like as not didn't appreciate her butting in.

She kneaded, willing him to relax.

Allie entered and tucked a quilt around Virg, then stood behind the settee. That was all it took for Louisa to do the same for Morg and for Bessie to stand with James.

Now, they were all here—except for Doc's Kate—whether the men liked it or not.

There was nothing but silence in the room.

"Damn it, this affects us, too," Bessie said. "We got a right to be here."

Mattie caught Fitch's gaze. "So what happens next?" The sooner they all knew what was coming, the sooner they could set to figuring what they had to do about it. Bessie'd be safe, since James wasn't charged, but Mattie, Allie, and Louisa could lose both their respectability and their husbands.

She wasn't going to let that happen, not if she could help it.

"It's a complicated system, with several layers," Fitch said.

"First, there's a preliminary hearing before Justice Spicer tomorrow. The Cochise County district attorney will bring evidence to prove probable cause to refer the matter to the grand jury. Spicer will decide if there is sufficient evidence to do that. Like Drum said, the preliminary hearing is pretty much a formality. Then, the case is referred to the grand jury. If they indict, the case goes to trial. Assuming it goes to trial, we mount our defense there."

Wyatt leaned forward. "It's clear as day we were just trying to disarm them. Why the hell else would we go down the block? You could see the damn guns!"

"Behan says they were on their way out of town," Fitch said. "If that was the case, they'd be entitled to take their arms with them."

Virge shook his head. "They weren't leaving. They were walking through town, gathering guns and pledging to fight Wyatt, Doc, and Morg. I'm chief of police. It was my place to disarm them. Mine or Behan's and he wasn't doing it."

Doc's attorney, Drum, waved a hand. "None of this matters right now. Let's start making a witness list for the trial. With politics being what they are here in Tombstone, that's where we're headed."

Mattie wrinkled her brow, working it out. "They don't get to defend themselves at this preliminary hearing? Justice Spicer just moves it along to the next phase?"

"Stay out of it, Mattie." Wyatt's voice was calm but she understood the quiet force in the words.

Tarnation. The man had no sense whatsoever.

Fitch glanced at her, then at Wyatt. "They're good questions, actually. Mostly, the focus of any defense at this stage is to challenge the evidence brought up by the prosecutor. The hearing is about deciding whether or not there is cause to send the case to the grand jury. As far as Spicer himself—he's a justice of the peace, not a judge. He's got no law degree. That means he almost always sends the matter forward."

"But he doesn't have to?" Mattie asked.

"No, he could decide the evidence doesn't warrant the charge."

"Mattie, we're wasting time here. We need to start preparing for the trial."

"Hush up, Wyatt." Bessie hissed the words. "Let her work this out. Who the hell do you think helped James raise that $10,000 for your bail? She got you more than enough to handle the defense expenses, too."

Allie pinned him with an acid glare. "She got some of Doc's bail raised, too, though I don't hardly know why she bothered. Took money out of the bank to make up the rest—which by rights was hers as well as yours. You messed with her future, ordering her to do that. If you get hanged, she won't have nothing left."

"We all got a right to be here and it won't take but a few minutes of talking," Bessie said.

James patted Bessie's hand. "Our wives are right on this. And we ought to be listening to them. Lord knows I should listen to Bessie a lot more than I do."

Wyatt blew out a breath and slumped back against the chair.

Finally! It took Wyatt forever sometimes. "So Spicer *doesn't* have to send it to the grand jury? He *could* decide there isn't evidence enough?"

Frisk shrugged. "Given the prosecution witnesses that came forward at the coroner's inquest, we'd have to combat that evidence."

"Could we do that?" Morg asked. "Go on the offensive rather than sitting back and letting the prosecution control things?"

"We could. It'd be unusual to mount a defense at this stage but there's nothing to say we couldn't, as long as Spicer would allow it. It's *his* courtroom."

"Is that what you're thinking, Mattie?" Bessie asked.

"Mostly, I'm thinking a grand jury is going to have folks on it that support the Cowboys. Same with a trial jury. If there's a way to avoid having all those people involved—"

"What's Spicer's politics?" Allie said. "He a friend of the Clantons?"

Wyatt turned, his eyes brightening. "Not at all. He supported Bob Paul and partners in the tobacco shop with the Wells Fargo agent Morg and I work for. We've always gotten on together."

Doc's attorney shook his head. "It's a risk. If we mount a defense at this stage and Spicer rules against us, we'll have shown the prosecution our hand. They'll use it against us later."

"I think I can take apart the prosecution witnesses," Fisk said. "Ike Clanton's not too bright. Once I get him blathering, I'll be able to get what I need from him. I believe I can pull favorable testimony from the others, as well. We'll need defense witnesses."

"What about us testifying?" Wyatt asked.

"Risky. Prosecution can ask you anything they want and with the words you and Doc and Morgan exchanged with Ike, that could backfire."

"If we can avoid a jury, let's do so." Wyatt rose and crossed the room. "Let's go straight at them. Put us on the stand, let us tell our story!"

Mattie's stomach lurched. He was all impulse, no forethought.

"I can't do that, Wyatt. Not with what was said. And, if you're on the stand, they'll ask about who fired first. I'd rather avoid that question coming up when you're under oath."

"There's no way for them to tell what happened without being questioned?" Mattie asked Fisk. "No way to get around it?"

"They can make a statement but that's it."

Drum shook his head. "A statement isn't a defense. It's a

damn oral statement."

The group quieted. There didn't seem any way around it. They'd need to rely on witnesses and however far Spicer's sympathies reached.

A risk.

"I can ask for Spicer to be liberal in his interpretations of what's allowed since he's a justice of the peace and not a judge. Maybe we can stretch out the statements a little."

"There anything saying how long it can be?" Mattie asked.

"No, but he'll balk if we go too long," Drum said.

Wyatt paced. "Let's gamble on it," he finally said. "I like the odds."

Mattie did, too. At this point, she and the other wives had little choice but to bet their entire stake and let it play out. She caught Wyatt's gaze. "If there are no rules in any lawbooks, why don't you place a heavy bet? When you make that statement, tell every damn thing the Cowboys ever did and how they had run-ins with you every time you tried to enforce the law. Tell 'em about all the threats Ike made against you these past months. If that doesn't justify taking away their guns, nothing will."

Wyatt glanced at Fisk. "Could we do it?"

"We can try." Fisk looked around the room. "But you have to know, all of you, that if this doesn't work, we'll have tipped our hand and given it all away."

December 29, 1881 (two months later)

Pounding sounded on the front door. Fear snaked its way through Mattie.

After a month and some thirty witnesses, Doc and the Earps had been released from all charges, but there had been death threats ever since.

She stumbled out of bed, saw it was still half-dark. Grabbing a wrapper, she lit a lamp and crept through the predawn light. She fumbled with the bolt on the front door. Wyatt had made her promise to keep it slid all the time, ever since Spicer dismissed the case.

"Come on, Mattie, open up!"

Wyatt.

Mattie pushed against the sticking lock and it finally slid open.

Wyatt near fell into the house, his clothing dark with what looked to be blood.

Her pulse raced. "What happened?"

He shut the door and faced her. "They shot Virge. God, Mattie, they near killed him."

Virge, the most peaceful of the brothers. Allie's man. "Oh, Wyatt, no!" She ushered him into a front room chair and knelt in front of him. "Tell me."

Even in the dim lamplight, his face looked haunted. "We were on our way back to the Cosmopolitan after the game at the Oriental closed up. Not more than a block, Mattie. A goddamn block. Suddenly shots rang out. A shotgun. Virge got torn up bad."

Mattie swallowed. "He's alive?"

"He got hit in the back and his thigh, nearly tore his arm to pieces. He wouldn't let them take it off, but they took out most of his bone all through the elbow. The doctor's been working on him for hours."

She sat back on her heals, tears stinging.

Wyatt hung his head. "There were three of them. They found a hat with Curly Bill's name inside it."

The Cowboys. She reached for Wyatt and he took her hand. "What can I do?" she asked.

"You can get your things and move into the Cosmopolitan

with the rest of us." Virge and Morg had moved their wives into the hotel earlier in the month, when the threats had grown more intense. Wyatt had moved with them. Mattie and Bessie had refused.

She pulled her hand away. "I'm not moving into a room next door to your whore."

They'd had this argument before, when the men had come up with the plan. Wyatt had moved his whore in with 'em, right down the hall. Josephine Behan—Sadie Mansfield—it didn't matter none what she called herself. There was no way Mattie was going to live under the same roof as her. Hell, knowing Wyatt, he'd be back and forth between their rooms.

Wyatt stared at her, his eyes empty. "She's in California, with her folks."

"You sent her there to keep her safe?"

"Does it matter?"

She shrugged, guessing it didn't. But it said something about the place she held in his heart. Mattie stood, sighed. "How do you think that makes me feel?"

Wyatt stood but didn't pull her into his arms.

Mattie stared, the truth of it breaking her heart.

"Things died off between us a long time ago," he said. "You know it as well as I do."

"It doesn't make it right. You married me. Promised to provide for me. You've already left me without love. Next thing, you'll take away my roof and my support."

He rubbed at his neck. "There isn't time for this now, Mattie. Come to the hotel where I can protect you. I've got things to attend to."

"Revenge?"

"I need to get a temporary appointment as federal marshal in Virge's place, form a posse. I need to telegraph Ma and Pa and Warren. I need to get you settled."

"There's no sense in going. You're going to leave me there alone anyway."

"You'll be with Allie and Lou. James might move Bessie over, too. You won't be alone."

"That woman coming back?"

"She's not there, Mattie. Get your damn things packed and let's go. I won't leave you with nothing, I promise you."

She drew a breath, stood, and went down the hall to her room.

I won't leave you with nothing.

But he'd leave her all the same.

February 9, 1882 (six weeks later)

It didn't get no easier, that was the truth of it.

At first, Mattie had clung tight to Wyatt's promise, but a promise from Wyatt didn't count for much and it sure didn't help her pain. Yesterday, Ike Clanton had pushed to file murder charges again and Wyatt had mortgaged their house to pay attorney's fees.

She rubbed her jaw where another tooth was starting to ache and figured it was one more thing to bear. She needed a drink.

She padded down the hall of the hotel in her stocking feet and rapped on Allie's door.

Allie stared at her. "You don't look too good."

She didn't feel too good, either. "Can't sleep. Toothache. Heartache."

Allie smiled in sympathy. "What can I do?"

"Come have a drink with me?"

"I reckon I can do that sure enough. Let's all go. Downstairs."

Downstairs . . . lord but that would feel good. "The men will have a fit."

"I don't give a damn," Allie said. "Being locked up in a hotel room is worse'n being shut away in the house. They ain't gonna know, anyhow."

Mattie nodded. It didn't matter to her none if she got killed downstairs by one of Wyatt's enemies or if she got left to die on her own.

A half hour later, they clustered in the dining room and ordered whiskeys all around. If there was one thing Mattie liked about this family, it was that the women were of a mind. They shared past lives—except for Allie who said she'd been a waitress—and a fondness for drink and a need to manage their menfolk.

"Well," Bessie said, "here's to being married to the Earps."

It wasn't a celebration for Mattie, but she clinked her glass with the rest and downed the whiskey.

"Morg is sending me to his folks," Lou announced.

Newlyweds. Enough so that Morg still cared about Louisa. Of the four, it was Lou and Allie who had the best relationships, Mattie figured. Bessie and James were comfortable. She and Wyatt? Not too good.

"When are you going?" Bessie asked Lou.

"Day after tomorrow. This latest threat by Ike has Morg nervous. He doesn't think it will lead anywhere, but Ike's awful mad again."

Allie bristled. "Ike ought to be glad they got off after what they done to Virge."

They chatted, Mattie working up her nerve. "Wyatt mortgaged the house." She didn't say more, just waited.

Allie and Bessie nodded. No secrets among the Earps. Lou's hand went to her mouth, the only one who hadn't heard.

"How much did he put you in debt?" Bessie asked.

"Less than four hundred, but it's debt all the same."

Bessie pondered. "He *could* pay that off with one night's winnings."

"His luck hasn't been too good of late," Mattie said. "Edgy as he is, watching for an ambush."

Nobody said much of anything to that. None of their men had been having much luck.

"It'll work out," Lou finally said.

But Mattie wasn't too sure. "He promised me he'd see I was cared for."

"Oh, Mattie, no!" Allie reached out to her, understanding what Mattie'd left unsaid.

"Shit," Bessie said, her gaze focused on the lobby across the room.

Mattie's skin prickled. She turned, not wanting to, but feeling a need to know.

Sadie Mansfield stood at the registration counter, a fancy gown hugging her curves. She laughed at something the clerk said, then gave him a wide smile.

Mattie soured, turned away. "I need another drink."

Allie poured it, and another for herself.

"Lou and I will follow her up, see what room she's in." Bessie motioned for Lou to follow and they left the room.

Mattie's eyes stung. "Well, if Wyatt wasn't sure about leaving me before, he sure won't be long making up his mind."

"I was thinkin'," Allie said. "You got papers saying you and Wyatt are married?"

Mattie shook her head.

"So if he leaves you, you won't be able to prove you were married at all?"

"No." It was the same for all of them, Mattie suspected. Recording such things seemed important when folks were young and had parents arranging church marriages. Preachers put things in a book. It had never mattered much to the Earps. Lord knew she couldn't go back and get papers now.

If Wyatt left her for that woman, he could just walk away,

without anything but his own promise to break.

Yep, a promise from Wyatt didn't count for much.

Mattie glanced at Allie. "You reckon it has to be a marriage license?"

Allie shrugged. "I don't rightly know. I reckon anything that says you're married, long as it's official."

Far as Mattie knew, there were no papers with her name on them. None even with Wyatt's, except arrest records and such. Except for the debt he'd taken on yesterday. A man had recorded that. Wyatt had showed her the note saying he owed the money.

Him, not her. But she *could* have the man add hers. If her name was on it, she'd owe the money, too, but it would also say right there on paper that there was a Mrs. Wyatt Earp.

And him leaving her with nothing would become a whole lot more difficult.

★ ★ ★ ★ ★

Part Three: Unraveling

★ ★ ★ ★ ★

Allie

Them last days in Tombstone was a sort of unraveling. The months after the shooting of the Clantons were bad enough, but come spring, all hell broke loose. Josie never did tell much about that time. She couldn't. It didn't fit in with the Wyatt she wanted the world to see and she couldn't much lie about it. So she just skirted on around it.

Chapter Twenty-Four

Funny how now two accounts of a story never match up.

Josephine
Saturday, March 18, 1882 (about six weeks later)
Tombstone

I'd seen the Earp wives watching me, trailing my movements ever since I returned from San Francisco. Their resentment of me was palpable. I didn't understand it when it was clear Mattie didn't want Wyatt. She hadn't even bothered to move into the Cosmopolitan until Virgil had been shot. Why the family scorned me was beyond my ken. It strained things between Wyatt and me, making nights like tonight—when Wyatt was late—even worse to bear. He shared my bed every night, but the possibility that one of the brothers might sway him to end our now-public affair was ever-present.

I knew he was just delayed, but a small hard kernel of doubt had sprouted and wouldn't let me be. I paced my room, fighting it.

Something wasn't right. If any of them were persuading him not to come tonight, I needed to change his course. Wyatt was mine and Mattie could go to hell.

I grabbed a wrap and strode out into the hallway. At the top of the stairs, I draped my shawl over my arm and glided down as if I hadn't a care in the world. One of the other dealers was at the faro table. I sidled up to him, intent on locating my man.

"Where's Wyatt tonight?" I asked, feigning casual interest.

The dealer raised his eyebrows, knowing better. A warm pride simmered. Wyatt was mine and everybody knew it.

"He's meeting Morg and Doc over at Campbell and Hatch's for a round of billiards."

My pulse increased. Doc didn't like me, made snide remarks about me all the time. I'd been right to be concerned.

I kissed the dealer on the cheek, whispered a thank you into his ear, then headed back out. It bothered me that Wyatt hadn't said a thing earlier about meeting his brother. The billiard parlor was just a few doors down from the Cosmopolitan. I'd wander over and lure him back to my room. Tomorrow was his birthday. He'd enjoy my gift a hell of a lot more than a game of billiards.

Like usual for a Saturday night, Allen Street was busy, filled with the drunk and half-drunk alike. No one bothered to ask for my time. I was Wyatt's and they all knew it.

I turned into the saloon. "In the back?" I asked the bartender.

The man nodded, tipping his head toward the billiard room. I was halfway there when shots rang out.

Oh, God, Wyatt!

My heart raced and I sped to the back room.

Morgan was on the floor next to the billiard table, another man downed near him. Blood was everywhere.

Wyatt knelt beside his brother. "Morg. They shot Morg," he muttered to no one in particular.

I rushed forward and someone caught me. "Let him be. You can tend him later."

"But—"

"You'll be in the way." The man shoved me to the side of the room.

Hot anger surged and I turned back to Wyatt, then stalled. The man was right. A group of men struggled to lift Morg and carry him to a couch at the side of the room. I glanced around to see if anyone else had been injured. Two bullets had shattered windows, one of them lodging in the wall behind me.

"Missed Wyatt by this much," one of the men next to me said. His hands indicated inches.

A shudder ran through me. First Virgil, now Morgan. And they'd meant to get Wyatt.

"The Cowboys?" I asked.

"You ought to get back to the hotel, Miss Sadie. It isn't safe here," the man said.

I shook my head. "When I know Morg is all right."

A doctor rushed into the room and began examining Morg, while another customer tied a tourniquet around the thigh of the other downed man. "Bullet went clean through Morgan."

Wyatt glanced at Morg, took a step, then saw me. He stopped. Pure agony filled his face, his mouth hanging open, his eyes haunted. Then he closed his mouth and went to his brother's side.

I hung back, waiting. I could do no more. Once they'd tended to Morg, Wyatt would need me.

The doc called for a lamp, turned Morg on his side. "It doesn't look good, not from the angle of it," he told Wyatt. Then he leaned in and spoke to Morg. "Can you move your legs, son?"

Morg moaned, the sound harsh and guttural. He choked on it and Wyatt wiped his mouth.

"His legs aren't moving. I think the bullet went through the spine," the doctor said, the words soft in the quiet of the room. Most folks had cleared out, Doc Holliday among them.

Minutes later, Virge and James rushed into the room, followed by the wives in their nightclothes.

I moved back into the shadows, unsure of my place now that the entire family was here. I knew I should return to the hotel, but my feet stood firm.

"Do you . . . know who . . . did this?" Morg managed.

Wyatt leaned forward. "Yes. I'll get them."

"That's . . . all . . . I ask."

Morg's voice softened and I heard no more. Tears streamed down my face. They knelt there with him until he breathed his last, the rest of the room in silence. In all, it took less than forty minutes.

"Get him out of here," one of them said, his voice resigned, too soft for me to recognize.

It took little time to move Morg. The wives went with his body while the brothers clustered, making plans.

I waited, my heart breaking, helpless until they left, leaving Wyatt alone.

He turned, saw me. "You waited." The words came out on a soft breath.

I moved from the dark edge of the room and pulled him into my arms.

He shuddered, dropped his head onto mine. Sobs racked his body.

My soul nearly split.

When he was cried out, he sighed and pulled away. "There are things to be done, Sadie. One by one, they're trying to kill us." He stared at me and I saw fear in his eyes. Fear and a hatred I'd never seen before. It echoed mine.

"James will take Morg to our folks from the station in Contention City. I think we can make the 12:30 train. Virge and Allie will get packed up and leave Monday. With Virge's arm the way it is, he's too easy to pick off. Bessie and Mattie will close the rest of things up."

My heart clambered and a cold sweat hit my skin.

"And you?" I didn't ask the real question. *What about us?*

"I made a promise to Morg. I'll stay until it's kept."

The words didn't need to be said. *I'll get them.*

Josephine
Monday, March 20, 1882 (two days later)
Tombstone

I ate a late breakfast and returned to my room. Wyatt and the others had left earlier to take Virge and Allie to the train. There'd been a funeral procession yesterday morning, as James and the wagon with Morg's body had left town to catch the train. A pair of Wyatt's friends had gone along, just in case there was any trouble. I'd watched from the window. Wyatt hadn't revealed his plans and had refused to discuss our future. I was on pins and needles.

He'd left me early yesterday morning, well before dawn.

Wyatt and I had had little time. There'd been a tenseness about him, a brittle distraction edged with purpose. And perhaps rage. It was a side of him I'd never seen. But if Wyatt needed to revenge his brother, I would stand with him. And I would give him the space to do it. Even if it meant waiting without knowing what was coming.

"Josephine?" A rap sounded at my door.

I opened it to find Marietta Spencer. She huddled, arms wrapped around herself like she was chilled. She sported a bruise on her face.

"What is it?" I asked, glad to have something to focus on. I guided her into the room. "Pete beat you again?"

Marietta's marriage had not been the bliss she'd imagined on that stagecoach trip we'd shared. Pete Spencer had turned out to be a violent man. He was friendly with the Clantons, but Marietta and I had remained friends despite all that.

She nodded, her eyes red and swollen. "And my mother. Yesterday."

I ushered to the bed, sat next to her. "What can I do?"

"I did not come here for you to do anything for me. I came to tell you something. I am only sorry I could not get here sooner, but Spence wouldn't let us leave." Marietta used her pet name for her husband. "This morning he passed out and finally Mama and I could get outside."

"You should be taking care of you, not worried about telling me anything. That can wait."

"It can't. Spence will be very angry when he finds us gone."

A chill crept through me. "You're scaring me."

"On Saturday, Indian Charlie and Frank Stilwell came to our house with a man named Freeze. They were whispering and I did not hear what they said, but they were excited and left the house with many guns."

"They carry guns most of the time, don't they?" Much as I liked Marietta, she always took the long way around to get to the point.

"I did not think anything of it then. But Spence came home late in the night, just after the shots that killed Morgan Earp. He acted strange, like he was frightened, and his teeth were chattering. Then the others showed up, a few at a time. All of them were pale and trembling and they talked about leaving their horses outside of town where no one would see them. It was very strange. And then, in the morning, Spence was angry. Angry but not drunk. He woke me at six o'clock and said he would kill me, and Mama, too, if we told anyone about what we heard."

I stared at her. "Are you saying they killed Morgan?"

"I think so, yes. A few days ago, I saw Spence point out Morgan to Indian Charlie. I think they were planning it then."

Wyatt would need to know.

"Did you report this?" I asked her.

Marietta nodded. "I have been to the law. There will be an inquest, but I am afraid something might happen to Mama and me before we can then testify."

"You really think Pete would kill you?" He'd beat her plenty of times but murder? My skin crawled at the thought.

Tears flowed down her face. "I think we will be safe. We will stay with Kitty, but I wanted you to know what I saw, to tell Wyatt. You have been a friend."

"I'll tell him."

"I also heard whispers on the street when I was coming here. You must tell him that Frank Stilwell is in Tucson and Ike Clanton is going to join him. I think they plan to kill Virge tonight, when the train stops there."

Fear snaked through me. Virge could hardly get around, let alone defend himself.

"Should I go to Sheriff Behan's office again?"

I thought about it. Johnny and the Cowboys were in thick. "I don't trust Behan," I told her. "I'll take care of it myself." I grabbed her shawl and ran out of the room, leaving Marietta sitting on the bed.

I just hoped I could get the telegram off to Contention City to warn Virge before the train left the station there.

Mattie
Tuesday afternoon, March 21, 1882 (the following day)
Tombstone

"Mattie?" Wyatt shouted from the door of their hotel suite. "Where are you?"

Mattie rushed from the separate bedroom. He'd been due back in Tombstone last night, promised he'd let her know all was safe. She'd been worried to death this whole time. At the look of him, she caught her breath.

Good lord.

Wyatt's clothes were stained with sweat and trail dust, but it was his face that stalled her heart. His eyes held a haunted glaze. His jaw trembled. "God, Mattie."

She crossed to him, folded him in her arms. In that moment, nothing that was between them mattered, only that he'd come to her, that he needed her. He was shaking.

"Dear lord, Wyatt, what's going on?"

"I shot Frank Stilwell."

Mattie swallowed. No wonder he was trembling.

"Tell me what happened."

"Yesterday, a telegram came in for us at Contention City. It said the Cowboys were planning an ambush in Tucson. Warren and I and the others got on the train with Virge and Allie, just in case."

She held him close, fearing what he'd say next. It was obvious things had gone wrong. "They're safe? Virge and Allie? Warren?" She didn't ask about Doc and the other two friends. Family mattered most.

"At Tucson, it all looked quiet. I figured it had been a false alarm. We all had dinner across from the depot, then put Virge and Allie on the train to California. We were getting Virge settled into his seat and there was Stilwell at the window. Hell, Mattie, I saw red! I took off down the tracks after him. We all did."

"He shot at you?"

"The five of us cornered him. He told us he'd done the deed. Killed Morg. I shot the son of a bitch. We all did. I need to get things packed up. Stilwell whined like a baby when he was begging for his life. He said Curly Bill, John Ringo, and Hank Swilling were in on the killing of Morg. We're riding out after them."

Mattie threw a few clothes together for him. She recalled the gossip from earlier today and glanced back at Wyatt. There were other names he needed to know. "Marietta Spencer testified it was her husband, along with Stilwell, Indian Charlie, and Frank Bode."

"We heard, as soon as we got back into town. I sent for a warrant from the U.S. Marshal's office, but we have to get a posse rounded up. Can you finish packing for me? We're going to meet for dinner, then head out."

She nodded, but a hard knot tightened her gut. Wyatt had left too much unsaid. "A legal posse?" She hoped like hell they'd thought this out.

"We're going, Mattie, whether the warrant gets here on time or not. They murdered Morg and I won't let that stand. The shooting in October, them maiming Virg. It's gone too far."

A knock sounded at the door and it opened. Wyatt's brother Warren poked his head in. "Sorry, Wyatt, Mattie. Just wanted to let you know that friend of yours at the telegraph office just flagged me down. A wire came in for Behan a couple hours ago. Your friend's stalling on delivery of it, but he can't delay too much longer."

Wyatt's face paled.

Mattie shivered. "What is it?"

"The Pima County justice of the peace has issued a warrant for our arrest for the murder of Frank Stilwell."

Josephine
Tuesday, March 21, 1882 (that evening)
Tombstone

Wyatt and the others who had been in at the train in Tucson were clustered at a back-room table in the Cosmopolitan restaurant. One without any windows. I paced the lobby, waiting to hear what they planned to do.

The evening had been tense. A tight knot had formed in my gut and I couldn't sit still. I'd never felt such anxiety for anyone. No one I loved had ever been in danger.

Love? Was that it? Was that why the tension bound me up?

Johhny Behan, *Sheriff* Behan, sauntered into the lobby. "Well, if it isn't the lovely Sadie Mansfield," he said, snide as I'd ever heard him.

I wanted to slap his face.

"What do you want, Johnny?"

"He in here? Wyatt Earp?"

I shrugged. "How would I know?"

Johnny curled his lip and hatred bubbled. How had I ever desired him? "Oh, I think you know just about everything about your newest protector."

"I haven't any idea where he is." I let the words drip out and watched him steam.

"When he comes out from that dining room, you tell him I want to talk with him. I just got a telegram from Tucson we need to discuss."

"*If I see him,* I'll send him to your office." I gestured as if it was of no matter to me, but we both knew better.

"No, I'll wait across the street."

I drifted toward the stairs. "Well, *if* I see him, I'll let him know."

"You do that, Sadie." Johnny made a snorting sound and strolled out the front door. I watched from the window. True to his promise, he crossed Allen Street and positioned himself against the horse rail. The damn son of a bitch should be rounding up a posse to pursue those Marietta had named!

My gut clenched. *Damn.* Johnny had clearly decided which side he was on.

I glanced at the closed door of the private room, looked back out the window. Johnny was out there right where he said he'd be, where everybody could see the fine job their sheriff was doing. Where there were too many witnesses for Wyatt to resist.

I took a step toward the closed-up room. Wyatt had told me to leave them be, so they could figure out what to do. But that was before Johnny knew about the telegraph. *Now,* he'd arrest them the minute they stepped from the hotel.

I drew a breath and strode to the door, knocked twice.

"Who is it?" someone asked. Charlie Smith, I thought.

"Josie. I have news."

He opened the door enough to let me in, then closed it behind me.

"Behan got the telegram," I said. "He's waiting on the street."

Wyatt's head whipped up and he met my gaze. "Figured he would."

I drew a heavy breath, let it out. "Do you want me to distract him? So you can ride out?"

"Any word on whether Wyatt's been authorized to create a federal posse?" Dan Tipton asked. As deputy federal marshal, Wyatt had wired for official authority to do what Behan would not.

I shook my head. "Nothing yet, as far as I know."

"Hell," Wyatt said. "I was counting on that coming before Behan got involved."

Tipton met his gaze. "So what now?"

My heart raced and I stepped closer to the group. "Behan won't see justice done. You know he won't. He'll throw the entirety of you into jail and won't do a damn thing to track down Morgan's murderers."

Wyatt pounded on the table with his fist. "I'll be goddamned if I let that happen. Get your things, boys, we're going."

"Behan will be right behind us," Smith pointed out. "We'll need to go out the back. Sadie can have someone bring horses around."

I glanced from one to the other, weighing it. I knew Johnny, knew Smith was right. But I also knew Wyatt's despair at losing Morgan.

"I promised Morg," Wyatt said, his voice breaking with the words.

And if he didn't keep that promise, he'd never be free of regret. "I'd go after the sons of bitches," I said. "Authorization or not. You know it will come."

My mind scrambled, working out the politics of it, how it would be seen. "Johnny has no guts to act on his own. He mentioned the telegram, but he didn't say anything about having a warrant in hand. Tell him you'll surrender to Bob Paul. He's the sheriff in Pima County and that's where it happened. If Behan doesn't have a warrant in hand, he won't be able to do a thing."

Like a good lie, a good political move went a long way toward creating an acceptable situation.

"That'll work." Wyatt stood. "Get your things, boys. We're riding."

Mattie
Thursday, March 23, 1882 (two days later)
Tombstone

Mattie'd been fit to be tied. Her and Bessie both.

From the news Bob Paul had brought. Wyatt had crossed the line, killing Florentino Cruz at Pete Spencer's lumber camp yesterday morning. It didn't set well with her. Being married to a killer wasn't the life she'd planned on having.

"Do you think it's true?" she asked. She'd always trusted Bob and she reckoned as Pima County sheriff, he'd know better'n most.

Bob looked back at her from his chair in the sitting area of

Bessie's hotel room. "It isn't Wyatt's way of handling things, but I've never seen him this worked up before. It's like Morg's death unraveled something in him."

Mattie nodded. That's how she'd been seeing it. When it came to keeping the law, Wyatt was the most levelheaded. The one who always looked for settling things. "It's because it was Morg. And Virg before him."

When it came to family, Wyatt's emotions got too knotted up.

"Behan's rounding up a posse to go after them."

"You going?" Bessie asked.

Bob shook his head. "Not with that bunch. They're nothing but thugs and I'll have no part of it."

He was right on that account, but it would come down to how it looked to folks. "I reckon that's all Wyatt's group is looking like. The newspapers are all calling it a vendetta."

"In truth, Mattie, that's what it amounts to. Stilwell was after Virge. There are enough witnesses to that. I think they could have brought him in rather than killing him. They should have surrendered to me."

"I told him that. He told Behan as much on Tuesday night. Then he up and left town."

"I'm not sure how they'll survive out there," Bob said. "Smith and Tipton were supposed to secure a loan, return with cash, but Behan nabbed them. The judge released them for lack of evidence. Behan never had the actual arrest warrant in hand. I imagine they're back with Wyatt by now, but the group's got no money for supplies."

"Did you talk to them while they were in jail?" Bessie asked. "Did they tell you what happened?"

"They were evasive, but it sounded like Cruz had been a lookout, hadn't fired any of the shots that killed Morg. Wyatt and the others shot him out of anger during the interrogation."

Mattie's stomach clenched up. "That makes them guilty of

murder for sure this time." She winced at how careless the words were in front of the sheriff, then passed over the worry. Bob was a friend.

"They'll keep on until this ends, however it ends. I don't see any chance of them coming in at this point. I thought you'd want to know." Bob stood, picked up his hat.

Mattie walked him to the door. "Thank you, Bob. I know it wasn't easy for you to come here and tell me this."

"I'll stand by Wyatt, Mattie. I owe him that and this isn't in character. He's walked on the shady side of the law before but not like this."

After Bob had left the room, Mattie turned to Bessie. There was no way to get past that the law didn't matter to Wyatt now.

"I'm not staying," Bessie said. "I'm going to California so I can keep James out of this mess."

"I figured that'd be your choice."

Bessie crossed the room, took Mattie's hands. "What are you going to do?"

"Bob Paul is right. Wyatt and the others will see this through right on to the end of it, until all the Cowboys are dead. Maybe even 'til Wyatt's dead."

"You gonna wait for him or leave him?"

Mattie shrugged. "I been waiting for him since I married him, one way or another. Waiting for him to get rich, for him to turn us respectable, for him to quit straying, for him to love me. I'm tired of waiting."

"I can't decide for you, Mattie."

"I'll come with you. I guess since I've waited through everything else, I can wait one more time." Maybe when he was shed of the vengeance and Tombstone, he'd be shed of that whore he was with, too, and they could start over new.

★ ★ ★ ★ ★

Josephine
April 1882 (the next month)
Tombstone

Wyatt didn't return to Tombstone. Instead, the news drifted in about the vendetta and the deaths that went with it. I'd expected it. What I hadn't anticipated was the aftermath around town.

By mid-March, the fine folks of Tombstone had begun treating me like a pariah. At first, there'd been snubs—uncomfortable after the months of semi-respectability. But then, there were death threats. Afraid, I'd moved in with Kitty and Harry under the cloak of darkness. Kitty spread it around that I'd left town.

Tombstone was tense and nearly everyone who'd been associated with the Earps had fled. I would, too, just as soon as Wyatt sent for me. A friend had wired my family on my behalf, asking for money. My trunks were packed and I'd go to him as soon as the pardon came through.

I was desperate to hear from him, pacing as I waited for Kitty to return. Wyatt sent all messages to Harry's law office and she checked daily for word from him.

The door sounded and I spun as she entered. "Any word?"

Kitty hung up her shawl and crossed the room. She laid a thin letter on the table next to my chair, then sat next to me.

I picked it up, my hands shaking. The return address said Albuquerque. I slid a letter opener under the seal.

"Open the damn thing," Kitty said.

I unfolded the paper and began to read. Wyatt, Warren, and Doc had traveled north, the others splitting off. He'd given an interview to a reporter, had an argument with Doc. The details that followed caught my attention. Reading, the tremble spread.

"What is it?" Kitty asked.

"There were words. About me." Stunned, I lowered the letter. Doc had never been a friend, but I hadn't expected him to interfere like this.

"They argued about you?"

I sighed. "There was a discussion about Mattie. About what Wyatt should do. Warren spoke for Mattie, said Wyatt owes her an obligation. Doc didn't much care about what happened to Mattie, but he had nothing but filth to say about me."

Kitty blew out a derisive sound. "That sounds a lot like Doc. I wouldn't worry about it."

I read the words again, looking for any way to avoid my brewing anger. I couldn't. I let it swarm before I spat out a response to Kitty. "He said I was a Jew-whore best left behind. Cheap and out for Wyatt's money."

She snatched the letter away. "Oh, honey, no!" Setting it on the table, she grabbed my hand. "Wyatt cares about you. If they fought about it, you can be sure that's what matters."

I shook my head. "He and Doc have a bond, ever since Wyatt saved Doc's life."

"It's not the same as a bond between a man and a woman. You said they fought."

I drew my hand away, took a breath. I hadn't read past the sentence with Doc's insult. Rage still simmering, I picked up the letter. Surely Kitty was right. Wyatt wouldn't stand for Doc saying such things.

I read the next bit and my pulse slowed a bit. "It was bad enough that Doc left!"

"You see!"

I lowered my gaze and read the rest. Shock rushed up my throat, choking me.

"What? What is it?"

I stared at Kitty. "Doc left, but his words stayed behind.

Wyatt doesn't want me to come. He says he has to honor his marriage." Hot tears ran from my eyes. "He's done with me."

★ ★ ★ ★ ★

Part Four: New Realities

★ ★ ★ ★ ★

Allie

After Tombstone, nothing was the same. There was new realities for all of us.

I reckon that's when the lying really started. At least the lying that mattered most.

Chapter Twenty-Five: Mattie

Hope isn't a lie.

July 1882 (three months after the letter to Josie)
San Francisco

Waiting wore on Mattie. It wounded her, deep in her soul that Wyatt had been in the city for some two weeks before sending word to her, but she'd decided to pretend she didn't know. That way, the small betrayal wouldn't come between them. It was time for a fresh start and she didn't want to let the past ruin things.

The stink of fish was heavy at the wharf where she waited for Wyatt. She swore San Francisco smelled near as bad as Dodge City, except it was fish that crawled its way up a body's nose and stayed put there. For some reason, the fish markets reminded her of decay, though she knew the fishmongers tossed out what had slipped past its time. Maybe the stink plain lingered.

She looked up, saw Wyatt striding toward her, and her innards tumbled with a mess of joy and frustration. "You're here, you're finally here," she said.

Wyatt folded her in his arms. "I'm glad you're safe. The family is treating you well?"

"They always do. There are no worries on that end."

They walked a ways, found a bench, sat.

Wyatt was handsome as always, but there were new lines in

his face. The months of constant travel had been hard on him, Mattie figured. And the burden of what had happened.

"I felt so bad for you," she said, "that you were going through all that happened without no one there."

Wyatt's mouth stretched but the line was thin. "Warren stayed close, up until I came here to Virgil's."

"You figure it's safe here?"

"Safe enough. There are no federal warrants, so I'm fine as long as I don't return to Arizona."

They were skirting around things, their old comfort gone. Mattie sighed, unsure how to regain what they'd had. She wasn't even convinced they could. "Are you shed of Arizona then?" she finally asked.

"I meant to go back, wanted to. We have property in Tombstone, the house, the mines, part interest in the Oriental's gaming. I thought it would blow over and we'd be done with it by now."

That would be a blessing, to be done with all of it. She reached for his hand. "You regret it? All that came after?"

"I promised Morgan there'd be justice for him. It wouldn't have happened otherwise, not with Behan."

Lines of regret filled his face, telling her his revenge hadn't given him what he'd sought. She didn't know how to fix that for him. It was something he'd have to live with.

"Killing was never part of your nature, Wyatt."

"It never had to be," he said with a sigh.

"It's weighed on you."

"What's done is done. I won't do any more of it." He squeezed her fingers. "I figure to live on gambling and what comes from the mines. I'm done with the law. There's too much entanglement, too much politics. I was never any good at that."

"Will we settle here, then?"

He shifted, said nothing.

Unease rippled under Mattie's skin. "Wyatt?"

"These past months, since April, I've chased the future round and round. I'm not sure we have one anymore." He stroked her hand, but it brought no comfort to her.

"You're done with me? Just like that?" She drew her hand away.

"It's not *just like that* and you know it. We haven't been solid for years."

She knew the truth of his words but it made things no easier. "You seeing her still?"

"I told her we were done. I meant to salvage things with you, but the longer I thought on it, the more I don't know if we can work things out. You hate my gambling and I don't see any other living for me."

Mattie thought on it. They'd survived fine these last years, with no desperate scrambles for money. A spark of hope surfaced. "You're a better gambler than you used to be."

"It isn't the life you wanted."

"Maybe it's time I settled on another life. We're never going to be high class anyway. I didn't mind it so much, in Tombstone. Folks didn't look down on us for it."

"It might mean moving around again."

"We're older, wiser. We'd just have to keep money back."

Wyatt shifted. "I don't know, Mattie. I don't know if there's enough feeling left between us."

Emptiness threatened again, but she pushed back on it, digging for hope. "You got any love left for me?"

"I care about you. I made vows to you. But there hasn't been love, not real love, for a long time. Caring about someone isn't enough, not when there are so many differences between us."

"And you've just decided all this without talking to me?"

He caught her gaze. "Would it have changed any of it?"

He'd never wanted to talk things out. But more than any

other decision, this was one she needed to be part of. "I love you. I don't want this to be done."

The words settled on him and they sat in silence for a few moments.

Finally, Wyatt spoke. "I need time. My heart is still so full of grief and hatred that it's shoved everything else away."

It wasn't a promise but it wasn't a castoff, either. Mattie reckoned she'd have to settle for that and hang on, wait a little longer. "So what happens to me?" she asked. "I can't stay with your family forever. That wouldn't be right."

"I'll send money every month. You can get a place. Give us time to think on this."

"You said you'd meant to go back to Arizona. If the pardon came, would you? Maybe if we were to go back to Tombstone, where you've got the gambling interest and the mines, it would be easier between us?"

"Aw, Mattie. I don't know. It'd be a struggle."

"Sometimes, struggles are worth it." She patted his leg.

Wyatt nodded. "I won't close my mind to it. For now, Virge and I are going to open a faro game here in San Francisco. I think it'd be best if you and I stay apart until I get this worked through."

"If that's what it takes, I'll wait on you."

August 1882 (the next month)
Prescott, Arizona

Mattie figured it was up to her to get things back on track while Wyatt stewed in his regrets. Last week, fed up with waiting, she'd asked James to buy her a train ticket to Arizona, and taken things into her own hands. If she was going to get Wyatt back, she'd best get him out of San Francisco. He'd hide there forever unless that pardon came through from the governor of

Arizona Territory.

She glanced up from her chair in the waiting area of the governor's fancy office, feeling out of place. She had figured it would be a lot harder for the governor to refuse a pardon if he had to do it to her face.

The bespectacled secretary approached. "I'm sorry Mrs. Earp, but the governor isn't able to see you."

"Not able to or not willing to?" Mattie asked. It was the third time this week the self-important little man had refused her. She *had* to get in to see Governor Tritle or Wyatt would never get the pardon. She put a stop to her toe, which had started tapping of its own accord a half hour before and stood so as the gatekeeper couldn't look down on her.

Once on her feet, she looked him in the eye. He wasn't very tall.

"He's simply too busy today."

"You told me that two days ago. Told me yourself to come back today."

"We didn't anticipate things would come up. Perhaps if you came back tomorrow."

Mattie felt the heat rise in her. He was putting her off and she knew it this time. At first, she hadn't thought a thing of it. The second time, it annoyed her but now she was pissed off. She let loose of the respectable façade she'd been hanging onto. Pretending at being a lady hadn't worked thus far.

"I'm not coming back again tomorrow. Not without making a big to-do about it. Maybe I'll bring a newspaper man with me. I might bring a few friends to fill up this here office, maybe camp here all day long. I reckon I could get word to some of the opposition party . . . that's what they're called, I think . . . and let them have a heyday with how you won't let folks in to see their own governor." Mattie didn't have friends here, but she'd heard other folks brew up threats of a hullabaloo and figured she had nothing to lose. And Pa Earp had told her, if she got in a bind, to act like she owned the place. She reckoned this was a bind.

"I'm sorry, I can't—"

"You really want me to stir up a hornet's nest about this? Hasn't the governor got enough to deal with without having to take on news stories and political fights? When you could have prevented it? You know you'll lose your job."

There, now his eyes widened up.

"I'll see what I can do."

"Why don't you just let me in right now? I'm mighty tired of waiting."

He stood there, seemingly unsure.

"You got a preference for which newspaper man I go to, or should I just round up all of 'em?"

"No need for all that." The words rushed from his mouth. "I think the governor can see you now."

Mattie marched straight for the inside door, before the secretary could call her bluff.

He hurried to pass her, opened the double door with a flourish. "Mrs. Wyatt Earp to see you, Governor."

Tritle sat behind a large wooden desk. He looked annoyed.

Mattie kept her pace firm, passed by the secretary, and sat in the chair across from Tritle. "I'm Mattie Earp and we have things to discuss." She turned to the secretary. "You can go now."

Tritle leaned back, clearly amused. "Most people don't get past him. I don't think I've ever seen anybody send him scurrying."

"A body does what it has to."

The governor settled back into his chair. "Are you married to Wyatt or Warren?"

"Wyatt. Warren ain't married."

"Well, Mrs. Wyatt Earp, what can I do for you?"

"I came to talk about the pardon."

Tritle raised his brow. "What pardon would that be?"

"The one you're issuing."

"Ah, now, Mrs. Earp, you know that's not going to happen."

"I figured that's why I had to come. Sometimes it pays for a wife to be heard."

They stared at one another before he continued. "Were you in Tombstone, Mrs. Earp?"

"I was. Sat at home waiting with my sisters-in-law for our men when they were out enforcing the law, dealing with that unholy mess near every day."

"That unholy mess is exactly why I can't issue a pardon. The entire town is overrun with lawlessness, outlaws and lawmen alike."

That was for damn sure, but it wasn't the point Mattie needed to make. She leaned forward. "I've never seen men more dedicated to the law than Virgil and Wyatt Earp. When the county sheriff wouldn't tend to getting things under control, they done what they had to, deputizing Morg to help. I'll allow they ought not to have included Doc Holliday, but Doc was loyal as a dog to Wyatt. The others, the ones that stepped up after Virg got crippled and Morg was killed . . . all by the same ones that no one else tried to stop . . . they were all after one thing. Controlling that lawlessness you're talking about."

"Until they crossed the line."

Mattie refused to be cowed. "What were they supposed to do? Bring them in so Johnny Behan could let them go?"

The governor waved his hands. "I have no choice in this."

Mattie blew out a breath. "Politics. Making sure Tombstone doesn't get named territorial capital over Prescott." Since coming to town, she'd learned all about that knot. Tombstone had petitioned to become the new capital and Tritle was determined to prevent the effort. He'd raised a fuss about the unrest there, even wrote to Washington about it.

"I won't deny that," Tritle confirmed. "But I can't reverse myself. I asked the president to condemn what happened. He did. All of it. I can't pardon any of them without looking like an ass."

Anger churned, but Mattie forced herself to stay calm. "So you'll sit there while good men stand branded as outlaws? You should be praising what they were trying to do. Don't you see that? If you work out how you tell your reasons, you can look good doing it."

"I can't, Mrs. Earp. I won't."

With that, her self-control slipped. "And the other lives you're destroying?" she asked, frustration filling her tone. "Virgil hasn't received his compensation for being injured on the job. He can't work. What're he and his wife to do? Warren and Wyatt are living day by day. I'm left with no support. I can't even sell the house without him coming back to sign the papers and he can't do that, not being a wanted man."

"He made his choice, Mrs. Earp." Tritle rose, crossed the room to the door. "There will be no pardon. I don't care what happens to Wyatt and Warren. Virge's folks will see to him." He grasped the knob and drew the door open, motioning for her to depart.

"As to your well-being, most women in positions like yours find a way. Miners are lonely men, Mrs. Earp. They pay well for female company."

Chapter Twenty-Six: Josephine

Reality is what one creates.

Early 1883 (the new year)
San Francisco

San Francisco remained as vibrant as I remembered it—enough so that I refused to move in with Rebecca and the family again. I turned to my old friend Lucky Baldwin. He rented me a small apartment just down the street from his theatre and I drowned my sorrow by spending my nights in his box. As to Lucky—well, he did like the ladies, and Sadie Mansfield was not a woman easily ignored.

Except by Wyatt.

Grief and resentment warred within me. Despite the obvious benefits of being favored by Lucky, I couldn't settle in. Especially once I heard Virgil Earp was in town. In the fall, area papers reported both Warren and Wyatt had passed through, always after the fact. But if I knew Wyatt—and I did—he'd be back and I was determined to locate him. He'd be in one gambling hall or another, I was sure.

I would *not* be brushed off like some common whore. Not by Wyatt.

The problem was, if I was going to troll the gambling halls in search of him, I needed to know how to play. Otherwise, I'd be a whore asking for men. If I played, I'd attract less attention.

"So, will you take me?" I purred in Lucky's ear.

He gave me a lopsided smile. "Why would you want to go gambling when you can spend the night at the theatre?"

"I'm curious," I lied. "I want to see what the excitement is all about."

"Gambling is a man's game, Sadie."

"Not like it was. You know the best places. And you know how to play well."

"I'm lucky."

"Skilled. In so very many ways." I let my hand trail down his arm. "Please?"

He ignored me, brushed me away as he stood. "Leave it be, Sadie. Faro is a game that can suck a person in. There are too many crooked dealers out there and cheating is rampant."

"You're no fun at all."

"I'm not teaching you to play faro and that's that. Go dress for tonight. I'll see you in the box." He pecked me on the cheek and left to prepare for his evening. Lucky was temporary and we both understood that, but the security he brought was what I needed. Still, his enthusiasm had waned and already he tended to treat me as a ward rather than a paramour.

I knew I shouldn't mind. It was easier this way. But the sting of it bit at me.

I slammed my wardrobe door shut, wincing at the bang. It wouldn't do to break the mirror. When the glass failed to fall, I breathed easier and returned to dressing. I'd chosen a deep merlot gown, one with a neckline low enough to draw attention but not so plunging that it invited offers.

My curves had become more defined with maturity and I was pleased with my shape, though my short stature made for a squatter hourglass than I would have liked. I blew a kiss to the mirror and headed into the busy streets of the city, away from the theatre district. I wasn't much in the mood for sitting through yet another night of the current play. If Lucky wouldn't teach me faro, I'd have to learn it on my own.

The gambling clubs were scattered across the city. I'd heard Virgil was operating a game in the area south of Chinatown and I'd find it, eventually, but it wouldn't hurt to stop at a few other places first to learn what to do. I'd watched plenty but never played and the last thing I wanted was to look like a desperate fool prowling for Wyatt.

Even if that's what I was.

The hills Ella Howard and I had scampered over so effortlessly were a chore in my corset and I rued I'd not hired a hansom. I'd not even considered how tiring it would be. I slowed, taking my time, and turned into the first establishment I saw. I could learn here as well as anywhere.

Inside, gas lamps lit the single large room. Men flocked along the bar at one side, whores among them. Tables were clustered to the left, a variety of games being played. A scattering of women sat in the games, some of them seeking customers, a few intent on the games.

None looked respectable.

I sighed. Without Lucky taking me to the best clubs, this would be the way of it.

I wandered in, seeking the faro tables. They were lined up along the far wall, the telltale faro boxes centered on each. Men glanced my way and I smiled back, projecting confidence I didn't feel. I sidled into an empty chair.

"We have about ten turns left," the dealer said.

"I'll wait."

I ordered a whiskey and watched the play. There were three players, each placing bets by placing tokens on thirteen cards that were outlined on the green cloth of the box. I struggled to keep up with the variety of bets. Some chips were placed at the center of the cards—that was an even bet, one for one. But there were corner bets that involved two cards diagonal from one another and row bets on several cards and coppering bets with pennies atop the chips. Around me, the other players called out phrases I'd heard many times, all signals on the amounts staked. The basics were easy. A card was dealt and winners were those who'd bet on that card. Unless it was the loser card, in which case the dealer won.

By the time the last turn of the game was over, I'd downed half my drink and determined I'd best start with even bets. So far, everything looked kosher in terms of the cards coming out of the spring-loaded box one at a time. I didn't see any way for the dealer to cheat.

"You ready little lady?"

"I'm always ready." I flashed him a smile as the man next to me sniggered. I flashed him a scornful glance and purchased my chips.

He raised one eyebrow and we placed our bets.

The dealer flipped out the first card and discarded it. Then he dealt out the loser card—the one that determined the chips that would go to the house. The man at the end of the table groaned; he'd lose a chip. Finally, the dealer laid out the card that signaled the win.

Easy enough. Chance, pure and simple.

But as the game went on, I realized the skill involved was in keeping track of which cards had already been dealt. In the games I'd watched in Tombstone, Wyatt had sometimes used a wire-and-bead mechanism to indicate the play but this dealer had none. This, then, was the core of it—where players who lost track made careless bets.

Players like me.

The twenty-five turns ended with me down twenty-one chips. Even with my careful one-for-one bets, I'd managed to lose most of the time. Two hours later, my purse was empty.

"I could buy you a few chips," the man with the eyebrow

said. "We could find a way for you to make it even."

I shook my head. Not tonight.

Instead, I downed the last of my current drink and staggered toward the door. I'd had a bit more than I'd planned. That might account for my inability to follow the play. Tomorrow, I'd drink less. It was an easy game. I just needed to keep my wits about me, learn to keep track of the cards.

How difficult could it be?

After a week of playing, I hadn't mastered that skill. I was drawn by the pace of the game and was following the lead of other players, upping the stakes on my bets when they did, covering multiple cards in a bet, and the challenge of beating the system was exciting.

I entered a small dark place on Pine Street, just a room in the front of a house, the sort of place that would get shut down for operating without a gambling license. A makeshift bar—a plank across two barrels—stood in the corner. Two faro tables filled the rest of the tiny room.

I made my way through the dimness and settled into a chair, pulled out my reticule, and handed a fistful of money to the dealer.

"I wondered when I'd see you," a familiar voice said. "I didn't expect it would be here."

A shiver sped its way up my spine. I looked up and caught Wyatt's gaze. "I did."

"You gonna get the game going or not?" one of the men said.

"I think I'm going to close things down. Virgil has a spot open." Wyatt tilted his head toward the other table. "The lady and I need a few minutes."

"Lady, my arse!" The man's gaze made its way over my body but he moved nonetheless.

Once he was gone, Wyatt took the empty seat and stared at me.

I shivered again as the silence stretched. "I heard you were in town," I finally said. "I knew I'd see you at some point."

"I didn't think it'd be at a faro game."

"I doubt you get out on the town to do much else."

His gaze roamed my body. "You've been looking for me?"

"After a fashion. You ought to have known I don't take orders well."

"I didn't want you staying in Tombstone. Not with the way things were there."

"You didn't have to tell me it was over."

"I thought it was best. I owed Mattie."

Pain bubbled and I realized I didn't much like knowing she played such a big part in it. My jaw set. "So you went back to her? She's here with you?"

"I meant to."

My heart skipped a beat. "Meant to but didn't? Is that what you're saying?"

"I told her I needed time."

I let the subject drop, needing time to let my emotions settle. "How are you?" I asked instead. "It's been almost a year since I saw you. I haven't been able to get you out of my mind. You didn't even write to let me know how you were. Damn it, Wyatt, I've been worried sick. The only thing that's kept me sane are the reports in the papers. At least I knew you were safe."

"We went to New Mexico . . . you know that . . . then Colorado. Once things cooled down, Warren and I ventured out here. We're trying to keep a low profile, but since there's no federal warrant, we're safe as long as we don't return to Arizona." His voice was cool, distant.

After a while, I had to ask. If it was really over, I needed to know. "And what about us? You knew this was where I'd come.

You couldn't seek me out?"

Wyatt sighed. "I should go back to Mattie."

I snorted, unable to bite back my resentment any longer. "Like hell. You don't love her and you know it."

"I told you, I owe her. A man doesn't leave his obligations."

"So you're not with her?"

"Not at the moment."

"Then it seems to me you *have* left her." I couldn't make sense of it. Either he was with her or he wasn't.

"I send money. Told her to give me time. She's waiting for me."

I leaned toward him. "People get divorces all the time."

"I can't do that."

"Why the hell not?"

"Damn it, Sadie, quit harping on me. I've made my decision."

I sat back. He was angry and it'd get me nowhere to stir that pot. He obviously didn't love her. I'd need to try a different tack. "All right. Don't divorce her. But you don't plan to be faithful to her for the rest of your life, do you? Vows didn't stop you before. Why would they now?"

He shrugged.

What had happened to the Wyatt I knew? "Is this something that's tied up with Morgan dying?"

"It's tied up with every one of my remaining brothers taking me to task. With Doc feeling strongly enough about it to sever our friendship. With me taking responsibility for the first time in my life. Had I done it before, I might have avoided the mess I created."

"Tombstone? You didn't create that mess! You stumbled into it without the means to handle it. Leave it be. It's over and done with. Forget about Tombstone."

"And what about what I dragged Mattie through before then?"

Life didn't turn out as anyone expected. I'd learned that. And I'd learned that if a person dwelt on it, they'd fret forever. "All of it is done. You can't change what happened so just erase it." I stroked his arm. "Start new. Send Mattie money if you feel obligated, but don't cripple your life feeling sorry about it. You've clearly decided you won't be with her."

"So I just forget about all that happened?" He sank his head into his hands.

"It's in the past. No one needs to know about it. Invent a new past. Who's going to know the difference but Mattie and the family?"

He looked up. "You'll know."

"Oh, Wyatt, I'm real good at making folks believe what I want them to." I laughed, letting the moment stretch.

"You'd still want me?" he finally asked. "After all I've done? After the men I killed for Morg?"

My heart stalled. "Is that what this is really about? You know as well as I do that I supported revenging him."

"Saying it and living with it are two different things."

"I told you to go."

"People say I'm a killer." Anguish filled his voice.

I took his hand. "People say things all the time. Doesn't make it true. You were tracking down outlaws and murderers."

"Was I? What about those I wasn't sure of?"

"You were sure of them all. You did what had to be done. You are a hero, Wyatt Earp. Act like one and the world will see you as one."

"And if I'm not?"

"In my eyes, you are. That's all that matters."

He looked into my eyes and the corners of his mouth lifted. "And me still being married?"

"I can forget that. We can forget that. Who else really knows?"

"I guess nobody."

It wasn't quite true, but it would be. I'd see to it. I smiled back at him.

"I'll never be a lawman again," he said. "That means a pretty unstable life, lots of moving around, relying on gambling income."

"I'm used to moving around—it's all I've done these past eight years." I leaned forward and kissed him, deep, inviting. Cheers and catcalls erupted around us. Then I drew back. "I'm willing to bet my stake on us. Turns out I rather like gambling."

Late 1884 (close to two years later)
Eagle City, Idaho

Wyatt hadn't exaggerated when he said we'd move around. Eventually, Bessie and Jim joined us—Warren, too—their misgivings about me shuttered away. The brothers were too close for them not to adjust, whether or not they agreed with Wyatt choosing me. We found common ground in making our shared ventures profitable. As towns went, Eagle City wasn't much, not like the other towns we'd been through. But we all knew Eagle City was full of opportunity. It was a boomtown. Between gold, drunks, and lust, we'd all make a fortune.

Bessie and I eyed the empty tent. Jim and Warren were out staking claims with Wyatt. Bessie and I were taking care of the business end of things. She had the business sense we'd need, I had the flare.

"It's got plenty of room," I noted.

"It's a damn circus tent." Bessie wasn't particularly pleased with the purchase but it was a done deal, so we had to find a way to make it work.

"Yeah, but fifty feet across is good space." In fact, fifty feet was a damn big area.

"There won't be room for a stable, not without upstairs rooms."

I sighed. I should have known Bessie would focus her skills on trying to make it into a whorehouse. "Look, Bessie, I know this isn't what you had in mind when you and James agreed to come, but let's be inventive. We can put in a good-sized bar, set up several faro games, keno if James wants to deal that."

"The money's in running girls," Bessie insisted.

"The money is offering something different. Let's plan on three games. I don't think Wyatt will trust just anyone with dealing."

"Doc isn't coming?" She changed subjects but I suspected we'd return to the brothel eventually. Bessie didn't let things lie for long.

I shook my head. "I doubt it. We saw him in Gunnison and he's not well. Besides, he doesn't like me." Hated me was more like it.

"Doc don't like half the folks he meets." Bessie glanced around the tent. "Well, we'd better plan on selling a lot of drinks. The men paid a fortune for this white elephant."

I clapped my hands together. "That's it! We'll call it *The White Elephant.*"

"I still say we need whores."

I ignored her. "Do you think we can find a piano? Or musicians with their own instruments? We could make it a dance hall."

"Recruit girls for dancing?"

It wasn't exactly what I'd meant but it would work. "There are places in San Francisco that do that. The girls get the men thirsty, encourage them to buy drinks. For every drink, they get a small percentage. The more drinks they sell, the more we all make."

"Don't seem too profitable to me."

"Depends on the price of the drink. Boomtown like this, drinks will be high. Women will be in demand. Men will like the idea of being able to dance with them. Hell, I won't whore but I'd dance."

Bessie bit her lip. "What if we build a small shack out back? Two small rooms. If one of the girls wants to take a customer, we can get a piece of that."

I knew she'd keep at it until I gave in. Whoring had been her fallback for too long. Mine, too, but I was done with it. "Works for me, as long as I don't have to do it. And as long as we don't get shut down or fined."

"You've never run a place, have you?"

"No."

"There's money in it, Sadie, lots of money."

I bristled. "I prefer Josie. Only Wyatt calls me Sadie."

"Whatever toots your whistle, honey."

Glad I didn't need to explain, I focused on her input. She was right, I'd never run a place—even Tip Top had been managed by the bartender. And, truth be told, I was happier not to be associated with it. "You run the side business, I'll run the dance hall," I offered. We'd get along better that way as well, I suspected. I wasn't Mattie and we both knew it.

"I can handle that. Jim will want to take charge of the bar."

"Wyatt will want to manage the gaming."

"Warren?"

"He'll come and go, I expect. Let's let the men work out his role."

"Then we're set." The men were used to their narrow spheres, Bessie and I to our individual interests. It was a scattered way to manage, but it would work. "Let's round up some tables, get a bar built, and put out the word we need dancers and musicians."

I nodded. It would be an adventure, the kind Wyatt and I thrived on. And the best part was that the gambling enterprise would be ours. Even when I lost, we'd win.

Chapter Twenty-Seven: Mattie

Sometimes, surviving depends on what you tell yourself.

Spring 1887 (three years later)
Globe, Arizona

Waiting out Wyatt was no easy thing. Mattie hadn't reckoned it would be, but there were times it pure drained her. She'd settled in Globe, with Kate Elder, Doc's woman, of all folks. Big Nose Kate, they called her. The woman still had a habit of sticking it in places where it didn't belong. But Mattie sure wasn't going to begrudge that big nose. If it hadn't been for Kate sticking it into Mattie's business, she'd have no place to be.

The pardon hadn't come. The security she'd planned by putting her name on that mortgage note hadn't come; the house had been repossessed three years back. And Wyatt still hadn't come. She'd waited, sure he'd send for her once he settled. But instead, he'd taken Sadie.

Sadie had chased him down in San Francisco, from what Allie wrote. And with Wyatt being unsure of things in their marriage, he'd been helpless to her wiles. Wyatt always did have a weakness in that area. Mattie had figured he'd tire of her, as he had every other whore, and come back to her. She hadn't expected it would take this long.

Oh, he sent money every month—a sure sign that he still cared about her. But the money didn't stretch far. She figured it was all he could spare. The gambling circuit had always been fickle with him.

"You ready?" Kate called from the hall.

"Just about."

Mattie took a swing of whiskey from the bottle on her bureau and let it slide down her throat. Doc was coming to Globe for a visit. She had a few more teeth that were rotting away and she'd ask him to pull them out. No sense keeping them now. She was thirty-seven years old, her youth long gone.

Hell, she looked like an old woman.

Felt like one, too. Between her mouth and the aches in her female area, she wasn't sure which was worse. Way too much whoring, she guessed.

"Mattie? Let's go!"

"I'm coming." She took another swig of the whiskey and chased it with a swallow of laudanum. Not much, not with the whiskey, but enough to hone down the edge of the pain. Being out and about would stir up the throb down below and there was nothing Doc could pull there.

She glanced in the mirror, saw a matron standing there, dressed nice but looking old.

Tarnation.

She should lose some weight for when Wyatt came back.

There were lots of things she should do, she reckoned.

She left her room for the dark hallway of the St. Elmo Hotel. Not really a hotel, just a fancy name Kate had dreamed up for her brothel. Still, Kate had given up a room to her and didn't demand Mattie take johns.

She did, more often than she'd like to, but not every night. Only when the money ran low. It made her feel small and cheap to do it, but she held her head high most times.

Kate was pacing in the kitchen when Mattie came down the back stairs. She eyed Mattie, all trussed up in the new dress. "Don't you look like a picture."

"Too much?"

"I told you when you bought it that it was a fine gown. Quit fussing." Kate grabbed their parasols from the table. "I say we should get our pictures done. Celebrate a bit."

"What am I celebrating?"

"Getting your rotten teeth pulled!" Kate giggled, the throaty sound hinting at her foreign accent. She'd lost much of it over the years, but it was still there in her laugh.

They left the hotel and headed down the street. Globe wasn't as big as Tombstone, but silver strikes had made a mark here, too. Mattie and Kate enjoyed the occasional night out at the theatre and were well known at the eateries. The town had provided Kate with a good living for eight years now and she'd managed to stay away from the taint of Tombstone. She'd made a good decision, not staying with Doc.

Besides, Kate and Doc never did too well when they were together for any length of time. There was a bond between them, but time away made it better.

Mattie figured that's sort of how it was with her and Wyatt now. Each of them with their own lives but still connected. Maybe Doc would bring word from Wyatt that he was ready for her to come.

Kate strode ahead, grabbing Mattie's hand. "Here! Let's do our pictures." She pulled Mattie into the small shop. Mattie winced as the movement stirred the ache low in her belly.

Inside, Mattie shivered. The last time she'd had her photograph done, she'd been a virgin, on the edge of becoming a whore. Her skin prickled at the memory of being posed, the photographer's hands on her, his eyes boring into her, making her feel worthless. Then, what she'd let him do in exchange for the proper photo. It'd scraped her soul bare.

"Miss Kate! It's good to see you." The photographer looked around. "I expected you to have a girl in tow."

Mattie forced herself to take a breath.

"Not today. Today is just us. Mattie and I would like our images done, for the fun of it." She turned to Mattie. "Have you ever?"

"Once. I had two sets done. One for my use, one to send with my sister." It was all over with, had been nothing really, not compared to what she'd done later. What she'd done since.

He took them into the back room, arranged pillars and chairs, posed them proper and ladylike.

When they were finished, Kate drew out her reticule and paid him, shaking her head when Mattie tried to pay for her own. "My treat. For being my friend."

Mattie thanked her, marveling at how strange it was to think of Kate that way. All those years ago in Kansas, Kate had belittled her. Now she was dependent on Kate and it'd switched up how they were together.

"I'll have the photographs ready for you ladies in a few days," the photographer said.

Outside, Kate said, "Shall we meet the stage?"

"Why don't you go on? Meet Doc without me. I'll wait in the restaurant. I reckon the two of you might want a few moments. It's been a long time."

"Thank you, Mattie. If we don't come by half-past the hour, you might want to head back to St. Elmo's. If Doc's feeling half as excited as me, we might skip lunch." Kate laughed again.

Mattie watched her walk to the stage stop, pushing back at the jealous twinge that was tightening her heart. She didn't have no right to feel that way. Kate had been a true friend these past years and she was due her measure of good feelings without Mattie begrudging her.

She entered the hotel restaurant and secured a table near the window, where she could keep an eye on the stage stop. That way, if Doc and Kate hightailed it back to St. Elmo's, she'd know. She reckoned maybe she could use up some time before she went back, give them time enough together first.

Lord, her tooth ached. It'd be good, having Doc tend to it. She should have brought her bottle of laudanum. Instead, she ordered a whiskey.

The stage pulled in, right on time, just as Mattie drained the first glass. She ordered a second.

Kate near bounced on her feet while she was waiting for Doc to disembark.

But he didn't.

Instead, Wyatt stepped out of the stage, followed by Sadie.

October 1887 (a few months later)
Pinal, Arizona

Looking out the stagecoach window, Mattie could see Pinal wasn't much. Oh, it stretched out a ways but some of the buildings were boarded up and the dust seemed to be blowing everywhere. It seemed to her the town was dying. Not the best place to be starting her life over again. But there wasn't much choice. She hadn't had the money to go farther.

Kate had sold her ownership of the St. Elmo back in May. Doc was in bad shape, had sent Wyatt to plead his case to Kate. She'd gone to care for him, as she had once before. This time, she figured he wouldn't survive.

Mattie eased out of the stage, moving slow so as not to disturb the pain.

She'd stayed on, at the St. Elmo, for as long as she could. But things had changed once Kate sold out. There hadn't been any way she could earn her keep, not with the spells of pain that flared up. Once she'd been turned out of the brothel, she'd had to face up to the fact that she couldn't afford living in Globe. Oh, she might have been able to whore on her own, but men didn't much want her no more. There was something wrong, a discharge that came out of her now, thick and foul.

The driver tossed her bag down. Mattie gritted her teeth, hoisted it up, winced.

But at least she wasn't in the stage, bumping up and down.

It was a block to the Pinal Hotel. It'd take every penny she had left, but she'd stay a few nights. With so many empty buildings in town, she'd find an abandoned place right soon, one that wouldn't cost her much. And a town like this, there wouldn't be many brothels.

She figured there'd be a few desperate miners unwilling to travel to Globe to meet their needs. They wouldn't be too picky. They'd pay for an old whore with rotten teeth. Not much but they'd pay. She'd survive. That's what it'd come to, she reckoned. Surviving.

Seeing Wyatt and Sadie had nearly destroyed her. She'd sat there, unable to move, and drank herself into a stupor. They hadn't stayed. They'd boarded the next stage and left after delivering Doc's message and persuading Kate to go to him.

But the feeling of betrayal had remained with Mattie. It had clawed at her. Him being with that woman and Sadie being all gussied up in a fancy dress while Mattie had to take in men to survive.

She reckoned she was nothing but a bitter old woman now.

That's what he'd done to her.

She moved down the block, slow and steady. Main Street boasted two stores still open and a few saloons. The largest was the Bank Exchange Restaurant and Ale House—a prideful name for such a dirty looking place. Way down the block, after some empty buildings, she spied the St. Louis Brewery. That was pretty much it. A sad end to a town that had once seen a big silver boom.

There was a doctor, she saw. Maybe he'd be able to do

something about her female problems. Maybe there'd be a dentist to pull her teeth. She could hardly eat anymore. At the least, between the doc and the mercantile, she'd be able to get some laudanum. Whiskey should be plentiful enough.

She was on her own, now.

July 3, 1888 (the next year)
Pinal, Arizona

Mattie watched the nameless man shuffle out of her tiny shack. He closed the door behind him, more than some did. She rose up, sat on the edge of the bed. Her shoulders shook and the tears she'd dammed up while she'd laid with him burst out, hot on her cheeks.

She was tired of her life slipping away, little by little.

There was none of what Wyatt had promised.

All these years, she'd been lying to herself, telling herself he loved her, that he'd do right by her, that he'd come back for her.

Lies, all of it. It'd taken him leaving her to live like this for her to realize it.

She reckoned she'd finally found a small measure of respectability, such as it was here in Pinal. Though men used her, she kept it so quiet, even the sheriff looked past it. Neighbors befriended her, helped her keep up her little place when she was in too much pain to maintain it herself. No one much looked down on anybody here. 'Course the town was dying as much as she was, so those who remained pretty much relied on and supported one another.

It wasn't the magic elixir she'd imagined it would be, being respectable. Maybe it was that it came too late. But, then, Tombstone hadn't brought happiness, either, and she'd been respectable there. She had been convinced it would all be perfect one day. Well, it wasn't and it never would be.

She ached. No, she *hurt like hell.*

She hadn't wanted to lay with the man last night but she'd sold her fine silver bracelets to pay the rent and needed laudanum. Lord knew he hadn't much wanted to lay with her, but he'd been drunk and eager to shoot his wad before he passed out. And he'd given her enough for her to pay Frank Beeler for the laudanum she'd asked him to buy, so she didn't have to walk to the mercantile.

A knock sounded and Frank poked his head around the door. "Hey, Mattie, you doing any better?" He looked a bit peaked and she knew he'd likely been drunk earlier. He entered, bottle of laudanum in hand.

"I hurt." Mattie took a swig of whiskey from the bottle on the rickety stand next to the bed and handed it to Frank. "You look like you could use a little."

Frank took a swig.

"Will you get a glass, Frank? Mix a little laudanum into some whiskey?"

"How much?"

"About twenty drops I think."

Frank fetched a glass, mixed up the concoction. To Mattie's way of thinking, he was a bit stingy with the laudanum, but she guessed there was always more, if she needed it. He gave her the glass, watched her down the mixture.

"Sit with me a bit?" she asked.

"Not long. I got work today." He settled into a chair, telling her about the gossip. Things blurred a bit in the telling and the pain clouded over. She thought she said something about Wyatt ruining her life but she wasn't sure.

When she woke, Frank was gone. She sat, her eyes tearing at the sharp stab the movement brought.

Damn. She wished she hadn't wasted all those years believing the lies she'd told herself. Maybe if she'd trusted her gut more, life might have turned out different.

She reached for the bottle of laudanum, drained what was left into the glass, and filled it up with what was left of the whiskey.

That'd have to be enough, she reckoned.

Epilogue: All Truth Erased

ALLIE

After Mattie died, Josie plumb erased her. She'd usurped Mattie's place right off, calling herself Josephine Earp from the start and always claimed they married for real on Lucky Baldwin's yacht in 1892. None of us believed it.

That security Josie wanted was never solid. Wyatt bought up fancy saloons and gambling places in San Diego while he and Josie lived big in San Francisco but lost them all to taxes. They moved around, following gold strikes in Idaho and Alaska and Nevada. They opened that White Elephant dance hall and saloon with Bessie and Jim—I never did know if they'd run girls out of either and you can be sure Josie never told. She never told about gambling their money away, neither, but Wyatt had to cut her off a bunch of times.

Over the years, she invented stories about her wealthy German merchant family, but we all knew she grew up a dirt-poor Pole with a pa who couldn't keep a job. She always had a fit when any of us called her Sadie, like it was too common. But maybe it was to hide what she done before she supposedly married Wyatt.

Don't know what it was that bound them two together, with them arguing like cats and dogs. She could be a spiteful woman, Josie could, and Wyatt liked to call her Sadie to rile her up, I think, or maybe because he liked the image of her as a whore. I figure neither one of 'em was faithful to the other. I never did believe Lucky Baldwin was just a family friend, no matter what she said. And Wyatt, well, he wasn't true to Mattie and I never believed he was with Josie neither.

I always thought maybe he'd turn out to be a good pa, but Josie lost two babies and only had Johnny Behan's son, Albert, and her sisters' kids to dote on. Wyatt spoiled the nieces and nephews when he got the chance, raced horses and gambled, and did "special" jobs for the Los Angeles Police Department. Later on, they were friends with Hollywood bigwigs and oh, did Josie's stories grow then. When that Stuart Lake feller wanted to write about Wyatt's life, Josie was like a hawk. It all became Wyatt being a devoted lawman who didn't touch liquor. She didn't tell about Wyatt being a whorehouse pimp, his arrests, or Mattie. She hid Mattie real good and nobody knew about Wyatt being "married" to Josie when he was still married to Mattie.

After Wyatt, the last of the Earp brothers, died peaceful-like at the ripe old age of 80, Josie still kept at it, filing lawsuits when she didn't like what was being written about them, meeting with folks to write her own story, losing track of the lies. She said it had to be that way, that none of us could tell how things really were or it would hurt the family. It shames me that I gave in to her. She didn't care none about the family. It was all about her.

In the end, Mattie disappeared from the telling as if she never existed and Wyatt Earp became a version nowhere near the truth. He turned out a hero, become a legend. I never did know if Josie really loved him or if that was a lie, too.

All I know is that none of it was necessary.

AFTERWORD ON THE EARPS

Mattie Earp died alone in Pinal, Arizona, on July 3, 1888 after a fatal overdose of laudanum and whiskey. Josie and Wyatt remained together, living in California, Idaho, Alaska, and Arizona. Wyatt died in Los Angeles on January 13, 1929 and Josie on December 19, 1944. Wyatt's legend was created in 1931 with the publication of *Frontier Marshal.*

Wyatt's parents remained in California until their deaths: Virginia (Jenny) died in 1893 and Nicholas in 1907, after remarrying to Annie Cadd the same year Virginia died. Wyatt's oldest brother (half-brother) Newton and wife, Jennie, moved to California. Jennie died in 1898 and Newton in 1928, a month before Wyatt's death. Younger sister Adelia Earp Edwards lived in California where she married, dying in 1941; her daughters were favorites of Wyatt and Josie.

James and Bessie Earp settled in Colton, California. Bessie's daughter, Hattie (called Hettie in this book), married Thaddeus Harris in Tombstone in 1881and they divorced in 1889. James and Bessie joined Wyatt and Josie in mining ventures in Coeur d'Alene, Idaho, in 1884. Bessie died in 1887 and James remarried. He died in 1926 in Los Angeles.

Virgil and Allie (his third wife) also lived in Colton, where Virgil opened a detective agency. The two traveled a nomadic life throughout the West for many years. They had no children of their own but did welcome Virgil's twenty-year-old daughter from his first marriage when she located Virgil in 1899 (he'd not known about her prior to then). Virgil died in 1905 in Nevada. Allie died in Los Angeles in 1947 at age 96.

Youngest brother Warren Earp lived in California after events in Tombstone, as hotheaded as his brothers and frequently in trouble. He joined James and Wyatt in Idaho. He married Kate Sandford in Idaho in 1887 but was living in California without her by 1892. He died of a gunshot wound in Arizona in 1900.

Doc Holliday died of tuberculosis in Glenwood Springs, Colorado in 1887, at the age of just 36. Kate Elder was involved with other men (possibly being briefly married to George Cummings in Colorado) after Doc died, and died as Mary (her real first name) Cummings in Arizona in 1940.

AUTHOR'S NOTE ON HISTORICAL ACCURACY

Accuracy is illusive for both Mattie and Josie. Josie seldom told the same story twice and the stories she did tell seldom matched the historical record. Mattie's existence, of course, was buried. I attempted to remain true to historical fact whenever possible but so many facts were either missing or contradictory. In the end, I chose the most plausible story and built my plot accordingly. Though there are facts in this telling, it is much fictionalized. No known facts were contradicted.

I chose not to include Wyatt's first wife, Aurilla (Urilla) Sutherland, in my telling. Since they were married such a short time before her death and there seemed little deception connected with her, she was not part of the hidden history and thus not a fit for the book's theme.

I chose to make Sarah/Sally Haspel a separate person rather than an alias of Celie/Mattie since I could find no evidence of Celia in any of the Peoria arrest records and did not believe she could have avoided those. As well, family lore suggests she may have spent time with Wyatt's parents. As to running away with the circus, I chose to follow a family story: there was an Orton circus in that area of Iowa at the time and it was plausible. I have no idea what motivated Celie to run away but felt it had to have been more than a thirst for adventure. I know nothing of what she felt about her lifestyle nor whether or not she really did abuse laudanum or commit suicide—that she used the drug is known as is the problem with her teeth; family suggested uterine problems. That she died after drinking both laudanum and alcohol is a matter of record. This is my take on her.

Josie told so many differing stories of her past and used aliases, making research difficult. Much of what she told biographers contained hints but seldom matched the historical record and most of her stories were contradictory. News accounts were useful in pinning down dates for her time in Arizona and Josie's bits of truth had to be shaped around those dates. Where her own telling didn't match the historical record, I reshaped her timeline. She was especially elusive in telling how and when she left home, whom she left with, her travel routes, and what she did to support herself. But she left clues in her mentions of Pauline Markham's theatre group and her use of names (usually partial names such as Leah Hirshberg for Dora Hirsch). Most people mentioned in the book did exist in the historical record including Ella Howard, Hattie Wells, Josie Roland (Jennie in the book), Dora Hirsch, Lucky Baldwin, Kitty and Marietta, the folks in Tombstone, Doc and Kate, and Johnny Behan. There is no firm confirmation that Sadie Mansfield and Josie Marcus were one and the same, but I believe it is highly plausible they were.

I changed a few names in my telling to avoid duplications. Josie Roland became Jennie. Four persons were named Henrietta: Hattie Wells retained her name, Josie's sister became Hennie, Bessie's daughter became Hettie, Johnny Behan's daughter retained her name. I manipulated a date in early 1882 (by a few weeks) so that Josie's return from San Francisco fit into the storyline. I chose to set Hattie Wells's brothel on Powell Street though it may have been on Clay Street.

SUMMARY ON SOURCES

Two sources were invaluable. Historian Sherry Monahan did an excellent job of examining the Earp women in her book, *Mrs. Earp: The Wives and Lovers of the Earp Brothers.* E.C. (Ted) Meyers's book *Mattie: Wyatt Earp's Secret Second Wife* held many valuable details and led me to newspapers, court records, and family members.

Other books consulted included *I Married Wyatt Earp: The Recollections of Josephine Sarah Marcus Earp* (Glenn G. Boyer); *Suppressed Murder of Wyatt Earp* (Glenn G. Boyer); *Tombstone Travesty: Allie Earp Remembers* (Jane Candia Coleman); *The Last Gunfight: The Real Story of the Shootout at the O.K. Corral—And How It Change the American West* (Jeff Guinn); *Wyatt Earp Speaks!* (John Richard Stephens); and *Wyatt Earp: The Life Behind the Legend* (Casey Tefertiller).

Many primary sources were cited by the historians above and were only re-researched if I needed more information than cited. I reviewed copies of relevant police magistrate dockets from the Bradley University Library in Peoria, Illinois, and a variety of Kansas newspapers, census and genealogy records, and the original manuscript of *Tombstone Travesty* (Allie Earp's story) from the Frank Waters papers at the University of New Mexico. A variety of online articles (weighed for accuracy) provided clues for further research and assisted with information on the Orton circus, circuses in general, and the locales within the books.

BOOK CLUB QUESTIONS

1. This telling challenges much of the legend of Wyatt Earp most readers know. What are your thoughts on the Wyatt Earp revealed here?

2. Most readers will be familiar with Josie as an adventurous actress as portrayed in the two Earp movies of the 1990s. What are your thoughts on Josie as presented in this telling?

3. Mattie was portrayed in those same movies as a bitter addict. Has this telling changed your opinion of her? How so?

4. There were many layers to the events leading up to the gunfight in Tombstone. How has this telling changed your understanding of the Earp/Clanton rivalry?

5. Had Josie and Mattie lived just fifty years later, how might their lives have been different? Do you see any similarities in opportunities for young women in desperate circumstances today?

6. Do you agree or disagree that deception played a major role in the lives of both Mattie and Josie? Was that deception necessary or was that a false belief? Why or why not?

ABOUT THE AUTHOR

Pamela Nowak was born and raised in southwest Minnesota and currently resides in Albuquerque. She has a B.A. in history and was a teacher, preservationist, project manager for the Fort Yuma National Historic Site, and administrator of a homeless shelter prior to her writing career. Her four historical romance novels have won numerous national awards and garnered critical acclaim for her ability to weave actual people, events, and places into her plotting. Now writing women's historical fiction with a heavy basis in fact, she's returned to her roots.

The employees of Five Star Publishing hope you have enjoyed this book.

Our Five Star novels explore little-known chapters from America's history, stories told from unique perspectives that will entertain a broad range of readers.

Other Five Star books are available at your local library, bookstore, all major book distributors, and directly from Five Star/Gale.

<u>Connect with Five Star Publishing</u>

Visit us on Facebook:
https://www.facebook.com/FiveStarCengage

Email:
FiveStar@cengage.com

For information about titles and placing orders:
(800) 223-1244
gale.orders@cengage.com

To share your comments, write to us:
Five Star Publishing
Attn: Publisher
10 Water St., Suite 310
Waterville, ME 04901